Praise for the novels
of Jo Beverley

"*Forbidden Magic* is wickedly delicious! Jo Beverley weaves a spell of sensual delight with her usual grace and flair."   —Teresa Medeiros

"Beverley weaves a stunning medieval romance of loss and redemption. . . . Sizzling!"
     —*Publishers Weekly* (starred review)

"A fast-paced adventure with strong, vividly portrayed characters . . . wickedly, wonderfully sensual and gloriously romantic."
     –Mary Balogh

"Intrigue, suspense, and passion fill the pages of this high-powered, explosive drama. . . . Thrilling!"
     —*Rendezvous*

continued . . .

Secrets
of the
Night

Jo Beverley

A TOPAZ BOOK

TOPAZ

Published by New American Library, a division of
Penguin Putnam Inc., 375 Hudson Street,
New York, New York 10014, U.S.A.
Penguin Books Ltd, 27 Wrights Lane,
London W8 5TZ, England
Penguin Books Australia Ltd, Ringwood,
Victoria, Australia
Penguin Books Canada Ltd, 10 Alcorn Avenue,
Toronto, Ontario, Canada M4V 3B2
Penguin Books (N.Z.) Ltd, 182–190 Wairau Road,
Auckland 10, New Zealand

Penguin Books Ltd, Registered Offices:
Harmondsworth, Middlesex, England

First published by Topaz, an imprint of New American Library,
a division of Penguin Putnam Inc.

First Printing, July 1999
10 9 8 7 6 5 4 3 2 1

 REGISTERED TRADEMARK—MARCA REGISTRADA

Printed in the United States of America

This book would not have taken full form without my husband's willingness to drive me round and round the Yorkshire dales; without my critique group making me keep focus; and without the generous advice of fellow writer Sue Stewart, who knows so much about the intimate life of horses.

And, of course, without my editor, Audrey LaFehr, who can always see ways to make a novel stronger.

Thanks to all the above, and to old friends Glyn and Jeff Dobson, whose hospitality helped me get back under the skin of the north of England after so many years away.

Chapter 1

It was a simple matter to sin, wasn't it? Didn't they call it the "primrose path of dalliance"?

In the swaying, rumbling coach, Rosamunde Overton sat at equal distance from all panes of glass, fleeing back home, cowardly virtue still intact.

She'd been afraid of coach windows since the accident that had scarred her face, but she hadn't realized how afraid of everything she had become. A person confined to bed loses the strength in their legs. She, huddled away for eight years in the quiet of Wensleydale, had lost all strength when it came to meeting strangers.

Especially when it came to sinning with them!

Sagging in her seat, she gazed at a landscape that seemed to reflect her mood. Scrubby sheep runs on rising ground were hung over by dismal clouds, remnants of the storm that had slowed her journey. Daylight was only a crimson memory, moonlight a pale promise, so she moved ponderously in the corpse-gray time between.

Sin had seemed straightforward enough when she and Diana had planned it. Her husband, her home, and all the people at Wenscote needed a child, but her husband couldn't give her one. So, she would wear a mask and surrender to the anonymous wildness of a Harrogate masquerade. As Diana had promised, there had been men interested in sinning with her. Interested—though none realized it—in helping her get with child without the man involved knowing who she was.

She closed her eyes. It should have been so *easy*!

Yet instead of encouraging any of them, she'd flitted

from partner to partner, nervously seeking a seducer more to her liking. What on earth had she expected?

A handsome prince?

A dashing Lovelace?

A noble Galahad?

As the evening whirled on, she'd realized such dream lovers didn't exist, but by then she'd become too aware of the real men's faults. Fat bellies, bad teeth, lascivious eyes, wet lips, dirty hands, knock knees. . . .

Even with a number of glasses of wine firing her blood, she'd lost her nerve and fled. At first light, before Diana stirred, she'd ordered her carriage to take her back into the dales, to safety, to Wenscote.

Wenscote, a sanctuary she didn't deserve since she wasn't willing to save it. Without a child, the estate would one day pass to Edward Overton, her husband's nephew. Edward would immediately turn it over to his severe religious sect. Her husband was not a well man, and her failure might even hasten his death. Might kill the kindly man who'd given a wounded sixteen-year-old shelter. Dr. Wallace said that the worry was aggravating Digby's internal problems and dizzy spells.

It should have been so easy!

Rosamunde surrendered to an idyllic picture of a happy Digby, enjoying watching the child grow and learn about its inheritance. Perhaps with a child to think of, he'd even follow the doctor's orders about plain food and little drink. Tears stung her eyes, but tears of longing. The key, however, was not wistful dreams but sin and consequences, and there she'd failed—

Snapping out of her useless thoughts, she let down the window. "Stop!"

"Stop, milady?" asked the coachman.

"Yes, stop! Immediately!"

The coach jerked to a halt, coming to rest at a slight angle, so that Rosamunde's maidservant, bonelessly snoring opposite her, almost toppled her considerable bulk onto her mistress. She braced to hold Millie off, then eased her back onto her own seat.

"Is there a problem, milady?" Garforth shouted down.

"I thought I saw something lying by the road. Perhaps a person. Send Tom back to see."

The coach lurched as the young groom leaped down. Leaning out, Rosamunde followed his progress in the gloom. "A little further, Tom. No, further out. Near that gorse!"

"Heck, it is an' all," the groom said, sliding down a slight dip and crouching. He looked up. "It's a man, Mr. Garforth!"

Rosamunde opened the door, held up her wide skirts, and jumped down to the road. "Is he dead?" she called as she ran over.

"Dead drunk more like, milady. Though what he's doing way out here . . ."

Rosamunde peered into a boggy dip. "He'll catch his death. Can you get him up?"

Tom shoved his big hands under the man's arms and lifted. He was a strapping fellow, but wet as his load was, and a dead weight, it took even him a while to drag the man onto the road. Rosamunde fell to her knees beside the bundle that reeked of wet wool and gin.

Grimacing, she felt his chilly wrist for a pulse. Alive, at least. Muttering at the dismal light, she checked by feel for wound or injury, but found none. As Tom said, dead drunk, even though they were miles from the nearest inn.

"What we going to do with him, milady?" Tom asked.

"Take him with us, of course."

"Nay, you don't want to do that. Who knows what he is? Not from these parts, and that's a fact."

And that pretty well consigned him to the devil. Rosamunde looked Tom in the eye. "Are we of the priests and Levites, then, to pass by on the other side of the road? Or are we Good Samaritans? Tell Garforth to back the coach to here."

With a shake of his head, the groom trotted off. Despite her biblical references, she was sure he was anxious to confer with the senior servant about her mad behavior. It wasn't mad, however. She couldn't abandon this man, even if he was a "furriner" and a drunk. Nights were cold up here, even in summer, and soaking as he was, he might not survive.

As the coach began to creak backward toward her, the horses having to be coaxed to this unusual maneuver, Rosamunde studied her living parable in the fading light. Could he, like the man on the road to Jericho, have been set upon by thieves?

Unlikely. Even the dim light would have shown bruises or blood. No, he was doubtless just a wretch who'd drunk too much.

Not a vagrant, though, despite the stink and the stubble on his jaw. With careful fingers she assessed his sturdy cloth breeches and jacket. Respectable clothes with a modest trim of braid and horn buttons. His waistcoat was plain, his neckcloth untrimmed by lace.

It all spoke of a steady man with employment and responsibilities. That puzzled her. In her experience, drunkards came from the lowest and highest ranks of society, not from the hardworking, middling classes she knew best.

He was wearing riding boots. Perhaps that explained things. Perhaps he'd toppled drunk from his horse.

"A proper mystery, aren't you?" she muttered, and gingerly checked his pockets. She felt particularly awkward about sliding her hand down the ones in his snug-fitting breeches. She couldn't help but touch the shape of his flaccid manly parts. It was all for nothing. Apart from a plain handkerchief, his pockets were empty. Perhaps he had been robbed at that, or had drunk down to his last penny.

She used his handkerchief to gently wipe some of the mud off his face. As the coach slowly eased beside her, the lanterns threw a pool of flickering light on her task.

Oh my.

Despite stubble, scrapes, and a minor bruise on his cheekbone, he was doubtless some woman's darling, this one. Not a glorious face, but a pleasing one, with regular features well arranged, features that even in unconsciousness hinted at smiles rather than frowns.

Suddenly tender, Rosamunde cradled his stubbled cheek in one hand, pleased she'd be able to return him to the people he smiled for. She could only hope he'd be wiser for his experience. He wouldn't have a chance if he caught an inflammation of the lungs.

"Hurry, Garforth!"

"I'm doing my best, milady."

She could tell he was no better pleased with her charity than Tom had been. Would they really have left the man here to die?

Once the coach was in position, Garforth tied the ribbons and risked leaving the horses long enough to help hoist the man in. No easy task, with him six foot and well-built. The procedure managed to wake Millie—a miracle in itself!—and after spluttering and exclaiming, she pulled out the blankets kept for colder journeys and wrapped them around him.

"He'll be ruining the seats otherwise, milady," she complained.

Rosamunde had the man put on her seat, then settled herself next to him, easing his upper body across her lap. That way she could stop him from being thrown about. Her hand touched his neck and she gasped at how cold he was.

"Is there somewhere nearby where we can find help?"

"Next place without going off the road is Arradale, milady," Garforth said, "and by then you're only five miles from home."

"Stop there." Rosamunde tucked the blankets tighter. "An hour could make the difference. In fact, stop at the dower house. It's the closest."

Arradale House was the home of her cousin, Diana, Countess of Arradale—that rarest of creatures, a peeress in her own right. The dower house was almost their playhouse, the place they still went to relax and be girlish for a day or two. It was always kept ready.

Garforth touched his tricorn, and soon the coach creaked into motion again. Speed would get the wet man to warmth sooner, but because of the accident, Rosamunde could no more insist on speed than she could have sex with a masked rake. She'd been telling herself that she could try again to sin, that next time it would be less of a shock and she'd do it. Now, however, she

had to wonder if some fears could never be conquered
by will alone.

Rejecting thoughts of failure, she concentrated on
something she could do, laying her hand again on the
man's chilly neck. His pulse was there, but weak. People
could die of cold.

"What do you think, Millie?"

The maid had her arms folded over her huge bosom.
"I think he's gallows bait, milady. You'd better be out
of reach when he comes out of his stupor."

"But what if he doesn't? Could he die?"

Millie wasn't really hard-hearted, just ill-tempered
about this disorganized journey, about them being on
the road at night instead of tucked up in a cozy inn
somewhere. She leaned over to peer. "Looks strong and
healthy enough to me, milady. Happen he'll live, unless
he gets a lung fever."

Rosamunde held him closer. He was a stranger and
probably a wastrel, but she had found him and she
would see him safe.

She had to be able to do something right.

It seemed an age before the coach swayed into the
lane leading to the dower house. Rosamunde was sure
the man's pulse was weaker. She eased from under him,
and as soon as the coach halted, leaped down and ran
over to thunder the knocker. There were no lights, but
she knew the caretakers would be there in their own
quarters.

The door was opened by gaunt Mrs. Yockenthwait,
peering suspiciously into the gloom. "Why, Lady
Overton!"

"I've an injured man in the coach. Can Mr. Yockenthwait help bring him in?"

In moments, the blanket-wrapped man was being carried through the door.

"The kitchen," said the housekeeper brusquely.
"Can't have all that dirty water on the good floors."

Tom and wiry Mr. Yockenthwait carried the bundle
down a corridor and into the stone-flagged kitchen,

warm with the heat from the big hearth. The men then hurried off to help Garforth with the horses.

"You'll be staying the night, milady," said Mrs. Yockenthwait, and it wasn't a question. "It's late to be traveling."

"We've come from Harrogate, and the rains turned the roads into mire. Then we stopped to pick up this man. He was just lying there!" Rosamunde heard her own weak panic and made herself take a breath. "We have to get him out of his wet clothes."

"No doubt of that," said the woman, rolling up her sleeves. "Come on, Millie."

Millie had settled her bulk into a chair, but she prepared to heave herself out of it.

"Rest, Millie," said Rosamunde. "I'll help."

Mrs. Yockenthwait gave her a disapproving frown, probably for pampering Millie Igby, though it might be because she was about to handle a naked man. "I'm a married woman, Mrs. Yockenthwait," Rosamunde said firmly, hoping no one guessed that in eight years of marriage, she'd never seen a man's body. "Anyway, don't you have a maid to help you now your daughters are married?"

"Jessie goes to bed with the sun, milady. I insist on it, for she's to be up with the sun, too. We're about ready for our beds ourselves."

And God-fearing folk, it was clear, did not travel after sunset.

Rosamunde ignored the woman's bark, which had never been matched with a bite, and stripped off her gloves, hat, and cloak. As an afterthought, since there were no strangers here—or no conscious ones—she shed the lacy cap with the frills and lappets that hid the sides of her face. She traced her major scar, however, up to the corner of her right eye. What would happen if he regained consciousness and saw her looming over him?

She gave herself a little shake, and knelt to help the older woman unwind the blankets. Being stronger, Mrs. Yockenthwait lifted him, while Rosamunde struggled to peel the sodden clothes from his upper body—jacket, waistcoat, neckcloth, and shirt.

When it was done, she was hot and winded, but he was still clammy with cold. She helped Mrs. Yockenthwait rub him briskly with warm, rough cloths, and felt rewarded when he began to shiver, even if his teeth did chatter alarmingly.

"That's good, isn't it?" she asked.

"Aye, but we need to really warm him. I'll fetch dry blankets and some wrapped bricks."

Soon his upper half was swathed, and the teeth chattering stopped. Rosamunde grabbed a towel and dried his brown hair.

Then they started on his lower half.

It was terribly difficult to get his boots off. Rosamunde was afraid that they'd twist or even break his ankles, but it had to be done, and when they tossed them aside to leak onto the tiled floor, his stockinged feet didn't seem to be out of shape. It took very little time then to rid him of the rest of his clothes. Though Rosamunde tried not to look at his private parts, she couldn't help getting a glimpse.

The hard thing that always seemed to hurt was rather endearing, lying soft against his hairy thigh. . . .

She hastily looked away, hoping Mrs. Yockenthwait took her red cheeks for exertion. She again helped with the brisk drying, deliberately taking the feet and calves, conscious of a strange, illicit pleasure in his well-made body. She'd never considered that a man's body could be so artistic, though she supposed she should have when it was so often portrayed in art.

When they turned him to dry his back, she decided that he could act as model for the sort of painting that hung in Arradale House. They had no such art at home. Digby preferred horses, landscapes, and family portraits. He'd commissioned a traveling artist to paint them as a couple—she from the good side of course.

Wrapping the warm blanket around the man's legs, she sighed at her hurt over that. Had she wanted her blemishes recorded for posterity? No, but in some strange way she had wanted to be recorded as she really was.

She pushed away her idiotic thoughts and helped turn

him on his back. "He's shivering less," she said, "but I think that's because he's warmer now."

"Aye, but he'd benefit from a hot drink." Mrs. Yockenthwait tried to feed him some tea, but most of it dribbled away.

Rosamunde hovered anxiously. She'd heard of someone lying naked with a chilled person to warm them. She could imagine Mrs. Yockenthwait's reaction to that suggestion!

Suppressing a smile, she brushed hair off his forehead. In the heat from the fire it was drying into curls of a pleasant russet brown. His clean face was every bit as handsome as she'd imagined, even with bruise and stubble. She couldn't possibly let him die. If necessary, she *would* strip naked and wrap herself up in the blankets with him.

Sliding her fingers down to his neck, she found it reassuringly warmer, his pulse stronger.

While Rosamunde's touch was tentative, the housekeeper pushed her work-worn hand under the blankets, right onto his chest. "Better," she said after a moment. "Sometimes drink seems to preserve them. Now," she said, pushing to her feet, "let me get you some tea, milady."

Rosamunde stood, too. By country time, it was late. Millie was already snoring.

As she accepted the tea, she said, "Millie and I will use our usual beds, but I suppose we'll need one for him, too." She looked at the long bundle near the fire. "How long do you think he could stay unconscious?"

"He could sleep the night away, milady. You want to put him in a *bedroom*?"

Rosamunde started, realizing it was extraordinary to provide such comfort for a vagrant. She looked at him again, a man with no hint of his status other than good looks. He could be the roughest, foulest kind of person. Something about him, however, suggested otherwise, and it was more than a face shaped for smiling.

She suddenly realized it was his hands. They were tucked away now, but as she remembered, they were not at all rough and the nails were neatly trimmed and tended to. And he'd been clean. Oh, he'd been mired up from his misadventure, but when he'd started out on his journey, he'd been as clean and well-groomed as any decent man.

"A bedroom," she repeated firmly. "Millie and I can take care of him. I don't want to give you extra work."

"Her?" Mrs. Yockenthwait said with a scathing look at the snoring maid.

"It's not her fault. She gets tired. And cold, even bundled in shawls."

"Aye, her mother were the same. But she can't be much use to you."

"She has to work for someone, and I have little need of fancy care."

The woman shrugged. "Leave him down here, milady. He'll do well enough on the floor, and it's warm by the fire."

"When there are beds upstairs? That seems uncharitable."

Rosamunde knew her insistence must seem strange, but she was coming to understand her own reasons. He was of respectable origins, she was sure, and not out of place above stairs. More than that, he was *hers*. Her cause. Her living parable. Down here, he'd be out of her orbit, firmly consigned to the servant ranks. Upstairs, he would be hers to care for, just for a little while.

"Happen he's not used to a fine bed," the woman said with Yorkshire stubbornness.

Rosamunde was a Yorkshire woman, too. "Then it'll feel all the better to him, won't it?"

Mrs. Yockenthwait shook her head. "You always did have too kind a heart, Rosie Ellington." But she said it with a hint of a smile, and her use of the familiar, childhood name was warming.

They'd run wild over this part of the North Riding, she and Diana, tumbling into trouble more often than not. The people here were used to picking them up and dusting them off, and sometimes, if they'd put themselves in danger, sending them home to be punished.

Dinah and Rosie in trouble again. Except that Dinah

was in Harrogate, doubtless washing her hands of her cowardly cousin.

The men came in, and Mrs. Yockenthwait served them tea and cold pie. Rosamunde shared the simple fare. Once the meal was underway, however, Mrs. Yockenthwait took down the long warming pan from the wall. "I'll just see to the beds, then."

Rosamunde leaped up. "I'll do that, Mrs. Yockenthwait. Millie will help." She shook her maid until she spluttered awake.

"Did I doze off, milady?"

"Only for a moment. But you must come help me prepare our beds for the night. Mrs. Yockenthwait has her own work to do."

"Good of you, dear," said the woman, arching to ease her back. "And I'll make up more hot bricks, too."

Millie insisted on carrying the heavy warming pan up the stairs. Rosamunde followed to be sure she didn't tip it. They went first to the front bedroom Rosamunde and Diana always shared. She tried to let Millie do the work, but the slow, almost snaillike pace broke her in the end and she seized the handle. "Why don't you get Tom to bring up our bags, and make everything ready. I'll finish the beds."

Millie nodded and lumbered off.

Rosamunde ran the warming pan around the bed in the spare room, glad it was summer so there'd not be too much damp and chill. With a few bricks to help, it should keep him cozy.

Then she also ran it around Millie's bed in the smallest room. The poor woman had such trouble keeping warm in the night, even though she slept in layers of clothes.

Leaving the warming pan in the bed the man would use, she hurried downstairs wondering whether she should send word to Wenscote to let Digby know where she was. She'd planned to stay in Harrogate for a fortnight, however, so he wouldn't be expecting her. And it was late for a message.

She paused at the bottom of the stairs, accepting that she didn't want to send a message. If she did, Digby would send servants to help. They'd take *him* off her hands. . . .

She shook her head. She was thinking of him as more than a drunk by the wayside. They said that clothes maketh the man, but once her parable had been stripped of his ordinary clothes, he'd seemed more rather than less.

Romantic folly! She was busily translating his russet curls and splendid physique into a combination of Hercules, Horatio, and Roland! A noble knight errant—

At that, she froze.

Knight errant?

She'd sought someone like that at the masquerade.

Why wait for another masquerade?

It was such a wicked notion, she hardly dared look straight at it, but it swirled around her, taking shape like steam hitting a winter window and turning to lacy patterns of solid ice.

After all, she *had* to do something. Doctor Wallace warned that Digby could drop dead at any minute. She'd known it anyway, with his red face and breathlessness.

At any minute.

And then Wenscote would belong to Edward and the New Commonwealth.

On her recent journey, she and Diana had visited an estate that had already been taken over by the sect. They'd found that the tales were true. If anything, the truth was worse than she'd thought.

Members of George Cotter's New Commonwealth had to give up life's pleasures in favor of work and prayer, and any infractions were punished. She'd heard that if parents didn't punish their children harshly enough—punish them for things like a girl taking off her cap, or a boy his collar—then the Cotterite "saints" did it for them, and the blood ran.

Rosamunde had seen some Cotterite children, tight inside concealing, restrictive clothes even on a hot day, looking as if they were afraid to breathe for fear of earning punishment. The only escape for the poor, trapped people was to move, to leave the land their families had lived on for generations, for centuries.

She couldn't let this happen to Wenscote, especially

as she was in no personal danger. With her widow's portion, she would be free to leave, while the servants, and especially the tenants, would be trapped. She had the means to keep everyone safe, and had failed. Now she had been given a second chance.

A man. A stranger, who'd soon be on his way.

She had to at least *try*! She'd never be able to live with herself if she didn't.

So. Though she was already trembling inside at the thought, she stuck the intent in her mind as a fact. She *would* do it. The only questions were about practicalities.

Such as how to get him to cooperate.

According to common wisdom and warnings, most men, especially young men, were desperate to get between a woman's legs. In fact, it seemed they often had to be fought off, and some would resort to trickery and even abduction to have their rakish way. Every young woman knew that being alone with a man was sure to lead to wickedness and a swelling waist.

Which was exactly what she wanted. It should be as easy as picking ripe berries. And yet, she couldn't help doubting. . . .

"Milady? Are you all right?"

At the housekeeper's question, Rosamunde started, realizing that she'd stood in the hall long enough to have found sheets and made the beds, never mind warm them. Sure that her wicked plan flickered around her like hell-flames, she walked briskly into the kitchen and asked the men to carry her knight, her savior, her potential partner in sin, up to his bed.

Chapter 2

She hurried ahead to give that bed an extra warming. It would never do for him to fall into a fever. She let the men slide his blankets off decently beneath the covers, but then arranged the warm bricks and tucked him in snugly.

"Do you know him, Mr. Yockenthwait?" she asked. For this to work, he had to be a stranger, someone never likely to visit these parts again.

Seth Yockenthwait shook his head. "He's not from hereabouts, milady. And he'd hardly go unnoticed, a handsome rascal like that."

Rosamunde looked at the man again and realized Seth was right. She'd been assessing his parts, but now she saw that they went together remarkably well. She was particularly struck by the curve of those smile-shaped lips.

Kissable.

She stepped back from the bed. Oh no! It was one thing to prepare to be a sacrifice, another entirely to lust like a wanton dairymaid for sweet kisses! This wasn't right—

But then she caught herself. *You don't get out of it that way. You'll do it, my girl, even if he's a noble knight incarnate!*

Tempted to laugh at the craziness of her thoughts, she led the way out of the room. No one must ever suspect that she had a personal interest in the man.

"We don't know anything about him," she said, as coolly as she could. "He could be the worst kind of scoundrel, and I won't put anyone here in danger." She locked the room from the outside and put the key in her pocket. "There. You needn't worry, Mr. Yockenthwait."

"Right you are, milady," the man said, in the manner of a Yorkshireman who reckons women are daft, but is too wise to make a point of it.

Almost trembling with nerves, Rosamunde watched the men go downstairs, then let Millie prepare her for bed. She sent the maid to her own room and waited. Once she was sure everyone was settled for the night, she took a deep breath—

And faltered.

She couldn't do this. She really couldn't!

You're not committing yourself to anything, goose. You're just going to check on your patient.

Even so, it took a whole quarter of an hour, as measured by the tinkling chimes of the clock in the hall, before she found the courage to move. Then she forced her feet out of her room and to the door of his. She took no candle, for he might have woken and he must not see her. She turned the key as silently as possible, then slipped into the dark room, closed the door, and stayed there, back pressed to the wood as if glued.

No movement hinted that he might be awake.

Feeling like a sneak thief, she crept forward to draw back the curtains a crack, to let in thin moonlight.

He'd turned over in the bed. She supposed that was a good sign, but when she gingerly touched him, checking his pulse and temperature, he didn't stir. He was comfortably warm and would likely live.

So, now what?

She carried a chair close to the bed and sat there, considering his shadowy form, bolstering her resolution.

Wenscote was in terrible danger. Everything had been comfortable until the spring, because the heir had not been Edward but another of Digby's nephews, William. William, a hearty dalesman like Digby, would have taken over Wenscote and cared for it in the same generous way.

William Overton, however, had suddenly died, perhaps because he was so like Digby. At an inn near Filey, he'd eaten a large meal, drunk deep, and suffered a seizure, leaving Edward heir to Wenscote. Edward, born and raised in York, was now devoted to the New Commonwealth.

With William's fate as warning, Digby was trying to change his ways, to live more moderately, but he did enjoy life's pleasures. Having Edward Overton paying dutiful visits and lecturing him on the benefit of plain food and drink made him more inclined to indulge out of sheer irritation.

And then there was his belated longing for a child.

Digby had never seemed much interested in marital matters, and in recent years such things had ceased entirely. Driven by the thought of Edward, however, he had tried a few times. Her cheeks heated in the dark at memory of those failures.

Poor Digby.

That was when he'd taken to hinting Rosamunde toward this course.

"You're a young woman, pet. It'd be only natural if you had an eye sometimes to the handsome young men."

And: "Perhaps God will be kind to an old sinner and send him a miracle."

Rosamunde pondered her miracle with a wry smile. It was only fanciful to imagine the man in the bed a gift of the heavens. He'd doubtless been by the road because of folly, and what she was planning was a sin, no matter how worthy the cause.

Did the end justify the means?

Yes, she really thought it did.

But then she stiffened, seeing a problem.

The masquerade had been attractive because she could have remained a mystery, even to her lover. With an inheritance at stake, that was essential. When this man left, he'd know where he'd been, and could easily find out whom he'd been with.

She settled her chin on her hand and tussled with the problem, wishing Diana was here to help. She was a much more devious plotter. What would Diana come up with?

A false name! Both for herself and this place. That

would be easy, especially if she kept him in this room and didn't let the Yockenthwaits near him. In fact, the taciturn couple could probably be relied on to keep the secret if asked. Millie would do as she was bid.

What name? What would throw him well off the path if he thought to find her, but not endanger anyone else's reputation? With a touch of wicked humor, she chose the name Gillsett. Gillsett was the name of eccentric elderly sisters who ran a remote farm in Arkengarthdale. Anyone who sought her up there would find a dead end.

That left the problem of setting him free without his knowing where he'd been. Of course. She'd simply get him dead drunk again.

Like a tumbling stream, certainty flowed through her, strong and clear. It was right. It would work. It was meant to be.

Anyway, once away from here, he wouldn't search for her. The world was full of men who ignored the women they had lain with, who ran from the babies they fathered. She couldn't remember a single case of a man making an effort to track one down.

So—she rubbed her hands nervously down her thighs—it was just a question of getting him to do the necessary. That should be no problem. Men were like bulls and rams, weren't they? Given a chance at a female, they took it. If he woke up to find a woman in his bed. . . .

Rosamunde's heart began to pound and she swallowed to ease a dry throat. Could she really do that?

She must.

She wouldn't be a coward anymore.

She drew the curtains tight again, then took off her dressing gown, placing it neatly with unsteady hands on the chair back. After a frozen moment, she eased under the covers, onto the very edge of the warm feather bed.

If anything, it was too warm, so she removed one cloth-wrapped brick. Then she tried to get comfortable. It was not strange to sleep with someone, for she'd done so since her marriage, but here the man was settled in the middle.

She wriggled as close as she dared—

Mercy me! She'd forgotten he was naked. It shouldn't make any difference, but it seemed the wickedest thing imaginable to be lying next to a naked man.

No. Not the wickedest.

She was trying very hard to commit adultery.

That was the wickedest.

She made herself prepare her mind for the act. No panicking at the last moment!

It was a simple business. He'd pull up her nightgown, move over her, and poke around until he got it in. He'd push in and out a bit until his seed escaped, then roll over to go back to sleep. Perhaps he'd even forget it had happened.

All she'd need to do would be to let him.

She took some deep, steadying breaths, telling herself again and again that she could do that. Let him. After a moment, to make it even easier, she eased the front of her nightgown all the way up to her waist.

When nothing happened, she made herself edge even closer so her naked thigh was in contact with his.

Then she softly laughed at herself.

What? Did she expect him to wake from his drunken stupor as if she were smelling salts waved under his nose? What an idiot she was! He was dead drunk still, and was probably going to sleep the night away. He could hardly be overtaken by lust until he was conscious.

Blinking back some tears—part laughter, part pain—she decided she might as well go and sleep in her own bed.

She didn't though.

It was easier to stay with the familiarity of a warm body beside her. And heaven knew when he'd wake. It could be late tomorrow, but it could be within hours. She had to be here when he did.

Perfectly aware that she was behaving strangely, Rosamunde turned to snuggle closer to her unconscious, wastrel knight, her unsuspecting lover, her heaven-sent savior. Gently, she let his warmth and soft breathing lull her into sleep.

Dark.
Pain.

Agony!

He raised his hands to hold his splitting head together, astonished to find that it wasn't in fact expanding and contracting with every heartbeat.

Where the devil was he?

What had happened to his head?

When he opened his eyes a hink, he saw nothing. Blind! Was he blind?

But then his frantic eyes caught a slit of lighter darkness. Surely a crack in heavy curtains showing night outside. Please God, let it be so.

Pain in his belly. Cramps. Not as bad as his head, but bad enough. He prayed not to be sick. If he threw up, he'd likely choke because he was never, ever going to move his head again.

Staying perfectly still, he began to notice other things. He was in a bed. Quite a comfortable bed.

He was naked. They wouldn't put a grievously ill man to bed naked, would they?

Someone was with him.

They lay a little apart, but he could hear regular, sleeping exhalations. A woman? It would explain his lack of clothing, but. . . .

What the devil had he been up to?

It could be a man—a fellow traveler, a fellow drinker, collapsed with him. He risked movement, stretching out an inquiring hand.

Female surely. He picked up the faint scent of flowers that had spoken to his instincts. In a nightgown. Strange, that. He couldn't remember ever enjoying a woman and leaving her nightclothes on.

Perhaps she was excessively modest, but that wasn't his type either.

Who was she?

He had no idea.

No idea even of possibilities.

'Struth, what a mess!

He must have drunk a barrelful to have a head like this, and to not remember the woman. What was he going to say to her in the morning?

Where had he drunk so much? He should know that.

He should remember starting to drink. He scrabbled for a place, a name, a picture—

And fell into a terrifying void. Where his memory should be, lay only emptiness.

Panicked, he clung to a fact he did feel sure of. He didn't drink to excess. He hadn't been truly sozzled since that time in Italy on his Grand Tour. He'd been sixteen and he'd thought the effects had cured him of overdrinking for life.

Was he in Italy now, sozzled on fine wine in a palazzo in Venice?

No. Years had passed since then.

Many years.

He was in England.

Yes, he was sure he was in England, and a grown man. He slid a hand down to his chin, feeling the strong bones and the roughness of stubble. A fact presented itself. His twenty-ninth birthday was not long past.

Why were some things so certain and others lost? He knew he was in England, but not where. He knew his age, but little of what he'd done with over ten years. Perdition! He started to shake his head and stopped with a hiss of agony. His brain felt both scrambled and faded, as if heavy veils hung between himself and the fragments of his life.

What did he remember? What?

Taking farewell of his family in London.

He had a family—brothers and sisters. He could even see faces, but when he asked for names he got only nonsense. An elf? A bright elf? A sinful elf . . . ?

He couldn't stand this. He tried to sit up, then stopped, frozen by pain. Oh God. Oh God—

He slowly eased his tormenting head back on the pillow, went back to lying very, very still. His head shrieked with every breath.

Perhaps he was gravely ill. But then, who was the woman in his bed? His nurse?

Hardly.

Who was she?

Who was *he*?

That simple question sprang into life, then fell tangling

into that ominous void, stiffening him with terror. Terror of following the question into that deep, black hole where he wouldn't exist at all. He reached out for something real. Anything. Her cotton nightgown.

"Oh. You're awake."

The woman had moved, and now she took his trembling hand in hers. He clutched at her, ready to weep with gratitude.

"Where am I?" he whispered, afraid of the pain of speaking louder.

Silence. Had he imagined her? He gripped her soft hand tighter. . . .

"Gillsett! Please. You're hurting me."

Immediately, he relaxed his grip. "I'm sorry. I . . . I can't see."

Her other hand brushed his forehead, a gentle touch that seemed blessedly familiar. Was this his wife? Surely he'd remember if he were married. It was not unpleasant, though, to think of being familiar with that warm voice and soft, caring hand.

But no. Her gentle touch merely reminded him of his mother, dead many years ago. Her soft voice would soothe him in fevered nights. Speaking in French, however. Was he French . . . ?

No, surely not.

"It's just dark, sir," the woman said, definitely in English. "It's the middle of the night."

He was making a fool of himself. Here he was, doubtless in an inn with a doxy, suffering the hell of a drunkard's head, and acting as if demons were after him. The pain, however, was real, and his stomach still churned ominously.

"I seem to have drunk too much."

"Do you not remember, sir?"

Oh, hell. Could he avoid letting her know that he didn't remember her or the merry bedgames they'd doubtless shared? "I'm sorry. My head . . . It hurts."

"It's all right." She touched him again in that tender, devastating way, sliding her cool hands over his and easing them down off his head. "Try to go back to sleep. You'll feel better in the morning."

"Is that a promise?" He even found a bit of humor for the comment, and that felt in character. But then the foulness bit at his throat and he rolled sharply away from her despite the agony in his head. "Going to be sick!" he choked out.

He fought it, and by some miracle she was round the bed and had the chamber pot ready by the time his stomach overwhelmed his will.

At least the racking, burning vomit seemed to take some of the agony with it. When he collapsed back onto the pillow, blades no longer stabbed through his skull. Only mallets hammered it.

The stink fouled the air, however. This was possibly the most embarrassing thing that had happened to him in his adult life. "I do beg your pardon. . . ."

"It's all right." He heard humor and groaned. Quite the figure of fun he must be. Doubtless he'd been smooth enough last night when he'd coaxed her into his bed, and now here he was like a puling, sickly child.

A damp cloth wiped his face. Then she raised his head slightly and cool glass pressed near his lips.

"More," he said, when he'd drained the water.

He heard a chink, and the promising gurgle. He was grateful she was working in the dark, for the thought of bright light made him wince. In moments she presented another full glass, and he drank it, then sank gratefully back onto the pillows.

Down pillows.

Inns didn't have down pillows.

"Where am I?" he asked again. She'd answered before, hadn't she? He'd forgotten.

"Gillsett."

That didn't sound like an inn. It sounded like a residence. A farm. Even a gentleman's house . . .

"What is your name, sir? Should we notify anyone?"

At least he didn't have to tell her he didn't know. He was sliding back down into that annihilating void.

Chapter 3

Rosamunde straightened and shook her head. She planned adulterous wickedness and ended up custodian of foul chamber pots. Perhaps her dull life was not the result of her accident, but simply her fate!

But at least she'd carried off the lie about where he was.

She'd never been a convincing liar. She hated deceit, and her stumbling tongue and guilty blushes had given her and Diana away time after time. Tonight, however, she had told her untruth in a calm voice and darkness had hidden her burning cheeks. Perhaps she could carry this wild plan off after all.

But not immediately.

The plan would have to wait until he recovered, so she might as well continue with chamber-pot duty.

She opened the window to freshen the air, then put on her dressing gown and carried the noisome pot away. She could hardly leave it to stink up the corridor, so taking the small nightlamp, she crept downstairs and placed it quietly outside the back door.

She returned to her room, took the clean pot from under her own bed and going to his room, placed it by his side. Should she stay in case he was sick again? Well, she wouldn't. The wretch had drunk himself ill, and he could puke himself sober without her help!

Thoroughly disgruntled, Rosamunde snuggled into her own bed—which by now was unwelcomingly cold. Her sense of the ridiculous soon returned, however. Why had she imagined that a sick man would awake cured and full of amorous intent?

Such foolishness.

She wished he had, though. Then, it would be over.

She turned, punching her pillow, feeling wretched about something. . . .

Then she remembered. Remembered thinking about her dull life. It was the sort of thought she didn't normally let out.

She had a lovely life. A kind husband. A comfortable home, and a prosperous estate that provided plenty of useful work. Loving family nearby. Good friends all around.

The accident could have made her a recluse for life, but Digby had rescued her with his kind offer of marriage.

What was a recluse, though? Even someone who lived in a community could be considered a recluse if she never left it. If she was afraid to. The recent trip to Harrogate had been her first venture out of Wensleydale in eight years.

So? She turned and punched her pillow again. Plenty of people were content to stay close to a good home. There were people in Wensleydale who'd never even been to Richmond!

So—the truth was that she wasn't happy living that way. Instead, she felt barred from the world by her face.

She fingered the scar ridges to the right of her eye. They weren't the problem. It was the long one down her cheek that made her hide away, even though her family and Diana kept saying it wasn't really so bad.

Even Digby, however, preferred to sit to her left.

Dear Digby. As a friend of her father's and an honorary uncle, she'd loved him all her life. But not, she was coming to realize, as a wife should love a husband. She hadn't known that at sixteen, however, hadn't know how wrong it would feel when he claimed his husbandly rights. It had never been terrible, just not something she and Sir Digby Overton should be doing.

She'd been relieved when the activity had ceased and they could be comfortable together again.

Until now.

Now, however, she had to have a child. She *owed* it

to Digby, to Wenscote, to everyone who had been so kind to her these past eight years.

Anyway—and this shamed her—she wanted Wenscote for herself. Without a child, when Digby died, she'd have to leave. Leave her sanctuary. Leave the place where she had powers and responsibilities.

Digby was a fair landlord, but not an adventurous one. It had been Rosamunde who'd started sheep-breeding projects, and growing winter fodder. She'd put the cottage industries—cheese making, spinning, and weaving—on a more orderly footing, and made sure everyone received a fair price. And, her true enthusiasm, she'd started breeding horses.

It had all come about out of boredom, but she knew she'd stumbled upon her life's purpose. Where was she going to find the like if she lost Wenscote? It wasn't even considered proper in most circles for women to be directly involved in animal breeding.

So there it was. In the open at last. She wasn't being a martyr. She was serving her own ends. True, many people would benefit if she went through with this, but at heart she was being ruthlessly selfish.

So be it. She still had reason enough, and the means.

A stud animal, she thought firmly. She was used to evaluating rams and stallions, and this one was healthy and well-formed. What more did she want? Was she still hoping for a dashing knight on a white charger?

A dashing knight would doubtless be a great deal of trouble. Her drunken wastrel would do his business, like Samuel her best tup, then move on to another ewe without a thought.

She heaved herself onto her back with a wretched sigh, wishing she could get to sleep. Problems were niggling at her, however.

Even she knew young men didn't leap onto every woman they encountered. A fine state of affairs that would be! She suppressed a chuckle at the thought of a country fair—or even church on Sunday!—with all the men acting like Samuel in a field of fertile ewes.

It wasn't funny, though. She had to work out what to

do. Should she dress provocatively? Would she have to be naked? Should she touch him first? Kiss him first?

Oh, she did wish Diana was here. Though unmarried, Diana met a lot more men and flirted with most of them. She'd even mentioned books on intimate matters. She'd surely know how to encourage a male. Whatever it took, however, Rosamunde was going to do it.

Even if she had to go up to Arradale and raid the library for those mysterious books!

Fear.

He lay still in the darkness, a bitter memory of enemies hovering over him.

Silence.

A foul taste.

Vomit.

'Struth! Embarrassing memory flooded back. He'd cast up his accounts in front of a woman.

Had she been real?

Tentatively, he reached out and found he was alone. Thank heavens. He'd dreamed it.

But the taste was still there, and the memory of a calm, pleasing voice was devilishly clear.

The touch of a breeze made him turn his head. His much less painful head. In the dark, curtains stirred, giving glimpses of a slightly lighter outside. Someone had opened the window to freshen the air.

So, who was she, and where was he?

Clearly in the country. The air and quiet told him that.

The woman had named the place, but that too eluded. Gill-something? Gillshaw?

He burned with a need for the security of knowledge. Despite comfort and tranquility, he lay tense with fear, under a haunting sense of danger in the shadows.

Was it real?

He didn't know.

Just as he still didn't know who he was. That seemed ridiculous, so he pushed and poked at his mind, demanding his identity.

He stirred only dreamlike memories, but snatched at them greedily.

Riding a country lane on a sweet summer's day.

When?

An old stone house with ivy-covered walls.

Where?

Birds singing in the trees. A blue coat spoiled by a brush against wet paint.

Had he cared?

Swaying in a good, solid coach, applying himself to paperwork. He paused on that. It showed a hardworking, conscientious fellow, and that felt true. Not this drunkard in a whore's bed. . . .

Silver plate on a laden table, glowing in candlelight. . . .

He sucked in deep breaths, forcing himself to break off the frantic struggle to weave these scraps into whole cloth. He knew with eerie certainty that they weren't connected.

Who was he?

What was his *name,* dammit?

The veils parted and his name popped out like an impish child saying, "Were you looking for me?"

Brand Malloren.

He groaned with exquisite relief.

He was Brand Malloren. The knowledge settled in his mind, carrying dancing ribbons of detail. He was Brand Malloren, third son of the Marquess of Rothgar. The old marquess. His oldest brother held the title now.

That rich dinner had been his last meal at Malloren House in London before heading north. As the ribbons wove into a complete story, he grasped each detail, desperate for more of himself.

He could see the dining room as clearly as if he were sitting in it. Silver dishes of excellent food, all bathed in warm candlelight though, it being summer, fading sunlight lightened the room as well. His oldest brother the marquess sat at the head of the table, Cyn and Cyn's wife, Chastity, at either side, Elf opposite. That was the "elf" he'd thought of before. His sister Elfled. Cyn not "sin," Bryght, not "bright"—Arcenbryght, his other brother.

How long ago had that been? Had Bryght's wife had

her child? Had all gone well? She was a small woman for childbearing. . . .

He struggled to remember something else, but everything between that pleasant meal and this dark, mysterious room lay blank, as if it had never existed.

But he remembered talking at that dinner about a trip north.

Was he now in the north? He thought he remembered a touch of it in the woman's voice, though she'd spoken like a lady. So, he was likely in Yorkshire or Northumberland. But where? And who was his nurse? And what the devil had happened to him?

He forced himself to sit up and after a moment, found the pain in his head bearable. Massaging the dull ache, he still struggled with the idea that he'd drunk himself insensible.

If he couldn't change the damnable darkness in his mind, he could surely light that around him. Groping, he found a table, and searched with his fingers for the candle and tinderbox that should be there. Nothing. He stretched further. He felt the brushing chill of glass a moment too late, and cursed as it shattered on the floor.

His fingers scrabbled over the smooth table for something else. Something he could use as a weapon. The door creaked open and a pale figure appeared, backlit by a weak night-light in the hall.

"Are you awake, sir?"

At the soft, remembered voice, he almost wept with relief.

Why this mad panic? What had happened to him?

"Sir?" She was coming over and he realized he hadn't answered.

"Yes, I'm awake. Don't come closer. There's glass on the floor to the right of the bed."

She stopped, only a gray shape now, for she'd closed the door. He reviewed matters with a suppressed groan. First he'd thrown up. Now he'd created a dangerous mess. He'd better crawl away from here as soon as possible and never return.

"Are you feeling sick again?" she asked. "The chamber pot's down there."

He tested the idea, and was pleased to be able to say, "No. I must thank you for your care of me."

"It's no trouble. Did you need something?"

My mind back. He could hardly say that. "Perhaps a light?"

"It's the middle of the night."

How could he say he was suddenly afraid of the dark? "I'm sorry for disturbing you." He wished he could remember her name, remember what they were to each other. Anything.

She came closer, round to the left of the bed. He watched the ghostly paleness of her hand and arm reach out so she could lay a hand on his forehead, and remembered the pleasure of her earlier touch.

"I'm much better," he said. A smooth hand. A lady's hand, though many doxies had soft hands, too.

"Certainly you have no fever."

"Where did you say this is?"

"Gillsett."

Gillsett. He repeated it to himself a time or two, determined not to lose it this time. "And where is Gillsett?"

"Arkengarthdale."

One of the more remote Yorkshire dales. Mostly sheep country. Strange to know geography and land use, but not where he had been recently and why. He felt strangely certain that he had no business reason to be in Arkengarthdale.

He had to ask the obvious question. "And you are . . . ?"

"Miss Gillsett."

He must certainly have dreamed the business of having this composed, well-bred lady in his bed. Miss Gillsett of Gillsett was doubtless a kind-hearted lady of sensible years and impeccable virtue. She'd likely faint if she learned he'd imagined her in his bed.

"Have you remembered *your* name, sir?" she asked.

From embarrassment and a dislike of being fawned on, he'd rather not say. But he had no choice. "Malloren." When she didn't react, he relaxed and added his first name. "Brand Malloren."

"Do you have family or friends who will be worrying, Mr. Malloren?"

He was actually Lord Brand Malloren, but certainly didn't mind being thought a simple mister in this embarrassing situation. The question was an interesting one, however. If his family knew he was sick they certainly would worry. They were far away, however, and he'd left his entourage in Thirsk. With luck, neither family nor staff would ever find out about this debacle.

"No. I'm traveling alone on business."

And, with another shift of the veils, he suddenly remembered some of his affairs. Visiting his brother's estates around England. Checking accounts and the care of the land. Arguing with conservative tenants about change. Reviewing breeding programs and the yield of experimental crops.

He remembered, too, that he often left his staff dealing with routine matters and visited suspect or interesting places without warning. Something about that snagged, like a painful jerk on a new scar—

"Business in the dales, Mr. Malloren?" Her voice distracted him before he could grasp what had snagged, and why it was important.

"Damnation!" He bit off more angry words. "I'm sorry. My nerves are on end. Truth is, dear lady, my wits are scrambled and I don't know enough about myself to make a sensible story of it. What happened to me?"

"I don't know. I found you by the roadside, unconscious, miles from anywhere. You were soaking wet with night coming on."

That was not the story he'd imagined at all. "By the roadside . . . in Arkengarthdale?" He knew enough of the land to see the picture. Sheep-dotted fells climbing up to boggy moor. Scattered, rugged farms and little traffic. "Then I most sincerely thank you, Miss Gillsett, for saving my life. I apologize even more for the trouble I'm causing you."

Rosamunde stood there, considering his dim shape in the dark. Diana always said she loved honesty too much, and it was true. She could dance along a lie for a while, but then truth would swell up in her like a pot boiling over. As it did now.

Was it possible to do this thing at least partly based on truth?

"Are you sincerely grateful, Mr. Malloren?" she heard herself say. Her hands were clasped tight together and her heart pounded.

"On my honor."

She swallowed. "Then would you consider doing me a service in return?"

After the briefest hesitation, he said, "How could I refuse?"

"You can," she assured him. "I don't want you to feel obliged if it is impossible for you."

"Why not tell me what it is you want?"

With truth in control she almost blurted out, "A baby." She had sense enough, however, to know she mustn't say that.

What, then?

Diana had said some women wanted men just for themselves. For the act.

What where the right words, though?

"I want . . ." When it came to it, she could only think of the sheep. "I want tupping," she blurted out, then covered her mouth with a horrified hand. "I'm sorry. Of course you wouldn't—"

"I don't see why not," he said, remarkably calmly. "I have to point out, however, that it can have implications, especially for an unmarried lady."

She thought for a moment, then said, "I'm not unmarried."

"Ah. Not *Miss* Gillsett."

"No."

"Widow?"

"No." That truth spilled out before she could stop it.

"A neglectful husband, then."

She hesitated. In most ways Digby was the sweetest, kindest man, but she knew what he meant. "Yes," she muttered, hand still half over her mouth.

Then she realized how this would look to him, and felt her face flame. She must appear to be a woman with a flaming hunger for carnal matters, a woman so desperate for it that she'd proposition a stranger she had found drunk by the road!

She almost fled then, but reminded herself that it was true. Not in the way he'd think, but true all the same. And what did it matter what he thought? After this, they'd never meet again.

He was silent, clearly thinking just what she expected. "So?" she prompted, and it came out harshly.

"Now? 'Struth, no." She heard him mutter something she couldn't catch. It was doubtless just as well. A tear leaked from one eye, and she fought the urge to sniff. She was making a thorough mess of this.

"You have been kind to me," he said, as if weighing each word. "I will gladly be kind to you in turn, dear lady. But my head still aches like the devil, my brain feels scrambled, and I'm not at all sure I won't cast up my accounts again if I try to move."

Of course he wasn't well enough. Rosamunde wanted to crawl under the bed in the hope that a monster truly did live there, ready to gobble her up. She also wanted it done and over with so she could get him out of the house tomorrow, and out of her life forever.

It didn't matter what she wanted, though, or how this embarrassed her, or how much she disliked it. She just needed to get it done and hope and pray that a baby resulted. Clearly, however, she'd have to be a nurse before she could be an adulteress.

"If your head hurts," she said, as coolly as she could, "would you like a powder?"

"I can't guarantee that my stomach will tolerate it, but I'm willing to try."

He sounded so *calm*. Was he not shocked to his soul by this?

She was.

"I'll be back in a moment then."

When she left, Brand eased back onto his pillow with a groan that wasn't entirely pain. Plague take it. But how could he say no? He was not unaccustomed to frustrated wives, and if he liked them out of bed he was happy to give them pleasure in it, but this case. . . .

He had no idea what she even looked like. It didn't matter much, but it made him uncomfortable. Oh well, by the time he was in a fit state to tend to her, daylight would resolve that. Nor should it matter that he didn't know her. He couldn't with truth say that he'd been well acquainted with every woman he'd bedded, and what he did know of this one was only kindness.

With a rueful smile, he accepted that it was his weakness here that bothered him. He wasn't used to dealing with amorous women when naked, sick, and half out of his mind.

He heard her return, and watched her shadowy figure fumble across the room. She'd doubtless had light in her own room and had lost her night vision. Why, then, hadn't she brought the light in here? Did she have something to hide?

"Here you are," she said, rather breathily.

Their exploring hands connected on the glass, and she started. Then he heard her give it one last stir with a spoon. "It's bitter, but it works. Get it all down."

He obeyed, then almost choked at the taste. "Perdition!"

"Will it stay down?"

He lay back and still. "We're arguing about it. What is that stuff?"

"Mostly willow bark."

After a moment, he said, "I don't think the chamber pot will be needed." He wished she would go away. "You don't need to hover over me."

She moved a few steps back. "Very well. Till tomorrow, then?"

Suppressing a groan, he said, "Breakfast and a toothbrush, dear lady, and I'll be entirely at your service."

She left and he feared his tone had been unfortunate, but plague take it, he'd nearly died, his brain was scrambled, and he'd just swallowed what tasted like deadly poison.

What did she think he was, a damned sexual automaton?

He drifted back to sleep imagining a scrawny harridan turning an enormous key that gradually raised and expanded his penis to quite terrifying dimensions.

Chapter 4

Rosamunde always woke early, and so she did, even after the most extraordinary and disturbed night of her life. She lacked her usual enthusiasm for the coming day, however. Covering her face with her hands, she wondered how she had brought herself to state her need like that.

Lord save her.

And it was still to do, though her courage had fled with the dark.

She crawled out of bed and drew back the curtains, revived a little by the first glow of a hopeful summer morning. Birds sang their hearts out and distant noises told her the Yockenthwaits were up.

Breakfast and a toothbrush, he'd said, and at the remembered tone, her cheeks flamed again. She'd demanded it as payment! If a man demanded it of her, she'd want to kill him, even if he had saved her life.

It was different for men, though.

Wasn't it?

Standing straighter, she took a deep breath of fresh air. Of course it was. They often paid for what she was offering.

She dressed herself in her simplest gown, with only one petticoat and a light corset underneath. With just the hooks to be fastened, she went to wake Millie.

The woman opened saggy eyelids. "Wha—? Milady? What time is it?"

"Early, but I need to speak to you, Millie. Do up my hooks, please."

The maid pushed herself up, shoving her huge nightcap back straight, and set to work. "Yes, milady? Is it that man? Is he worse?"

"No, not worse. Listen. I've told him that this is a place called Gillsett, and that my name is Mrs. Gillsett."

After three fumbling hooks, Millie asked, "Why?"

"It doesn't matter *why*. Just make sure to keep up the pretense if you have to help me with him."

"You can't be taking care of the likes of him, milady!"

"I already have." Her dress fastened, Rosamunde stood and turned. "He was sick in the night."

"You should have called for me to take care of that, milady!"

Rosamunde could imagine the performance that would have been. "It wasn't necessary. But I left the chamber pot outside the back door. If the Yockenthwaits haven't handled it, you should. The main thing is that you not let him know where he really is."

"If you say so, milady." Rosamunde could hear the dull befuddlement in the maid's voice, but she knew Millie wouldn't waste energy on questions. Millie worked herself and her many layers of clothing out of bed. "I'll be up and dressed, and look after that chamber pot, milady."

Rosamunde headed downstairs, trying to get her schemes straight in her mind. Even if Millie had to attend the man, she wouldn't chatter, but would she remember not to "milady" Rosamunde?

Well then, perhaps she'd be *Lady* Gillsett. Wife of . . . Sir Archibald Gillsett. Sir Archibald could be ancient, and spend most of his time taking the waters at Harrogate or Matlock.

That was why she was a neglected wife.

She rather liked this other identity. Lady Gillsett—a bolder, wilder woman than Rosamunde, Lady Overton. Lady Gillsett wouldn't have butterflies in her tummy at the thought of the man upstairs and what was going to happen. She'd be licking her scarlet lips in anticipation.

When was it going to happen? After breakfast? Rosamunde froze at the bottom of the stairs, hand over butterflies. That meant *daytime*!

Things that had seemed possible in the night seemed

very impossible in broad daylight. She and Digby had never done it except under cover of night. On the other hand, she wasn't entirely sure she could keep the man for another night. If he was recovered enough for . . . for what she wanted, he would surely be recovered enough to leave.

She could lock him in.

A captive lover, she thought, hand over mouth suppressing a wild giggle.

Lady Gillsett wouldn't blink at that. Lady Gillsett probably picked up handsome rogues all over the land and discarded them after use without a backward glance. Rosamunde went forward, trying to walk like Lady Gillsett, head at a saucy angle, hips swaying, pausing by the mirror in the hall to study the effect.

She rolled her eyes. Even from her good side it looked ridiculous. She had always been the wholesome type, and her nut-brown curls and round, rosy cheeks couldn't look at all wicked. She tried hiding her ordinary blue eyes with sultry lashes, but then she looked half asleep! She supposed if she had a low-cut gown, she could show off her generous breasts. But she didn't, so she couldn't.

He'd agreed, she reminded herself firmly. He didn't need to be seduced into it.

She found the kitchen bustling, steam puffing out of pots, tasty aromas of fresh-baked bread and frying bacon wafting from the hearth. A thin young maid busily cleared the men's breakfast plates—they'd obviously eaten and gone about their work—and Mrs. Yockenthwait punched down a huge crock of bread dough with her powerful fist.

"You're up early, milady. Give us a minute and Jessie can set up the breakfast room."

Rosamunde sat at the plain kitchen table. "I'd be happy to take my breakfast here, Mrs. Yockenthwait."

The woman's brows rose, but as she flung a cloth over the crock and put it back near the hearth, she said, "Right then. Jessie, lay a place with the good china!"

Rosamunde knew better than to insist on using the servants' ware. She was only trying to save them work, but right and proper order must be maintained.

While the maid was off getting the china, Mrs. Yockenthwait washed her hands. "Did you look in on that man, milady? I haven't had time yet."

"He was sick in the night, and later I gave him a powder for his sore head. Since then, he's just been sleeping it off."

"Aye, we noticed the chamber pot. Did you bring that down, milady? You should have woken one of us."

Rosamunde picked up a piece of bread left from the men's breakfast and buttered it. "He's no concern of yours, Mrs. Yockenthwait. Millie and I will take care of him."

At that moment, Millie lumbered in, swathed in shawls and went to the back door. She came back quickly, so the chamber pot must have been gone. "What do you want me to do next, milady?"

Rosamunde suppressed a smile at the "next." Millie made it sound as if she'd already done hard labor. "Sit and eat breakfast, Millie," she said, only then realizing that she was creating difficulties of etiquette. Young Jessie had just come in with the fine china, and now there was Millie to consider.

The maid laid a place for Rosamunde, then went to get another setting. Mrs. Yockenthwait scowled. Oh, how good intentions led to complex problems.

"Millie," said Rosamunde, "why don't you swing the kettle over the heat ready for tea. And help Jessie to make breakfast."

This seemed to reestablish order in the universe, and the atmosphere in the kitchen became comfortable again.

"Did he say who he was, milady?" asked Mrs. Yockenthwait, preparing a rank of bread trays.

Rosamunde almost told the truth, but then decided that the fewer people who had a name for him, the better. "He doesn't remember. Not even how he came to be in a ditch by the road."

"Not surprising, that, dead drunk as he was. And you'd best not to be getting too familiar with the likes of him, milady."

Familiar! Rosamunde knew she was blushing. "He's harmless. Really. He was most apologetic and embarrassed. Whatever caused him to drink so much, I'm sure it's not his usual way. In fact he said so."

"Happen he would," said the woman dryly. But then she admitted, "His clothes are good enough. Or were. They're mostly dry, and I've had Jessie brush them off and sponge them down." As the sizzle of frying bacon and eggs started, Mrs. Yockenthwait added, "Happen he'll want breakfast, too."

Rosamunde couldn't let either maid take it up. "I'll check after we've eaten."

She ate quickly, not having much of an appetite anyway, and being anxious to get back to Mr. Malloren before anyone else. As soon as she was finished, she leaped up, and over protests, assembled a tray for him.

Fried eggs and bacon might stir his stomach again, so she chose bread, well layered with butter and honey. She added a mug of tea with milk, deliberately choosing the servants' ware and putting a couple of lumps chipped off the sugar into the saucer. "I'll take this up and see what else he'd like."

"But, milady—" said Mrs. Yockenthwait.

Millie even heaved herself to her feet.

"I'll do it!" Rosamunde called with a smile, and hurried on her way.

Once upstairs, however, she paused for courage and for thought. She mustn't make any silly mistakes. With a start that almost spilled the tea, she realized that she'd nearly made the biggest mistake of all.

He mustn't see her face!

Only a part of this was because of her awkwardness over her blemishes. He must never know who she was. If for some reason he tried to find her, he'd draw a blank at Gillsett. Then he could search the dales for years, if he were mad enough, without finding this small house. But if he started to search for a lady with scars on her face . . .

She put down the tray and hurried into her room to find the painted mask she'd worn for the masquerade. She looked at it and grimaced, wishing she'd not played with it. She'd taken the plain, full face mask of shaped silk that Diana had provided, and amused herself by adding arched eyebrows, pinkened cheeks and a couple of fashionable black patches high on the cheekbone. It had seemed appropriate for a decadent, wicked masquerade, but now . . . ?

She put it on, and saw what she'd feared: a grotesque doll's face.

She shrugged. It couldn't be helped, and it must be done. She carried the tray to his room, balancing it on her hip as she unlocked the door.

The room was bright and the bed was empty!

Almost at the same moment she saw him, turning sharply from the window, a towel wrapped around his hips. It wasn't a terribly large towel.

Rosamunde didn't drop the tea and toast, but it was a close thing.

"I'm sorry," he said, clearly wickedly amused. "Should I plunge back into the bed?"

Eyes firmly turned away, Rosamunde said, "Yes, please."

Oh dear. So much for Lady Gillsett!

She made herself look boldly at him, watch him as he strolled to the bed and slipped under the covers, discreetly shedding the towel. Lady Gillsett would appreciate every inch, and Rosamunde had to admit that she did, too. She'd thought him well-made when unconscious, but awake and mobile he was remarkable. By the time he covered himself to halfway up his chest, she felt a Gillsettian pang of regret.

Only then did she marvel at how relaxed he seemed, and a knot of worry started. Between his first waking and his second, he'd forgotten the name of the place where he supposedly was. What if this time he'd forgotten his nighttime promise?

Would she have to go through the whole thing again?

Steadying her nerves, she carried the tray over and set it on his knees.

He put a hand to it, smiling up at her. "Better?" He was teasing, yes, but perhaps a little puzzled. Did that mean he *did* remember?

"You startled me."

"I couldn't find my clothes."

"They're in the kitchen being dried and cleaned—as best we can." She couldn't stop her hands fiddling with her skirt. "You were found in a muddy ditch."

He studied the tray, then picked up a triangle of honeyed bread. "I wish I could remember how or why. But clearly I could have drowned if I'd ended up facedown, and without that, I'd likely have died of cold. You have my eternal gratitude, Mrs. Gillsett."

Did that refer to their wicked arrangement? She wasn't sure she *could* start all over again, particularly in daylight. "I brought tea and bread, but if you want, we can provide something more substantial."

He added sugar to the tea and stirred it. "I'll admit to being hungry, but I'd better test my innards on this first." He glanced up. "I do most sincerely apologize for being so foully ill in the night."

He meant it. He was, she thought, embarrassed, too. About being sick? Or other things.

"You remember?"

"I think so."

Rosamunde gripped her hands together. "All?"

He was sipping the tea, but watching her. "I think I remember everything, yes."

It was clearly a very subtle question. After a moment to gather courage, she answered it. "Good."

With the slightest twitch of his brows, he settled back to tea and bread.

Was that all he was going to say? Rosamunde wanted to ask if he was *really* going to do it. And when. And how—

"Is the mask necessary?" he asked.

She touched it, strange beneath her fingers. "I don't want you to see my face."

"Then I assume you're not Mrs. Gillsett of Gillsett."

Rosamunde's heart missed a few crucial beats. "Why would you think that?"

"If I have your name and direction, what point in hiding your features?"

He was right! She should have known she'd make a pig's dinner of this. She tried to recover. "I never imagined you'd come seeking me."

"Even less reason for a mask."

Scrabbling for an explanation, she came up with, "What if we passed on a street one day, or met at an assembly? I'd rather you not be able to recognize me." Thinking of a phrase Diana sometimes used, she added, "It's a foible, sir. Humor me."

And it worked. Shrugging, he said, "I owe you my life, so I will certainly humor you." He glanced up. "In all ways."

Even though this was what she wanted, Rosamunde almost squeaked like a cornered mouse.

She watched as he ate, until he pushed away the tray. "That does seem to be staying inside, but I'm afraid I still don't feel I can do you credit. Is there any chance of the toothbrush?" He rubbed his hand along his jaw. "And a razor would be a blessing."

At these prosaic requests, Rosamunde wanted to burst into tears. Next he'd be making an appointment for, say, half-past-one in the afternoon!

After a moment she managed, "Of course. You can borrow my toothbrush and powder, and I'll have warm water brought for washing. I'm not sure about the razor."

"Doesn't your husband shave?"

Oh, Lud. How to answer that? "Of course. But he's away. He's doubtless taken all his razors with him. But I'll check!"

She escaped then, locking the door as if he might come after her. No chance of that! He was doubtless delaying in the hope that she'd change her mind.

And he'd guessed about the wrong name. Butterflies and billhooks! Whatever he was, he was no fool. She leaned back against the paneled wall, hand to chest. Diana had been right. The masquerade would have been *much* simpler.

She didn't, however, regret this course.

That searing vision of his almost-naked form made her not regret it at all. Her feelings were truly wicked, but if she had to do this thing, she wanted to do it with her handsome wastrel.

She took off her mask and stuffed it in her pocket,

then rubbed her face in the hope of clearing up any marks. After a check in a mirror, she hurried down to the kitchen to order Millie to take him the toothbrush, tooth powder, and warm water for washing. "Oh, and he managed to knock a glass on the floor in the night, so clean it up carefully. Don't leave any bits." She turned to the housekeeper. "Mrs. Yockenthwait, can we find a razor for him?"

"Are you sure you want to give a man like that a blade, milady?"

"He's harmless." Even as she said it, Rosamunde knew it wasn't true. He wouldn't take the razor on a murderous rampage, but something dangerous wove about this Mr. Malloren. Drawn though she was, like a fly to a spider's web, she'd feel safer once he'd done the necessary and disappeared from her life.

Safer, but not necessarily happier.

Mrs. Yockenthwait provided her husband's razor, and Rosamunde quietly reminded Millie of the deception before sending her upstairs with the water and blade. She wanted to go herself, but it would look peculiar. Meanwhile, she searched for a way to keep the housekeeper from paying him a visit.

She'd still not found a plausible excuse when a plump young woman burst into the kitchen, red-faced and panting. "Auntie Hester! Auntie Hester! Carrie's having the baby!"

Then the lass saw Rosamunde. "Milady!" She bobbed a curtsy.

"My niece Dilly Beckworth," said Mrs. Yockenthwait, frowning. "Well, and this has come at an awkward time. I said I'd go and help, but . . ."

"But you must!" Rosamunde insisted, trying not to sound as relieved as she felt. "Jessie can take care of things here, with Millie to help. Quite likely I'll be on my way later today, anyway."

After a moment, Mrs. Yockenthwait nodded. "Right you are then. And you can always send up to the big house if you need aught. I'll just get some things."

She marched off, and her niece fidgeted around the kitchen.

"Is Carrie your sister, Dilly?" Rosamunde asked to put her at ease, and to cover a whole new set of alarming thoughts.

The girl curtsied. "Yes, milady. And it's her first."

"I hope all goes well with her."

Rosamunde, however, was thinking that a birthing was a grand place for gossip. Many women would gather, and then there'd be hours to pass talking.

"Is she near her time?" Rosamunde asked.

"I don't think so, milady. Her pains only started this morning."

Could be all day then.

Mrs. Yockenthwait came back in. "Are you bothering Lady Overton, Dilly?"

"No," Rosamunde said. "I was just asking about your niece's welfare."

"She'll be all right, God willing. A sturdy lass, and healthy." But then Mrs. Yockenthwait said, "Dilly, you wait outside." When the girl had gone, she said, "I'm a mite worried about leaving you here with that man, milady."

Rosamunde felt as squirmy as poor Dilly. "No need. I'm keeping his door locked. And if he gives any trouble, there are men nearby to help."

Mrs. Yockenthwait gave her a Yorkshire look. It could reflect worry, or it could be suspicion as to what Rosie Ellington was really up to.

There was no help for it. Rosamunde seized her courage. "Mrs. Yockenthwait, I'm thinking it might be better if people didn't know about him. About the man . . ."

"Aye, milady?"

Rosamunde tried to look calm and in control. "He spent the night unconscious or vomiting, but still. It might look a little strange if people heard about it. My reputation . . ."

After a moment, the woman nodded. "Happen you're right, milady. Best anyways to keep these things to ourselves. You hear, Jessie?"

"Yes, Mrs. Yockenthwait!"

"I'll have a word with Mr. Yockenthwait, too. Perhaps you should speak to your groom and coachman, milady."

"I'll do that. Thank you." Rosamunde spoke as calmly as possible, but inside she quivered with the certainty that Mrs. Yockenthwait *knew*.

Knew what she planned.

And why.

Which was why such a stern, upright woman was willing to turn a blind eye to sin.

The housekeeper took off her apron and put on a cloak and hat, barking out a stream of orders. "Jessie, you be sure to look after Lady Overton properly. And to put that bread in the oven when it's risen. And to take it out right. And don't forget to put that ham in for supper. And pick the beans. And . . ."

Eventually she ran out of instructions, gathered up the basket she'd prepared, and cast one last considering look at Rosamunde. "You take care, milady."

Rosamunde nodded, and watched her leave.

How excruciating to think that the housekeeper guessed what she was up to. On the other hand, it suggested the local people might be willing allies. No one wanted the New Commonwealth in the area, and dale people being dale people, there wasn't a family at Wenscote without links to every other family hereabouts. Dale people being dale people, they'd not want outsiders to know of their business anyway.

She cast a cautious look at young Jessie, but she had settled to her work. With luck, she didn't suspect anything.

Normally, Rosamunde would have put the girl at her ease, but it suited her to have Jessie somewhat in awe and fixed below stairs. "Millie and I will take care of the gentleman, Jessie. There's no need for you to come upstairs."

"Very well, milady."

Millie returned. "I've done as you asked, milady, but do you know, that wretch has hardly a stitch on! It's not right, you going in there."

Rosamunde blushed, but grasped the moment. "I'm sorry it upset you, Millie. I am a married lady, which you and Jessie are not, so I'll see to him." Before Millie could form an objection, Rosamunde added, "Meanwhile, there's mud on my blue petticoat. Please try to clean it. In fact, why not work in the kitchen where it's warm?"

Millie frowned, but she never really argued with anything. She shrugged and clumped off to find the petticoat. Rosamunde nipped round to the small stables and warned Garforth and Tom not to gossip about the man. When she returned, Millie was close to the hearth with the petticoat, a bowl of water, and some soap.

Everything was in place. It would take something drastic to cause Millie to climb upstairs again, and Jessie had no reason to.

Now what?

Rosamunde wandered to the drawing room, tangled in uncertainty. What on earth was the etiquette of this extraordinary situation? When should she go upstairs?

What would Lady Gillsett do?

Lady Gillsett would doubtless be up there now, ogling his body as he shaved, poised to ravish him at the first opportunity. Rosamunde, however, skulked here, her courage fled to the far sides of the earth, leaving a sick, trembling jelly in its place.

She squared her shoulders. Even with knocking knees and quivering insides, she was going to do this. Now!

She went upstairs, and faced the door to her captive lover's lair. Oh dear. She did feel like a Christian about to face the lions. Lud . . .

Smoothing her hands down her simple green dress, she wondered if she should change back into her nightgown. She couldn't. She couldn't go in there like that in daytime.

Whatever was to happen, she had to go through the door.

She tied on her mask with nerve-tremored fingers, then had to wipe them again on her skirt before she could turn the key.

Her heart thundered, and her lungs sucked desperately for breath.

She went in.

Chapter 5

He lay in the bed as if he'd not moved, but he was scrubbed clean and smooth shaven. Naked to the hips, hair curling lazily on his shoulders, eyes steady on hers, he stole what breath remained.

Don't faint! she commanded herself, and did get some control, but she was suddenly sure this was impossible.

With a quirk of his brow, he patted the bed.

Rosamunde sucked in a deep breath, summoned Lady Gillsett, and sauntered over to hitch herself up beside her lover. Still fully dressed.

Oh dear. Should she have stripped first?

Looking down, she saw her scuffed and sensible shoes on top of the bedcovers. No one could be seduced in their shoes! She hastily eased them off and tipped them over the edge of the bed, hoping he hadn't noticed.

Her stockinged toes felt shamefully naked.

Now, she supposed, she'd have to look at him.

Her eyes skittered sideways. Puzzled and surprised summed up his expression.

"My dear lady, if you want a merry tumble in payment for your care, I'll give you that. But why don't you tell me what you really want?"

Rosamunde turned fiery hot beneath the mask. Damn him for not being stupid.

It was tempting to tell him the truth, that she needed a child. But she daren't. Too much hung in the balance here, and her virtue and reputation were the smallest part. The welfare of all the people attached to Wenscote rested on this moment.

"Why do you doubt what I want?"

"A remarkable lack of lust."

She looked at him then, really looked at him—strong neck, broad shoulders, sculptured chest, and a soothing hint of plain soap. . . .

"I lust," she said, and it was true. It was an unfamiliar state, but she recognized it. A dizziness, as if her heart were not quite reliable. A strangeness on the skin, as if it might hurt to be touched.

Or not exactly hurt . . .

"Perhaps you do at that." Taking her hand, her left hand, he fingered her ring. "If it wouldn't offend, I'd like to know something of your husband."

What?

Why?

Would this man ever do the expected? Was he typical of men, or had she just snared a very unusual one?

Since he seemed set on it, she gave him as much truth as she could, unsteadied by the brush of his fingers on hers. "My husband is a good man, a kind man. But old. He doesn't . . ." That might ring alarm bells. "He rarely . . . er . . . claims his marital rights."

He raised her hand and kissed it, kissed it—deliberately, she was sure—by her wedding ring. "And you want me, here, now?"

The brush of warm lips against fingers. Such a little thing to stir her so. "Yes," she said, over a thudding heart. "I want you. Here. Now."

It was true, but now it was more than lust.

She was driven by rampant curiosity.

She had always been curious about everything, and now she needed to know about this. She needed to know if she'd experienced all there was, or if—as instinct, rumor, and sizzling senses said—there was more.

Still playing with her fingers he asked, "Is it safe? Now?"

"Yes."

He raised her hand again for a kiss, a slow and lingering kiss to her knuckles, and then his mouth slid to her pale inner wrist. She felt his tongue, wet on her skin. "Very well."

Already breathless, she braced for something swirling, something as overwhelming as the mysterious longings seething deep inside her, but he merely turned her away. "Let's get you out of your clothes." He began to unhook the back of her gown with calm, confident fingers.

On their own, shocked by his prosaic tone, her hands jerked to her bodice, ready to resist. She made herself submit. But did it have to be so businesslike?

A dozen times in the next minutes, she nearly balked. In bed, in the night, in the dark, in her nightgown, she'd been prepared. But here she was, in daytime, being stripped by a naked stranger!

In the end, she did break free, scrambling off the bed to remove her own petticoat and stockings, leaving only her shift. It was sensible cotton with a tie neckline and elbow-length sleeves trimmed with a plain ruffle. It hung like a tent down to below her knees, but she felt nakedly, wickedly exposed.

She dared a glance to see what he was making of all this.

So much for stories of lust-driven men! Here she was, as good as naked in broad daylight, and he looked as interested, as excited as . . . as a shepherd watching the sheep! Was it all nonsense? No, she thought with a silent groan, the problem was that she kept forgetting to be Lady Gillsett. A willing lover wouldn't act like this.

Again, she wanted to crawl under the bed.

She reminded herself grimly that it didn't matter if she was ridiculous, or if he lusted after her. Only that she get with child.

And he'd promised.

As if coming to the same conclusion, he flipped back the sheets. She slid under them, wriggling her shift down neatly—

There she went again! In the night, she'd pulled up her nightgown and snuggled up to him. Now she lay stiffly, covered, and as far away as she could manage without falling off the edge of the bed.

Brand regarded his mysterious bed partner with concern. Neglected wives who sought out men to satisfy their needs were one thing. What was he to make of this?

What he had to make of it, he supposed, was a good experience for her. He had no doubt that she had saved his life, and he remembered her gentle care of him in the night. He owed her a debt and she had specified the payment, one he could afford. It wasn't for him to back away, even though he felt strangely uncomfortable and unsettled by her manner.

He remembered the fear he'd awoken with. Was that the problem? Terror had faded in daylight, but a taste of it lingered. Perhaps that and his missing memories were upsetting him.

Was this a trap?

Why?

Blackmail?

It was hard to imagine how.

An attempt to trap him into marriage?

Her husband could be imaginary, though her wedding ring had the look of one worn for years. Or she could be a widow. Even so, how could she think to drag a man to the altar this way? Would an outraged relative charge in at a crucial moment and demand marriage or a duel? With regret, he'd fight, and if necessary, kill.

Or would the intruder stab him as he lay, claiming righteous provocation?

But who the devil would want to murder him? The Malloren family had enemies in high places, but it was hard to imagine any of them coming after him in the rural north. Besides, most of the enemies were owned, and handled, by his brother the marquess. As estate manager, Brand wasn't tangled in his brother's political machinations.

No, these formless terrors were the product of whatever had felled him the day before, and nothing to do with this poor woman. He couldn't let them get in the way of giving her the reward she wanted for her kindness, and giving generously.

He just wished he was sure he knew what she wanted.

Wryly, he decided that the only thing was to go slowly, so she could retreat if she changed her mind. That wouldn't be hard. Sweet though she was in nature and body, it would take a while for him to summon any real enthusiasm, especially with that grotesque mask.

As a first step, he eased her into his arms. She stayed stiff for a moment, then relaxed, seeming almost to snuggle into him. That was better.

Once she seemed at ease with his touch, he settled to enjoying her, to stroking and tasting her smooth skin, starting with the less alarming places, then slowly trespassing under the modest shift.

She didn't object.

He began to be very pleased about that. He always enjoyed the feel of a woman's soft curves, the satin of her skin, the warm, earthy smells of her more private places. The mask had only a narrow opening at the mouth, preventing kisses. That was a shame, but perhaps in time she'd relax enough to put it off.

Or perhaps she'd worn it deliberately for just that reason. Some women felt kissing was more intimate than sex.

Soon any notion of effort melted. She was lovely to his senses, shapely, musky, soft and sensuous. Pleasantly plump yet firm, like perfect fruit, she was just as he liked a woman, and though she was passive, he could sense response in the very way she shifted her body against his.

What a shame that such a delightful creature was wasted on a man who didn't appreciate her.

He eased a full breast free of her loosened neckline to nuzzle it, breathing deeply.

Perfect.

Absolutely perfect.

Rosamunde let him handle her like a rag doll, dazed and amazed. She didn't know what she'd expected—something like Digby's direct efforts, she supposed, but more vigorous since Mr. Malloren was so much younger. Not all this touching, stroking, licking.

But then she began to worry. When were they going to get to the important bit? His hands seemed to have been everywhere but where it mattered, and even there, hands wouldn't do it.

Those clever hands were doing other things, however, things that made her want to shiver and twitch. In the end, she did, and he asked, "Like that?"

Like? She hadn't been thinking in terms of *liking*. She wanted him to get on with it! She said, "Yes," to encourage him, only realizing a moment later that it was true.

She liked it.

Oh my. Instead of waiting tensely for the dreadful deed, she let herself savor his touch. His whole body, warm-rough-rubbing, making her warm-soft-humming, liquid as lapping water, warmed by his warmth, dizzied by his smell. . . .

Lord save her! This drifting, fevered feeling must be desire—the fire that inspired poets and rascals, and drove men and women into sin and disaster. This was the mystery she'd sensed, but never before experienced.

Here.

In her!

She looked at him, wanting to say something to express her wonderment, but was caught to silence by his rapt admiration of her breasts. She watched as he kissed one again and again, cradling it in his hand as if it were a fruit he desired to eat.

Her.

He cradled and hungered for her.

Hungry herself—for those lips upon hers—she wove her fingers in his hair and tilted his face up to hers, bending to put her lips to his.

Only then remembering her mask.

He drew away, but with a smile. "Can we dispense with the mask yet? You can trust me to be discreet. . . ."

He was already tugging at the strings, but she seized his hands. "No!"

He stilled. "Trust me."

She wavered, pained by his honest need, longing to be honest with him. But then, like icy water, she remembered what lay beneath the mask. Not just her identity— something that could ruin everyone—but her damaged face.

"No," she repeated firmly.

He shrugged. "Then there can be no lip kisses." Instead, he bent to kiss her nipple, drawing it deep into his mouth.

With a choked cry, Rosamunde went limp, but when it seemed he might stop, she clutched him to her. He laughed softly against her mouth-wet skin. "I fear your husband is not just neglectful, but ignorant, my sweet."

Digby? Digby should have been doing things like this?

He'd squeezed her breasts sometimes, but she hadn't liked it. He'd certainly never done the things this man was doing. Now, he was working the same magic on her other breast.

Assailed by sweet sensations, she laughed softly, recognizing a natural force, greeting it as a birthright long denied. He looked up, warm eyes smiling as if her laughter gave him genuine pleasure. Then he touched the important place at last, delicately, almost questioningly.

In answer, she spread her legs, but he didn't cover her and enter her. He just stroked her there. Without pride or dignity, she clutched him, silently begging. For the first time in her life she truly wanted a man inside her. It was an extraordinary need, an aching hunger, an instinct, almost, that could not, must not be denied.

He just touched, and stroked.

"Now," she commanded. "Do it *now. Now!*"

His eyes flashed heated humor. "Are you sure?"

It wasn't a serious question, and she didn't even try to answer. He grinned and moved over her.

Though braced for it, she didn't feel squashed or smothered. She even relished his weight in the cradle of her hips and raised them, seeking. As if in direct response, he guided himself slowly into her.

At last.

She relished every inch of it, but then, startled by the fullness of completion, she cried out. Laughing, he put his hand over her masked mouth. "Hush. No matter how safe you think we are, we can't have you screaming and yelling."

Rosamunde put her own hand over her mouth, because for the first time she could imagine screaming and yelling. She'd cried out the first few times Digby had claimed his rights, but that had been from pain, and after the first time, she'd tried to suppress her noises because it hadn't been his fault. That pain had stopped, but in the years after, she'd never made any kind of noise except the occasional grunt if he squashed her.

Now, she braced herself for the pounding thrusts, commanding herself stay silent.

It didn't happen.

He was back to her breasts again, nibbling and sucking and moving only slowly inside her. Now her hand served to stop pleas for more, for quicker, for harder.

Now!

She mustn't interfere. She couldn't afford another failure like Digby's recent efforts. She couldn't help but move her hips, however, feeling his so hard against her. How different it was without a round belly between.

How tightly he filled her. She supposed that Digby filled her, too, but with all the bouncing and pounding she'd never been so aware of it as now when she felt the friction of his slow movements, as she flexed her own hips in synchrony with his.

She stared up at him, looming over her, many inches taller than Digby, and broader. Perhaps it should be frightening to be so overwhelmed, but it wasn't. Instead, she felt sheltered. Cherished. At home. A creature safe in its burrow, lovingly tended.

Sliding her spare hand up his muscled arm to his broad shoulder, she silently thanked him for precious gifts. But then, caught by a startling pang of need she dug her nails in his flesh. He grinned, eyes afire, and thrust once, hard.

And she arched, lifting him off the bed, counting her own hot pulse pounding through her flesh like a drum, reveling in her liquid need tight around him. He coiled down and sucked at her nipple so hard it should have been agony, but it made her cry out against her hand and arch up harder, like the hard thrusts she'd expected from him.

And this time he met her.

At last he met her need for need, urgently, powerfully driving her back down where she wanted to be. Beneath him. Around him. Part of him.

He was saying things, urging her to things as he moved harder and faster.

Never stopping.

Never pausing.

She began to almost want him to stop. This was too much.

Too hard.

Too unrelenting.

Don't stop!

Oh mercy, mercy.

She was mad with something that must be completed, terrified of the hovering doom, racked with a pain that she loved, groaning with fear and pleasure. . . .

Sobbing with it.

Until—at last, at last—it happened!

No wonder she'd never started a baby, she thought with startling clarity just before she burned up in sudden, obliterating fever. She'd never done it properly!

She held on to that thought as she spun wildly through the fire, and afterward, as she wept into her mask. She wasn't at all sad and was glad the mask hid her folly.

She held on to the thought as a promise—a promise of the baby she'd surely created. Held it as she lay beneath his shuddering heat, feeling as if she'd melted entirely into a puddle of sated senses and sweat.

Truly, that had been the most remarkable thing that had ever happened in her life, and she was very grateful not to have missed it.

He was kissing her neck, her breasts again, but she just wanted to stay a puddle, a surely pregnant puddle. . . .

He rolled onto his back, taking her with him, holding her close. After a languorous while—a moment, an eon—he whispered, "Delightful mysterious lady. More?"

"What?" Even talking seemed too much effort.

He slid down a bit, holding her up on his arms, and suckled her dangling breasts.

"Oh no." Rosamunde had never imagined doing it more than once a night. Or day.

"Oh yes."

"We can't."

"We can."

"*I* can't." And she couldn't. She felt as wrung out as a boiled sheet on laundry day.

"Yes, you can." He nipped at her, making her want to giggle. "I'm not niggardly when it comes to paying debts. You must let me pay in full."

"You've paid. . . ."

"For my very life?" He ignored her feeble protests, lowering her and soon trapping her in need again.

Twice to make sure. Why not?

But when he rolled her onto her back, he used his hand between her legs, slowly, slowly, so she was whispering pleas and even cursing his control before the brilliant end.

As he stroked her and soothed her, she said, "But we didn't do it. Did we?"

"Do what?" Though she was too embarrassed to look at him and talk about this, she could hear the humor.

"Er . . . the whole thing."

"Didn't you like it?"

She knew it was pointless to lie, but tucked her head down as if there was a point to hiding her masked face.

He raised her chin. "You know, your husband could do that for you, even if he can't do other things."

Rosamunde tried to imagine prosaic Digby indulging in such antics.

"No?" he asked.

"I don't think so."

"Some men don't deserve their treasures. But most of it you can do for yourself."

"That's a sin!" How absurd, when she was here, sinning.

"More?" he asked.

Limp and almost quivering, she shook her head and meant it. "You're trying to kill me."

"I've killed no woman yet. Turn, my dear." He didn't wait, but turned her and raised her onto all fours. From behind, he covered her, nipping her protesting neck like a stallion with a mare. "More?"

Stiff in shock, Rosamunde resisted a moment longer, but he wrapped an arm around her and brushed her sensitive nipples while his new erection stirred between her thighs.

A moan escaped her and he licked around her ear, whispering, "More? Please?"

"More," she agreed, and he entered her, quick and fast this time. Like a bitch, or a mare, or a ewe with a tup she let him master her and take her, until they collapsed down in shattered ecstasy, him half over her.

Tangled like that, they slept.

Chapter 6

Rosamunde awoke, sticky and aching in odd places, still half under his big body. She wondered if she and Digby had been doing it entirely wrong all along. Certainly she'd never felt the changes this man had made in her. Perhaps, even, people were supposed to do it from behind like animals. Animals, after all, rarely seemed to have trouble conceiving.

Books. Diana had said she had books. Rosamunde decided her education had been sadly lacking and she needed to read those books.

Shifting slightly, tenderly—in more ways than one—she looked at her lovely lover. Brushing a tendril of hair off his forehead, she found it damp with sweat, but his face seemed relaxed, perhaps slightly smiling. Surely he'd found pleasure and satisfaction in paying his debt so generously. She knew men didn't care much about whom they did this with, but still, it warmed her to think that her body had pleased and satisfied him.

He had given her so much, and she wasn't at this moment thinking about the child she so desperately needed.

Remembering the extraordinary sensations, she felt her body stir, greedy for more. Stroking down her own belly, she tried to soothe it, like a restless creature that could not have what it demanded.

And it could not.

This was an idyll, a moment out of time. Soon her lover would be gone, and to do her duty, she must become once more the placid, comfortable wife of an older man who could not, or would not, do these things.

No one must ever imagine her to be capable of this wanton wickedness.

He'd said she could do it for herself. Tentatively, she slid her hand between her legs, wondering if that was true. As she stroked her slick and sensitive flesh, she thought perhaps it was. Even so, she doubted it would be even nearly the same.

Stroking herself, she looked again at her lover. Her secret lover. If only a woman could set up the equivalent of a mistress.

Smiling wryly at such a ridiculous thought, she removed her hand and fought her wicked urges. She must keep her thoughts on Wenscote. That was all that mattered. Resting her hand on her belly, low down where her womb lay, she prayed that a child was starting there.

"Sore?" His lids rose heavily, sleepy and sated.

"Not really." She said it to reassure him, but then realized how it sounded.

"More?"

She laughed because it clearly was a joke, but she also made sure to roll away and out of bed, for she was tender enough and drained enough to not relish another bout.

At the moment.

Stop that, Rosa. It's done now.

Over.

Forever.

She tugged her shift down decently, then glanced at him. Shift or not, there wasn't a bit of her he did not know.

Except her face.

How strange, bizarre, she must look to him.

He was on his side, head propped up on his hand, looking as if there was nothing strange about her at all. "Do you want me to leave now? I could stay until tomorrow. . . ."

She paused in tying the laces at her neckline. Was that more generosity, or had he liked it enough to want more for himself? That idea wrapped around her like a thick blanket, comforting and tempting her. It had nothing to do with saving Wenscote. It was simple delight at maybe being desired.

"Have you remembered more of yourself then?" she asked, finishing the neat bow.

"Vigorous exercise seems to be doing the trick." With a wicked twinkle, he added, "A little more might complete the process."

She shook her head at him, but couldn't help mirroring his smile. She hoped it showed in her eyes at least. "So you're not being missed at the moment?"

"I don't think so. I manage estates for a nobleman, and I was visiting a couple of places in the Vale of York. We're not in the vale, are we?"

"No." Should she even consider letting him stay? It was dangerous. It was tempting. . . .

"I thought not. I was staying in an inn, The Gimmer's Horn near Northallerton. That's the last I can recall, so I suppose that must have been where I got drunk."

"That must be thirty miles away. You have no idea how you came to be near here?"

"None. Perhaps a bit more vigorous exercise . . . ?"

"Oh, stop it!" She laughed, and threw a cushion at him, sweetly astonished by her joy in his teasing.

And tempted. So very much. He could stay. They could—

Wicked.

Dangerous.

"No one would miss you?" she asked, shaking out her petticoat and stepping into it, trying hard to be practical.

He sat up cross-legged, the blue cushion held to cover his genitals. "I have some people waiting for me in Thirsk, but they won't worry for a while."

He could stay. She was weak to even think about it, but this would be their only chance. Once he left, it would be forever.

His body was so very beautiful, his smile even more so, and he was so . . . sweet. An inadequate word for such a man, but what else described the honeyed warmth he'd created in her? It ran through her veins, loosening places she'd never known to be so stiff, so cold.

He suddenly smiled as if he knew and tossed the cushion back at her, revealing surely the beginning of another erection. "More?"

Rosamunde put the cushion on its chair and hastily tied her petticoat strings at her waist, trying to tie something tight in herself. "You couldn't have walked from Northallerton to here," she said, trying to keep things to the practical.

"Well, I could, but I don't think I did. What date is it?"

"August eighteenth."

"I remember going to bed on the sixteenth. So I must have ridden here yesterday on horseback or in a coach. I'm not sure I should leave until I remember all of it. Perhaps I have a dread enemy."

Despite his light tone, something struck an alarm. "Do you?"

A sudden stillness in his features echoed her, but then he shrugged. "Not as far as I know. Aren't you going to help me jog my memory?"

"Be serious!"

"I am. Though serious isn't quite the right word." He touched himself. "Firm perhaps. Come back to bed."

His frank boldness was making her blush, but stirring fire inside as well. "I can't." There were a hundred reasons, but she seized the easiest. "It's too risky."

"Ah. I suppose your reputation requires that you are not seen in my room very much. Later then?" He managed to make it plaintive, like a child begging for a treat, but there was nothing at all childish about the light in his eye.

He was dangerous. She should get his clothes, lend him some money, then arrange for someone to drive him to Thirsk. She should.

She tried to moisten her dry mouth and finally succeeded. "If you're sure you can stay . . ."

"I'm sure I should regain all my memories before leaving." Despite his hand still resting lightly on his erection, he spoke seriously, and indeed, if there had been foul play, he was right. "So," he asked. "When?"

A laugh escaped, a half-exasperated one. How could sin be so carefree? "Not till the night. And even then—"

"When darkness falls," he interrupted firmly, shifting and arranging a swirl of sheet for decency.

She put her hands on her hips. "Oh, so suddenly it's for *you* to decide, is it?"

"If I don't, you'll dither away our time together."

"This is wrong," she said weakly, his very ease and confidence threatening her. Surely sin should be all spines and cold, hard edges.

"That's for you to decide. I'll leave now if you want. Don't worry about my safety. If I made an enemy who dumped me in the dales, I doubt he's hovering to finish the job he assumed the rain and cold did for him."

So, it was her choice. She remembered with shock that once this had been her demand. Payment. A cold, hard bargain in the night. She tried to return to that place, that safe place, but soft warmth cradled her. "It probably is wrong," she said, meeting his eyes, "but I don't care."

He smiled again, a delighted smile that even seemed to chase away sin. "I'm pleased." After that simple, stunning affirmation, he added, "But if you want much more excitement, my dearest lady, you'd better feed me."

Dropped back to everyday concerns, she grabbed her gown and hurried into it. "Of course. You must be famished. What?"

"Anything sustaining. Come here and I'll help you."

She was struggling to fasten her corset and the hooks down the back of her gown. She needed help, but was that all he would do?

On trembling legs, she went to perch on the edge of the bed, back to him. She expected—half hoped for—attack, but instead just felt his fingers deftly attending to the clothes he had so recently loosened. He tightened her corset laces, and knotted them. Then he fastened the ten hooks up her back, brushing aside her hair at the nape to do the last two.

"You've done this before."

"Of course."

No shame. No repentance. It should make her think of sin, but instead it made her think, almost tearfully, of marriage. Of the sort of marriage that perhaps some people had, where shattering lovemaking could be followed by conversation and commonplace kindness.

When he finished, she began to rise, but he cinched her waist with his hands.

Ah. Attack.

"I must go and find you that sustaining food," she said, heart beginning to race. Moments ago she'd felt satiated. Now, she wasn't so sure.

"Gracious hostess. But there's no need to serve me. I could come down to the kitchens."

"No!"

"Why not?"

"In a towel?"

"I could wear the sheet as a toga."

"Don't be silly." She pulled against his hold, but he had her trapped.

He put his lips against the side of her neck and whispered, "Why do you keep locking the door?"

Her shoulders tensed despite that soft warmth. "You're a stranger. You could do anything."

He laughed softly. "You haven't seen everything I can do. Yet." His tongue teased her, and his thumbs made tiny, unignorable circles on her back. "Sweet Lady Mystery, am I perhaps your prisoner?"

She jumped. "No! I . . . I just don't want you wandering the house."

"Really? Do you know what I think?"

"What?" It escaped as a half-choked whisper.

Thumbs playing gently, shiveringly, he said, "I think I'm your love-slave. Captured on the wild moors to serve your wanton pleasure."

The resonance with her own thoughts, with reality, shocked Rosamunde into really trying to pull away.

He kept her close, an arm tight around her waist. "Call it indentured servitude, then. Is not that the truth? I owe you a debt, and you require payment in service."

"But you've—"

"Paid part of it. I bind myself to your service." He turned her, lowering her breathless to the bed. "Until dawn tomorrow, I am yours. Command me, mistress. What do you want in the secret hours of the night?"

"Nothing!"

"Liar," he whispered, shifting more heavily onto her. She sucked in air. "I want to go and find you food."

"Parts of you look very tasty."

"Nourishing food!"

"Mistress commands that I don't lose my strength?"

"No, I—"

"Mistress thinks I am too thin?"

Half laughing, Rosamunde pushed at his chest. "Stop it! You're being ridiculous. *You* said you were hungry."

"I will starve if it be your will."

His warm eyes met hers, urging her to join in the game. Could men and women play games?

"Do you wish me to starve?" he asked.

She tried to wriggle sideways. "No, of course not."

He stopped her. "I am grateful for your mercy, mistress. So, when I have my strength back, what will you want of me?"

"Nothing." It was still a lie.

He knew it. A sparkle in his eyes said that, but he lowered his lids and managed to look downcast. "Alas. I have failed to give pleasure. Bring back the razor, mistress, and I will put an end to my miserable existence."

"Never. From now on, you grow a beard."

"Then it will have to be hanging. I will hang myself with the sheets."

"Then I will take away all the sheets."

Shining eyes met hers. "Ah-ha! You *do* want me naked!"

"No!" Laughing, Rosamunde tried again to squirm free of his body and his nonsense. "As your mistress, I command you to live. There!" It was only as she triumphantly exclaimed this, that she realized he'd lured her into his games.

She stared up at him, seeing that this, too, was part of his payment, his generous payment. How long had it been since she'd enjoyed such a lighthearted, playful moment?

Falling happily into the spirit of it, she wriggled out from under him and off the bed, and victorious, he let her go. "I know what you are, sir!" she declared.

"You're a traveling mountebank, and your friends at Thirsk are your theater company!"

"Alas," he said, sitting up again, hand on heart—or more devastatingly, on his gorgeous muscled chest. "I am a mere amateur. In acting, that it."

"And in lovemaking, sirrah, I suppose you are a *professional*?"

He laughed aloud. "No, mistress mine. In that, too, I am an amateur. But not *mere*."

An amateur. One who did things for love, not money.

He didn't mean it that way, but it broke the spell. There was no question of love here. It was for payment, payment for his life. And she was not here for amusement, to be carried back to childish ways, but for a desperately needed child. What's more, she must never trust such a smooth-tongued rascal. Oh, he was good-natured and charming, but he was undoubtedly a rascal. He could be a highwayman, or a dissolute gamester, or the sort of man who slipped from place to place, breaking hearts and escaping creditors.

"What food do you want?" she asked, ruthlessly dragging matters back to the prosaic. She sidled around to find her shoes and put them on.

He placed his hands together and bowed over them. "Whatever my mistress desires."

She deliberately listed the food she liked least. "Pease pudding? Eel? Tongue?"

He peeped up mischievously. "Tongue. I like tongue."

Rosamunde blushed down to her toes. Oh, why could he do this to her?

"However," he continued, "I will pass on the eels. Oh, and speaking of 'eels—not the local delicacy made of cow's feet, I beg you."

"Cow heels," she said, struggling not to let him make her laugh again. "Pickled trotters, then. How would that be?"

"I confess, I have never met a foot I wished to eat." Then his eyes flashed merrily. "Nibble, now . . ."

Rosamunde's blushing toes—recognizing that they were being spoken about—curled. "Oh, don't!"

"No? Your wish is my command, mistress. Until dawn

tomorrow, I am yours. I will not touch you, top or toe, without your consent. And you, you are free. . . ."

"Free?" she breathed.

"Free to do with me entirely as you wish."

Rosamunde saw that he meant it and immediately had a vision of licking his naked body. Every inch of it. After a breathless moment, she stepped forward, and saw a welcoming, interested light in his eyes.

She was hovering on the brink, her mind filled with wicked longings of licking his naked body as he lay passive beneath her, she with all her clothes on, armored against him. Could she do to him what he'd done to her? Could she watch him dissolve?

His brows rose as if she'd spoken her wicked dream and a wave of heat flooded her. It really wouldn't be that terribly dangerous to spend a little more time up here with him, would it? Millie and Jessie wouldn't—

Then a sound broke through. Familiar, tinkling bells.

"Oh no!" she gasped, shocked right back to icy reality.

"What?" He surged from the bed, all fun discarded, immediately dangerous.

"My mother!"

He froze, then stared at her. "Your *mother*?"

"The bells on her pony's harness. Butterflies and bill-hooks, I should have known!"

Racing to the window, she heard him echo, " 'Butter-flies and billhooks'?"

She peeped around the corner of the curtain in time to see her mother's one-horse chair jingle down the lane toward the front of the house. "She has someone with her, too!" She whirled to him. "What am I to do?"

He was almost helpless with laughter. "A *mother*. And a guilty daughter!"

"How could she know?"

He seized her shoulders. "Calm down, Lady Mystery. Perhaps she doesn't. If she does, I'm merely your sick patient." He looked her over quickly, even turning her to inspect the back, then pushed her toward the door. "Go. She won't be able to guess what you've been up to." But then he added, "Will she want to come up here?"

Rosamunde, already with the knob in her hand, gave a little moan. "If she knows about you . . . she *can't*." But Rosamunde wondered if Mrs. Yockenthwait might have thought a mother excluded from the secrecy. "If she knows I have a sick man here, she won't think I've cared for you properly."

"How little she knows you," he said, with a toe-curling smile. "But if she's going to come up, you need something to mask the smell."

Rosamunde paused, absorbing the fact that the room smelled of sex. "Mercy!"

"Do you have any gin?"

"This is no time to get drunk!" But then she saw what he was about. "No. Wait!"

She ran into her own room, the one she and Diana had shared here since they were children, and pulled out a bottle of port. From a daring childhood pleasure, it had become a sweet tradition before bed.

Daring. They hadn't known the meaning!

As she rushed back with it, the door knocker rapped.

Still naked, he'd opened the window wide and had clearly stirred the potpourri in the dish on the mantel. She didn't know if it would be enough. She thrust the bottle into his hands, trying desperately to think of something to suggest.

He pushed her back out through the doorway. She ran down the stairs, then skidded to a halt at the bend and raced back up to lock the door. Her knees knocked and her heart thudded with all the panic she'd felt at twelve or so, involved in some terrible mischief, and about to be found out.

Terrible mischief, indeed. This capped them all!

What on earth would her mother say if she found out?

Rosamunde plunged down the stairs and into the drawing room just before poor overworked Jessie trotted through the hall to answer the door. Sucking in huge breaths, she pulled off her mask and stuffed it in her pocket. A glance in the mirror showed the pressure marks it couldn't help but leave. With a mutter, she pulled it out and put it on again.

She had just sat down and opened a book, when the door opened.

"Hello, Rosie," said her dumpling mother, bright eyed and cheerful. "We heard you were stuck here with some mysterious half-dead stranger on your hands, so we had to pop over and see."

Chapter 7

We? Oh no. Behind Mrs. Ellington was Rosamunde's nosiest sister.

Still, she leaped up with what she hoped was convincing surprise and pleasure. "Mama! Sukey!

Sukey, six months pregnant, was already inspecting the markings on the bottom of one of the china ornaments. "Why are you wearing that mask, Rosie? It looks horrid."

With a shaky laugh, Rosamunde took it off. "Just being silly. I thought strangers were coming."

"Very silly," said her mother, sitting down. "If they were strangers, you wouldn't let them in, would you? Anyway, it's time you accepted that your scars are not bad enough to curdle the milk." But then she shrugged, for she'd said it before. "So, dear, tell us about this invalid. Mrs. Yockenthwait seems to think he's a brigand."

"Like a highwayman?" Rosamunde queried lightly. "He wouldn't get far in that trade when he was clearly tossed from his horse."

"Is that what happened?"

Nervous Jessie bobbed a curtsy. "Would you like tea, milady?"

"Yes, thank you," Rosamunde said, hoping that might stop the inquisition. "Tea would be lovely."

As soon as Jessie left, however, her mother asked, "So, who or what is he, dear?"

She had to lie again. "I have no idea. He has no tools or goods with him. Nothing at all, in fact, apart from the clothes on his back and a handkerchief. He either drank it all, or had his pockets emptied for him."

"Doesn't he know who he is?" Sukey asked, turning from an inspection of a row of books. As well as being nosy, she was very shrewd and could winkle out a secret in a moment. Rosamunde prayed there was no evidence of her wicked morning, and that for once in her life she could hold to some untruths.

"He was unconscious through the night," she said in an uninterested manner, "and he seems confused still."

"Or likes the enjoyable bed he's landed in," Sukey pointed out.

Rosamunde felt her face flame again, and smiled brightly to compensate.

"Where have you put him, dear?" her mother asked as Jessie hurried back with a tray loaded with china, teapot, and cakes. Rosamunde welcomed the chance to leap up and help her.

"In a bedroom upstairs."

"Rosie!" Sukey exclaimed. "You soft-hearted numb-skull."

"I didn't see why not. He's not a vagrant."

"How do you know?"

"His clothes are decent."

"Perhaps he stole them."

Rosamunde had never thought of that. "He speaks like a gentleman. And he doesn't have a working man's hands."

"Then he's a wastrel."

Since Rosamunde basically agreed, she couldn't think of a retort.

"Stop bickering, girls," their mother said. "I don't suppose Diana will mind Rosie putting her charity case in a good bedroom—unless he has lice."

"Of course he hasn't," Rosamunde protested.

"So, is this paragon of innocence up to receiving visitors?" Sukey asked, coming to sit near the tray. "What does he look like? Is he dashing and handsome?"

"When puking?" Rosamunde asked.

"Is he puking still?"

"No, and he's handsome enough." Rosamunde doubted she'd get Sukey out of the house without a glimpse so there was no point in lying.

"Balding?"

"No."

"Squint?"

Rosamunde stared at her sister. "No!"

"Bad teeth?"

Rosamunde almost snapped out another no, but caught herself. "I don't think so."

"In that case," said Sukey, licking cream from her fingers, "he'll count as an angel in these parts."

"I don't recollect any of those flaws in Harold," Rosamunde pointed out, referring to her sister's husband.

Sukey took more tea. "But I always said I married an angel."

"So," interrupted their mother, sipping, "when is your angel likely to take wing?"

"Tomorrow, I hope. I want to be home."

"Of course you do, dear." Her mother nodded, gray curls bobbing under her plain hat.

Rosamunde felt suddenly defensive. "Digby isn't expecting me. He won't be worrying."

"Of course not, dear."

Rosamunde expected her mother to offer to send a message, and when she didn't, she stiffened. She'd thought Mrs. Yockenthwait might have suspicions, but surely such notions would never cross her own mother's mind! She was not one for looking at the underside of things.

"So," said Sukey, draining her teacup and rising briskly, "let us ascend to heaven to visit the angel."

Rosamunde had expected it, but she tried to resist. "Why?"

"You haven't had Dr. Wallace in. If the poor man's been vomiting and is still abed, you maybe should. Mother and I can give our opinion."

"He's doubtless asleep."

"Then we'll have a quiet look. Does he have a fever?"

Rosamunde stared at her sister resentfully. Getting Sukey out of the house without a glimpse was as likely as ascending to heaven on the spot. Still, she was struggling for a way when her mother dabbed her lips with her serviette and rose to head out of the room.

"Has he a cough, dear?" her mother asked, climbing the stairs in a no-nonsense manner. "I heard he was soaking wet when you found him."

"That's true." Rosamunde hurried after, speaking as loudly as she dared in case he needed warning. "But as far as I can tell, he's escaped consequences."

"They could still come. Lungs are tricky."

"Not without a fever, I don't think," Sukey said, and Rosamunde realized that this investigation wasn't entirely nosiness. Sukey was three years her senior and had two children, and their mother had given birth to eight and lost two. They both knew a great deal more about nursing than she did.

"He was sick in the night, but not since," she told them.

"Drink will do that," said Sukey, "and getting rid of the poison does them good."

Rosamunde wondered if there were aspects to Harold Davenport that she hadn't guessed.

"He had a terrible headache," she volunteered. "I gave him a powder. The headache one. It seemed to help." She fumbled as much with the key as she dared.

"Locked, dear?" asked her mother.

"Can't be too careful with strangers." Rosamunde offered a brief prayer and opened the door.

The curtains were drawn, throwing the room into dimness, but the window was wide open, so they billowed a little. Birdsong trilled in, along with fresh summer air. In the room, Rosamunde's twitching nose mainly detected potpourri and port, though she thought other wicked aromas lurked underneath.

Her secret lover was tucked firmly in the bed, eyes closed.

"Oh my," whispered Sukey, tiptoeing close. "Not quite an angel, but plenty handsome enough for a mortal man."

Rosamunde saw the corner of his lips twitch and prayed harder—that he be able to control himself.

"Handsome is as handsome does," said her mother prosaically, opening the curtains a crack to give more light. "The good-looking ones are usually nothing but trouble." She came over and picked up a corner of the sheet to inspect a purple stain. On the table nearby, the bottle of port stood empty alongside a used glass.

"What possessed you to give him more drink, Rosie?"

"Hair of the dog?" Rosamunde suggested weakly.

Her mother shook her head and laid her hand on his forehead. "Cool, as you said. And his color's good. I don't think there's any cause for concern as long as you keep him away from drink. We'd best go before we wake him."

"Is he naked?" Sukey whispered as they retreated to the door.

"He hardly dumped himself by the roadside with a nightshirt in his pocket." Rosamunde got them out of the door and shut it, knowing he had to be fighting laughter.

"I'm sure Mr. Yockenthwait has a spare."

"Seth Yockenthwait's six inches shorter and half as wide."

"So, they say angels don't have a—"

"Hush!"

"Sukey Davenport," said Mrs. Ellington, shaking her head, but eyes twinkling, "sometimes I wonder at you."

Sukey just laughed. "Someone stripped him out of his wet clothes and into that bed."

Rosamunde locked the door and headed back downstairs. "Mr. Yockenthwait and Tom settled him in the bed, but Mrs. Yockenthwait and I stripped and dried him. I'm hoping the story won't get out. People do talk."

"Indeed they do," said her mother. "We won't gab of it, and Hester Yockenthwait only told me because she thought perhaps a mother should know."

Know what? Rosamunde wondered faintly.

Her mother kissed her cheek, perhaps a little bit more firmly than usual. "Take care, dear."

"So," said Sukey, brushing a kiss against her cheek, "is he an angel?"

"He's just an ordinary man," Rosamunde said firmly as she went with them to the door. "Nothing more."

And that, she thought as she waved them on their

jingling way, proved that she was becoming an excellent liar.

Once the chair had disappeared round a bend, she blew out a breath and slumped against the wall. In all her planning, she'd never imagined having to deal with her mother in her house of sin! She wanted to rush upstairs because . . .

Just because.

Smiling, she acknowledged that she wanted to laugh over it with him. An angel, indeed. But first, he deserved a good meal.

She was checking with Jessie as to what could be provided in a hurry, when the kitchen door was opened. She turned with a start, thinking her mother and sister had returned, but it was Diana, Countess of Arradale, who swept in. Dressed in a magnificent burgundy riding habit braided in gold, she slapped embroidered riding gloves against her palm with a jeweled hand.

"Good day, Jessie," she said to the suddenly flustered maid, but then she turned a stern eye on Rosamunde. "I want to speak to you."

They were quite alike in height and build, but Diana carried herself higher, as if being a peeress added inches. Of course, she also favored high heels, even on her riding boots. She headed autocratically out of the kitchen, heels clicking, assuming Rosamunde would follow. With a wry look at the maid, she did. She was about to be given a stinging lecture on cowardice.

In the drawing room, Diana tossed her glittering gloves onto a sofa. Her mannish tricorn followed, revealing hair of a more reddish brown than Rosamunde's, neatly pinned up in a complex arrangement. "You ran away!"

"Yes," Rosamunde said meekly.

"How could you! It would have been perfect. At least two men were desperately seeking the Columbine."

Yesterday, Rosamunde would have felt justly crushed by this, but now she was having to suppress a smile.

Diana was no fool. She gave Rosamunde a sharp look and sat down. "What have you been up to?"

Rosamunde swallowed. "Getting a baby. I hope."

"What? You left *with* someone? Who?"

Rosamunde sat opposite. "Not *with* someone," she whispered. "I found him on the road." She quickly gave her cousin the story.

Diana's jaw dropped in shock. "And you think *this* specimen safer than my guests? Really, Rosa! How feather-witted can you be? He'll probably strangle you and steal the silver!"

"No! Really. He's a gentleman and has excellent manners."

"So do some highwaymen." She rose sharply. "I'd better see him—"

"No."

Diana halted, then subsided with a questioning look.

"I don't want you interfering, Diana."

"This *is* my house, you know."

Rosamunde had forgotten that detail, so she switched to petitioner. "Please?"

Diana's blue eyes narrowed. "You're up to something."

"Of course I'm up to something! I'm up to"—she found it hard to say the word—"adultery."

It hadn't felt like adultery.

"But it's so dangerous. You're bound to be found out."

"No, I'm not. Why would anyone think I'd . . . do that with a sick man I rescued?"

"Is he sick?"

"Not anymore. But I'm keeping him in his room as if he is." She bit her lip. "He's my secret love-slave."

Diana's eyes widened, then she burst into laughter. Rosamunde joined her in a wild storm of healing laughter that reminded her of their younger years.

When they sobered, however, Diana shook her head. "*He* knows, dearest. That was always the blessing of the masquerade, that the man wouldn't be able to tell anyone, or make trouble."

"I know. But I think it will be all right. I've been wearing the mask, and I hope to get him away from here without his knowing where he's been or who he's been with."

"How? Where does he think he is?"

"Gillsett."

"Where the Misses Gillsett live? You wicked, clever scoundrel! If he goes there looking for his masked lover, he'll get a shock. So, have you done it yet?"

Rosamunde jerked under that blunt question, coloring. But she nodded.

Diana swirled over to hug her. "Brave girl! I hope it wasn't too unpleasant."

Rosamunde bit her lip. It almost seemed too precious to speak of, but it was too great a treasure to keep from her cousin. "Diana, it was the most remarkable . . . I never knew . . ."

"Rosa! You haven't been so foolish as to fall in love with this wretch, have you?"

"Of course not. And he's not a wretch. He's a gentleman."

"Ha!"

"He is." Diana's meaning had sunk in, however, giving her a qualm. "I'm not in love. That would be ridiculous. I hardly know the man." She had to wonder, however, just what it was, this tender feeling that made her want to smile and smile, and share things with him. "It's just the act," she said, as much to herself as to her cousin. "I finally understand why some people plunge into folly over it."

Diana's brow wrinkled. "You do? Can you explain it to me?"

But at this point Rosamunde ran out of words. "It's special. A physical feeling . . . that . . ."

"Not the same as with Sir Digby?"

"No." But that seemed terribly disloyal. "Not that . . . I mean—"

She was saved by Jessie knocking and peeping in. "The tray's ready, milady. Should I take it up?"

Rosamunde leaped to her feet. "I'll do it."

Diana rose, too. "Don't think you're escaping, Rosa, leaving me with such a string of mysteries and teases! Do you at least know his name?"

Rosamunde halted, tray in hand, knowing she'd look the lowest sort of trull to have been romping in bed with a man without even knowing his name. "It's Malloren," she said. "Mr. Brand Malloren."

She hurried out, but heard: *"What?"*

Oh no.

As Diana cried, "Rosa! Come back here!" she fled upstairs, plates sliding, liquid sloshing from the spout of the pot. She didn't want to know what had made Diana shriek like that. She didn't want to know!

Was he really a highwayman? Were wanted posters stuck up all over England blazoning his name?

After the briefest pause to tie on her hated mask, she flipped the key in the lock and dashed into the room, slamming the door closed with her behind.

"What is it?" he asked, instantly alert despite only having a sheet wrapped around him like a toga. He was by the window again, but had kept the curtains drawn, and was peering out through a chink.

"Are you wanted?" she gasped, tray still clutched before her.

"Wanted?"

"By the law."

"Not to my knowledge." He came over and took the disordered tray from her, placing it on a small table, and tidying it. "Since my recent activities aren't completely clear yet, I can't swear to it. Ah, pork pie. Thank you." He took a big bite and swallowed it before adding, "So? What's to do?"

"It doesn't matter."

He took another bite, clearly not convinced. "Then won't you sit with me while I eat?"

After a struggle with herself, she sat down opposite, touching her mask to make sure it was in place. She wanted to stay. She also wanted to put off hearing Diana's bad news. Just for a little while.

"It's hard to tell with that damned mask, but I'd say you look shaken. Did your mother give you trouble?"

Rosamunde stopped twisting her hands together and smoothed her skirt. "No. Of course not."

"She seemed a pleasant lady. I'm glad you have her."

"So am I." She wasn't sure it was right to ask personal questions, but after a moment, she did. "Do you?"

"I did. She died when I was quite young."

"I'm sorry."

"I missed her. I still do, I suppose. She was a wonderful person. Joyous, loving, strong. It would be precious to be able to visit, to share things, to do things for her."

It touched her deeply because he said it simply as he ate, as if this were something taken for granted between sons and mothers. Her instincts weren't wrong. Highwayman or not, he was a good man.

He swallowed the last of the pie and looked up, eyes twinkling. "And the other lady is assured I'm not an angel?"

"My sister Sukey." Rosamunde knew her eyes were twinkling, too. "She took my word for it."

"So they'll not make trouble?"

"No."

He poured some thick chocolate and sipped, considering her. "Do you want to change our arrangement now your mother is on the scene?"

"No."

"I'm charmed to think I'm such a wonderful lover that you are ready to take risks over me, but why?"

Rosamunde ran a finger down the rough heat of the chased-silver chocolate pot, wondering how much truth was wise. She wanted to give him as much as she could. "I've never had a lover before, and I doubt I will again."

"You're young still."

"And married."

After a pause, he said, "Forgive me for being crude, but to an elderly man."

"He's only fifty-five." She hoped it didn't sound like a complaint. She didn't wish Digby dead, but honesty said that she wished she'd never married him. It lay bitter on her soul, the ingratitude of that. More bitter still, however, was the loss of what she might have been if she hadn't been such a coward after the accident.

"Fifty-five to your what?"

She jerked out of her thoughts. "Twenty-four."

"How old were you when you wed?"

"Sixteen."

" 'Struth, my dear. Why?"

Rosamunde had never questioned it before, that desperate need for a safe haven—away from her smothering
family, but also away from the world, from the need
to meet strangers. Now she did, but it was too raw to
poke at.

"Why not?" she replied briskly. "Many ladies marry
young, and some prefer an older man. The point is that
I *am* married and to a good man. I can't risk this again."

She thought he might argue the point, but then he
leaned back, sipping his chocolate. "I won't tattle. My
word on it. So, do you regret it?"

"Not at all."

"Good." He drank the last of his chocolate. "Then
what do you command?"

For a moment she didn't understand him. Then she
blushed. "Nothing."

"Nothing? I warn you, my dear, charming though you
are, my duty ends at dawn. I've remembered my affairs
and have an appointment I must keep. If you try to hold
me here, you'll have an enemy, not a willing slave."

"I won't hold you." *But you won't like my way of
letting you go, alas.* However she arranged it, he would
be an enemy then, and it would be better so.

She stood and picked up the tray. "I have someone
in the house and must spend time with her. And it's
important, in case your presence gets out, that I very
obviously am not spending much time up here."

He grinned. "It's all the fault of my angelic good
looks. No one would believe your innocence."

"Quite. If you were homely, it would be a great deal
easier."

"I can cross my eyes," he said, proving it. "Unfortunately, I can't hold it for long."

Rosamunde just shook her head. No wonder he'd
ended up drunk in a ditch. He didn't have a serious
bone in his beautiful body, and doubtless was a feckless
wastrel. It seemed a terrible shame.

"May I at least have my clothes?" he asked. "The
Roman look is out this year."

"Shame," she said, allowing herself a brief, apprecia-
tive study of the Roman look. When he laughed, she

added, "Your clothes are definitely the worse for their adventure, but I'll send my maid up with them."

"So, when do I get to serve you again?"

Rosamunde grasped the tray tightly, almost like a shield. She had a well-developed sense of right and wrong, and she knew that further encounters with this man would be wrong. She could argue that it increased the chance of a child, but she knew in her heart that if she gave herself to him again, it would not be for that. It would not be for Wenscote. It would be from raw desire, and a hunger to store up warm nourishment for the coming barren years.

She should tell him that there would be no more service, that he'd be attended entirely by Millie from now on. . . .

"Tonight," she whispered. "Once everyone is in bed." After a moment, she added, "They go to bed early."

"Good. More hours until dawn."

The whole night? Was it possible?

She backed for the door as if leaving a dangerous animal. When she balanced the tray on her hip to manage the knob, he came quickly to help her, astonishingly elegant in his toga-sheet.

The question that seethed in her burst free. "Why would your name alarm someone?"

He paused, his hand on the knob. "Whom did it alarm?"

He stood so close that one bare arm and shoulder brushed her. An urge to lean toward him almost defeated her will, to lean and rest her cheek against his smooth skin, to draw in the remembered warmth and comfort of his body.

Oh, this was wrong! She mustn't allow herself a *lover*.

"Never mind," she said and swept through the doorway. She locked the door, though it was pointless now. The danger was free, and was in her.

Chapter 8

Before Rosamunde had time to collect her thoughts, Diana popped out of her bedroom, snatched the tray to place it on a table, then dragged her into the room. "Brand Malloren!" she whispered.

"Yes." Rosamunde's mind was still dazed from her encounter. *Why* couldn't she allow herself a lover, just once in her life? Wasn't it every woman's right?

Diana was staring at her. "You have no idea, do you?"

"About what?"

"About the Mallorens!"

Rosamunde slumped on the window seat and prepared to face the truth. "What has he done?"

"Done?" Diana's fine brows tangled. "I'd think you'd know that better than I."

"Away from here, I mean."

Diana shook her head and settled elegantly on the other end of the cushioned seat. "Lud, I forget that you never go anywhere. I don't suppose you read newspapers either, do you?"

"He was in the newspapers?" Rosamunde felt rather sick. She'd never been inclined to think of highwaymen as romantic. They were, after all, just thieves, and often murderers. But perhaps if he was the dashing kind of highwayman it wouldn't be too bad. "What crime did he commit?"

"Crime?" Diana came close to gaping. "Rosa . . . ! No, as far as I know Brand Malloren hasn't been in the papers. But his brother has. Often. You must have heard of Rothgar."

"What's Rothgar?"

"Not *what.* Who. The Marquess of Rothgar."

Rosamunde stared at her. "Are you trying to tell me that he,"—she waved in the direction of her prisoner's room—"is a *marquess*?"

"I dread to think where your brain is." Diana leaned forward. "Pay attention. If he's Brand Malloren, his *brother* is the Marquess of Rothgar. His oldest brother, of course."

"Of course," echoed Rosamunde. "But his clothes are so simple. I don't understand. . . ."

"Nor do I. But the Mallorens are famous. Or infamous. Lord Bryght—"

"Lord?" Rosamunde exclaimed.

"Lady Elf is a very pleasant lady," Diana rattled on. "She's the only one I've actually met—"

"Diana!" Rosamunde shouted to get her attention, then lowered her voice. "Are you saying I have a *lord* in that room?"

"If you have Brand Malloren, you have, but—"

"That's terrible!"

"Well, he's not a real lord. He doesn't have a seat in Parliament or anything."

"Is that supposed to be consolation?"

Diana suddenly laughed. "Oh, love. I doubt he's going to haul you into court. And you certainly have fine taste when it comes to capturing love-slaves."

"I *rescued* him." Rosamunde didn't, however, doubt his rank for a moment. It explained so much. There wasn't a servile bone in his confident body.

"Rescued, captured . . ." Diana waved a glittering hand, for she always wore an abundance of rings. "You relieve my mind! You've become so dull, but this is fully worthy of our childhood exploits. A Malloren as a lover. What a brilliant choice."

"I didn't *choose* him," Rosamunde protested, knowing her cheeks were red.

One of Diana's arched brows quirked. "Are you saying that as soon as you hauled him out of the ditch, you thought, 'A man. Good. I'll have him in my bed by tomorrow.' "

"Of course not!" Rosamunde leaped up to pace out

her embarrassment. "Very well. I did decide that he was . . . not unbearable."

"Quite. What on earth, though, was Lord Brand Malloren doing drunk by the side of the road in simple clothing? I don't know the man, but it seems unlikely."

"Perhaps he's been cast off."

"The marquess is rumored to be very protective of his family. In fact, you'd best pray Lord Rothgar does not take offense at your treatment of his brother. He's said to be merciless on such matters." She lowered her voice. "Some say he's mad."

"Mad!"

Diana laughed. "I'm teasing, sweetheart. I've never met the marquess, but I haven't heard of him foaming at the mouth. I gather it was his mother who was mad."

Rosamunde stared. "Lord Brand's mother was *mad*?"

"Oh no. They're half brothers."

Rosamunde sagged. "Thank heavens!"

"Well really. Isn't it unfair to be judging someone by their parents? Has Lord Brand seemed insane to you?"

Rosamunde wondered if she knew what sanity was. "No, but—"

"Then judge him on himself."

"I'm an animal breeder, remember?" She suddenly hugged herself. "Just think! I could have made a child who carried insanity in its blood. I thought about the physical, but I never considered his sanity or moral qualities. Temperament can be bred for, you know, as well as physical form. You did say you'd heard nothing bad about him? About Lord Brand?"

"No, but he doesn't seem to move in society."

"He said he manages estates for a nobleman."

"There you are, then. He's a country bumpkin like yourself. He'll probably delight in talking about crop rotation, turnips, foot rot, and such."

"I'm more interested in whether his child will."

Diana rolled her eyes. "I'm sure you'll make certain it does, poor thing." She rose and twitched her skirts into line. "I am concerned, however. We have to make sure the Mallorens can't find you once this is over."

Rosamunde shivered. "I've done my best. He doesn't know where he is, or whom he's with."

"True, but if he thinks to ask about men found by the roadside and cared for, you're sunk. Admit it. My masquerade was a much better plan."

"Probably, but with luck, most people will never know a man's been here with me a' all. The servants have agreed to keep it to themselves."

"Can they be trusted?" Diana's frown expressed doubt.

"I think so. They don't want the New Commonwealth here any more than we do."

Diana sat down, staring. "You explained it all to them?"

"Of course not! But they're not stupid, you know. I think Mrs. Yockenthwait guessed, and my mother and Sukey."

"Aunt Ellington!"

Rosamunde pressed her hands to burning cheeks. "Isn't it terrible? But . . . but she seemed to approve. I don't know whether that's comforting, or proof that the world has gone mad."

Diana blew out a breath. "Well, you might have pulled it off then. Still . . ." She pursed her lips, a familiar glint of mischief lighting her eyes.

"What?" asked Rosamunde with foreboding.

"It wouldn't be hard to spread rumors. As insurance. A man found by the road by a lady. Perhaps here, perhaps near Ripon, perhaps in Niddersdale, or Airedale. By Lady Hauxwell, or Mrs. Tring, or even one of the Misses Gillsett. . . ."

"Diana!" But even as she protested, Rosamunde was thinking it might work.

"You know that people believe the stories they're told, then pass them on with changes. And every dalesman believes that wickedness and wonders go on in the other dales. When you had your accident, half of North Yorkshire thought you dead, and the other half thought you blind. A good number believed you were running away with a lover. Or that both of us were."

"I pray that rumor doesn't revive. My plan depends on my impeccable reputation."

"Which you certainly own." Diana moved close and took Rosamunde's hand. "It was my fault—"

"No—"

"Yes! I was the one urging speed for no reason at all. It should have been me—"

"Silly! It should have been neither. It was a freakish accident, both the coach overturning and the glass slashing me. You were knocked unconscious and could have suffered even worse from that."

"But didn't." Diana touched Rosamunde's cheek. "I do wish you'd put it behind you, love. Time has faded the scars. They really aren't as bad as you think."

Rosamunde suddenly saw how much it would ease her cousin if she lived a normal life. She'd never realized before how deeply Diana felt it. "I'll try," she promised. "But not yet. For now it's essential that I remain respectable, reclusive Lady Overton."

"But—"

"Thank heaven I didn't tell anyone but you his name!" Rosamunde had to interrupt Diana. She didn't want to think of her scars and decisions now. It would be too painful.

Diana shrugged and let it go. "It was wise. I'll set some trusted servants to start the rumors. If word ever does leak out about a man's presence here, it will just be one of many vague tales."

"Thank you."

"So, the only remaining problem is him. You can't just wave him out the door, or he'll know."

"Especially as we are miles from anywhere. I have to take him somewhere." She worried her knuckle for a moment. "I could blindfold him."

"Would he submit to that?"

"Probably."

"You seem interestingly sure of him. But it wouldn't work. He'd still have a fair idea of how far he'd traveled. The nature of the land. He'd hear sounds. I'm sure he's not stupid."

"No, he's not. So, O wise one, how do I confuse the poor man?"

"You found him drunk. Leave him a jug of gin, and perhaps he'll drink himself silly again."

Once that had been Rosamunde's plan, but now she shook her head. "He's never once asked for wine or spirits. Does that sound like a drunkard to you?"

"Unfortunately, no. I suppose you could knock him out, but . . ."

"But no! I wouldn't have the slightest idea how, and it's horribly dangerous. Look at how addled you were after our accident. And poor Bob Wigglethorpe, he's never been the same since that beam fell on his head."

"Well then, I could ask old Mistress Naisby for a potion."

Rosamunde wasn't happy at the thought of drugging the man, but it seemed the lesser of the evils. "Perhaps you'd better, just in case. I hate doing that to him, though."

Diana leaned to kiss Rosamunde's cheek. "You're fretting again. Remember, you've done the main part and can't weaken now."

"Screw my courage to the sticking point."

"Exactly. But remember, this is not Shakespearian tragedy. Rosie and Dinah are going to emerge triumphant. Just as long as Rosie doesn't have one of her fatal attacks of honesty. Promise?"

Rosamunde thought wistfully of the simple beauty of honesty, but she nodded. "Promise."

When Diana had left, Rosamunde was tempted to just sit in the window seat and fret the day away, but she had to be seen in case any of this ever came out. Anyway, she thought as she tidied herself and left the room, he wanted his clothes.

In the kitchen, she studied the plain garments, confirming that they were not the style and quality expected of an aristocrat. Perhaps despite his family, he truly was a simple man. Her willful mind settled on that, on the fact that they might not be wildly divided by their stations, but then she forced herself to stop such folly. Rank was the smallest obstacle in their way.

She was married.

She was seeking a child in order to save Wenscote, and she could only carry that off if no one in the world would imagine that Lady Overton might take a casual lover. Even if those barriers fell, she was a farmer's daughter—a gentleman farmer, but still a farmer—and Brand Malloren was the son of a marquess.

And, she reminded herself, he had no lasting interest in her. He was paying a debt and amusing himself. That was all.

She sent Millie up with the clothes.

Now, she needed to be seen out and about. She put on her cap, the one that hid the edges of her face, then went to wander in the part of the garden that ran close to the passing road.

A number of vehicles and people on foot came by. If they saw her, she greeted them. They were all people she knew, and none of them seemed at all suspicious. It was not unusual for her to spend a day or two here with Diana.

Perhaps she should suggest that Diana move into the dower house to make it even more proper. She didn't want that, though. She didn't think she could go through the night if Diana was sleeping in the next room.

She settled to doing some weeding until she was interrupted by Millie stumping down the garden path, muttering again about half-naked men. "He wants something to read."

"Read?" Rosamunde echoed blankly, though it made sense. The poor man was recovered, but stuck in that room with nothing to do.

"Should I take him something from the library, milady?"

"Yes—" But then Rosamunde thought of a complication. "No! No, I'll go and choose something for him. Thank you, Millie."

As Rosamunde hurried to the few shelves that passed for a library in the dower house, she knew she'd just escaped another disaster. These books came from the big house and were embossed with the word "Arradale" and the family crest.

She ran through them, hoping desperately to find an unmarked stray, but of course there was none. She could cut out a front page, but she hated the thought of mutilating a book.

What now?

With sudden inspiration, she left the house and walked the half mile to Arradale itself. She entered by the kitchens and asked for Diana.

"Ridden out to inspect the hay, milady," said the butler, who had appeared with that instinct butlers seemed to have. "The dowager is available."

Rosamunde wished she could just ask for some recent papers, but she would have to speak to her aunt.

Round as her sister, Lady Arradale managed to carry her weight with the presence expected of a countess, and her hair by some miracle of cosmetics, was still the rich brown of her youth.

"So, dear," she said, accepting an airy kiss near her delicately powdered cheek, "rumor says that you are having a little adventure."

"Adventure, Aunt Arradale?" Rosamunde queried as she sat on a brocade-covered chair, a jiggle of nervousness stirring deep inside.

"Mariah stopped by, and told me of your invalid. Very charitable of you, dear."

Of course her mother would visit her sister when so close, and of course she'd tell her what was going on. But what exactly had been said? Rosamunde desperately tried to judge her aunt's tone, but she'd always been hard to read.

"It's rather tedious, really, Aunt," she said in a bored tone, "but I feel I must stay at the dower house until we can send him on his way. Tomorrow, I hope."

She'd thought she was grown up, but this business was pitching her back into childhood. Rosie and Dinah, in trouble again.

Rosamunde's parents had always been soft-hearted and hated to punish their children, but Lord and Lady

Arradale set high standards for their only child, and enforced them. If Diana had been in trouble, it was certain that Rosamunde had been involved, too, and so everyone—including Rosie and Dinah—had agreed the penalties should be the same. If a whipping was called for, however, it had always been Aunt Arradale who'd dispensed it.

Now Rosamunde could almost imagine her aunt calling for a birch!

But that jerked her memory to the New Commonwealth and their harsh way with children. Even under Aunt Arradale's firm hand, punishment had never been severe. Just enough to make them truly sorry for whatever they'd done wrong.

"Problems?" her aunt asked perceptively, and Rosamunde gathered her wits.

"Not really, Aunt. Well, there's Sir Digby." Rosamunde leaped into an innocent subject eagerly. "I wish he would eat and drink more moderately. The way his color rises, the way he wheezes when climbing the stairs, it does worry me."

"With reason. The earl was in a similar state, and it took him from us."

Rosamunde had forgotten, and was sorry for stirring sad memories.

"And," said her aunt, "when Sir Digby dies, his heir is an adherent of this new extreme sect, I understand."

"Edward Overton, yes. It is a worry."

"You should get with child, dear," said her aunt blandly.

Rosamunde, feeling hot all over, had never dreamed of speaking of marital matters with her august aunt. "We are trying. Digby and I. . . ." It was true, after a sense.

"It's fortunate that men are not like women, and seem able to procreate in their older years. How fortunate he is to be married to a healthy young woman." She inclined her head with a very slight smile. "To you, dear."

Was that royal approval? This was the most extraordinary conversation of Rosamunde's life.

She moved bluntly on to the purpose of her visit. "My

invalid would like to read a newspaper, Aunt. I came to ask if I could borrow yours."

"Of course, dear." Lady Arradale rang the golden bell by her hand, and when a footman responded, sent him on the errand.

"So," she asked, "who is he?"

Rosamunde steeled herself to lie. "He doesn't seem to remember yet."

"From?" asked her aunt.

"He doesn't know that either."

"And a victim of drink." Her brow furrowed a little. "Perhaps he prefers not to give his identity. Be careful, Rosamunde."

"He does claim not to drink much as a rule, Aunt Arradale."

"Well, he would, wouldn't he?"

It amused Rosamunde how all the older women were so skeptical about men.

Shrewd eyes assessed her. "Have a care, my dear. Rogues and rascals are often charming, which makes them all the more dangerous, especially if they are handsome, which I gather this one is. If you wish, you may send him here for the night."

Rosamunde was saved by the footman returning with a small pile of papers on a silver platter.

Aunt Arradale waved them over, and Rosamunde snatched them, standing. "Thank you, Aunt. It hardly seems worth moving him, and Diana's going to help return him to civilization tomorrow."

"Is she? Too much to hope that she'd leave such an unusual situation alone. However, since you know neither his name nor his direction, where, pray, are you going to return him to?"

Oh Lord. "Thirsk. He seems to think he comes from there, so we hope he'll be recognized."

"And if he isn't?"

"Then I'll leave him there with some money. I can hardly keep him here, Aunt Arradale!"

"I do hope that the two of you are acting according to your age and dignity."

"Of course, Aunt!" Rosamunde exclaimed, definite vi-

sions of the birch swirling. But then an idea stirred.
"Perhaps," she said, thinking it out as she spoke, "*I*
should move here for the night. It does concern me a
little, being there with him now he has recovered
consciousness."

Aunt Arradale nodded with obvious approval. "Very
sensible. You can never be too careful about reputation,
and it will be pleasant to have your company for
dinner."

Rosamunde hadn't quite intended that, but the words
had the aura of a royal command, so she had to agree.
She gave her thanks and good-byes and threaded her
way back out of the grand house, turning things over in
her head.

Yes, she thought, emerging into sunshine on the
sweeping terrace that led down to the east lawns, it was
the right thing to do. If news of his presence leaked out,
the fact that he'd been vilely ill the night before, and
she'd slept elsewhere tonight would help deflect suspicions.

Why, she wondered, did people assume that nighttime
was the only dangerous time?

She hurried across velvet lawns and through the carefully managed wilderness, happy to be seen by a number
of gardeners, but strangely unsettled by her visit to the
big house.

Why?

Pausing on an ornamental wooden bridge, she watched
the racing water, pondering. She'd known and accepted
the style at Arradale all her life—in fact, as a child she'd
used its grand staircases and marbled halls as a place to
play. She'd never pined to live that way, preferring the
simpler ways of her childhood home and Wenscote.

So why did it disturb her now?

Ah. Because Arradale was Brand Malloren's accus-
tomed style of living. Or something even grander. It em-
phasized the gulf between them.

She shook her head at the way her foolish mind kept
taking that path. The gulf was as wide as an ocean,
formed by dishonesty, the pressures of her cause, and
the absolute fact that she was married.

And that they were strangers, she reminded herself, walking on briskly, heels rapping on the wooden planks, then turning silent on the leaf-mold path. Brand Malloren had a gift of seeming familiar, but this time yesterday she hadn't even known the man. She was crazily building a romantic fancy over a disreputable stranger. What was worse, both Diana and Aunt Arradale might have guessed it.

Bad enough to be known as adulterous, even in a noble cause. Intolerable to be thought stupid!

She stopped by the old oak near the Hawes road, struck by another thought.

Why had he not told her he was Lord Brand Malloren? Why had he kept some of his identity hidden? Probably—why had she not thought of it earlier?—his simple clothes were a disguise. So, what had Lord Brand Malloren been up to that led to him ending up unconscious and in danger of death?

She doubtless didn't want to know. After all, the son of a marquess could be many other things—a highwayman, a smuggler, a felon running from the law.

She was in danger of being bowled over by a charming rogue. She must *not* let herself start to trust him. She was doubtless being a fool to trust him as much as she did. A wise woman would have nothing more to do with him.

Rosamunde, however, wasn't wise enough for that.

She plucked a buttercup by the path and spun it so it shone in the sun as she considered how to sneak back into the dower house after dinner to enjoy a seductive tryst.

Chapter 9

She was almost at the house, skirting the hawthorn hedge between the side garden and the road, when a voice hailed her, "God be with you!"

She turned, and on the other side of the hedge saw a horseman in a tall, black steeple hat. For a moment she thought it was Digby's nephew Edward Overton, but he would have called her by name, and anyway, this man was stockier.

A New Commonwealther. Here. It was like a call to battle, a reminder of the seriousness of the situation.

"Sir? Do you need something?"

He was an ordinary enough man with quite a kindly expression and very fine, vivid, brown eyes. His plain gray suit was simple and well-worn.

"Is this Arradale House, sister?" She stiffened at that address, then remembered that they used "brother" and "sister" instead of more formal forms of address.

"The dower house." She knew it was irrational, but she felt as if he knew exactly what was going on.

"A handsome property. And you, I think, must be the countess's cousin, Lady Overton."

Rosamunde put her hand swiftly to cover her cheek, astonished that she'd been talking to a stranger without giving it a thought.

"Yes, I knew you by your scars," he said, without embarrassment. "Edward Overton has mentioned them."

She made herself lower her hand. "You know my nephew?"

"Very well. I am staying at your home at his invitation."

"He has no right to invite guests!" she said sharply before she could stop herself.

"Just for the night," the man said, as if he hadn't noticed her discourtesy. "We travel to Lancashire to preach, and broke our journey at Wenscote so Edward could visit his ailing uncle."

"Sir Digby is not ailing, as I hope both you and Edward have seen."

"It is a blessing, but he would do better for a simple diet, as we have tried to tell him."

Blast them both. Though the advice was sound, Edward had a way of giving it that always upset Digby, and this man wouldn't help with his bland, impervious amiability. Thank heavens they were leaving in the morning.

Then something else caught her attention. "I didn't know Edward had taken to preaching."

"He is assisting me, and training for the future. We all expect Edward to soon be high in our ranks."

By virtue of his rich gift of Wenscote. Rosamunde kept a bland smile pinned in place. "I'm sure he's delighted."

"Our pleasure comes only from service to the Lord. We will leave at first light tomorrow. Will we see you at Wenscote tonight?"

"I am spending the night at Arradale House."

"Then let me thank you now for the hospitality of your home. It shows all the beauty of a woman's care."

"Then you may express your thanks to Mrs. Crofton, the housekeeper, who has been there a great deal longer than I, and who does most of the ordering of it."

He inclined his head slightly, perhaps in acknowledgment of her parry. "I will do so. I gather from your husband that you tend the garden, however, and are interested in animal breeding."

"True." She wished he would go, but also wished to learn more of him. He represented her enemy, the first New Commonwealther other than Edward that she'd ever met.

"Then I wish all the more that we had opportunity to talk. It is a strong interest of mine, and one day your work will be turned to the purposes of the Lord. God's blessings on you, sister."

With that, he clicked his horse onward. Rosamunde listened to the clop of his horse's hooves moving away, seething at the thought of her work profiting the New Commonwealth. The encounter disturbed her in other ways, too. He could not possibly suspect, but she wished a New Commonwealther had not encountered her here today. If—when—she revealed her pregnancy, would he make any connection?

No, for he'd not know a man was here.

Still, she shivered.

And he'd been a different sort of man than Edward. Though Edward had the means to hurt them all, she generally found him ridiculous with his ostentatious simplicity and humorless preaching. That man, with his simple manner and warm eyes, could sway the susceptible, persuade the reluctant. He'd even made her feel her scars were nothing.

Dangerous, that.

He was a dangerous man. She was used to thinking of the New Commonwealthers as rather stupid.

She hurried on her way, wishing Digby would ban Edward from the house. Digby had hopes of turning him from the sect, of course, hopes that she was sure would never come true. At the moment, it was all Digby could think to do to prevent disaster.

Soon, please God, all that would change.

Should she go up to Wenscote to check on the situation? It would only take an hour or so. It was impossible, however, because there'd be no good reason to come back. She'd have to send a letter, however, explaining her comings and goings to her husband.

So many complexities.

That man had said he and Edward were to leave tomorrow. It would be all right. She grimaced as she wiped her shoes and went into the kitchen. She wanted it to be all right so she could stay, and she wanted to stay for wicked delights.

She'd never have believed before yesterday that she could so quickly and thoroughly tumble into sin.

          *   *   *

Rosamunde found Jessie and Millie at the kitchen table, enjoying a cup of tea. Jessie leaped up as if caught in a sin, but Rosamunde waved her back to her seat. "I assume there's been no trouble from upstairs."

"Not a sound, milady. Do you want tea?"

"Yes, thank you. In fact, I'd better take him something." The mere thought of visiting him sent her foolish heart racing.

"I can do that," said the maid, who'd gulped her tea and was now busily preparing new. Rosamunde supposed there was no way the girl could sit comfortably in this situation, but she wasn't about to let anyone steal a few precious moments with Brand.

"I'll take it up," she said, wishing she had the strength to do otherwise. "I have the newspapers for him."

"There's plenty of books in the library, milady," Millie pointed out with a disapproving glower. She always thought people took advantage of Rosamunde.

"Not to his taste, I'm sure. However, I do have that book on animal breeding that I bought in Harrogate. I'll see if he would like that." At least she hadn't yet written her name inside.

Jessie had finished the tray, so Rosamunde picked it up and hurried out of the kitchen. She should probably have let one of the maids take it, but she couldn't resist a few more minutes of his company.

Couldn't resist. . . .

Anyway, she rationalized, the less the maids saw of him, the less likely they'd be to let slip any details.

Oh, what a tangled, tangled web!

And there was the dratted mask. She put it on, unlocked his door, and entered his room.

He rose, and she paused, blinking at the change in him. The clothes might be simple and stained, but in some way they made him an altogether more formidable figure. He seemed bigger, but also more distant. His hair was tamed by a dark ribbon, and despite the low quality of the garments, something made it clear that he was an aristocrat. The way he stood? The aristocracy were taught, boys and girls, to stand and move so as to command. She saw it in Diana, and even Aunt Arradale had learned it after her grand marriage.

Whatever the cause, he effortlessly dominated the room. He was a stranger.

"Tea?" he said pleasantly. "When a person has nothing to do, food becomes important."

Rosamunde came to herself and placed the tray on a table. "And newspapers."

"Wonderful lady!" He smiled at her, but she felt more like a praised servant than a thanked equal. "Can you be even kinder and keep me company?"

Helpless to resist, Rosamunde sat and prepared the tea, taking foolish pleasure in such a simple task. "I can't stay long," she warned as she stirred the swirling leaves.

"I suppose not." He sat at ease, one leg crossed over the other. "Who was that I saw you talking to outside?"

Her spoon rattled against the china pot. He'd *seen* her? After a moment, she realized that he couldn't have seen much at such a distance, and she'd been wearing her obscuring cap.

She continued to stir the leaves, half mesmerized by the dark, spiraling liquid. "Talked to? When?"

"Just now. In the steeple hat."

She looked up sharply, but didn't see the suspicion she thought she'd heard. "It was just a New Commonwealther."

"Ah yes. The Cromwellians."

She realized the tea was probably overbrewed by now and hastily poured it. "I'm not sure they're that, though they want people to live the strict Puritan life. Milk? Sugar?"

At his indication, she added them.

"So," he asked, taking the cup from her, "he's a neighbor? You have the New Commonwealth in this area?"

"Not yet." Immediately she wished she'd just said "No."

"They seem to be spreading. Steeple hats and starched caps all over the place."

"Yes." Surely there was no harm in discussing a social phenomenon, and yet it rested so close to her secrets that she did not dare. She seized the plate of biscuits and thrust it at him.

He took one, but said, "I'll admit to having some sympathy with their cause."

"Sympathy?" She almost spilled the ginger snaps in his lap. Was *that* the reason for his plain clothes? Mercy, what had she done?

"You sound shocked."

She gathered her wits, searching his face for clues. "You don't strike me as a Puritan."

"I suppose I don't," he said, with a laugh. "And I'm not. But I don't much care for the excesses of today either. The government has restricted sale of gin, yet poor people still drink too much."

She put the plate down with a *clink*. "So it's allowable for the higher orders to drown their troubles in spirits, but not for the common man?"

"Are you a radical? If a simple man drinks every day, likely his children will starve. If a nobleman does it, his dependents may not suffer unless he games at the same time."

She couldn't resist. "What you're saying, of course, is that noblemen are useless."

His lips twitched at what he clearly thought was a private joke. "Only some of them, dear lady."

"And what of the nobleman who employs you? Is he an idle drunkard who knows not what he owns?"

More humor. "Assuredly not."

"Yet *you* were found drunk."

"I told you I don't drink to excess."

"Will he dismiss you, then?"

He put down his cup and looked around. "Where do you keep the rack and thumbscrews? This is clearly an inquisition."

Rosamunde wondered why she had turned teasing into attack. "I'm sorry. But you did appear to be drunk. It puzzles me."

He gave a rueful grimace. "It puzzles me, too, for it isn't in my nature. I have this vague memory of being in a tavern, but that doesn't mean I was there to drink deep. It's a place to meet others, or to eat a simple meal."

"And there are no taverns within miles of where I found you."

"Then we have a mystery to add to the many." He shrugged. "I doubt it's important."

"Even though someone moved you, drunk, from there to the cold, wet moors?"

"Perhaps I rode. I had a horse. A dun gelding hired in Thirsk. Has such a horse turned up around here?"

"Not that I've heard."

"He might have returned to more familiar parts."

"But why would you have been coming up here?"

"Where is here?"

She almost told the truth. "G— Gillsett." Of course, she had to stammer!

"Don't lie," he said without heat. "You want to keep your identity secret. I accept that."

"I'm sorry," she said, and she was. She was miserable. She'd always regarded truth as precious, as part of the deepest, warmest bonds. *You don't even want such a bond with this man,* her stern part said.

Yes, I do, whispered folly.

"Where will you want to go tomorrow?" she asked, reminding folly that tomorrow this would be over.

"To Thirsk. I have an appointment to keep there. I likely will be out of a job if I let matters run wild much longer."

"You do suffer from a harsh master, then."

"Harsh? An understatement! I only pray he never hear of my misadventure."

"He would turn you off?"

"He'd turn me inside out. Clearly, I was stupid somewhere."

He was probably speaking of his brother, the daunting and vengeful marquess. "He won't find out from me, at least." Rosamunde rose, knowing she must leave, but miserable over it. Or rather, miserable over this talk of him leaving.

Tomorrow.

Forever.

It seemed wrong that this could end so absolutely, so soon.

"Is our time up?" he asked, as if responding to her secret thoughts. She let herself believe that he minded, too, just a little.

"Not quite. I have a book that might interest you."

Brand watched her leave, irritated at himself over the wistful note he'd heard in his own voice. She was a married woman, and he wasn't going to carry her like a hump on his back when he left.

His interest in her sprang from boredom. Nothing more.

He turned his mind to the thought of his brother's reaction if he ever learned of all this. Bey would be scathing if he heard that a brother of his had let himself be drugged.

That had to be the explanation, however. Probably some form of opium. Plain drink couldn't have had the effect he'd suffered. So, he thought, leaning back and nibbling another biscuit, who had drugged him? And why? If only he could remember whom he'd been drinking with.

The money in his pockets had gone, but it had been a small amount, not worth a plot. Anyway, thieves wouldn't take the trouble to carry him so far from the place of attack.

And why, plague take it, had his mysterious lady been talking to George Cotter?

She returned with a large, leather-bound volume, clutched rather like a shield. "I don't know if this will be of interest. It's agricultural."

"My bread and butter, dear lady."

"Oh. I suppose so." She walked over and thrust it at him. "It's new, so you may not have read it."

He looked at the title. "*Planned Breeding Programs— A Gentleman's Guide.* Interesting." Opening the book, he added, "So new, the pages are uncut. I will need a knife."

She left and returned in a moment with a razor-sharp, long-bladed one designed for just this purpose. He could very easily have slit her throat with it. He didn't point that out, but it reassured him. She couldn't be up to serious mischief and be so naive.

He wasn't even certain Cotter was a wrong 'un, but her conversation with the man bothered him. Thus far, he hadn't been more than idly curious about his gentle jailer, but now he needed to know more.

"Is this book a gift for someone?" he asked, slitting pages.

"For myself."

That did surprise him. "You breed stock?"

A movement, a slight rearrangement of spine and shoulders, told him she was uncomfortable with the question. Not surprising. It was hardly a conventional occupation of ladies. "It is an interest of mine, yes."

"Sheep? Cattle?"

"Sheep and horses."

"Racehorses?" Intriguing.

"No. Draft horses."

Astonishing. He loved being astonished. "I have a soft spot for the mighty beasts."

She sank into a chair, perhaps without realizing it. "I think they're beautiful. I laugh at racehorses with their spindly legs and nervy temperament."

"Common spirits? I don't think you have a nervy temperament."

"Are you saying I'm like a cart horse, sir?"

He laughed. "Only in their most admirable qualities. I know, for example, that your legs are not at all spindly."

She pushed down her skirt, as if anxious that she might be showing her legs. She was a conundrum, his captor. He wished he could linger here a month to discover all her secrets. To keep her longer, and to test her a little, he asked about the most famous authority on animal breeding. "What do you think of Bakewell?"

"Very little, which seems to be his purpose, for he keeps his business and his methods to himself. I gather he's doing good work with horses, but that his improved sheep are too fatty for meat."

"Perhaps we'll find use for mutton fat. Do you breed for meat?"

"Not primarily."

"The new factories and mines mean there's strong demand for it."

"I know, but it doesn't interest me."

"Wool, then."

She nodded firmly. "I'm trying to improve softness without sacrificing the sturdiness of the beasts. I've imported stock from Ireland, but the quality of the wool seems more dependent on the living conditions of the animals than on the breeding."

"Good food, coarse wool. But there's plenty of need for coarser wool, and the staple's longer."

"There's also need for the fine. England is a great wool-producing nation, but we import vast quantities of the finer types. Don't you think we should produce wool for fine shawls as well as worsteds and blankets?"

"Definitely."

She had leaned forward in her enthusiasm, but now she stiffened. "You're laughing at me!"

He raised a hand. "No. I'm delighted by your excitement. What about the horses? Are you using continental stock?"

"Lord—" She noticeably broke off. "Another breeder here has a Friesian stallion. I'm breeding to that with native draft stock, but I'm thinking of bringing in a stallion of my own. We need more strong horses, especially up here. Oxen are useless."

Did she run her own estate? What of her elderly husband? Perhaps he was feeble, so she'd taken over, and was proving to be an admirably managing female.

"Are you thinking to enclose any of the property?"

Again, she nodded, in that definite way quite contrary to her flustered behavior about more intimate matters. "I think the tenants will agree. The days of strip fields and open grazing are over. Are your employer's estates enclosed?"

"Some. He has a great many estates. As you say, it's usually the best way. How can anyone cope with a landholding broken into little pieces scattered over a large area?"

"And with all the animals grazing together. How can anyone run a breeding program . . . ?"

They fell into lively conversation until a chiming clock somewhere in the house caught her attention. It was sometime later that she shot to her feet as if someone had stuck a pin in her behind. "I can't sit here talking all day! What will people think?" She even put her hand to her mask, as if fearing it might have melted away.

As perhaps, in a sense, it had. Enjoying her company, he'd felt as if he'd seen through the cloth to the features underneath. That he really knew her.

He rose, wanting to ask her to stay, but speaking from his nobler side. "Knowing people, they'll think the worst."

She almost flew to the door. Hand on the knob, however, she paused like a wary bird. "I'm moving elsewhere for the night."

"Ah." The disappointment was disturbingly sharp. "I am truly sorry about that."

Like a bird pecking, she added, "I'm coming back. After dark. I think."

"Do." Against his will, he added, "Please . . ."

But by then she had completed her flight and the lock clicked shut. Had she heard the betraying word? He half hoped not. This was madness, and he knew it.

A marvelous kind of madness, however. A marvelous adventure. He should write it up as a book—*A Gentleman's Adventures in the Yorkshire Dales.*

What was the ending, though?

No glorious triumph, alas. It ended tomorrow when he settled into his mundane tasks, and she returned to her elderly husband.

He picked up her book and opened it, treasuring the unexpected meeting of minds it represented, and the charming, enticing differences that went along with it. She shared his beliefs and aims, but was hindered by a softer heart. She wanted to look after every single person who worked on her land, even the feckless. He doubted she was ruthless enough to make notable steps in animal breeding. She wouldn't cull the weak.

None of that made him like or admire her the less.

And was all this to end at dawn?

It must. She was married. This had only ever been a

fleeting visit to a forbidden, secret place. Tomorrow he must leave. Doubtless stacks of work awaited him, and he had an appointment in Thirsk he must not miss.

He'd not pursue his mysterious lady, but he'd have to look into the matter of his abduction. On the surface, it made no sense. He'd been involved in a routine inspection of a property he might want to buy.

In his usual habit for such trips, he'd dressed simply and ridden to the area on a hired horse. He liked to find out the true situation, not the one presented by an anxious seller. He didn't deceive anyone on these trips, though, and even used his own name. The sort of people he was interested in talking to—innkeepers, farmers' wives, laborers, craftsmen—wouldn't recognize the name Malloren. If they mistook it for Mallory, however, he didn't correct them.

He'd not expected any surprises, for his local agent had looked into the property thoroughly. However, now that he thought of it, as part of his enquiries, he had been asking questions about a neighboring estate. Rawston Glebe had recently been taken over by the New Commonwealth.

As he'd said to his lady, he didn't totally disagree with the Cotterites. They were good farmers, and they took in farm workers displaced by the changes in England. Apart from the inclusion of families, their strict communal life was almost a revival of the great medieval monasteries of this area—Jervaulx, Rievaulx, Fountains—and no one could deny that the monks had created agricultural prosperity out of harsh lands.

The only thing Brand had against the New Commonwealth was that when they took over an estate, they forced evictions on those unwilling to convert. It wasn't right for people to be turned off their land, land they'd worked for generations. Moreover, stability and continuity bound together the English countryside. It served no good purpose to disturb things, and the Cotterites were turning the north upside down.

Of course the current tenants were allowed to stay, but only if they followed the sect's strict teachings.

Brand didn't much care for fashionable decadence, but there was no sin in laughter and play.

His mind slid to his mysterious lady, who seemed a stranger to laughter and play. Could she be a Cotterite? She didn't wear their uniform, but her dress was more modest than fashionable. If there was some connection between the New Commonwealth and his abduction, might she have been part of it?

He shook his head, unable to see George Cotter condoning unlawful sex. If Cotter wasn't at least honest in his beliefs, Brand had lost all judgment of people.

Brand had found the man surprisingly intelligent and undoubtedly sincere. He argued passionately and cogently that land wasted on parks and pleasure gardens should be given to sober, hardworking tenants. That was hard to argue with. In fact, Brand had experienced a similar meeting of minds with Cotter as with his mysterious lady. Cotter, too, was an ardent but clear-sighted believer in agricultural improvement. As with the monasteries, he was using his disciplined followers to bring about change far faster than usual.

Faster than Brand could, having to deal with the countrymen's stubborn adherence to ways of the past. He was often pushed to his limit by phrases such as: "What were good enough for our fathers should be good enough for us, milord." And: "That's not the way we're used to doing things round here, milord."

Commanding total obedience certainly had its appeal.

Brand shook away his wandering thoughts. His mysterious lady couldn't possibly be part of any plan of George Cotter's. In fact, the New Commonwealth had nothing to do with his affairs other than the fact that they owned an estate next to one he might buy for his brother.

And, of course, the fact that his brother was coming north with the King's commission to investigate the sect for subversive tendencies.

Brand leaned back to contemplate that. Could word of Bey's mission have spread? He was ordered to meet his brother in Thirsk tomorrow at noon, which is why his amusement here must end at dawn. No matter where this place was, it must surely be no more than six hours' ride from Thirsk.

Bey doubtless wanted Brand's impressions of the north and the New Commonwealth. Once done with that, Brand would have a hectic schedule to catch up with. Including, he thought with sudden interest, visits to various stockbreeding estates. Might he turn up at such an estate and come face to face with a certain mysterious lady . . . ?

He'd like that.

Very much.

Too much.

He put down the unread book and stood to pace the confining room, fighting the knowledge that, despite her wishes, he couldn't walk away from this. He needed to know more, if only to be sure that she suffered no harm from this adventure.

Perhaps he could convince her to trust him. Perhaps he could become a discreet friend. If her husband really was elderly and indifferent, perhaps they could—

He stopped himself. That way lay madness. A man couldn't become obsessed with a woman whose face he'd never seen, whose name he did not know.

Clearly, he could.

A married woman, he reminded himself, making himself sit down to read the solid book.

Damn, the pages were still uncut.

Damn it all to Hades!

He grabbed the razor-sharp knife and began to slice open pages, wishing he could slice through reality as easily, slice through to a place where his mysterious lady wasn't married, and wasn't secretive. To a place where they could enjoy delightful conversations of all kinds, whenever they wished.

For the rest of their lives, before, during, and after delightful lovemaking.

Chapter 10

Rosamunde had halted in the corridor outside the bedroom, fighting a mad urge to rush back—not to her captive lover, but to that dazzling surprise, a man she could talk to. She'd forced her steps on, but in a daze of wonder. A man who shared her interests, who didn't scoff at or belittle her enthusiasms.

She'd always known even Digby was humoring her. He'd raised no objection to her interest in stockbreeding, nor to her expenses, but it had always been clear that he regarded it as another man might regard his wife's interest in buying new curtains or bonnets.

Her modest successes merited only a "That's good, Rosie," said as he read a newspaper or magazine.

Rosamunde had become so used to this that she'd never dreamed it could be different. She'd certainly never expected a meeting of knowledgeable minds with the charming rogue she'd taken as lover.

Now, out in the garden, she admitted that everyone might be right in their warnings, though profoundly wrong as well. They feared she was in danger of falling in love with a handsome rogue. If she fell in love with Brand Malloren, however, it would be as much with his company as his body. More, in fact. She was too practical to toss her life away for physical delights. But for companionship—for respect, shared interests and laughter . . . Those were treasures that could last a lifetime, and were precious beyond all.

Nearly all.

Vows, duties, and responsibilities *must* come first.

By the stone arch that led into the kitchen garden, she paused to wonder at herself. Here she went again, weaving ridiculous dreams. There was no meeting ground for them.

Not one scrap.

Except that there was, and they had found it, and she liked him so very, very much.

Standing straighter, she swallowed folly. This was no good, no good at all. He was leaving tomorrow, and for now she had beans and blackberries to pick.

She'd asked Jessie if she needed anything from the garden, and the maid had asked for the beans. Walking to Arradale earlier, Rosamunde had spotted a laden thicket of brambles. Afraid to go upstairs to change or get her cap—afraid she'd weaken—she'd protected her cream colored dress with a kitchen smock, and borrowed a mob cap from Jessie to shield her face.

From the sun, she told herself. It was time to get over this obsession with hiding from strangers, for Diana's sake if not for her own.

She picked the beans and left them in one basket, ready to collect on her return. Then she went to fight the brambles. Alone in a quiet corner of the estate, however, she found herself fighting insanity as much as thorns. .

Even if she were pretty and single, Lord Brand Malloren would never be for her. Never! She might be cousin to the Countess of Arradale, but that was the result of a wild mismatch between the old earl's younger son and the pretty daughter of a local gentleman farmer.

It didn't raise the family up high. The Ellingtons were still just solid farming stock. Her own marriage to Sir Digby Overton was more than she'd normally have looked for.

Nor did her friendship with Diana make her a suitable match for a marquess's son. Certainly, if she wished, she could move in high circles, and perhaps attract a husband there, even with her blemished face. She'd not expect a noble suitor, however. Her portion had been a mere thousand pounds. A man like Brand Malloren could expect ten times that.

She was so distracted that thorns caught her smock and her flesh, digging deep, so by the time she'd freed herself, blood mixed with the purple stains on her fingers. She licked the wounds clean, tasting the mixture of blood and juice, and the salt of tears.

She sucked in a deep breath. *Stop it, Rosa! Stop it right now.* If heaven is kind, you are carrying a child that will be Sir Digby Overton's heir. Your duty is to the child, your husband, and the estate. Once Brand Malloren leaves, you will not think of him again.

Ever.

Firm in that resolution, she picked the last of the ripe berries and headed back to the dower house.

Firm?

If she were really firm, she wouldn't keep her tryst tonight. She paused in what she and Diana called their faery glade, a concealed spot in the wilderness where a little stream tumbled over rocks, surrounded by wildflowers. They'd always thought faeries must live here, and had whispered wishes into the chuckling water.

They'd come here once to wish that Rosamunde's scars would heal to smooth skin. Childish folly.

Cleaning her stained and scratched hands in the cold water, Rosamunde wished for the mature strength to do right. She had as much success at washing away her wicked hunger as she did at washing away the stains.

It was beyond her to give up her one last night.

Then she looked at her purple fingers and groaned. A fine wicked woman she was turning out to be! Was she going to have to go to him masked and *gloved*? The stains would fade in a day or two, but for the moment she was an uncorrectable disaster. Her mouth and chin were probably stained, too, since she'd sampled the sweet, juicy fruit.

At least stains on her mouth and chin wouldn't matter. The mask would hide them. The mask that prevented kisses.

She did so long to kiss him, and to be kissed back.

Oh, but like a child, she wished for impossible things. She wanted to be a beautiful woman. A seductive woman, even, the sort men longed for on sight. But even without scars, she wouldn't be. She had freckles from being in the sun, and since it didn't matter, she'd never pampered her skin with creams.

Didn't crushed strawberries get rid of sunburn and freckles? She eyed the blackberries, then laughed at herself. The only good *they* would do would be to cover her freckles with purple splotches. He'd probably think she had the plague!

Oh, but it was a seductive dream, suitable for a faery glade. Flawless skin, softened by years of creams. This other Rosamunde's hair would know only rainwater, rainwater in which rosemary had been steeped to bring out the rich colors. For the final rinse some extra perfume, perhaps. She already used gillyflower in her hair rinse, but a seductress would have heavier weapons than that. Rose? Carnation? Mignonette?

And clothes. Smooth, exquisite silken clothes such as Diana wore, with embroidery even on the layers that people would not, should not see.

She remembered being stripped by her captive lover and hid her face in her hands. What had she been thinking of? Her corset was four years old and mended in places. Her shift and petticoat were of plainest, practical style.

Pitiable.

Pitiable.

Could she bear to be taken again out of pity?

She uncovered her face to look up through green leaves to the fathomless blue sky. In truth, yes. In truth, she'd be taken any way it had to be.

She leaped to her feet and fled the place of foolish wishes, trying to escape wicked desires and deep mortification. As she emerged from the wilderness, someone called. Jerking out of her panicked thoughts, Rosamunde saw Diana waving and hurrying along the path to her.

She experienced a painful stab of envy.

Diana had the look of a seductress. She always protected her milk-white complexion with enormous hats. This one was white, tied with wide ribbons of straw-gold. The hat was scattered with silk flowers, and bow and flowers matched the trimming on Diana's floaty, low-cut muslin gown. Her breasts were a little smaller than Rosamunde's, but the bodice made the most of them.

That gown, Rosamunde thought rather spitefully, would be ruined in a moment by blackberry picking.

"There you are!" Diana declared, shaking her head with a laugh. "Blackberry juice, grass stains, and a servant's smock. Really, Rosa."

"Have one." Rosamunde offered the full basket, half hoping her cousin would accept and drip juice on herself.

With a twinkling smile, Diana took one gingerly between her fingertips and popped it in her mouth without any mess at all. "Mmmmm. They're at their best. If Mrs. Yockenthwait's making her blackberry pie, I'm staying to eat here."

"She's off with a niece who's having a baby."

"Oh. Who? I could visit. New babies are so special. You should come, too. They say it makes a woman more likely to conceive."

"That's an old wives' tale." Rosamunde popped a berry into her own mouth, amazed at how plainly she could refer to her wicked enterprise.

Indeed, Diana blinked at her in surprise.

"Well," she said after a moment, "all right." She pulled a small, stoppered bottle out of her pocket. "This is from Mistress Naisby. Guaranteed to knock him into a deep sleep. She warns that to keep him unconscious for many hours you'll have to give him the whole amount, and he'll not feel too well when he wakes up."

Rosamunde reluctantly took it. "She didn't have anything gentler?"

"Not that will last long enough. And this has a taste. She suggests giving it to him in spicy soup or punch."

"Lud! How am I supposed to do that?"

Diana pointed at the basket. "Blackberry cordial. With all that spice and a healthy shot of brandy, he'd not taste hot pepper."

Rosamunde looked at the plump berries as if they'd become tools of the devil. "Oh dear, oh dear. You can't imagine how kind he's being. Why can't I just trust him?"

"Well, why can't you?"

Rosamunde grimaced. "Because it's not my risk to take. Too many people's futures depend on this." She tucked the bottle in her pocket. "Who drinks blackberry cordial at dawn?"

"At dawn? Why at dawn?"

"Because that's when he insists on leaving." They strolled on. "I visited the big house and your mother invited me to stay the night."

Diana rolled her eyes. "How did you get out of that?"

"I didn't. It will help to deflect suspicion. But you'll have to help me sneak out."

"Dinah and Rosie." Diana chuckled. "We've done that a time or two, haven't we? I'm quite envious of you, you know, slipping out for a naughty tryst."

Rosamunde stopped and faced her. "Don't be."

Laughter faded. "Is it so horrid? You seemed so—"

"It's not horrid. That," said Rosamunde, reluctant to say the words, "is the problem."

"Rosa! I warned you."

"You can warn me that the sun will rise. It's not likely to do any good!"

Diana stared at her. "I'm sorry. . . ."

"No, no! I'm sorry. I've no call to snap at you. It's just . . ."

"Yes, I see. Perhaps later—"

"Don't!" Rosamunde exclaimed. *"Don't* speak of Digby's death."

Diana turned white. "I'm sorry. But really . . . no! I'm sorry. But . . ."

Rosamunde hated herself for upsetting her cousin. "But he's so much older, and will doubtless leave me a widow. I know. But Diana, even so, nothing could ever come of this. He's a nobleman!"

"My father married Mother."

"And lambs are sometimes born with two heads. Anyway," she said sighing, "even if he were mad enough to consider it, it won't appeal when he comes to his senses. I'm lying to him, I'm using him, and I intend to drug him in order to keep my secret."

"Rosa—"

"And don't forget my face. If he could forgive all else, he'd hardly be able to overlook that."

"Truly, Rosa, it's not as bad as you—"

With a wild laugh, Rosamunde turned into her cousin's arms and clung to her. "Oh, I feel so wretched! And from so many confusing wounds."

Diana held her close. "You've done what needs to be done, dearest. You don't need to do more. I'm sure it won't make any difference. Look, we'll—"

Rosamunde pulled free, wiping her cheeks. "But I *want* to! That's what's so terrible. I want to. I want it so badly I'm willing to risk my reputation, and Wenscote, and my chance of heaven for it!"

"Oh," said Diana, stunned. "So it is like that after all, is it?"

Brand watched from the window as two women strolled down a path toward the house. At a greater distance he'd seen them pause, then embrace, almost as if one had given the other bad news. Was one of them his mysterious lady?

As they came closer, trees and shrubs veiled his view. They were of a height and size, but one wore a fashionable white gown and an extravagantly wide hat tied with yellow ribbon. It successfully hid her face, but he didn't think she was his lady. The other looked like a servant and carried a basketful of something dark. Blackberries?

Clearly neither was his lady.

His.

No. Resolved not to be sucked into folly, he returned resolutely to his book. It was just the sort of material that usually interested him. He'd been reading for a while when the lock turned. He rose as she entered, damning the pleasure that instantly sparked at the sight of her. She walked toward him, and he noticed that her fingers were stained.

Blackberries? Had this, after all, been the woman in the smock in the garden? If so, why had she fallen into that deep embrace? What had distressed her?

How could he take away her pain?

"Is the book passing the time, sir?" she asked.

"Yes, thank you." He found himself studying her masked face, seeking emotion, seeking identity. Unless her mask was skillfully padded, it showed her features—round of cheek, a little short of nose, squarely firm of chin. The artificial coloring gave the illusion of reality, but the result didn't look like a human being at all. Only the eyes did, and they were ordinary, showing no distress.

"My maid will bring your dinner shortly," she said. "Beyond that, please try not to bother the servants here. They are few, and busy."

"You're leaving now?" He really shouldn't feel as if his world would suddenly be empty. He had better control of his mind and his emotions than this.

"It is time."

"When will you return?" Not, *will* you. She *must*.

Her hands moved. If she were a lady of less self-control, he thought they would have fiddled with her skirt. "Later. After dark."

He let out his breath. "I'm glad."

Her eyes met his, and he thought perhaps he would recognize them again, if they looked at him that way. "Are you really?"

She was asking things of him to which she had no right. No right at all. But even so, he put out a hand. "Very really."

She just stood there.

"The idea is that you put your hand in mine."

Her hands moved again, this time as if they would sidle off behind her, into safety. "Why?"

"Because then, you would have to be over here, close to me."

"And what good would that do?"

"Then I could sit and pull you into my lap. I could hold you for a moment."

He saw her tighten, almost pull in on herself as if threatened. "Why?" It was almost a wail.

"Why not? What frightens you? Remember, mistress mine, you are in command. I am but your humble servant."

"You, sir, lack the concept of humility entirely!" But

she walked forward, reminding him again of a wary bird, tempted by seeds, but afraid of the hunter. As one last movement, she put the tips of her fingers on his hand. The stained and chilly tips.

He waited.

With an audible breath, she slid her hand farther and wrapped her fingers tightly around his. He sat, then gently, he drew her down onto his lap and settled her there where, he was startled to think, she was meant to be.

He almost held his breath, so aware was he of danger. There was nothing for him here but a few hours of pleasure.

With another man's wife.

Damn Sir Archibald, or whoever the man was.

He raised her hand to inspect purple fingertips, then sucked at them. "Blackberries. Dare I hope for blackberry pie?"

"Perhaps." Her head was down, and he felt sure she was blushing beneath the mask, soft and relaxed as a child against him. What a charming, inconsistent mystery she was.

Wrapping his arms around her, he held her close as if she were a large child. He had no idea why he was doing it, but then he realized that he'd wanted to hold her ever since he'd seen that embrace in the garden.

She'd needed comfort then, and he wanted to give her comfort now.

Her glossy brown curls brushed his face, smelling faintly of flowers. Her other perfumes were vague and natural and already recognizably hers. This was danger and he knew it. All he courted here was pain. Tomorrow he would leave, and for a little while he'd ache from loss of her. But only for a little while. Once he was back in his real life, with work, friends, other women . . .

He held her closer still.

Soft and firm. A peach of a woman who made his mouth water. Her head nestled a little closer, settling on his shoulder as her breathing drifted slow and at rest. Her momentary peace was palpable and precious. He could give her this. It might only be a brief respite from whatever troubled her, but it was his to give.

He wanted to say many things, surprising things.

He wanted to tell her that he'd never held a woman quite like this before, that if a woman had been on his lap they'd been engaged in love play. That he wanted love play, but that for the moment, he valued this above all.

He wanted to ask her again to take off the mask and trust him, not only for the trust, but because he had a desperate need to kiss her, to join his mouth to hers in that most soul-deep melding.

He'd never thought of kisses in that way before.

He was tempted to tilt her head and kiss the painted lips of the mask in frail hope that it would be any kind of substitute.

He wanted to demand the reason for the mask, for the desperate embrace in the garden, for her hungry, bold, unpracticed insistence on sex. What were her troubles, her trials, her sufferings? If he knew, perhaps he could sweep them all away with a godly—or at least a lordly—hand.

He generally had little interest in his noble status and wealth, but it would be precious if he could lay it at his lady's feet.

He wanted to pledge himself to her happiness. He wanted more. Only by desperate will was he preventing himself from begging her to abandon everything—her marriage, her life, her friends, her family—and run away to live in scandal and shame with him.

He breathed deeply, fighting to protect her from himself.

He'd never imagined he had such a foolish romantic quivering within. She would be ruined, and his pleasant life would be destroyed. He had work he enjoyed and which fulfilled him; leisure enough and friends to share it with; a loving family; and the general approval of his fellow man. The last thing he needed was scandal.

There could be worse than scandal.

Perhaps her husband wasn't too old to come after him and demand a duel. He'd doubtless be able to kill the man, but he wouldn't. Honor would not permit that. Not when he was in the wrong.

Did he want to die for love?

Short of that, he could face a court case for alienation
of affections. She and he would become the tattle of the
town and he'd have to pay a punitive fine. He suppressed a groan at the thought of Bey's reaction to such
a sordid imbroglio.

There'd be items in the lower newssheets, crude illustrations on the windows of the printing shops. Specula-
tive illustrations of him and his adulterous lover in their
bed of sin. Coarse illustrations of a Yorkshire wanton,
huge breasts and hamlike legs exposed.

If he were the nobody she thought him, it might be
possible for them to steal a life together. Few people
would care. A Malloren, however, was always a source
of interest, and there were plenty of people eager to cast
a dart at the Marquess of Rothgar, a power in the land
and confidant of the King.

Their relationship simply couldn't be.

He nuzzled her soft brown curls, assailed by loss, astonished to feel the sting of tears in his eyes.

Rosamunde leaned against him, fighting a desperate
battle with tears. A few had escaped, but the mask
would hide them. She would not sob, even though her
chest ached with the swell of it.

She tried not to think, because there wasn't a thought
that wasn't painful. One broke through, however, like a
bell in the night. If only this could be, this closeness, day
by day. This was her birthright. It was every person's
birthright, to have someone to hold them with tender
care. . . .

But then she found the strength to fight back.

If she wanted to be held with tender care, Digby
would do that. Digby, her kindly husband, whom she
was supposed to be helping here, not betraying in her
heart. She fumbled herself desperately out of Brand's
arms, off his lap. After a startled moment, he helped so
at least she didn't fall.

"I have to go," she said, knowing it was inadequate.
She looked at him, suspecting that he'd see the unshed
tears in her eyes. It was suddenly important, despite the
folly of it, that he know about the tears.

"You will return?"

Were his eyes a little moist? Were they? What did it mean?

She should say no.

She should say farewell.

Now.

"Later," she said, swallowing again. "It . . . it might be quite late. . . ."

He put his hands together and bowed. "As you will, mistress. At whatever hour, I will be yours, be everything you desire." There was no humor in it this time, however, nor in the words he added:

"But don't forget. For our sins, it can only be until dawn."

Rosamunde left the room with dignity, still fighting tears when out of sight. She would not cry. Not even in private. But she slammed the door of her room and ripped off the hot, sticky mask, then rubbed her face hard, forcing the tears back into the aching well where they belonged.

She would *not* cry!

If she started to cry, all would be lost. It would prove that all was lost. . . .

Lost.

Lost.

No! *This* wasn't important. It was a phantasm. Reality was important. Wenscote, and Digby, and all the people there. People she loved. Reality was the child who would save them all.

His child.

Brand's child.

She seized the bedpost in both hands and squeezed it, letting the pineapple carving bite into her flesh, squeezing, squeezing until pain overwhelmed folly, until she could at last breathe again and stand calm, her purpose clear in mind.

No more risks. She might not risk discovery by returning tonight, but she risked something worse. Something deep in her heart that might shatter honor.

She would move to Arradale and leave only to go home.

She would let Diana manage the business of disposing of this inconvenient secret lover.

Inconvenient.

Secret.

Lover.

She sat on the bed with a defeated thump. *Why* had he held her like that? She wanted to wail the question, for it had caused such wounds she could imagine dying of them. Even so, she would not have missed his embrace, at cost of her life.

Indeed, now she knew the madness poets wrote of, the madness which drove men and women of power into the flames of disaster. But it wasn't *love*. No one could love someone they'd known for such a brief while.

It was folly!

It was idiocy!

A weakness of the mind.

A conflagration of lust.

She must not return. She must go home to her husband.

But she, who had lived her life on moral principles, who had always had the strength to do the right thing, was burning with need and could not resist the flames.

Splashing cold water on her face proved too feeble a gesture against such heat and fire, and a tiny, despairing laugh escaped. Even if she could fight the fire, she must return. Not for lust, but because, quite simply, she had promised.

She would betray Brand Malloren in other ways—she had no choice—but not in that.

She had promised and she would keep her word. She would be his mistress until dawn.

Chapter 11

$\mathbf{D}$inner and an evening in stately Arradale should have been interminable, but Rosamunde found it a steadying time. Here were order and manners and convention to quench some of the unruly flames.

She, Diana, and Aunt Arradale were joined by her aunt's companion, Mrs. Lampwick, an intelligent, self-composed woman; and Mr. Turcott, Diana's secretary, whose devoted hobby was to research the history of this part of Yorkshire. Conversation at table was easy, erudite, and never touched on the emotions.

Except, Rosamunde thought, that there might be some sort of connection between Mrs. Lampwick and Mr. Turcott. It did seem, after all, that the lady had been helping the gentleman with some of his research. Though both were cool in their manner, sometimes she caught their eyes lingering on each other for a moment, or a range of excitement and intensity in their exchanges not shown when they spoke to others.

Would she have been so attuned to it a day ago?

As the meal progressed, it turned her gloomy. What a wonderful marriage those two might have—two equals with shared enthusiasms, together in everything, and free to love. Why was that denied her?

Because at sixteen, devastated by her wounds, she had run away from life, run behind the high stone walls of Wenscote. She had made her bed, however, and must lie in it. Choices must be lived with.

But I was only sixteen!

Even so.

The older couple disappeared after dinner, supposedly to separate occupations. Rosamunde wondered, then pushed such suspicions away. Just because she had become a wicked wanton was no reason to doubt the honor of two respectable, middle-aged people. If there was anything between them, they would move through the acceptable stages to the altar, not fumble and tumble among dusty family archives.

The mere idea must have made her lips twitch, for the dowager asked, "What amuses you, Rosamunde?"

They were in the drawing room, glorious with Chinese wallpaper, taking tea in tiny, delicate cups. As was her nature, Rosamunde told as much of the truth as she dared. "I wondered if there was a romance stirring between Mrs. Lampwick and Mr. Turcott."

Aunt Arradale's eyes twinkled. "You see it, too, do you? Yes, it is my dearest hope. Two more harmonious people cannot be imagined."

"How lovely," said Diana. "We must see what we can do to push them together."

"They are old enough to manage for themselves, dear."

"But I like to arrange lives. Left to themselves, people so often make a muddle of it!"

"Sometimes muddle is just what is needed. What *you* need, Diana, is a family of your own to manage."

Diana raised her chin. "You know I will not marry."

"Such foolishness. What use your precious independence when you are alone and bored?"

"I'm not bored. I live a very interesting life."

"Then don't interfere in the lives of others. Why not play for us, dear."

Diana rose with a flurry of silken skirts. "Very well. But considering how often you have lectured me about tidiness, Mama, I think it very inconsistent of you to preach muddle. Come, Rosa. Let's play an orderly duet."

As they walked toward the harpsichord, Aunt Arradale's voice pursued them. "The difference, Diana, is that human affairs are *supposed* to be muddled. That's when matters work out for the best. In a tidy world, your father would never have married me. He'd have married the Duke of Langton's daughter and been miserable."

Diana rolled her eyes at Rosamunde, then turned to look through the stack of sheet music by the instrument.

Rosamunde, however, pondered her aunt's words. Her own marriage was not at all muddled. It had been a tidy solution to her problem, and had been orderly from the moment she'd left the church on Digby's arm. It was also lacking. She wasn't used to thinking of it like that, but it was. It had never occurred to her that mature lives were supposed to be anything but orderly, but if someone as clear-sighted and intelligent as Aunt Arradale thought so. . . .

As Diana pulled out a sheet of music and sat down, Rosamunde had to suppress a laugh. If muddle was proper, her life at the moment was the epitome of propriety! She sat and looked at the music, then began to pick out her part. As she and Diana made order out of the muddle of notes and settled into the sprightly duet, she glanced out of the long windows, across the well-tended grounds, straining to see a particular window through the trees.

What was he doing? Thinking?

Her notes clashed with her cousin's and she hastily paid attention to the music. Not about duty, she prayed as she followed the notes. Nor payment of a debt. Please let it be more than that. She knew it was. Perilously more.

The windowpane shadows darkened and lengthened as golden evening sank into red. Soon would come night.

Night, secret night.

The prime occasion of secrets, muddle, and sin.

When dimness caused the dowager to ring for candles to be lit, Rosamunde excused herself to go to bed. Diana immediately said she would go up, too. The dowager looked at them, and it was as if fifteen years had evaporated. Rosie and Dinah up to mischief again.

All she said, however, was, "Good night, my dears."

Once they were safe in a bedroom, Rosamunde said, "I'm sure she guesses. This is *terrible!*"

"You thought Mrs. Yockenthwait guessed. And even your mother."

"But this is *Aunt Arradale!*"

Diana rolled her eyes. "Do you, too, sometimes wonder whether she has a birch tucked away?"

Rosamunde laughed, but heard it swirl toward wildness. Rubbing clammy hands on her skirts, she tried to steady her mind. The moon was slight, and though she knew the grounds well, she wanted to cross the park before full darkness settled. "I must go."

"Yes. This is quite extraordinary, you know."

"Of course I know!"

"I mean, watching you go, knowing what you are going to do." A quick frown tangled her brows. "At least you're getting to *do* it!"

"I got to do it on my wedding night."

"This clearly isn't the same. There's something about you now."

"Something . . . ?" Rosamunde looked down at herself as if it might show. "What?"

"You've changed. Of course, your mind is elsewhere, but you move differently. It's a little thing, but it's changed you."

"Oh, I do hope not!"

Diana whirled and picked up Rosamunde's shawl, wrapping it tenderly around her. "Ignore me. Go! I'll make sure no one notices your absence. And don't forget the soporific."

Rosamunde patted her pocket, though she hated the thought of using it. "I'm not—"

She had been about to say that she wasn't doing this out of choice, but of course that wasn't true.

"Yes, you are!" Diana smiled. "I'm sorry, dearest. Truth is, I'm envious. I don't suppose he'd care to move in here for a day or two."

It was clearly a joke, but a fierce "No!" escaped Rosamunde, leaving her brutally exposed.

"Oh love," said Diana softly, "don't."

Rosamunde tightened the shawl, unable to resist a check of her appearance in the long mirror. Because it was Arradale, she was wearing one of her finer gowns, a pale pink silk, trimmed with cream lace and pearls. It still wasn't how she wanted to appear tonight. It was a young girl's dress, the style that Digby favored for her.

"It's just a silly infatuation," she said, turning away. "I think we women are inclined to fancy ourselves in love with the men we do this with." She cast a quick, wry look at the frustrated Countess of Arradale. "A warning to you, if you like."

"That if I took a lover, I might fancy myself in love? I find that hard to believe, but I'll bear it in mind." She hugged Rosamunde and pushed her toward the door. "Go. Enjoy it for both of us!"

Rosamunde laughed and left the room to slip rapidly through the warren of a house she knew so well. She left by a small side door and gravel crunched beneath her feet as she followed the path that encircled the house. Then she struck off across springy grass toward the stand of trees that screened the dower house.

Then, even through night-dark trees, she saw a glimmering light.

He'd placed a candle in his window and it shone like a beacon to guide her.

Brand had set his candle close to the window.

He'd seen his lady leave earlier, accompanied by the fat maid who'd brought his dinner. He hadn't seen either of them return, despite almost constant vigil. It was frustratingly possible that she'd return from another direction, and ridiculous to think that she might lose her way.

It was night, though, and not long past the new moon. He hated the thought of her out alone in the dark.

He tried to be rational and concentrate on the book, but despite the interesting subject, words passed through his mind like water.

He concentrated harder. The writer had some intriguing ideas about achieving specific improvements in stock through careful breeding. It was a chancy business, however, as everyone knew from life. A strong-featured man might marry a pretty woman and have pretty sons, and heavy-faced daughters.

What sort of children would they . . . ?

No.

But they could have made a child.

If so, it would be counted as her husband's. No business of his.

Easy to think, less easy to live by.

Perhaps in nine months or so he should seek her out to make sure all was well. If it was, he'd not endanger her reputation.

He muttered a curse at his own duplicity. If he found her again, he'd be back in the morass. Perhaps he should break out of here now and run. It wouldn't be hard to escape.

Hand marking the place on the page, he tried to summon the will-power to leave. And failed. Nothing would stop him draining the unsatisfactory cup.

The book, he reminded himself.

Planned breeding programs.

Targeted breeding wasn't new. People had tried for champion racehorses for centuries and, for even longer, devotees had bred pit bulls and fighting cocks for strength and aggression. In those cases, however, they were willing to discard hundreds of failures in the search for one champion. A farmer needed a better success rate than that. The book suggested scientific ways to increase the success rate.

He managed to fix his interest on the text and was startled when the key turned and she came in. He looked first at her face and hit the frustrating grotesquerie of her mask, so he quickly looked lower for hints about her mood.

Nervous, but not as awkward as the first time.

In the process he couldn't help but notice that she was wearing her first low bodice, which made the magnificent best of her figure.

Hot desire hit like a lightning bolt.

Silk, he thought desperately, trying to keep control. Pink silk. Lace. Bows. Pretty. Feminine.

Not right for her.

Not for his mysterious lady.

She might be pretty, and she was certainly feminine, but she possessed more womanly strength than the gown suggested, and more character, too. He'd dress her in earthy colors. Subtle greens, warm browns, cream. Blackberry purple . . .

He was just sitting there. Putting the book aside, he rose to give her the honor of a full, courtly bow. "Welcome, mistress."

She seemed frozen, too, and he wondered if she almost hadn't come. Should he move between her and the door to prevent escape?

Then she jerked into movement, hurrying toward the candle. He caught her wrist as she passed. "It was daylight before."

"It's not daylight now." Her tendons ran stiff beneath his fingers.

"Candlelight is very becoming."

Her head tilted back as if she prayed. "I need," she whispered, "darkness."

Why had it been possible earlier in daylight, but not now? What had changed? He wanted very much to love her by candlelight, but he let her go, licked his finger and thumb, and pinched out the flame. "Now, mistress," he asked in the dark, "what else do you command?"

With the lack of light, his other senses sparked. He fancied he could hear the rustle of her gown as she breathed. Certainly he could smell the flower perfume that would ever after be linked in his mind with this strange affair.

With her.

"Should I undress?" she whispered.

"It is as you desire." Did his voice carry his bewildering tremor of raw desire?

What was he? A callow youth?

She moved suddenly, distressfully. "Tell me what to do."

He spoke his need. "Surrender. Give up your command. Give it to me. Be my slave for the night."

"Indentured servant," she retorted. Perhaps she took a step away.

"Slave."

His eyes were settling to the dark. He saw her turn

her head, as if trying to study him. "What if you do something I don't like?"

"Tell me. My aim will be your delight, I promise. Trust me."

That, above all, he wanted. Her trust.

"Why should I?"

The cold question hurt. "That is for you to decide."

She moved restlessly, over to the bed and back, skirts whispering of secrets and senses. "You won't do anything . . . to distress me?"

"I can't promise that. We have only a few hours in which to learn what distresses us and pleases us. Quite likely we will never meet again." He said it deliberately, and heard her stifled protest. "It seems a shame to spend our last night blandly. Though, if that is your wish, it shall be my command."

She stood still, so perfectly still that he could detect neither rustle nor breath. Then she turned, and sank to her knees before him. "I am yours, then. Pleasure me as you will, my lord. Until dawn."

My lord? He'd not told her of his title. But then he realized it was just part of the game. A synonym for master. A happy whimsy. It pleased him that she would use his true title throughout this special night.

He settled his hands on her warm, soft shoulders, slid them across satin skin, feeling her rapid pulse. No faster than his. As he circled her neck, tension set her muscles and she swallowed, but she remained acquiescent. He wasn't sure he was breathing at all in this stunning, meaningless moment.

Then: "Welcome, slave," he said, and took her hands to draw her up into his arms. He sat, settling her on his lap. His hand found the swell of her full breasts above her stiff corset.

If she were truly his, he'd command her to wear lower bodices. She had the figure for them. But then again, if she were his, he might want her beauty to be for him alone.

He was just holding her, his fingers exploring that discreet rise of flesh. With a bemused smile he realized that her total surrender had left him rather at a loss. What *did* he want to do with her?

Cherish her.

Forever.

Holding her closer, he rubbed his face gently in her silky hair. "I wish we had longer."

"Why?"

"Then we could waste more time like this."

She moved infinitesimally closer. "This doesn't feel like a waste of time."

"It doesn't, does it?" With closeness, lust had simmered down for a while. He moved his hand up, up to the tender skin of her nape, and the tangling tease of her hair, longing to kiss her. He wouldn't ask again that she remove the mask, for she clearly had her reasons. Perhaps she was a stunning beauty, known far and wide. Perhaps she was scarred by the pox.

Neither mattered.

He breathed in her scent and, ignoring the bothersome strings of the mask, tested her ear with his tongue.

She sucked in a breath. He smiled, and teased her a little more, exploring the curves and ridges, and the soft lobe. Then he sucked it.

Her hand clutched at his arm. He blew softly into her ear, a breath only, but he knew how it would sound to her, here in the dark, in the heat of their closeness.

"You can't," she said, unsteadily, "make love to an ear."

"Never say can't to a man on his mettle." And he proceeded to make delicate love to her ear, only letting his hands take the smallest part—one playing in the wonders of her nape, the other wound with one of hers, sensing her growing tension.

She suddenly laughed, a gasping laugh. "Stop!"

He nipped her. "You surrendered, slave."

"But please. I want more."

So he raised her hand, and freeing it from his tangling fingers, made love to it, to each separate finger in turn. He suckled and stroked each in his mouth, then moved between the smoothness of the back, and the hot sensitivity of the heart of her palm.

He nipped the pad at the base of her thumb. "I have a complaint."

She tensed. "What?"

"There was no blackberry pie for dinner."

She melted into laughter. "Oh, I'm sorry. Jessie mustn't have had time."

"You need more servants, mysterious lady."

"At this moment, I need only you."

His body betrayed him with a tremble. His already hardened penis responded. This couldn't go on much longer—

Well, why not?

Sitting up straighter, he eased her astride him. She tensed a little. Doubtless she'd never done it this way before. Hell, she'd doubtless never done it except passively under her thrusting, loutish, elderly husband.

He hoped that was true. If he could have nothing else, he wanted her senses, her heated memories, her secret dreams, to all be of him.

As casually and slowly as possible in his increasingly desperate state, he arranged her skirts so none of them came between her nakedness and him.

"What are you—"

"Hush, slave."

She went silent, but remained anxiously rigid.

Adjusting his own position, he spread his legs, spreading hers. Her hands braced against his chest, as if she might at any moment push away from him. He captured them, placing them on his shoulders. "No," he said.

Then, without getting up, he struggled out of his coat. His cravat followed, then his shirt, tugged out of his breeches and up over his head as she bounced and slid with his movements, driving him even wilder. Then he put her hands on his bare shoulders and almost melted at the sweetness of it.

After a moment, her hands moved, sliding slowly along his shoulders to the curve of his arms, then back to his neck to circle—or half circle—it in imitation of his earlier action. Her thumbs rubbed up and down the front of his throat, and she must surely feel it when he swallowed, feel his desperate pulse.

Then her hands slid behind, to his nape. He squeezed his eyes shut and prayed, in danger of coming just from that innocent, devastating touch.

Her naked heat was so close, so ready! He managed to stay still as she sensed him with her fingers. Then she leaned forward—unaware, he was sure, of how her movement almost destroyed him—and put her face to the base of his neck.

Now *he* braced to push away, unable to bear the thought of a kiss from the mask. He felt only her tongue. Carefully keeping the mask from contact with him, she was cherishing his skin with her wet tongue.

Control broke. Thrusting his hands under the silk and lace of her skirts, he freed himself. Then, groaning with relief, he guided himself into her hot, creamy folds, fighting to go slowly, then losing, all his awareness there, and there alone.

When her hands clutched his hair, he'd forgotten he even had a head.

She moved as if to take him greedily farther into herself, as if to move around him.

He pushed into her, deep into her, into the flaming clutch of her.

He groaned something. He hoped it was flattering, because he meant it to be—she was bloody perfect, and she was giving him perfect pleasure—but at the moment she was only that. His pleasure. He took and took, holding her hips to use her, until he dissolved into her and she into him, snared to him by his arms, her hair sticky in his questing mouth.

Dammit, but he wanted to kiss her!

He dragged back her head, wrenched up the bottom of her mask—something ripped—and put his mouth to hers. She cried out, struggling, but he kissed her anyway, claimed his right to kiss his woman, and after a moment she surrendered.

Bliss.

He drew back at last, feeling himself slip out of her below, sated, dissolved, complete. "I tell you true, sweet lady, I will always recognize you if we chance to kiss."

She fumbled, and he knew she was pulling her silly

mask back into place. "That's safe enough, then," she
snapped. "I don't go around kissing strange gentlemen."

"I'm no stranger to you. Not anymore."

He'd broken the rules, however, so he seized her skirts
in case she tried to run.

All she said was, "Promise you won't do that again."

"Didn't you like it?"

"Yes."

He groaned at her wonderful honesty, pulling her into
his arms. "Then why not? Why? What point to a mask
in the dark?"

"I have my reasons. You must promise."

"But you are my slave. You surrendered."

"Not to that."

"To everything."

"No." She tried to move and found she couldn't.
"Don't . . ." she whispered. "Don't spoil this."

He wanted to insist, to truly master her to his will. He
thought he could. Despite that, he knew he couldn't.
"Tell me why you must wear the mask."

"I can't."

"It's dark. I can't see you. Blindfold me, if you want!"

"It's not that. Stop this! If you don't, I'll have to go."

He froze the angry words that burned at his lips. "But
you don't object to kisses?"

"Not as such."

"Then tell me how I can kiss you. I need to kiss you."

She lay against him, her breathing as fractured as his.
After a silence he made himself not break, she said, "Let
me go, and I'll try to fix the mask."

He wanted to argue further, but this clearly was her
limit. Much as he hated to, he helped her to stand, then
listened as she left the room.

She might not return.

What did it mean when a man risked a night of lus-
cious sex for the chance of an honest kiss?

He sat and sank his head in his hands, hardly able to
believe all this. He'd never had a taste for over-
wrought drama.

He didn't have a taste for it now.

He was sunk in a genuine tragedy.

He believed this magic between them would have sprung up no matter where they'd met. If fate had been kind, it would have been at an assembly, a tea party, or even a country fair. He could have wooed and won her in the proper manner.

Instead, they had this. Masks, drama, and tormenting secrets in the night.

Chapter 12

The door opened and he said a brief prayer of thanks that at least she had returned. She fumbled her way over, and a searching, unsteady hand brushed his cheek. Catching it, he drew her gently back onto his lap, realizing with a wince of embarrassment that his clothes were still disordered. A courteous gentleman with a trace of brain left would have tidied himself while she was away.

"You can kiss me," she whispered, "if you still want to."

Hardly daring to hope, he explored the path with his fingers, up her arm, across her shoulder, up the front of her slender neck, to her firm chin. Skimming to one side, he found the mask still there, cut so only her chin and lips were exposed. Despite her tension, he followed the ragged edge up, over her nose and down the other side.

It was a more common style for a Venetian mask than full face, and he wondered why she hadn't worn one like this in the first place. Curiously, he explored a little more with his finger, and found full, soft lips. Kissable, vulnerable, generous lips. He'd known how they would be. Tracing around them, he detected no secrets except that her lips twitched as if he was tickling her.

He longed to demand an explanation of her strange obsession, but he wouldn't risk this precious gift. Tilting her head, he put his lips to hers, hovering a moment as if at a shrine. It was she who wove her fingers in his hair and pulled him closer.

Though still aware of the mask, he surrendered. Perfect, perfect lips soft under his. A treasure of a hungry mouth. Deepening and blending, the kiss became a mating of its own, perfect in its way, so that when they slid apart, he felt almost as satisfied and drained as after sex.

Almost.

Her hand traced his face. "Thank you. You were right. I would hate to have missed that. Any of this. I want you to know that. It has to stop at dawn, but whatever follows, you have given me something very precious."

So suddenly it should have been audible, his willpower broke. "It doesn't have to stop at dawn."

Her hand stilled. "It does."

Holding her palm to his lips, he said, "Come away with me. It will be a scandal, yes, but in my circles, people accept scandal."

"Your circles. Someone told me Brand Malloren is a lord. That his brother is a marquess."

"Yes."

"Why didn't you tell me?"

He was surprised that it might have hurt her. "No bad reason, I promise. I didn't want to discomfort you. And I'm not so elevated. I'm my brother's land manager, that's all."

"Manager of a great deal of land, I'm sure."

"If we're talking of honesty, why not give me your true name?"

Her hand slipped free. "I can't. That's the simple, honest truth. Not for my sake, but for others. And for their sake, I cannot run off with you."

Anger stirred. This was no dithering, tempted wanton. This was a woman who would hold by her intent. Had he actually liked the fact that she was strong?

What confined her so absolutely?

How could he break it?

"Would you run off with me if you were free?" he tried. "Not unmarried, but free of whatever binds you?"

"Is anyone ever free . . . ? But yes, if not for heavy obligations, I might. It's bitter to me that I could be so weak, but that's the truth. I am bound, though. I want you to promise never to try to contact me once we part. Please. It's important."

He put her gently off his lap and stood to disrobe her. "I can't promise that. For the sake of what we have, for your honesty, I will try to do your will. I promise to try, but I can't promise to succeed. I'm not used to being weak either, but you have made me something of a stranger to myself. I have no control." His fumbling hands on her gown echoed his words.

As did her tremors. "I am the same. It's wrong. . . ."

He only half heard her, being more intent on the urgent loosening of her corset strings.

"I'm discreet," he argued, tugging the strings until the corset was loose enough to pull over her head and toss away.

"Discretion isn't enough. I wish you would promise."

"I don't make promises I cannot keep. Do you?"

"No."

"Then promise me one thing."

"What?"

He put his arms tight around her from behind. "If you don't leave with me," he whispered into her neck, "promise to send for me if you are ever in need. Of anything. *Promise.*"

After deep breaths, she asked, "How could I?"

"A message to Malloren House in London will always reach me. Marlborough Square. Or addressed in care of the Marquess of Rothgar. Promise." He knew his arms were tightening. He couldn't stop them.

"We shouldn't—"

"Only in need. *Promise!*"

"It won't happen!" Struggling against him, she gasped, "I have a good husband and loving family. I won't need you. I'm not alone in the world!"

Abruptly, he loosed her. "Then I wish you were." He fought the petticoat strings at her waist and managed to knot them. Frustrated—with the lace, with the dark, with her—he snapped them with his bare hands.

"Stop that!" she protested. "You're going to leave me in rags!"

Ignoring her words, he lifted her so the petticoat dropped, then dragged off her cotton shift so she was finally, perfectly naked to his hands. He stilled them at her waist, caught almost breathless by the moment.

"Promise me," he said again, trying to sound like the

reasonable man he generally was, not the wild one he was in danger of becoming. "Promise me that if ever you have need, any need, you will send for me." He slipped his hands up slowly to fill them with the perfect generosity of her breasts. *"Promise me."*

He could hear her breathing, feel it through his hands. "What if I summon you to be my love-slave any time I feel the need?"

"I can imagine nothing more delightful."

"This is folly. Folly beyond reason!"

"Promise."

"Oh, very well!" she snapped. "But it will do you no good. I will never be in that desperate a state."

"I should hope that you're right, but I don't. I'm not sure I can live without you." He was mad to reveal that. Clearly mad. He didn't care.

"This is *all*. Tonight is all we have."

Rage flared because he feared she was right. He didn't understand her situation, her family, her husband, but he knew her. With his soul and his bones, he knew her. Whatever had driven her to this—and "driven" was not too strong a word—she wasn't a woman who could live openly in sin.

Intolerably, she would never be his. With the dawn, she would disappear, pick up the pieces of her life, and banish him from her thoughts. But not from her memory or her dreams. He'd make damn sure of that.

He let her go and began to strip. "Our situations are different," he said, choosing words like weapons as he pulled off his drawers and stood finally as naked as she. More naked than she. He wore no mask. "I'm not likely to stay celibate. I can find release tomorrow if I want it. What of you?"

"I don't need *release*."

"Liar."

He took a step closer to her shadowy shape, and she inched back. He shouldn't be doing this. He should be snatching the time to give her sweet loving, not loosing his anger. Not trying to push her into admitting her need, her temptation. Not trying to whip her into wild ruin.

She stopped her retreat and her chin went up. "I didn't find release in what we just did." Now her tone was as harsh as his.

She was right. He'd not given a thought to her satisfaction. A dismal first.

"I suppose it's as well," she continued coolly. "After tonight, I will not do this again, so it is better, really, that it be something of a disappointment."

He captured her wrist. "Don't poke a lion, sweetheart, unless you want it to roar." He dragged her toward the bed. She fought him.

"Slave?" he reminded her.

"Mistress?" she spat back. "My lord?"

Abruptly, unfairly, he let her go. "Leave then."

His breath stopped. Might she actually . . . ? If he sank on his knees and begged . . . ?

But after a silent moment, she stepped closer, found his hand, and linked it once more around her wrist. "My lord?"

He almost swept her into his arms, but that wasn't the game they were playing just now. "Slave," he whispered. "Love-slave." Let her interpret that as she wished.

Then he pulled her toward the bed, the bed he'd already turned down in welcome.

Pushing her down on her back, he tugged her hips to the edge then spread her thighs wide with his hands. He heard her suck in her breath, and waited. He wasn't so far out of his mind that he'd truly assault her.

Abruptly, she relaxed, surrendered. Touching her hand to be sure, he found it limp by her thighs on the sheet. He raised it, kissed it, then kissed her inner wrist as he had done so long ago, brushing his lips up to her inner elbow.

Then, her hand still in his, he slid his other between her thighs. "Are you obedient to my every wish, slave?"

"Yes, my lord."

"Then I command you to surrender. To enjoy." To himself alone, he added: *To remember.*

She didn't fight, so he roused her passion with his hand, pleasuring her breasts with his mouth. Her crushing grip on his other hand spoke her passion, flexing and squeezing wildly, guiding him to go fast or slow, soft or hard. As her hips' wild dance rewarded him, he eased the pressure, hoping she had her other hand ready to cover her mouth if she screamed.

Hell, if she screamed and brought witnesses down on them, perhaps that would get him what he wanted—her as his wanton mistress.

Then he was rewarded with a deep groan, a sound he'd go odds she'd never made before. A secret, guttural groan for him alone. He'd have more. He was in control, he could do this for hours if necessary.

He drove her on, to bone-aching, tendon-straining tension, easing again to hold her back. Her feet came up to the edge of the bed and she arched off it. He stopped entirely.

"Down, come down, sweetheart."

With a sob, she settled her hips, rolling. "Don't . . . Please . . ."

"Hush. hush. Quietly," he murmured, nipping at her wet, swollen nipples.

"Beast."

"Slave."

"I hate you."

"You don't."

He began to pleasure her again, and was rewarded immediately with a shudder of desire. "I *won't*." She wasn't referring to hate but to orgasm. She was going to fight him.

He grinned. "Yes, you will."

And she did, though she fought him so that it became a wrestling match across the bed, one with very strange holds.

Only after her surrender—when she lay hot, sticky, limp, and completely his—did he move over to enter her.

"When I'm dead," she muttered, "tell Diana. She'll help you get away."

He had no idea who Diana was, but he had a true appreciation of her mettle. What a zest for life lay under her quiet manner. She deserved more than the half-life she lived.

"Come with me when I leave," he said, hovering, the

tip of his erection teasing her. "We can do this every
night. Every, single, night." He eased in, inch by inch.
Her hips yearned toward him.

"Then I'd surely die."

"No, dammit. You'd *live*!" And he thrust deep.

She climaxed again abruptly, long before he'd expected. Freed, he pumped to ecstasy, too, and sealed it
with a kiss as desperate as everything else between them.

She was right.

It could destroy a person, this.

But he'd die in ecstasy.

"What time is it, I wonder?" she asked.

Time had passed, he knew, without any idea of how
much. Minutes? Days? It was still dark, and she
sprawled limply beside him, still entangled. Her voice
sounded like he felt, drained almost to unconsciousness.

A distant church clock saved him the effort of trying
to answer. Twelve strokes.

"Midnight." She stirred slightly, as if adjusting her
body to a new skin. He put his hand on her belly and
stroked the silky curve, wishing he could see her like
this—luxuriating in her sated body.

He would see her like this. She was his. He only had
to prove it to her. Before dawn.

"Six hours or so to go," he said, sliding a fingertip
into her navel.

She squirmed away. "Don't!"

He trapped her. "Why not?"

"It tickles."

With a laugh, he weighed her down and kissed her
navel, flicking his tongue inside. She shoved him and
they wrestled until he let her pin him down. She was
agile and strong, and not afraid to fight dirty. Another
delightful surprise.

Then, straddling his legs triumphantly, her hands pin-
ning his arms to the bed—though she must know he
could break that hold any time he chose—she lowered
her head to kiss *his* navel, to tease it with her tongue.
His belly muscles tightened and his penis stirred again.

"You like that?" she asked.

"I like that."

With what sounded like a purr she began to lick his torso, long strokes and short, wriggling sinuously over him as she tried to reach every little spot.

"Why are you gasping?" she asked, mischief in her voice.

"Because I feel like a landed trout."

"Wet?"

"Desperate."

"Should I stop?"

"Never." He deliberately echoed her earlier words. They were both fighting the dawn.

"What else would you like?" she asked, tongue back to swirling around his navel.

"Touch me."

She didn't pretend to misunderstand. Releasing his wrists, she shifted to explore his genitals with curious, sensitive fingers. He concentrated on holding back need as long as humanly possible, letting her cup and flex his balls, stroke him to the tip and back.

His control broke. He grabbed her, rolled her, and plunged into her, into orgasm.

And so it went through the night—playing, exploring, teasing, tormenting. It was the wildest, sweetest passion he had ever known, with a woman made for love, and ready to love with joy and abandon. She found delight in every new twist he thought up for her, and added a few of her own through sheer inventiveness.

There had to be quiescent times, however, and in the sleepy deep of the night, he found himself cradled in her arms, talking. He was perfectly aware that she was giving little in the dreamy flow of words, but he was willing to use his own story to win her if he could. He'd strip himself down to his soul if it would make her his.

He told of his pleasant childhood, and received some unspecific memories of her own in return. He was glad to hear that she'd enjoyed her younger years, and not at all surprised to find she'd been something of a terror.

He told her of his parents' sudden deaths from fever, the abrupt and absolute change in everything, and was comforted by her hands and her gentle kiss in his hair.

He knew she had at least a loving mother still, yet she seemed to understand the paralyzing shock it had been.

Perhaps she understood what it had meant to him and the others, especially the young twins, when Bey had fought to keep them together.

"Bey was only nineteen."

"Bey?"

"My older brother—half brother actually—the Marquess of Rothgar. We're all named after Anglo-Saxon heroes—our father's particular interest. I feel fortunate to have ended up with Brand. Poor Bey, being the oldest, received Beowulf, which Father would use in full, with resonant pleasure, as often as he could."

She chuckled. "So instead he took the name of an Eastern prince."

"It suits him very well. Having come into his responsibilities young and abruptly, he's an autocratic devil. He didn't have the power and authority when our parents died, but he stood firm all the same. I was only twelve and grief-stricken, but I gather everyone wanted to split up the family, to take us off his hands. He set himself to keeping everything as unchanged as possible.

"At the time I simply accepted it," Brand said, staring sightlessly into the past. "He even kept the awareness from us that there was any threat of change, though we suspected and worried. The twins went missing for a whole day. They were eventually found in a cupboard under the pantry stairs, but it had already been checked, so they'd been moving around. It must all have been a terrifying responsibility for him. He'd not exactly been the epitome of responsibility before."

He stopped himself then, despite the seductive dark, for the whole story wasn't his to tell. He'd only gathered later that his brother held himself responsible for their parents' deaths, not without cause. He'd picked up a fever in one of his wild adventures, and had hovered near death. His stepmother had nursed him lovingly, saving his life, but caught the disease herself. The devoted marquess had ignored the doctor's orders to stay away, and he had succumbed.

The younger children had been firmly kept in a distant

wing, which had made the shock more terrible. When they'd been banished there, their half brother had been seriously ill, which was bad enough. When they emerged, their wonderful parents were dead, and Bey—still pale and thin from the sickness—was Marquess of Rothgar and their only protection against the world.

"It must have taken a lot of courage," she said, hand playing soothingly in his hair.

"An amazing amount. No one would have blamed him for letting the family be split up. In fact, I think he was criticized for not doing so. A lot of people thought him too wild to care for us."

Again he stopped himself, before he mentioned madness. Bey was not mad. There had never been any sign. But his mother had gone mad, and that hung over him like a threatening shadow. His mother hadn't seemed deranged either until she had killed her newborn child.

"People do what they have to do," she said. "Find the courage when they need it."

"Some people." Then he wondered if she was talking about herself and longed for the key to unlock her guarded mind. He pushed down that spurt of resentment and went on to relate some of his more innocent adventures.

"And how did you come to be your brother's land manager?"

"I don't know how familiar you are with the way of aristocratic families. To preserve the family power, nearly everything goes to the oldest son. The younger sons and daughters receive a portion, usually from property their mother brought to the marriage. In that way, the original holdings are not broken up. Younger sons are supposed to make their own way. The church, the army, and the navy are the usual paths."

"I don't quite see you as a vicar."

He laughed. "And Bey didn't want any of us in the army or navy. Says they are barbaric and ill-run institutions. I've always had an interest in agriculture, so I ended up with that."

"What would have happened if you'd longed to be a dashing officer?"

"Exactly what happened when my youngest brother took that route. Flaming rows and physical confinement."

"Mercy. What happened?"

"Cyn's a major now."

"So your brother is all bark and no bite?"

"No more than I am, dear lady." He nipped her to make his point. "Bey has particularly sharp fangs and uses them. But in the end he wants what's best for us. Cyn loves the army, and I'm happy with enclosures and turnips."

She nipped him back. "I'm glad you have a fulfilling life."

He'd begun to reacquaint himself with her breast, but he paused. "It will be unsatisfactory without you."

She didn't even respond. He'd returned to the subject often enough through the night, battering her will with his need, unable to believe that in the end he would lose. With a sigh, he set to doing the only thing he could—searing the memory of him into her body, mind, and soul.

Gathering memories of her into his own.

But even when every minute is precious, nature will have her way, and people are not automatons. Eventually, still touching, half-laughing over their latest contortion, they stilled, and sleep stole the rest of their night.

Rosamunde came awake, instantly aware of everything, tears aching behind her eyes.

They had only the sheet over them, and she felt a little chilled. He lay on his front, apart from her, but his arm draped over her, for comfort and possession.

Possession.

Again and again in the wild night he'd asked her to leave with him, demanded to know what tied her so firmly here, what bond could be so much stronger than the one they had forged.

After a while she'd stopped trying to argue with him. She couldn't give him the truth, and she wasn't sure he'd see the force of it if she did. In the wild tradition of

High Romance, he expected her to toss everything away for love.

Love.

That's what it was. She could no longer deny it.

And outside, silver dawn signaled the end.

She eased over, wanting to study him in the fragile misty light. What had happened to them, not just last night, but over the past few extraordinary days?

An intimacy had grown, a familiarity that went deeper than the skin. It was something a little like the closeness she had with Diana—a bond that physical distance, or change, or even disagreement could never touch.

That was a friendship begun in the cradle, though, not a brief encounter. How could she feel this way about a stranger? It was all there, however—the gift of laughter, the discovery of trust, the miracle of instant communication, of shared interests, of secret understandings. A security that defied any challenge.

She swallowed and breathed back tears, refusing to tarnish the treasure with denial. They had found something precious here, she and Lord Brand Malloren, a connection never dreamed of, come about through pure chance.

And it was as useless as seed thrown on rock.

In normal circumstances, they would never have met—the marquess's son and the gentleman-farmer's daughter. Certainly they would never have cracked their conventional shells to find the bonding-flesh that lay beneath. And now she must seal the shells closed again, seal them with betrayal.

If he'd promised not to seek her out, perhaps she could have avoided this. Diana would not have approved, but she would trust his promise. Throughout the night, however, he'd fought her will, and she couldn't believe he wouldn't try to find her.

Therefore, she had to make sure he couldn't.

She had to drug him.

Just for a moment she imagined the insane alternative. She could roll closer, kiss his skin as she had so often in the night, breathe his smell that she would now recognize anywhere, explore the muscular contours of his

body for the sheer delight they gave her fingers, and tell
him that she would surrender past the dawn.

That she would run away with him. That she didn't
mind leaving everything she knew and loved as long as
she was with him. That she would become a fallen
woman, shunned by all decent society, as long as she
could fall into his arms.

And, terrifyingly, it would all be true. At this insane
moment she felt all of that. Of course, she would regret
it later, but threat of future pain would not bar her from
present ecstasy if that were the only price.

It wasn't though.

She could tear herself from home, life, and reputation,
and perhaps consider it all well lost for love. She could
not tear herself from duty.

Her duty to Digby and Wenscote.

She sighed. Could she tell him the whole truth and
trust that he would understand, that he would make the
sacrifice with her?

It was tempting, for her trust in his promises ran ocean
deep. She couldn't be sure, however, that he'd see things
as she did. Perhaps he'd think it more important to claim
his child than to save a small estate in Yorkshire. Perhaps—he'd hinted at it in the wilder night—he'd use
scandal to trap her.

She couldn't afford the risk.

Tears making her mask clammy on her face, she eased
herself from under his arm. He muttered, but didn't
wake. She drew the blanket over him, put on her shift,
then slipped quietly from the room. She'd laid out a
simple brown traveling gown in her old bedroom, one
that she could dress in by herself. Millie was remaining
at Arradale during this risky enterprise. Once decent,
she crept down to the kitchen, praying that no one was
up yet. She'd cut it close with that indulgent spell of
what-ifs.

In the kitchen, all was quiet, the hearth still cold. As
quietly as possible, she found some cold meat and bread,
and the blackberry cordial she'd asked Jessie to prepare
the night before, adding brandy and some extra spices
to the recipe.

She tipped the potion in the jug, stirred it, then sipped the tiniest amount. It was rich and delicious, and anything extra was covered by the strong flavors.

She hated to do this to him, though.

Pushing aside her qualms, she went upstairs and found him half-awake, tousled, prone, with his chin on his hands. "You are an early bird, aren't you?"

"It's nearly dawn," she pointed out, struggling to hide a fierce pang of longing and sorrow. "You set that as the end."

"What idiot said that it is always darkest just before the dawn?"

There was no point to that. "I've brought you some breakfast. Just simple things. The servants aren't up yet."

He stirred to sit up and she took the tray to him.

"Aren't you eating?"

"I had something," she lied. Food would choke her.

He bit into the bread and chewed, looking at her. "I would like to see more of your face."

"I know." The growing light was dangerous. He might see the edge of the scar that the mask no longer quite covered.

He shrugged and took another bite. "So," he said, when he'd swallowed it, "what now?"

He hadn't touched the glass.

"My carriage will take you to Thirsk."

Another mouthful and a shrewd, thoughtful look. "Won't that make it easy for me to guess where I've been? I warn you, I have quite a good sense of direction."

"You'll be blindfolded," she lied.

He shook his head, clearly seeing how little point there was to that. If only he'd drink! Diana would have the coach at the front any time now. Heavens, she needed to get him dressed, before he passed out. If he ever drank anything.

"That's blackberry punch," she said. "I . . . I had it made especially for you."

He smiled, a little sadly, but picked up the glass and

took a sip. "'Struth, sweetheart, but that's likely to knock me out again. It's hardly a breakfast drink."

Though she hated the manipulation, Rosamunde tried to look hurt. "I thought . . . since there was no pie."

He laughed and took a deeper draft. "I suppose if I don't have to ride, it'll do no harm."

Fighting tears, she brought his clothes over and he climbed out of bed to begin to dress. "Don't stand there like a nervous servant," he said rather shortly. She felt short, too, furious at fate.

She sat on the bed, watching him fasten his shirt.

"So," he asked, "when do we say our fond farewells?"

"Soon."

"You're not coming with me?"

"I can't. I must get home."

"To your husband." He took another bite of bread, then shrugged into his waistcoat and jacket, leaving them both unbuttoned. "He doesn't deserve you, you know."

"Don't."

When he picked up the glass and took another deep drink, Rosamunde knew he was drowning anger. Suddenly he turned the vessel and offered it to her. "Come, it's the closest we have to a loving cup. Drink in recognition of the night, and vow to me that at least you will never forget."

Rosamunde looked into his angry eyes, wondering frantically if he suspected. She saw only grief and longing, and her will trembled. Dear Lord, she couldn't do this!

But she already had. He'd already swallowed half the brew.

Abruptly, it seemed right that she drink, too, that she take a little of the betrayal she'd served to him. She covered his warm hand on the glass, drew it to her, and sipped from the rim still moist from his mouth.

Then, deliberately, she drank deeper.

She pushed it back to him. "You finish it. I promise, I will never forget."

She watched as he drained the drink, eyes on hers, but then she made herself slide off the bed. "I must check on the coach. I'll be back soon."

She left the room without a backward glance and didn't allow herself to falter. This had never had anything to do with her needs or feelings.

She didn't have to check on anything, but she should say good-bye to Jessie, and leave vails for her and the Yockenthwaits for their service. She also had the note she'd written for Digby, telling him she was going to Richmond with Diana for a couple of days. She collected coins from her room and removed the mangled mask, stuffing it in her pocket for disposal later. As she left the room, she searched herself for some effect of the drug.

Nothing. What were they going to do if it failed to work? Or took too long.

But as she started down the stairs, her balance almost failed her and she clutched the banister. Lud, how horrible! What was she going to do if it got worse than this? Diana would be cross over her quixotic sharing of the potion.

She concentrated as she went downstairs, hand tight on the rail, having to think about each step.

Jessie was building the kitchen fire, still rubbing sleep from her eyes. "Milady! I thought you'd spent the night at the big house?"

"I did." Rosamunde hoped her words didn't sound as tangled as they felt. "But Lady Arradale and I have decided to see our unwanted guest as far as Richmond."

The maid rubbed ashy fingers on her skirt. "Is there anything you want me to do, milady?"

"Just make sure this note is sent to Wenscote." She placed it on the table. "I've taken him some breakfast, and the coach will be here at any moment. I wanted to thank you for your help with him." She gave the girl a shilling, and put a crown on the table for the Yockenthwaits.

When the maid had thanked her, she made her way carefully into the front hall to wait for the coach, feeling horribly as if she were drunk, but more than drunk. No sense could be relied on. The early light shimmered, and when the coach appeared, it seemed to be surrounded by a multicolored mist.

As the coach drew up, Diana leaped down anxiously. "Did it work?"

"I think so." Rosamunde had her hand on the porch pillar for contact with reality. "I had to drink some myself. I feel rather strange."

Diana grabbed her arm. "You idiot! Why did you do that?"

"Never mind." Rosamunde looked beyond, and saw Tom—a rather wiggly Tom—who was doubtless even more convinced of her insanity.

"I brought a groom from the Arradale stables, too," Diana said, indicating another stalwart young man. "He'll keep his mouth shut. Anyone from these parts will do anything to avoid having the Cotterites here."

Rosamunde had to accept the fact that quite a few people suspected what she'd been up to, and would know for sure if she started to swell with a child. Thank heavens dalesfolk didn't give out much to strangers.

Focusing carefully, and wishing her feet weren't so far from her head, she led Diana and the grooms upstairs and opened the bedroom door.

He lacked only his boots, but toward the end, he'd guessed. She knew, because he'd staggered to the bed and torn all the covers off. He'd probably intended to rip the sheet still tangled in his hands.

She gently extricated him, determined not to cry. It was better like this. Now, he'd never want to see her again.

"No need to put his boots on," she said, hearing her own voice strangely calm.

Diana brushed his tangled hair off his face with a murmur of approval. Rosamunde wanted to slap her hands away, but she stood back as Diana had the two grooms lift him and carry him out.

"Oh, do be careful!" she gasped as one of his feet knocked against the door. Her sudden movement dizzied her, and she tipped heavily into a chair.

"What a tangle!" Diana said, hands on hips. "Never mind, love. I'll take care of it. When you're recovered, you can go on home—"

But Rosamunde staggered to her feet. "No! I'm coming."

"Why?"

Because I have to make sure he's properly taken care of, Rosamunde thought. Diana might decide to dump him in the middle of nowhere. He might come close to death again. She could sense a chill in herself, a deep, unnerving shiver. Even without rain, he might die of exposure.

"I just have to," she stated, knowing she sounded like a truculent child.

Focusing on Diana's face, she saw exasperation, but worry, too. "Heaven knows, in your present state, it's probably better to keep you under my eye. There's no knowing what you might do or say! Sit."

Rosamunde obeyed. She felt dangerously close to sleep, and this was the effect of only a couple of mouthfuls. Had she given him too much?

"Mistress Naisby," she said, finding it hard to shape the words, and watching as if down a flashing tunnel as Diana stripped the sheets off the bed.

"Yes? What?" Diana bundled them up and tossed them aside. She'd brought fresh ones. No, not fresh.

"Where did those sheets come from?"

"They're mine. They'll look as if they've been slept in for a few days, but nothing more."

Rosamunde watched the Countess of Arradale make a very untidy bed. She'd probably never done it before. She'd been meaning to ask something. Something important.

"Mistress Naisby . . ."

"Yes?" Diana turned, the bundle of soiled sheets in her arm and shook her head. "Faith, but you're in a state, love." She put her other arm around Rosamunde and hoisted her to her feet. "Come on. You can sleep it off in the coach. If all goes well, we can be back here tonight, and you can be home tomorrow. Sober."

"Not *drunk*," Rosamunde insisted.

"I know, love." Diana steered her toward the doorway.

"Mistress Naisby."

"What about the old witch?"

"How much did she say to use?"

"All of it to be sure to render a strong man unconscious for a considerable amount of time."

"Oh good," said Rosamunde miserably.

Diana held her closer as they worked their way down the stairs. "At least by this time tomorrow, it will all be done with. Except," she added in a whisper, "for the consequences, we hope."

Safe in the hall, Rosamunde put her hand over her belly, as if there might already be something there to feel.

"All done," she echoed. "Except for the consequences."

Chapter 13

She woke with a violent headache and a very tangled mind. Where was she? And why was the world bouncing around so painfully?

"At last."

Rosamunde forced her eyes open, turning her head toward her cousin's voice by her side, hissing with the pain. Poor Diana looked as bad as she felt.

In fact, Diana looked extremely peculiar.

"Are you *spotty*?"

Diana touched her blotched face. "Does it work? I thought it such a clever idea."

Rosamunde closed her eyes. She must be in a drugged dream. Diana would never be happy about pimples. Nor would she ever wear such a dull, plain outfit, and a mob-cap.

Her face was tapped gently. "Rosa! Stay awake. We have to fix you."

"Don't do that. Please." Rosamunde opened her eyes again and found that Diana was still spotty. All over her face. She had a particularly revolting pimple on her left cheekbone. Inflamed red with a pus-filled center. "Are you real?"

Merriment sparkled in this strange Diana's eyes. "Only in a manner of speaking. I'm your maid."

"What a peculiar dream."

Diana thrust the spots closer. "It's not a dream, Rosa. It's a disguise. Pay attention. We can't leave Brand Malloren somewhere and be seen in the same area. It's too easy a link. So I stopped off in Richmond—you were dead to the world—and sought a little help from a friend of mine. An actress. She found me these clothes, and painted my face. I don't think anyone will recognize the Countess of Arradale, will they?"

Rosamunde focused on the enormous pimple. "No. Especially as it will never cross their minds."

"Quite. No one who matters notices servants. We're approaching Thirsk, however, so we have to do you."

Rosamunde raised her hand to guard her face. "No spots!"

"No, no. Just a lot of ordinary face paint."

"I don't want face paint either!"

"Well, you must have it." Diana lifted a wooden box onto her lap and opened it. "You're my mistress. The sort of high-born lady who wears a great deal of *maquillage.*"

Rosamunde had the sinking feeling that this was all too real. "I don't like face paint. It looks horrible."

"Think, love! You can't show your scars, and a mask would draw attention, but heavy paint will hardly get a glance."

Rosamunde's mind, however, had jolted to other matters. "Where is he?" She sat up, despite the pain in her head. "What have you done with him? What have you done?"

"Nothing!" Diana said, pushing her back. "Hush. He's underfoot. And before you protest, I couldn't prop both of you up for four hours. He's safer where he is."

Brand Malloren was the cushion beneath her feet! He lay curled in the tight space on the floor of the carriage, but at least Diana had put a folded blanket under his head.

"Oh dear." She raised her feet, but there really was nowhere else to put them.

"Don't fuss. He's fine."

Rosamunde had to put her feet back on his shoulder, but she leaned down, despite her throbbing head, to test the pulse at his neck. Slow, but steady and strong. And this time he wasn't particularly cold.

She sat back up. "Put a blanket over him please."

Diana rolled her eyes, but she did it, finding a rich brown one under the opposite seat and dropping it over him.

"Oh dear," said Rosamunde. "This is so like what happened to him before. He was so ill. Oh, faith . . . !"

"What?"

"The symptoms. He *said* he was no hard drinker. He must have been drugged that time, too, and with something similar. He'll hate me."

"A good thing under the circumstances."

When Rosamunde tried to object, Diana interrupted. "Rosa, if he hates you, he won't try to find you."

"If he hates me enough, he might."

Diana looked struck by that. "And a Malloren. Lud. All the more reason for disguise!"

Rosamunde flinched from the pots of paint. What she wanted was to curl up with Brand and go back to sleep, to stay asleep until her stomach settled and her head stopped pounding. Perhaps never to wake up. She had to go through with this, however. For Digby and Wenscote.

"Can paint really mask my scars?"

"Dulcie showed me how." Diana uncorked one squat pot. "This stuff is a sort of paste that can be used to fill in wrinkles. Or scars. Turn this way." She tilted Rosamunde's face, then began to apply it thickly.

"I'm going to feel stiff as a board."

"Probably. You won't need to laugh or talk, so don't worry about it." Firm fingers smeared on the temple and cheek. "There. Almost gone." Diana pulled out another pot and applied a creamier substance all over Rosamunde's face.

"That's not lead, is it?" Rosamunde asked, pulling back.

"No! Come back here. Everyone knows the dangers of white lead by now." Diana moved back to consider her work. "It's working. Even I can hardly see the scars, and a casual glance would never detect them. And no one will recognize you, either. You look different. Older."

"Delightful."

"If I can be spotty, you can be a hag." Diana put away the two pots and opened some more.

"I don't feel at all well, Diana," Rosamunde said, queasy at the smell of the grease.

"We have to do this." Diana took Rosamunde's chin in a firm grip. Teeth in her lower lip with concentration, she tried to paint an eyebrow, then let out an unladylike curse. She opened the window and yelled, "Stop the coach."

"Stop the coach?"

"Stop the coach!"

It halted with a jerk. "Is something the matter, milady?"

"No. Just keep it still for a few minutes." With no further explanation, Diana set to work and Rosamunde felt the brush whisper over her brows.

"Better," Diana said. In moments she'd done the lips, too. "I've made them thinner and darker. A veritable hag!"

"Thank you, I'm sure."

"My pleasure to serve you, milady. What else? Ah yes, patches!" She produced a little box and some glue, and pressed a number of black patches around Rosamunde's face.

"Stop! Anyone will think I'm pox-scarred."

"Good. If they detect any scarring, that will explain it." She tilted her head to consider her work. "I think I have a gift for this. Drive on, coachman!"

As the coach rocked into motion once more, she produced a mirror from the box and held it up.

Rosamunde stared at a stranger. With pale paint, black brows, red lipstick, and scattered "beauty spots," her face looked garish. Fashionable ladies and gentlemen generally used some paint—it was part of being well-dressed—but this was extreme. However, she knew some did paint themselves this way, especially if they had problems to hide, such as scars from the smallpox. Or if they thought they could preserve an illusion of youth.

"I'm not scarred," she whispered, touching her cheek. "How very strange." The mirror showed ghosts of the wounds, but as Diana had said, to a casual glance, her face was unblemished.

"And no one will know you," Diana said. "I'm going to powder your hair, too. No grease. Just a light dusting to disguise the true color. Blue, I think."

"Blue?"

"I'm sure you're just the sort to wear blue powder."
She dusted it carefully, but a cloud still floated around
Rosamunde.

"If I sneeze, I'll likely scream with pain."

Diana stopped, and peered at her. "Pain?"

Rosamunde realized she'd not said anything about it
before. "I have a headache. A bad one."

Diana hastily put away the powdering brush and even
tried to waft the hazy cloud away. "You should have
said."

Rosamunde just leaned her head back against the seat.

After a moment, Diana said, "Look, Rosa."

Rosamunde opened her eyes to see that strange face
in the mirror again, this time crowned by faded hair.

"It is miraculous," Diana said, "even if by accident.
Dull, like your mother's hair. It adds decades to your
age."

"You're right." Rosamunde just wanted to close her
eyes and fight nausea.

"Just one final touch . . ." Diana dug in a pocket and
pulled out a glittering handful.

Jewels. Probably the ones Diana had worn this morning, for Diana loved glittering jewelry. She and Rosamunde jokingly called them her "sparklies" for, indeed,
for daily wear she paid little attention to value and se-
lected for glitter.

Now she clipped earrings to Rosamunde's lobes,
clasped a couple of items around her neck, and a few
more around her wrists, then slipped rings onto Rosamunde's limp fingers.

"I hate wearing a lot of rings."

"What a grump you're being. Just four, then. There.
Now you are the very picture of a decadent lady of fash-
ion, and as far from Rosamunde Overton as can be
imagined." Diana glanced out of the window. "We must
be close to Thirsk now. Time to dispose of our burden."

"He's not—"

"Yes, yes, I know," Diana said with a wave of a pale
hand made strange by the lack of glitter. "He's a prince
and a hero. But we still have to dispose of him."

"Here?" Rosamunde saw only fields. "He has to have shelter of some kind."

"Rosa, it's summer, and this isn't the moors!"

"Shelter," repeated Rosamunde stubbornly.

Diana muttered, but she studied the surrounding countryside. "There's too much traffic on this road, anyway. We'll have to turn off. Find a hay barn or some such."

She commanded Garforth to take a turning ahead.

"It's nowt but a track, milady."

"Take it." Diana peered out of the window. "There's a signpost. It has to be a road of sorts."

When they slowly turned off the highway, however, a jolt warned that Garforth had been right. Signpost or no, it was little better than a track, ridged and rutted by hoofs and cartwheels and set into stone by summer sun. Rosamunde tensed, refusing to complain of the jolts of pain as they bumped along. She deserved to hurt as much as Brand would.

"The signpost was to New-something," Diana said, clinging to the strap by her side. "A mile and a half. That's not far and surely somewhere along here we'll find a place to put him. Look, there's a barn. It will serve." She called for Garforth to stop.

Almost weeping with relief to be stationary, Rosamunde struggled to focus and saw a ramshackle wooden building in a field. It stood open on one side, showing it held only the remnants of last year's hay. She wanted to protest that it wasn't good enough, but made herself be silent.

It would serve.

It seemed very isolated, though. He could lie there forever.

She heard Diana giving instructions and moved her feet so he could be pulled out. She closed her eyes to stop herself from fussing. Then he was gone, and her feet settled on the empty floor.

She tried to keep her eyes closed, to leave it to the others, but it was impossible. She looked, and saw him being carried across the hummocky field by the two young grooms, Diana following with his boots. Even though they were strong young men, they couldn't help the fact that one arm dragged almost on the ground and his head lolled.

Rosamunde grabbed the blankets and struggled out of the coach. Once down the steps, she had to pause to let the whirling world settle, praying her stomach would not embarrass her. The thought of how sick he'd been the last time heaped burning guilt on her head. If she had the choice again, she'd not have done this to him, not even for Wenscote.

As soon as she could, she set off doggedly across the field, determined to make sure he was as comfortable as possible.

She saw the men toss him on the remnants of hay, and broke into a run. "Stop it!"

Diana turned. "Rosa . . ." but then she shook her head and grabbed the blankets. "Look, I'm going to tuck him in as snug as a babe."

Rosamunde ignored her cousin's disgruntled tone and watched, hand braced against a weathered post. Then she stared. "Diana! The crests."

"Bother." Diana pulled a corner loose and glared at the embroidered crest that was probably on every item she owned. She looked up at the two stoical servants. "Do something, Culver."

Without expression, her groom knelt to slice off the crested corner of each blanket, tucking them into his pocket.

"There," she said, standing and brushing straw off herself. "Can we go now?"

Rosamunde wanted to say no, wanted to tuck him in herself, wanted to give him one last kiss. In truth, she wanted to lie by him, ready to care for him when he awoke. He seemed comfortable enough at the moment, but she knew the kind of hell that awaited him. She'd witnessed it last time, and now was experiencing it her-self to some degree.

It had never been about her own needs, however, ex-cept for the wicked night that she had stolen from fate. As she deserved, it had only made things worse. She

allowed herself one last look, then turned and walked
to the coach without a backward glance.

After settling herself in her seat, she pointedly looked
away from the field as Diana sat down beside her, and
the coach moved off.

It was done.

It was over.

No looking back.

"Apparently we can't turn on this road," Diana said,
as the coach heaved up, then fell into another dip with
a bone-shaking jar. A moan escaped Rosamunde.

"Oh, love. Is it that bad?"

"It's only what I deserve. He'll be worse—Ah!" Another lurch sent agony through her.

Diana stuck her head out and commanded Garforth
to stop.

But after a brief exchange, she said, "We can't possibly turn the coach, dearest. But it's under a mile to the
next place, and we'll go as slowly as possible. Surely at
New-whatever, we must join a better road."

As the coach began to inch forward, Rosamunde tried
to keep her head as still as possible and not complain.

"I can never understand these things," Diana
muttered.

Rosamunde opened her eyes a chink and saw that
Diana was struggling with a book of coaching maps.
"What was the last place we passed? I can't find New-
anything near Thirsk. . . . Oh, Rosa."

Rosamunde knew from the tone that it had nothing
to do with the map. She realized she had tears on her
cheeks.

"It's just the drug. And the pain."

"Pain over what?" Diana demanded, dabbing at the
tears with her handkerchief. "He's just a handsome
charmer, but there's nothing there for you, love."

"I mean the pain in my head." It wasn't the whole
truth. She hadn't known grief could cause such physical agony.

A wheel caught in a particularly deep rut, jarring the
whole coach. She groaned.

"Devil take it!" Diana exclaimed. "And there's nothing we can do other than stop still for eternity."

"We could walk," said Rosamunde, and then, "Yes!" She started to fumble for the door.

Diana restrained her with one hand while shouting at Garforth to stop so they could get down. Soon Rosamunde was standing on the road, her head swimming, pain beating at her, but pain under her own control. "This is better," she said. "Better."

Diana put her arm around her waist. "Come on, then, love. On to the New-place."

Rosamunde accepted her help and trudged forward, tussling with tangled thoughts. She was suffering in mild form what Brand Malloren had after she'd found him. He'd been drugged before. By whom? And why?

Could he be in danger?

She stopped. "It's not right to leave him there."

Diana forced her onward. "Rosa, stop this! What do you think we should do? Deposit him tenderly at an inn with the whole world knowing who left him there?"

"We're in disguise."

"Not a good enough one for that!"

"But what if the wrong people find him?"

"Wrong people? What wrong people?"

Rosamunde tried to explain, though she feared she wasn't making herself very clear.

"Enemies," scoffed Diana, sounding distinctly grumpy—walking was not her favorite occupation and she doubtless wasn't wearing sensible shoes. "If so, it was by a chance thief. Why think of enemies and plots?"

"I don't know. I just *am*!" Rosamunde's head was pounding with each step. "Why would a chance thief move his victim to the middle of nowhere?"

"Perhaps the thief came upon him in the middle of nowhere."

"He said his last memories were at Northallerton. He was moved into the hills so he'd die."

"Then *why*," demanded Diana in something close to a snarl, "would this enemy who wanted him dead not simply slit his throat?"

Lacking an answer, Rosamunde sank into silence. She knew one thing, however. She couldn't leave this area until she was sure Brand was safe.

To do otherwise would carry betrayal to intolerable levels.

New-place—since it didn't have a sign they had no way of knowing its proper name—turned out to be a sorry collection of abandoned cottages on a half-decent road. To Rosamunde's fuzzy mind, it symbolized the disastrous state of her life.

"This hamlet was new back in the days of Bad King John!" Diana complained as she picked her way to the listing signpost which had arms pointing up and down the road. "Ah-ha! Only one mile to Thirsk. We can pick up the Ripon road there and head home."

Garforth steered the team in that direction, then halted and got down to poke worriedly at his wheels and axles while Diana hoisted Rosamunde back into the coach. Then Diana settled with a sigh of relief, taking off a high-heeled shoe to inspect her foot.

"I'm sorry," Rosamunde said, not particularly surprised to find that her nausea was building. Perhaps, since she'd drunk so little of the potion, she could fight it off.

As the coach creaked into motion again, Diana eased her shoe back onto her foot and pulled her gold watch out of her pocket. "That took nearly an hour. We're going to be late getting back home, especially as we'll have to stop soon and rest the horses again."

Was this the time to say she wasn't going?

Then Rosamunde turned cunning. Any suggestion that she wanted to linger to watch over Brand might lead to a quarrel. The autocratic Countess of Arradale was quite capable of carrying her home by brute force, especially if she realized Rosamunde's other plan—to let someone know where Brand was so he'd be taken care of.

However, she had a perfect, even honest, excuse not to leave the area. "I really don't feel well."

She must have looked the part, for after a quick glance, Diana didn't put up a fight. Perhaps she, too, quailed at the thought of many more hours in the coach. "Very well, we'll stop in Thirsk for the night. After all, we're in disguise. No one will see any connection between us and Brand Malloren."

Having achieved the first part of her plan, Rosamunde tried to make her crippled mind to come up with a way to inform someone of Brand's whereabouts. A cunning way that wouldn't reveal her part in it.

She had to admit that it wouldn't be easy.

Diana had opened her guide again, and was flicking through pages. "Thirsk. Thirsk. Thirsk. Let's see. . . . The only coaching inn seems to be the Three Tuns."

Oh dear.

Rosamunde had wanted Brand brought here because he'd said he had a party waiting for him and an appointment to keep. If there was only one decent hostelry, however, then his party could be waiting there.

She hadn't told Diana any of this, but she wasn't about to do so now or they'd push on to Ripon. With their clever disguises, she told herself, all would be well.

Diana called up to Garforth that they would stop at the Three Tuns, then turned to Rosamunde. "Now, all we need is a title for you." With a twinkle of mischief, she said, "What about Lady Gillsett?"

"No!" Rosamunde almost shrieked it, and her head went wild. After a moment, she added, "We don't want the slightest connection, remember? We need something ordinary. Unmemorable. Lady . . . Richardson."

"Very well. Lady Richardson, wife of Sir John Richardson of Lincolnshire. So, why don't we have any baggage . . . ?"

"Lost it." Rosamunde closed her eyes and tried to plan, but her mind felt shredded by pain and guilt.

"A mislaid baggage coach!" Diana agreed with almost unbearable enthusiasm. "Yes. How clever." Then she squeezed Rosamunde's hand and said in a whisper, "Poor Rosa. Not long now. See, we're entering the town."

Rosamunde raised leaden eyelids. Indeed, the coach was winding its way along a narrow, bustling street. Oh mercy, could she bear it? The rattle of hooves and wheels, the clang of a blacksmith's hammer, a wave of acrid-smelling roasting meat . . .

Nausea almost won; then, blessedly, they rattled into the large market square. It wasn't market day, so it was empty and relatively peaceful. In moments, they halted before the noble portico of the tall, square inn.

Rosamunde shuddered with relief. A bed. Soon she could lie in a bed.

Servants swarmed out to attend the noble guests. Rosamunde let Diana handle everything, but she was impressed and amused by the way her cousin managed to sound exactly like the uppity maid of a minor gentlewoman. Diana's tone became particularly sharp when the plump innkeeper insisted that though he could give the lady a private sitting room, he had absolutely no bedchambers for the night.

"No room at the inn," Rosamunde thought, the large reception hall swaying sickly around her. She couldn't possibly go any farther. Bracing herself against a solid white pillar at the base of dark stairs, she knew she couldn't even climb back into the coach. Faint kitchen smells were turning her stomach. Voices buzzed—Diana's sharp. The innkeeper's oily. Another voice. Male. Soothing.

Settle it, she thought desperately. Take a private sitting room if that is all they have. She was going to be sick. She remembered Brand fighting it. He'd lost. She'd lose. She'd much rather lose the battle in private.

Then Diana touched her arm. "Milady?"

She sounded a little peculiar. Not her accent. Her tone. Or would anyone sound peculiar to Rosamunde at this moment? "There's a gentleman here offering to carry you up to your bed, milady, if you will permit it."

"Bed?"

"He's given over his bedchamber to you, too."

Rosamunde turned her head painfully and saw a tall, dark-haired man bowing. A veritable knight errant!

He was a handsome man, but that had nothing to do with his status as hero in her eyes. He had given her a room, and would carry her up the stairs.

"If you will permit me, Lady Richardson?"

Rosamunde eased away from the support of the pillar and let him lift her into his arms.

"Allow me to introduce myself," he said as he began to climb the stairs. "My name is Rothgar."

Chapter 14

Eyes closed, Rosamunde was fighting an internal battle. She really should warn the kind gentleman. "I fear I might be sick, sir."

"If so, it will doubtless balance some of my many sins."

A hint of humor, almost a touch of the familiar, had her opening her eyes a crack. No. He was no one she knew, and she'd remember him if they had ever met. To her exaggerated senses, he looked as Lucifer might in an ordinary, dark cloth suit. Devilishly beautiful. . . .

"Are you a rake?" She'd never actually met a rake, but he fit her image of one and he'd mentioned many sins.

He angled her so they could enter a room. "In my own estimation, no."

He paused while quiet-voiced people fussed around, probably turning back the bed, perhaps running a warming pan through it.

"Do we judge for ourselves whether we are sinners or not?" she asked. Mired in her own confusions and guilts, it seemed important.

"What better guide than our own conscience? Your bed is ready, Lady Richardson." With a distinct hint of dark humor, he added, "And you must lie in it."

Rosamunde could have laughed at that. He thought her suffering the results of drink, just as she'd misjudged Brand. Justice and retribution indeed.

Someone took off her shoes, and then he placed her carefully on the soft bed. He was very strong, and wonderfully gentle, but the sheer bliss of the bed wiped out everything else. "Thank you, sir," she remembered to say, letting her eyes close.

His voice seemed to come from a distance. "I wish you a speedy recovery, Lady Richardson."

Rosamunde supposed he left, but she was entirely focused on fighting nausea. She hated to vomit, but now she also feared the agony it would shoot through her head. What Brand must have suffered, and he'd also not known who he was, or where. Even so, he'd maintained an essential courtesy that she knew was part of him.

What was her essential essence?

She had to move as people took off her gown and corset, but she managed to keep the nausea down. When offered a cordial of some kind, she tried it. Sweet with honey, it did seem to settle her stomach a little.

Perhaps it was going to be all right.

Then the covers were pulled over her, the window curtains drawn tight together, and peace settled.

"There," said Diana, touching her head gently. "Rest, love. You'll be better in the morning."

"Probably," said Rosamunde, sadly remembering taking care of Brand. Remembering that he was alone now, abandoned, and she was failing him. She was in no case to have him found.

Could she ask Diana to do it? When he woke, he'd be in a worse state than she was. No one would carry *him* up the stairs—

"Rothgar," she muttered, memory stirring. "But isn't that . . . ?"

"Hush," Diana soothed. "Don't worry about it. He didn't suspect a thing."

Rosamunde bolted upright. "Brand's older brother. The marquess!"

She was abruptly and violently sick.

Her head! Rosamunde came to consciousness, a consciousness focused on a throbbing head. Immediately her thoughts flew back to Brand, to how he had felt, to how he would feel when he came around this time.

She must do something. She must have him found, cared for. . . .

The attempt to move shot agony through her skull and she stilled, breathing deeply.

"Ah," said a soft voice in a broad local accent, "awake, are you, milady? Not feeling too lively by the look of things, either. You just lie a bit, dearie. There's nowt to fret about."

Nothing to fret about. "What time is it?" Rosamunde asked, eyes still closed.

"Midafternoon or thereabouts."

Midafternoon! She forced the panicked feeling down. There was still time to have Brand found before nightfall. To do anything, however, she needed her strength and wits back.

Had she dreamed it? No. Brand's brother was here, and one look at the marquess's strong features and eagle-sharp eyes had told her that though he had been kind, she did not want him as an enemy. She had made him her enemy, however. Now, she must not be found out.

It was almost too much. She had to somehow tell someone about Brand without arousing the suspicions of the ominous marquess. His effect on her had been so powerful, she almost felt he must have seen straight through their disguises.

Diana!

She quickly opened her eyes, and as she thought, saw a sturdy, middle-aged woman looking down at her. "Where's my maid?"

"Nothing's amiss, milady," said the maid soothingly, taking one of Rosamunde's hands in her own warm, rough one. "She went to find a headache powder for you at the apothecary, and asked me to watch you. Now, what can I do for you, milady?"

Rosamunde suppressed a moan. She knew her cousin. She was up to something. Probably spying on the marquess. Diana couldn't seem to take this situation with the dread seriousness it deserved. She took it seriously enough not to want to risk exposure, however, so this might be Rosamunde's only opportunity.

She began to slowly ease herself up. That headache powder would be welcome if ever it arrived. For now, however, pain or not, she must get up and find a way to send a note to the marquess.

Very indirectly.

When she'd achieved the vertical and the room had stopped wavering, she asked the maid for some tea.

"Of course, milady. Just the thing. Anything with it?"

"No." The thought of food made her stomach churn. "No, thank you."

When the maid had tiptoed out, Rosamunde considered her stomach. Though her innards still churned, she didn't think she was likely to throw up again. Brand had only vomited once.

With a groan she remembered broaching the subject of debt payment to Brand when he was in this state or worse. No wonder he'd seemed snappish about it. She could only pray she'd recover as quickly as he'd seemed to.

She was stripped to her shift, but she staggered to a chair by the window. Gingerly, she eased back an edge of the curtain. The sun was off this side of the building, so she wasn't assailed by light. She looked down onto a garden, however, and saw nothing of interest.

To find out what was happening, to make sure Brand was found, she'd have to leave the room.

How long would it take for him to come round? She'd been unconscious for about four hours during the journey and slept another couple. At the thought of how much he'd drunk of the potion, she winced with guilt. He was a big man, but even so, he could be unconscious all day and his pain would be at least as bad as the last time.

The maid came in again. "Oh, you're up, milady. You must be feeling more the thing. I've made a good strong pot of tea, but there's water to thin it if you want. And I brought a few plain biscuits in case you did feel like something to settle your stomach." She put the tray down in front of Rosamunde. "Would you like me to pour, milady?"

"Yes, please. Strong and sweet."

"That's the idea. Strong, sweet tea and a body's ready for anything."

In moments Rosamunde was cradling the warm cup and sipping the mahogany-colored tea, feeling the heat, the taste, and the sugar bring her back to life. Her headache eased. "It's wonderful. Thank you. What is your name?"

The maid curtsied. "Gertie, milady. And we do have good tea here. Mr. Sowerby—he's the innkeeper—he has his own blend. Very popular it is with those who like a good dish. Mind, his home-brewed ale is famous, too. That's good and strong as well. But now, I mustn't be chattering," she said and went to tidy the bed.

Rosamunde would like peace and quiet, but she needed news more. News about the marquess—why was he here? And especially news about a man found in a barn.

"Have you many guests?" she asked.

"Full to the rafters, milady. But that's because of a great lord who arrived today with ever such a lot of servants. Hard to see how one body can need so many people to look after him, and that's the truth. And we already have his brother here with another herd of people doing for him. Though he's not here at the moment. The brother. Now there's a nice man, Lord Brand. A lovely smile, and generous with it."

She smoothed a pillow, having repaired the bed so well that it looked as if it had never been used.

Generous, Rosamunde thought in sour and irrational jealousy. It was true, though. Brand did have a lovely smile, because he meant it.

"Not that it's not interesting to have all these fancy servants in the house," Gertie continued, tidying the washstand. "Some of them aren't above a bit of mischief, if you know what I mean. Mrs. Sowerby has the younger maids locked up tight at night."

Rosamunde encouraged the chatter. "What great lord is this?"

Gertie actually stopped work to reply. "Why, no less than a marquess, milady. Marquess of Rothgar. And according to his people, he's a mighty man in the south. If we're to believe his footman, he knows the King as well as I know Mr. Baines the butcher!"

Rosamunde almost choked on her tea at this comparison. "I suppose he's a great deal of trouble, then."

"Well, as to that, he only arrived a little afore you, milady, but I wouldn't say so. His servants are insisting on this and that for his lordship, but it's only what most lords want. It's his own bedding and pillows you're lying on, milady, for he gave up his room for you. He can't be as bad as he looks."

"Bad?" Rosamunde echoed, considering the marquess. He had done an act of kindness for her. Perhaps he wasn't to be feared.

The maid colored. "I likely shouldn't have said that, milady. But there's something about him, and that's the truth. I suppose it's an affliction to him, looking so like Lucifer."

So that impression hadn't been an effect of the drug. "Perhaps he likes the effect," she suggested. "I suppose it's useful to have people afraid of you."

"Not very comfortable, though, is it? Ah well," she said, adjusting a chair to her liking, "I doubt I'll have much to do with him. His own people will do for him, and we'll do for his senior servants."

Rosamunde, however, was following another line of thought. Lord Rothgar had only just arrived? Had he somehow learned of trouble and come north? But that couldn't be. It was a three-day journey from London, even with the best horses. He must have set out around about the time Brand was being drugged.

Despite logic, however, his sudden appearance seemed uncanny, as if it should be accompanied by flames and brimstone.

"And his brother?" Rosamunde asked, feeling as if just mentioning Brand might betray her.

"Lord Brand?" Despite her middle years, Gertie sighed. "Such a lovely man. So easygoing and pleasant to all. To meet him, you'd never know he was brother of such a mighty lord."

Rosamunde was hard pressed not to voice her agreement. "But you said he had a retinue of servants?"

"Oh yes, but more in the way of business. Clerks, accountants, lawyers, and such. But they have their own servants as well. Apparently Lord Brand runs his brother's estates—and there's plenty of those, I'm sure."

Clerks.

Accountants.

Lawyers.

Rosamunde poured herself more tea, fighting both laughter and tears. Her secret love-slave. Even when she'd known he was a lord, she hadn't understood. How was she supposed to know? He hadn't objected to a simple house with virtually no servants. In fact, he'd acted like the ne'er-do-well she'd first thought him, as if he'd nothing better to do in life than amuse himself with her!

Except when he'd firmly set the end at dawn.

Lord Brand Malloren, with a brother close to the King and an entourage of his own. Now more than ever she knew there was no connection between him and Rosie Ellington, other than a chance moment on a dark road.

And yet, and yet—she nibbled a dry biscuit—he'd not been acting when he asked her to run away with him. She remembered how he'd insisted on it, grown angry over it, returned to it again and again in the night.

Now, in light of his rank, she understood that he'd meant it. Such a powerful family would be used to shaping the world to suit themselves. They wouldn't care about the opinions of others. He doubtless thought she'd be honored to be his mistress. Certainly scandal would be a midge bite to him.

If Wenscote wasn't threatened by the Cotterites, would she succumb?

No. Without that threat, she would never have lain with him, lovely man or not. And she had to accept that if she'd not approached him, he would never have shown any interest in her. None, in fact, because without the need to hide her identity, she would doubtless have shown him her true face, her scarred face.

Suddenly, achingly, she longed to be back with Digby, back home, safe in the security of Wenscote where she could be herself.

Then she realized that Gertie was still chattering.

" . . . gone for days."

"Gone? Who?"

"Why Lord Brand, milady, as I said."

"He's missing?" She managed an idle tone.

Having run out of tasks, Gertie just stood, hands clasped on her white apron. "Nay, not missing. Apparently it's his way to ride out alone visiting places. He hired one of Mr. Sowerby's hacks, despite having two fine riding horses of his own. Incogno, or something, his people call it."

"Incognito." That explained his plain dress.

"Aye, that's it. But the marquess sent word that he'd be here to meet with him today, and he received that message before his last jaunt. So it is a bit strange that he's not back."

Rosamunde had to say something. "What could have happened to him?"

"Well, the world's full of wickedness, isn't it, milady? Three coaches were held up by highwaymen last month not far north of here, and the press gang came in at Filey. I do hope nothing bad has happened to him."

"So do I." Afraid her tone had been a bit too fervent, Rosamunde added, "Such goings-on. It makes me quite nervous to travel!"

Gertie came over and inspected the empty biscuit plate with approval. "Now, now, don't you fret. Travel by daylight, and you'll not come to misadventure."

In truth, if Rosamunde had followed that advice, she would never have had the adventure that started all this.

"But what of Lord Brand?" she prompted.

Gertie lifted the tray, worry settling on her face. "It's to be hoped he turns up soon, milady. From what his servants say, the marquess'll tear this part of Yorkshire apart if he don't. We don't need trouble like that."

Rosamunde shivered, remembering Brand's stories in the night about his oldest brother and his care of his family. Diana, too, had said he had the reputation of being protective and vengeful.

What would a man like that do to people who drugged his brother into sickness and pain, and abandoned him in an isolated barn?

Rosamunde rested her sore head on her hand. If only

she'd followed Diana's plan and done it at the masquerade. Then, Brand would not be in such danger. Please God, she'd have still found him and rescued him, but she'd have sent him safely on his way.

What would have happened during a day or two of his recovery at the dower house? Would they have talked? Would they have found the connection that still held, still tugged at her so painfully?

She might not even have stayed, though. She might have left him to the Yockenthwaits and carried on to Wenscote. Free of this turmoil, she would have been happy. . . .

She sighed. Her heart could not think that way. Despite the agony of loss, she could not wish her days with Brand away. She could not wish to be carrying a faceless stranger's child instead—she prayed—of his.

Selfish creature that she was, she could not wish it even to spare him suffering.

She could, at the very least, do something to ease his suffering. She stood, making sure not to wince or wobble. "I am feeling better, Gertie. I think perhaps I could continue my journey today."

"Nay, milady, you must stay the night. Swaying about in a nasty carriage is bound to turn you sick again."

Rosamunde hated the thought, but lingering here was far too dangerous. "I need to get home. Please help me dress."

Gertie shrugged. "As you will, milady." She soon had Rosamunde into her stays, petticoat, and plain gown. Checking her appearance in the mirror, Rosamunde was startled by the stranger there, and somewhat reassured. Even if she were to meet the marquess one day, he'd never connect her with Lady Richardson.

She wondered if Brand might, though. Or at least, recognize her as his masked lady. Lady Richardson's madeup face, with dense white cream, rouge, dark brows, and carmine lips was eerily like her painted mask. As the mask was ruined, so this one was badly mangled by sleep.

Rosamunde dismissed the maid, found Diana's pots, and did her best to repair the effect. The face in the mirror was horrible—a hag's face suggesting wickedness—but she did find comfort in it. There'd never been a trace of pity on Gertie's face.

With the face fixed to the best of her ability, Rosamunde searched the room for writing materials. None, not even Diana's traveling note case. How to leave a note without pen and paper?

The guests' parlor. Surely there were such things there.

She hesitated, quite simply afraid of venturing out with this strange appearance, and terrified of bumping into the marquess. She must, though. Brand could be rousing and suffering now. Rosamunde took a last fortifying look in the full-length mirror.

No one would recognize—

But then she smiled. Lady Gillsett! She looked exactly like her imaginings of wicked Lady Gillsett. Embracing that boldness, she sallied out to save her love-slave in distress. The inn seemed strangely quiet, and only one person passed her in the corridor—a young man with a ledger in his hand. A clerk, it would seem. Perhaps one of Brand's men.

She could stop him and tell him. . . .

Don't be a widgeon, Rosamunde!

As she descended the stairs into the hall, two redcoated officers approached, but waited courteously at the bottom until she passed them. Both gave her light bows, but showed hardly any interest.

No stares.

No pity.

An airy sense of freedom lightened Rosamunde's step. She was truly out in the adult world for the first time.

A footman stationed in the hall willingly led her to the guest parlor. It proved to be a charming room with long windows looking out onto the market square. Two country ladies were taking tea at a table by the window, and a rotund middle-aged man sat in a wing chair by the screened hearth, reading one of the papers provided.

The man ignored Rosamunde entirely, but the ladies—weathered faces and wiry hair—looked over with a smile and a nod. A faint smile and a brief nod. Rosa-

munde supposed she didn't look like the kind of woman
to have much in common with them, and that gave her
an idea.

Sitting at the walnut desk, she took a sheet of paper
from the drawer, and mended the battered pen. Then
she dipped the tip in the inkwell, and started to write.
She had planned a curt note from a third party, but her
hand and mind wrote the letter of her heart.

To Lord Brand Malloren,
    You will not forgive me, and that is as it should
be. There can never be anything lasting between us,
only the brief time we had. Know this, however, and
believe it I pray you, my lord. You have brought a
joy and light into my life that will live with me always. In the name of that joy, which I hope you
shared in some small part, I beg you not to seek
me out for vengeance or for any other purpose.
    I had no choice. I never had any choice,
    "Lady Gillsett"

She read it through and knew she should tear it up.
She couldn't, but she also couldn't leave it here for him
like a blatant calling card. She folded and sealed it, and
addressed it to Lord Brand Malloren. What address had
he given her in the desperate night? Malloren House.
There'd been more.

Marlborough Square! She wrote that, then "London,"
then slipped the folly into her pocket. She'd find a way
to send it, a way he'd never trace.

Now she wrote the letter she'd planned.

Lord Brand Malloren is to be found in a wooden
barn not far out of Thirsk, off a rough track between the Ripon Road and a place that starts with
New—.

Resisting the temptation to add unnecessary words,
she folded it, wondering how to direct it. Though it presented dangers, she addressed it bluntly to the Marquess
of Rothgar. If her plan worked, it would take time for

him to receive it. Time enough for her to be away from here. For once this note was sent, they must leave. Though she longed to hover and see Brand brought to safety, that was too great a risk. A risk to herself and Diana, but also to the important plan behind all this.

Now for the next move. She rose from the desk to pick up one of the newspapers, then sat in an armchair close to the older ladies, pretending to read. As she hoped, the man left first and no one else came in. Rosamunde gathered her courage and went over to the two women, who were just finishing their tea.

"Excuse me."

They both looked up. "Yes?" said the one on the right.

"Can we help you?" asked the one on the left.

Rosamunde sat, heart pounding with nervousness, trying to feel like the hard-faced woman she appeared. "You are just breaking your journey here?"

Two heads nodded.

"Yes, indeed, mistress."

"On our way home."

"Glad to be back."

They shared responses like old familiars. Sisters for sure, perhaps even twins. They were so ordinary and cheerful that Rosamunde longed to be ordinary with them, to be real. The paint, in truth, was just another mask.

"Do you go far?" she asked as if making idle talk.

"Far enough, mistress."

"Up into Arkengarthdale."

"We must be on our way soon."

"Or 'twill be dark before we're home."

Far enough, indeed. And somewhat remote. All the better for her plan. "You travel without escort?"

A chuckle. "Who'd bother an old pair like us?"

"Though we carry our pistols just in case."

"By coach?" Rosamunde asked.

"There's few roads up where we live. We ride."

The one on the left stuck out a leg, showing she wore tall riding boots under her skirts. "Astride, of course."

"Of course." Rosamunde was beginning to be fascinated and wished she could get to know these characters better. She had to achieve her purpose, however, and then get away from here.

"I, too, am leaving shortly," she said. "But I need to leave a message for a gentleman here. Without him knowing who it comes from." She was blushing under the paint at the implications, but was sure that on the surface she seemed all hardened wickedness.

Two sets of blue eyes widened.

"Goodness gracious."

"You haven't been foolish, have you?"

"It's plain to see you're married, dear."

She'd never thought to remove her wedding ring! She quickly elaborated on her story. "The very opposite," she said, trying for a tragic look. "I have come to my senses. But, dear ladies, I must leave him word."

"Very right."

"Very noble."

"To be sensible, I mean."

"So sad."

"Quite romantic!"

"We were to meet here and run off together," Rosamunde continued, "but no one yet suspects. He has only just arrived, which has given me the chance to see that it can never be." She sank her head on her hand. "My poor husband. My poor dear children."

"Oh, the little innocents."

"Ah, you poor thing."

Rosamunde faced them, ashamed of the lies she was spewing to these kindhearted ladies. And yet, beneath it all, lay too much truth for comfort. "For the sake of my reputation, for my husband and children"—she put the folded paper on the table—"no one in the inn must know who has left this note for him."

The lady on the left picked up the note and read the direction. "A marquess!"

"Alas, I was blinded by high rank."

"And other things, I'm sure."

"We caught a sight of your man, dear."

"A fine figure."

"But handsome is as handsome does, sister."

"True. He shouldn't be coaxing good women away from their homes."

"What can we do to help, dear?"

Rosamunde wondered wildly what the marquess might do about this slander on his reputation. Thank heaven, he'd never know who was responsible.

"I wondered . . . It is an imposition, but I hoped you might feel able to give the note to someone on the edge of town, with instructions that it be delivered here after a small delay. I fear he might pursue me, you see, and I might weaken."

"Wise to get clear."

"We'll do as you ask."

Now came the hardest part. She'd have to ask them to lie.

"If anyone asks later, can you not tell them anything about my appearance? I am somewhat disguised. . . ."

The woman on the left patted her hand. "Of course, dear. Don't worry about it."

"And don't lose strength."

"Go home to your husband and children."

"Your precious treasures."

"Neither my sister nor I ever married."

"Must be hard at times to be married."

"Men are, aren't they? Hard."

"Say difficult, Mary."

"Oh, yes. Difficult, Annie."

Though the sisters seemed unembarrassed, Rosamunde wanted to giggle at this.

"But sin can never lead to happiness in the long run," Mary said firmly.

This was so true, Rosamunde lost any desire to laugh. "Alas, I know it. Thank you for your help."

She felt tempted to hug the dear, compassionate women, but contented herself with a squeeze of one woman's hand. "Thank you again. It . . ."—her voice broke of its own—"it means so much."

With that she fled before she honestly wept.

Behind, the two sisters shared an intrigued look.

"Quite the little drama, Annie."

"Or tragedy."

"Hard to tell."

"He's the sort to ruin women."

"Dark. Handsome."

"More than that."

"True."

"Quite young, I think. Her. Beneath that paint."

"Oh yes. Hands always tell."

"And unhappy."

"Love. Not worth it."

Annie drained her tea. "I wouldn't have minded though."

Mary nodded. "Me neither. Me neither."

With that, they finished their tea. Miss Mary took up the note and Miss Annie paid the bill, and the eccentric Gillsett sisters picked up their riding crops and tricorns before clomping off to call for their horses.

Chapter 15

"We have to leave!" Diana gasped, rushing into the room dressed in what looked like rags.

Rosamunde turned sharply from the sitting room window, where she'd been foolishly hoping for sight of Brand being brought to safety. "Indeed we must." Then she took in her cousin's frantic state. "Why? What's happened?"

"The marquess is making enquiries, and he's brought in the *army*. We have to leave. Once away, we can get rid of our disguises and he'll never find us."

She flung an armful of clothes onto the bed—her previous servant's costume—and began to struggle out of the sacklike garments she was wearing.

"Is this another disguise?" Rosamunde asked, helping to remove a coarse calico apron, a dingy top, and a saggy brown skirt.

"This," said Diana, tossing the last item on the floor, "is the best that could be found when you threw up all over me."

"Oh, Dinah, I'm so sorry!"

Diana relaxed a little and threw her a smile. "You couldn't help it, and I must admit, it's been interesting being the lowest of the low." She tied the laces of her blue skirt over her snowy white shift, and quickly slipped into the brown overbodice lacing it down the front. "When I put these clothes on at Dulcie's, I never thought they'd feel so grand to me one day. Now, let's pack and get away from here."

Rosamunde watched in astonishment as her normally unflappable cousin dashed around gathering their belongings. "Yes, I agree we should leave," she said, "but the marquess will never suspect us, Diana."

All the same, awareness of her note pricked at her. Now was clearly not the time to confess but Rosamunde too wanted to hurry away from Thirsk. She helped pack.

"That man suspects everyone," Diana said, then dashed to snatch something from the empty grate. Pieces of paper?

Rosamunde's suspicions sharpened. "Diana, what have you been up to?"

Diana froze, then stirring memories fifteen years or more old, she tilted her chin defiantly and showed what she held in her hand. Her crest torn off a sheet of paper. "I've delivered a note to the marquess, telling him where to find Lord Brand. It just wasn't right—"

"You've *what*? Into his *hand*?"

"No, of course not! It was very clever. I'll explain later. But it's wending its way to him. And I just saw him with two army officers. I've ordered the coach. We'll never make it home today, but we have to leave."

"Indeed we do," said Rosamunde with a sick feeling that everything was going wrong. "I've just dispatched a note to him as well!"

"What!"

Rosamunde gave her cousin a rapid account of her plan as they both picked over the room for any betraying item. A button. A thread. As they worked, she received a tangled tale to do with ostlers and the London coach. Diana had apparently dropped her note in the stable yard as the coach was leaving. She had also clearly had at least one close encounter with Lord Rothgar.

"Oh, Diana," she said, giving the room one last scrutiny, "if only the devilish marquess hadn't arrived when he did! Even in a moment, he made me feel he could find out all my secrets."

"Devilish. Exactly the right word," Diana agreed, peering behind the bed.

Rosamunde picked up the valise. "Come on. Devil or not, he is hardly likely to come up here and search places like that!"

Diana was on her stomach, now, searching beneath

the bed. "He's capable of it, believe me. I saw him questioning the servants, looking for any tiny clue. He's offering silver for any news to do with his brother. The servants will clean cracks in the floor with their fingernails. Ah-ha!"

"What?"

Diana rose, triumphantly holding a shilling. "Riches!"

Clearly the strain was turning her cousin's mind. "Come along before you lose your wits entirely. A shilling, indeed."

Diana took the valise from her. "I'm the maid, remember?"

Prompted, Rosamunde banished terrified Rosie Overton and summoned Lady Gillsett. Thus armored, she swept out of the room and down the stairs. While paying the innkeeper, and handing out the vails to Gertie and the other servants, Rosamunde still couldn't help hoping that Brand would be carried in. Yes, it would be dangerous, but she'd weakly sacrifice every trace of safety for him.

No! She had to preserve the secret. Two notes were winding their way to the marquess, and without doubt he could be trusted to act on them and care for his brother properly.

She'd rather not, however, have encountered him on the way to the door.

"Lady Richardson," he said with an elegant bow. "I'm delighted to see you so improved."

Summoning Lady Gillsett as armor, Rosa extended her hand, glad for once of the absurd weaponry of Diana's glittering rings. "I am much improved, Lord Rothgar. I thank you for your kindness."

She surreptitiously assessed him with clear eyes. A fine gentleman in casual country clothes. Nothing frightening about that, surely. And yet, there was a presence to him, an aura almost, such as she'd never encountered in her sheltered experience.

"But is it wise to continue your journey?" he asked, lips brushing the air so very close to her skin. "It is already gone three."

Her nerves trembled. By accident or design, he was

blocking her way to the door. Did he know? He couldn't know!

"We planned to be in York by tonight, my lord," she said, drawing on every scrap of Gillsettian blasé. "If the road is good, we will make it, and with luck, our baggage cart is there awaiting us. My gown is sadly rumpled." He still held her hand, and she wasn't quite sure how to retrieve it.

"And a lady—or a gentleman—is at a sore disadvantage with only one set of clothes."

"I see you understand, my lord," she drawled in a world-weary manner. "One must dress plainly for travel, but one cannot exist in drab forever."

"But with such beauty as yours, Lady Richardson, mere clothes become irrelevant."

Heaven help her. Was the man *flirting* with her? It gave her an excuse to remove her hand and take a small step backward. She hoped it didn't show the panic she felt. "Hardly, my lord, or we'd all walk around naked."

A wicked light lit his dark eyes. "Not in the English climate, dear lady. But it could make Italy an even more entrancing destination." He bowed and moved to one side. "*Bon voyage,* Lady Richardson. I hope we meet again. In Italy, perhaps."

Abandoning the hazardous Gillsettian manner, Rosamunde said a hasty, "Good day, Lord Rothgar," dropped a slight curtsy, and swept out with as much composure as she had left. Her knees were knocking!

"Oh, well done," Diana whispered as they passed down the corridor leading to the stable yard.

"Hush," Rosa said on a breath. "Say nothing here."

The coach was ready, with Garforth giving the traces a final check, so they could climb straight in. Once settled, reacting purely to that ominous encounter, Rosamunde wanted the coach to race out, now, immediately.

Why ominous, though? The marquess had been a little over-bold, but he'd been addressing bold Lady Gillsett. Doubtless in his circles, risqué flirtation and innuendo were the normal way to go on. He'd obviously suspected nothing. All the same, her instincts screamed to be away, and Garforth was still steadily checking the vehicle.

Diana had pulled out her road guide. "It was clever, saying we're heading for York, but we'd better do so."

Rosa turned from the window to look at her. "That will take us in entirely the wrong direction."

"I know, but we have to be seen to be leaving the square as if going to York."

"He might watch?"

"Definitely. 'Devilish' is exactly the right word. You have the feeling he has three heads like Cerberus, and each with all-seeing eyes. But see,"—she thrust the map in front of Rosa—"we can cut across and join the Ripon road again."

"It could be a track as bad as that other one."

"This is a coach map. It wouldn't mark it if it were that bad. Anyway, it's our only choice. We don't have to get far today. Just away. If anyone should come after Lady Richardson, going south will throw them off the trail.

"And once away from here," Diana continued with satisfaction, "Lady Richardson and her spotty maid will disappear like dust in the breeze. Devil or not, the damned Marquess of Rothgar will never find us then. Never."

That had to be true, but still, as Diana gave Garforth the route and the coach finally creaked out of the Three Tuns yard, Rosamunde felt a shiver down her spine as if they left a shimmering trail for the man who would soon pursue.

The Marquess of Rothgar watched the strange Lady Richardson leave, accompanied by her even stranger maid, wondering exactly what mischief they were up to. It was idle curiosity, however, wiped away when Kenyon, Brand's manservant, brought him a grubby note.

A man is to be found in a broken-down barn off a track joining the Ripon and Northallerton roads about one mile out of Thirsk.

Instinct spurred him to lead the search himself, but he'd disciplined himself years ago to delegate, and to stay at the center of his web. He dispatched Kenyon and his best men to check the report, and another servant to find out where the note had come from. Then, he went up to his private sitting room—the one next to the bedchamber recently vacated by Lady Richardson— carefully presenting the impression of a man without concerns, and forced his mind to think through the implications.

Was the man mentioned Brand? Why else send it to Kenyon?

Had this any connection to the New Commonwealth sect? The King had sent him north to investigate it for treasonable activities but when he had written to Brand he had not suspected the extent of the danger.

Even so, Brand should have been warned. An oversight.

A tragic one? The note did not say whether the man was alive or dead. Why would the New Commonwealth attack him through Brand?

His servant returned to report on the note. "The lad picked it up in the yard as he says, milord. Took it to some others, because he couldn't read. 'Twould seem to have been dropped out of the London Fly that left half an hour ago."

"Take Denby and Lisle and go after it." Denby and Lisle were two of his grooms. His servants were never merely servants. "Note the names and descriptions of all on the coach, and watch for people who might be in disguise. Create as little upset as possible, and give everyone a crown for their inconvenience." He unlocked the strongbox and filled a pouch with coins. He passed it over, then added, "Ask Lieutenants Cripp and Haughton to attend me. They can accompany you to give it official gloss."

In moments the two uniformed officers were bowing to him. They'd been sent north in case official action was required against the New Commonwealth. He explained their role.

"With your indulgence, my lord," said Lieutenant Cripp, a sober-eyed, ambitious young man, "our duty here is to do with George Cotter and his followers."

"I have reason to suspect a link, Lieutenant."

Cripp clearly doubted it, but was wise enough not to push indulgence too far. He had queried his orders, so if it ever came to an inquiry, his skin would be safer.

Once the officers had left, Rothgar picked up the note again, scrutinizing it for anything more it might offer. Abruptly, he left his private rooms and went down to the entrance hall. The footman there leapt forward to offer assistance.

"Where would a guest here find writing paper and implements?"

"In the guest lounge, milord," said the footman, leading the way.

The room was deserted. Rothgar went to the desk and picked up a sheet of the paper. Not the same as the note. A much lower quality. The note he'd received was on the highest quality of paper, which intrigued him a great deal, especially as it looked as if identification had been torn off the top.

Crested paper. The London Fly. Brand. What could connect the three?

He should return to his room and logical thought, but worry sent him out of the inn, where he would see any arrival sooner. It was country teatime, and the place was virtually deserted, which suited his mood. He wasn't in the habit of pacing and fretting, but now, waiting for his men to return, he was close to it.

When his father and stepmother had died, his nearest half brother Bryght had been a dark, intense adolescent, difficult in his anger and grief. They'd only found closeness in recent years. Cyn and his sister had been seven-year-old twins, who'd frightened him to death, when he was only nineteen and responsible for everything.

Of his five half siblings, only Brand and Hilda never caused him trouble. Brand had been twelve, generous, sweet natured, and loving, which had been terrifying in its own way to the person who had chosen to steer him through the perils of young manhood. Hilda had been ten and blessedly calm and sensible.

They had been the ones who'd seemed to understand

his pain and fear, even though he'd never felt free to show it. They'd done their best to help.

They'd run after the twins, and eased Bryght out of his grim moods. When Rothgar was most uncertain of himself, most overwhelmed with administration and responsibilities, Hilda would appear with her beloved lute and play to him. Sometimes just her smile was enough, reminding him of why he was still fighting the well-meaning relatives who wanted to take them all off his hands.

Or Brand would waylay him with an urgent question to do with horses or weapons that required him to escape for a little while back to boyish things.

Like any parent—and he often felt like a parent—he tried not to play favorites, but the deepest places in his heart belonged to Brand and Hilda, the two with the sunniest natures, the two most like his magnificently generous and joyous stepmother.

Whom he, of course, had killed by carrying infection back to their home.

Had he killed Brand, too?

If his suspicions were correct, the New Commonwealth was ruthless in its holy purpose. He could see no reason for them to hurt Brand, but who else—

Hard-soled shoes clattered behind him and he turned swiftly, switching the hold on his gilded cane, which was also a sword stick.

The youth skidded to a stop, eyes wide. About thirteen, robust, healthy, rosy-cheeked from running.

"Yes?" Rothgar asked, immediately sheathing his tension so as not to alarm the boy.

"An it please you, sir. Are you the Marquess of Rothgar?"

"I am."

"Blimey," he breathed, eyes widening and searching.

"I left my coronet at home," Rothgar said dryly. "You have a message for me?"

Reminded of his purpose, the youth thrust out a neat, clean, folded note. "For you, milord. The footman back at the Tuns said you'd give me sixpence for it!"

Rothgar took the note, and read the direction. One

to Brand's manservant, one direct to him. Swiftly, he broke the seal and read. Different handwriting, but essentially the same message. This time, however, Brand was mentioned specifically.

Breath became precious. No hint here either as to his condition. Was this a form of torture?

"Where did you get this?"

At his tone, the lad stepped back. "I didn't do nothing wrong, milord!"

Rothgar realized he had crushed the paper in his hand and made himself relax. "I don't think you did. But before you get your sixpence, you will have to tell me where you obtained this note."

Still poised for flight, the boy said, "A lady gave it me, milord. An old lady on a horse. She said to take it to the Tuns, and make sure you got it. But to wait until the clock struck four. I only did as I was told, milord."

"How was she dressed?"

"Dressed, milord? Like a woman."

Rothgar felt a spurt of wry amusement. He supposed lads didn't pay much attention to clothes. "Do you know the New Commonwealthers?"

"Aye, milord."

"Was she one of them?"

He shook his head positively. "Nay, milord. She were dressed more like a man in skirts. Three-cornered hat and a braided jacket. She had riding boots on, an' all."

Curious. "Could it have been a man in skirts?"

The boy blinked. "Why would a man tangle himself up in skirts, milord?"

Rothgar took out a shilling. "Which road was she traveling?"

The lad's eyes gleamed. "Northallerton one, milord. Her and the other."

"The other?"

"There was another lady just like her. Two peas in a pod."

"In boots and tricorn and man's jacket?"

"Aye, milord!"

Rothgar tossed the boy the shilling, and watched as he ran off with a whoop. Such a simple way to bring excitement to a young life. In the meantime, he felt as if he were caught in a fever dream. Twin ladies dressed like men. Or twin men dressed like ladies?

Add a spotty kitchen maid who behaved somewhat boldly for her position, and her raddled mistress with young hands. They, however, could have no connection with this tangle.

He disciplined his mind back to the notes, which assuredly did. Two notes on different paper and in different writing, sent by different routes, but directing the search to the same spot.

And in all of this, no obvious connection to the New Commonwealth at all. Yet who else could it be? Could they have sympathizers outside the sect?

A suspicion stirred, and he returned swiftly to the inn to check the paper in the lounge again. As he'd thought, the second note had been written on the Tuns's notepaper. He inspected the pen. Newly mended and then not much used. A quick scribble confirmed that almost certainly the second note had been written here.

By whom? The inn was almost entirely taken up by himself and Brand, but coaches changed horses regularly and passengers ate. Doubtless passengers from the London Fly had spent some time in here. The two notes could have come from the same person.

But the handwriting was markedly different. One message was in neat, rounded lettering; the other in a finer, taller script, sloping vigorously to the right.

God. What did this matter at the moment? Where was Brand? Was he alive?

He couldn't help going to the doors of the inn to look out into the square. No sign yet.

He made himself turn away and saw the footman hovering in hopes of silver. "Who used the guests' parlor recently?"

"I don't rightly know, milord. People come and go."

"Think."

The man jerked under the terse command. "The Misses Gillsett took tea in there, milord."

Rothgar looked at him. So easy? Too easy, surely.

"Do they dress in mannish clothes and travel on horseback?"

"That's them, milord."

"Do they stop here often?"

"They don't travel much, milord, but when they jaunt off to York, they always break their journey here."

"Where do they live?"

"I'm not sure, milord. Up Arkengarthdale somewhere."

One of the remoter dales, one with no connection to the Cotterites, yet they must have been the ones to pass the boy the note. He'd suspect impostors, except that the footman knew them. They would have to be questioned.

"Who else?"

The man scratched beneath his powdered wig. "A gentleman, milord. One of the Fly passengers who was served his meal first. I think he read the papers. Then two of the ladies from the coach sat in there a while, waiting for their meal."

So. Three people from the coach. Any two of them could have sent the notes by different means. But why two? That was what fretted at him. The second note didn't give much more detail than the first, and the first was not likely to go astray.

The second note had been clearly delayed, and yet the first had as good as been sent to him direct.

"And that Lady Richardson."

He looked at the footman. "What of her?"

"She went into the parlor for a while."

"Is she a regular guest here?"

"Never seen her before, milord. Hear tell she's from down south."

"Do you know anything of her?"

The man shook his head regretfully, obviously aware that information brought rewards. "Only that her spotty maid's from Surrey, so likely she is, too. She—the maid—has been chatting to the servants here a fair bit. Seems her mistress lives a quiet life, so she enjoyed a chance at a bit of company."

Rothgar pondered the bold maid and the painted lady, wondering if they could have any part of this. He doubted any devout Cotterite would put on such a disguise, but he placed them in his mental picture just in case. Lady Richardson was undoubtedly up to something, but it was more likely to be extreme vice than extreme virtue.

It was his way to check everything, so he passed the footman a coin. "Pass the word among the servants that any new information about any of the passengers on the London Fly, or the Misses Gillsett, or Lady Richardson and her maid will be appreciated."

A clattering in the square alerted him then, and with a careful appearance of calm, he went to the entrance. Ice chilled him. Kenyon knelt in a farmer's cart, one hand bracing himself on the rough rim. He was looking down, face tense.

Rothgar's men rode alongside, somber.

The weather-beaten farmer halted his sturdy piebald horse by the portico and Rothgar stepped swiftly to look. Braced for the worst, but praying.

Brand lay on a bed of hay, pale with the fractured breathing of a man in agony. At least he was breathing. And there was no blood. A hand on his brother's neck found a slow pulse, but quite strong.

"The local doctor. Immediately." One of his men rode off at a gallop.

To Kenyon, he said, "Broken bones?"

"Not as far as we can tell, milord. The pain seems to be all in his head, but there's nothing there either."

Rothgar felt gently around Brand's scalp. As the manservant said, nothing. That could be worse than a clear cause.

"Bring him in."

Brand groaned when they moved him, his breathing close to sobs. For once helpless, Rothgar could only make sure he was handled as gently as possible, his head supported at all times.

Then he noticed that his brother had been lying between rich, golden-brown blankets spread over the rotting straw. A clue. A lead to vengeance. He picked them up and followed the men into the inn and up the stairs.

Brand was silent now, and Rothgar checked his pulse

again. His brother's eyes moved behind the lids. Half-conscious, thank heaven. Conscious enough, perhaps, to suppress weak noises.

"It's Bey," he said quietly. "You're safe now." He took one of his brother's trembling hands in a steadying grasp, and perhaps there was the trace of a squeeze in response.

Cold fury burned, but it would wait.

As soon as Brand was on a bed in a darkened room, eased carefully out of his jacket, his breeches loosened, Rothgar leaned over and put his hand to his brother's stubble-rough cheek. "Brand?"

On a thread of breath came the reply, "Who?"

"Bey," he said again.

His brother shuddered. "Thank God. I can't do this again, Bey. Stop it, please."

"I'm not God, alas."

If only they knew the cause. Drink? Brand didn't drink like this.

"Again," he suddenly noted. Recurring, intense head pain could indicate a fatal condition. Brand gave a choked sob, evidence of just how terrible the pain must be.

Rothgar squeezed his brother's hand to get attention. "What happened to you, Brand? I need to know."

The eyes scurried around behind the lids. "She . . . I . . ." After a lingering silence, Brand said, "It'll go away. Been here before. Don't worry."

"When do I ever worry? A doctor is on his way. Rest . . ." He suspected that by then his brother had fallen asleep or back into unconsciousness.

She? A woman?

He leaned down and kissed Brand's temple. "Man or woman, Brand, they will pay."

Chapter 16

The ruddy-faced doctor was little use, apart from confirming that Brand did not appear to have any physical injury or virulent illness, though his belly seemed tight. "I fear he has ingested something that does not agree with his system, my lord."

"Or it could be a ferment in the brain."

The doctor looked down. "That is possible, my lord." And fatal, as they both knew.

"Does this follow that pattern?"

The doctor looked up, clearly alarmed by the rank of his patient. "It is hard to tell, my lord, without knowing the symptoms leading up to it. But the belly is not usually engaged. I think part of the problem must lie there."

"What then? Drink?"

"Unlikely, if not tainted. Bad food rarely causes this extent of head pain." He leaned forward and pulled back Brand's eyelids for perhaps the tenth time. "Still constricted. Some medicine taken unwisely, perhaps, my lord. Or even some fungus."

"Poison?"

The doctor's hand began to shake. "It is possible, my lord. I have little experience with such things. However, in that case I . . . I really should purge him."

"It will be agony for him to vomit."

The doctor wrung his hands together. "It will be as you wish, my lord, but it will hurt him a great deal more if he has poison in his system and it continues to circulate."

Brand was moaning now, even though unconscious. Abruptly, Rothgar gestured for the doctor to give his treatment, then turned away. At some sounds, he turned back to see the doctor struggling to force the emetic down Brand's resistant throat.

"Stop." He strode over, took the glass and supported his agonized brother himself.

"Brand. Drink this," he said in the commanding tone he'd learned to use with his siblings. "It's unpleasant, but necessary." He put the glass to his brother's lips.

Brand turned away. "Tastes foul."

"You haven't tasted it yet, so how can you know? Do as you're told."

His brother's eyelids fluttered open a crack. "Is it really you? I thought it was someone else. . . ."

"Definitely me. And thus you must obey."

"I keep dreaming, Bey. . . ."

"I am no dream. Drink." He placed the glass against his brother's lips, and when Brand began to obey, tilted it. "All!" he commanded when Brand would have balked, and compelled him to drain it.

" 'Struth, Bey!" Brand complained. A moment later, he vomited all over him.

Continuing to support his brother through choking and sobs of pain, Rothgar said, "How fortunate you are that this is not one of my favorite suits."

"Hell and perdition. Don't make me laugh. I feel turned inside out as it is and my head is indescribable."

Despite the stink, Rothgar continued to hold him. "We had to expel the poison."

"I'd have been sick on my own."

"Would you?"

"I was last time."

"Last time?" Rothgar took the damp cloths Kenyon had found and wiped his brother's face. Then he fed him sips of water.

"I felt better after being sick last time, too. Need a long sleep."

Brand's eyes were closing again, so Rothgar laid him gently back on the pillow, which had been changed to a clean one. Most of the vomit had gone onto himself, so there was no need to move Brand to another bed.

"I'll be able to thank you properly, then, my lady,"

Brand muttered, so that Rothgar could hardly hear him. "Just don't turn that crank any more. . . ."

Once Brand had drifted off to sleep, Rothgar moved away and stripped off his outer clothes. His own man, Fettler, was already there with fresh garments and warm water for washing.

As he cleaned himself, he puzzled over his brother's words.

My lady? He immediately thought of Lady Richardson, but that was folly. Almost the classic fallacy of *post hoc ergo propter hoc*. Because one event occurred after another, it must be caused by the other. There were thousands of ladies in the north who were candidates for this mischief, and the last thing the guilty party would do would be to make herself so obvious in this inn.

Yet, someone had written that note on the Tuns's paper.

Crank? he suddenly thought. Did that imply torture?

In his shirtsleeves, he returned to the bed and inspected his brother's hands. Undamaged by struggle. He gently rolled up Brand's shirtsleeves. No sign of marks, inflammation, or bruising. Trying not to disturb him, he pulled back his loosened breeches and eased out the shirt to look at his torso.

Brand's hand came down quite firmly to stop him. "Optimist. Hag. Anyway, I want to beat you first."

Brows raised, Rothgar pulled up the blanket over his brother and left him in peace.

There was a woman involved for sure, but not torture. He didn't understand "hag" and "crank," but Brand's tone had been tender as much as anything.

Which could be difficult when it came to retribution.

He'd left the blankets in his private parlor, and once dressed, he went there and summoned Kenyon. "These were found with him?"

"Yes, my lord. Tucked snugly around him." Anxiously, the man asked, "Will he recover, my lord?"

"I believe so. He hadn't just been tossed there?"

"No, my lord. Carefully settled."

A woman, for sure. Something had been cut off one corner of both blankets. Almost certainly a crest. Moreover, the quality matched the quality of the paper used in the first note. So, Brand had been dallying with a grand lady, had he, and come to grief?

Vengeful relatives?

That would more likely lead to a duel than poison. And would a vengeful mistress or relatives tuck in their victim so tenderly?

He thought again of Lady Richardson. It would be irrational to be here and so obvious a target of suspicion, and yet there had been something about her that plucked at his questioning nature. What?

Her paint had been far too heavy for daytime wear, of course. At first sight, he had assumed she was returning from some revel, still suffering from drink. Now, however, he wondered if she had been in disguise. Though she'd worn jewels enough for a ball, her dress had been simple travel wear.

And her maid had been deuced odd. Such a spotty creature might be expected to be shy, to hide her face, and yet he'd caught sight of her a time or two looking around boldly and moving with a degree of crisp authority.

Trying to make the unmatched pieces fit some pattern, he ordered a long-delayed meal, and summoned Brand's secretary to share it with him.

The middle-aged man entered and bowed. "They say Lord Brand will recover, my lord."

"It would seem so, Mr. Vickery, though these things are never sure until over with."

"God be praised. He had eaten something to disagree with him?" Vickery sat to share the meal.

"And then tucked himself up cozily between fine blankets in a decrepit barn in an isolated field?"

Startled, Vickery followed Rothgar's gesture to the blanket and rose to inspect it.

"Do you recognize it?"

"Not at all, my lord, though it is of finest quality. A traveling blanket, I would assume, and it once held a crest of some kind. Cut off recently, too, since the material has not frayed."

"Quite," Rothgar said as the man sat opposite again.

"There would appear to be a lady involved. Do you know anything of my brother's recent amours?"

The secretary shook his head. "None, my lord."

Rothgar paused in serving himself soup. "You know of none?"

"I'd be deeply surprised if there were any, my lord. Lord Brand is not profligate in these matters. When traveling, he rarely engages in such amusements unless he should happen to encounter particular ladies of his acquaintance. He considers it too dangerous to take up local invitations without full understanding of the situation."

Rothgar filled his soup plate. "I didn't realize he was quite so cautious as that."

"Not always cautious, my lord," said Vickery with a fond smile. "Just wishing to be aware of the risks he takes. And in addition, he truly enjoys his work and it occupies a great deal of his time."

"I see. And he hadn't encountered any of his particular ladies recently?"

"None, my lord," the man repeated firmly.

Rothgar questioned the secretary throughout the meal, but gained absolutely no new information. By then, however, his riders were returning.

Lieutenant Cripp reported briskly on the occupants of the coach. "None admitted to any knowledge of the message, or involvement with the New Commonwealth, my lord. None appeared to be in disguise."

"How many women were there, and of what type?"

"Just two, my lord. One was wife to a lawyer traveling with her. Young, plain, and quiet. The other was a thin stick of a woman, middle aged and vinegary. She didn't think much to being stopped, even with a crown for her time."

"Thank you, Lieutenant."

The young man bowed stiffly. "May I ask now what connection this has to the New Commonwealth, my lord?"

"No, but you may continue your inquiries into the sect. Investigate the possibility of there being local gentry and nobility who are secret sympathizers."

"Secret sympathizers?" Cripp echoed in sparking interest. "By the deuce, my lord, that would complicate things."

"Precisely. Look into it, Cripp."

Rothgar watched the man leave. That should keep the officer's alert mind engaged. It was possible there was a conspiracy afoot that went beyond the sect, but he doubted it. Everything he had learned about them suggested they were strict and sincere about their exclusive way of life.

No, the attack on Brand was probably private business to do with some woman, and thus Rothgar didn't want Cripp poking into it. It was his to deal with. Sooner or later, the woman involved was going to suffer for his brother's pain.

By the time the coach reached the Ripon road—along a side road little better than a cart track, but passable— Diana had scraped off all her face paint and a good deal of Rosamunde's. "We'll leave some to hide your scars. It does work marvelously well."

Rosamunde looked in the mirror and had to agree, though she didn't like the pallid coating over her skin. "I can't spend all my days like this."

"But you could wear it when you go in public, and perhaps it can be tinted a more natural shade. We should stop in Richmond and have Dulcie teach you how to do it."

"No. I must get back to Wenscote. I worry about Edward upsetting Digby."

"If that Cotterite was telling the truth, Edward's gone."

"But for how long? He'll doubtless stop by on the way back."

Diana squeezed Rosamunde's hand. "But soon, if the gods are kind, Edward will no longer be a threat. That will comfort Digby."

Rosamunde winced. "The most extraordinary comfort for a wife to give her husband. Rejoice, for you have been cuckolded and will have another man's child to raise!"

"Isn't it what he wants?"

"The child, yes. But not the cuckolding."

"That makes no sense."

Rosamunde sighed. "I liked it, Diana. Oh, more than that! I fell in love with Brand Malloren. That's the sin. That's where I've cheated Digby. I worry that he will guess."

Diana's eyes never wavered. "You must not let him."

After a moment, Rosamunde nodded. "You're right. I must not hurt him. I will not even think of Brand Malloren again."

"Is that possible?"

Ignoring the jab of her cousin's question, Rosamunde said, "Anything is possible." She placed her hand on her belly. "Just pray, pray hard, that there is a child. I cannot go through this again."

"Anything is possible," Diana reminded her, and she was right. Heaven help her, but if this hadn't worked, she would have to do it again. Why was it so much more impossible than before? The situation hadn't changed.

But it had. There was no point in hiding from the truth within her own head. She loved. No matter how foolish, how illogical, she loved Brand Malloren. Adultery had been an offense against her wedding vows. Next time, however, it would be an offense against something deep and meaningful within her. Though logic said it wasn't so, she felt it would kill her.

Diana was consulting her map again. "I know a quiet inn off the main road. The Tup and Ewe. It's owned by old servants of mine. We'll stop there for the night." She looked up with a quick, confident smile, clearly enjoying matching wits with the enemy. "Search the roads as he might, the devilish Marquess of Rothgar won't find us there."

Oh, for this to be just an adventure, a matter of out-witting pursuit. Diana was wise, perhaps, to avoid love, marriage, and entanglements. Rosamunde left the details of the adventure in her cousin's hands and concentrated in sorting out her own mind. She firmly summoned visions of a long, happy future at Wenscote, with Digby, and a precious, healthy child and heir.

If she worked at this hard enough, perhaps over the years she'd reach the blessed state where Brand Malloren never entered her thoughts at all.

With a sense of déjà vu, Brand was nibbling toast and sipping tea, hoping his churning stomach would accept it, when his brother entered his bedroom and dismissed the servants.

"Is that preparatory to a stinging rebuke?"

"Only if you deserve one. I thought you might not want witnesses to your story."

"Story?"

Brand was enormously relieved to have Bey here—he remembered enough of the night for that. On the other hand, he wasn't ready to decide what to tell his brother. He wasn't even sure which parts of his memories were real, and which were dreams.

"The story of how you came to be found in a broken-down barn," Bey prompted.

"Was I? I have no idea."

"What of a lady with a crank?"

Brand stared at his brother. "What?"

After a moment, Bey said, "Very well. Tell me what you do remember."

"Some useful information about planned breeding programs," Brand said flippantly, seeking time to think.

"As your employer, I'm delighted. That is not what I mean."

Brand concentrated on the next piece of toast.

"Am I to understand that you don't want me to discover who did this to you and why?"

Exactly, though it was instinct more than logic. Brand had no difficulty remembering his lady, her sweetness, and their blissful conversation. He'd never forget their passionate entwining. A candle in the window. Blackberries . . .

Rather more fuzzily, he remembered some arguments about the future. He thought he'd wanted her to leave with him and she'd adamantly refused.

Logic insisted she'd drugged and disposed of him, but his heart rejected it. Time would solve the dilemma. Memory of his last waking hours, and of whatever he'd eaten and drunk, would presumably return in the next day or so.

"It's personal, Bey," he said at last, knowing his brother wouldn't like it. "My memories are still unclear, and I need to recall everything. Then I'll take care of it."

After a moment, Rothgar pulled out two pieces of paper and laid them on the bed. "Then you may want these notes. They were sent separately, both correctly telling me where to find you. One is written on high quality paper which has doubtless had a crest removed. The other is on the paper available in the guest parlor below, written with the inn's pen."

Brand picked them up and read them, but with only academic interest. If his lady had been so desperate to keep her secret that she had drugged him, she certainly wouldn't make herself so obvious.

But, cold logic insisted, if not her, who? Was Yorkshire full of people trying to drug him and dump him in out-of-the-way places? But she wouldn't—

Then, like a lightning flash illuminating a stormy landscape, he saw her, her roughly cut mask revealing only her firm chin and full, soft lips, offering a cup.

She'd urged it on him. Sipped from it herself . . .

Betrayal stabbed him like a blade.

"The note on expensive paper," Bey was saying, "was likely tossed out of a London coach just as it was leaving, but no one in that coach would own crested writing paper. The other was sent to me by a Miss Gillsett—"

Brand jerked his eyes up. "Who?"

"A Miss Gillsett. That means something?"

"Perhaps . . ."

"I sent riders after the Misses Gillsett—"

"Misses?"

"Twins."

Twins? Brand just sat there, assailed by the idea that he might possibly have spent those two days with twins. The mask might have been to conceal minor differences.

But no, surely not. It had to be one woman. He couldn't have such a powerful response to two. To two playing a game.

Could he?

"They admit to having sent the note," Bey said, "but say it was given them by someone else. They refuse as of the moment to say more."

"As of the moment? 'Struth, Bey. Do you have them in a torture chamber somewhere?"

"That worries you?"

It terrified him, but damnable hope persisted. "They're here?"

"No. They are doubtless in their home in Arken-garthdale."

Wasn't that where she'd said they were? Was it going to be as easy as that?

But twins. Drugs. Was it really so sordid . . . ?

"Brand," Bey interrupted sharply, "I am becoming irritated by your reticence. Tell me one thing. To the best of your knowledge, is this anything to do with the sect called the New Commonwealth?"

Brand almost said no, but then remembered George Cotter speaking with her. "Why?"

"It's your turn to give some information. Well?"

Brand recognized the change in his brother's tone. "I don't think it has anything to do with the sect."

"That's not good enough. I'm sent north by the King to look into their activities. He has considerable concerns. Not without reason since the old Commonwealth led King Charles the First to the chopping block."

" 'Struth, there's no danger of that, is there?"

"With the Jacobite cause not entirely dead, especially in the North, nothing is certain. So, is there any connection between your affairs and the New Commonwealth?"

Brand tried to put aside hurt and sentiment and be logical. "The Jacobites are mostly Catholic, and the Cotterites are far to the other extreme."

"There have been unholy alliances before now. Well?"

Brand leaned back, thinking. "I truly don't think there's a connection, but I can't be sure. You have to let me think about this, Bey. My brain feels scrambled, though not as badly as last—"

Perdition. He'd not meant to reveal that.

"Last time? This has happened to you before?"

"Leave it. Look, I met George Cotter before any of this happened. I'd go odds he has no thoughts beyond the spiritual and the welfare of the simple people."

"Are you a convert?"

Brand couldn't help but laugh and put his hand to his head. "Hardly. I could appreciate some of his ideas, but I don't approve of the severity of the sect's rules and disciplines. I do approve of the way they manage their estates, though."

"What a very one-furrow mind you have. Have you visited any of the New Commonwealth estates?"

"Just his own. He started all this by turning his own estate into a Puritan commune. It's well run and very progressive. You know how hard it is to get the rural people to change to new ways. He—"

Rothgar raised a hand. "I have no interest in agricultural theory at the moment. But whilst there, you heard no sedition?"

Brand thought for a moment. "No. But then, they take 'Silence is a virtue' very seriously."

"And you are not willing to tell me about the lady you have been dallying with."

At the abrupt question, Brand tried instinctively to throw up a screen between Bey and his mysterious betrayer. "What lady?"

"You talked in your sleep. Was she a Cotterite?"

He gave up the struggle. "Definitely not."

"Was it she who poisoned you?"

"I can't be sure."

Bey rose. "We will have to talk more of these matters. For now, who is Lady Richardson?"

"Who?" Brand knew that question had been tossed at him deliberately in the hope of startling the truth from him, but at least this time his confusion was real.

"A heavily painted lady, overtaken by an illness that might be similar to your own, though in milder form."

Brand was about to dismiss the matter, but then his breath caught. "Heavily painted?"

"Thick enough to conceal anything, including identity."

His heart was speeding. He could hardly believe it

might be so easy. "Medium height, medium build, generous breasts?"

"Yes."

"Wedding ring. Plain gold."

"Wedding ring, plus four very ostentatious ones. Brand—"

Brand shook his head. "She doesn't wear much jewelry. . . ." But how could he be sure he'd seen every side of her? Them? He pushed aside his tray, and threw back his covers. "She's here? Where?"

Rothgar stayed him with a hand on his shoulder. "She's gone."

Brand looked up. "Are you telling the truth?"

His brother's eyes met his. "Have I ever lied to you?"

"Where is she then?"

"I have no idea. She and her spotty maid have vanished into thin air."

"Spotty maid?" Brand's puzzlement changed to sharp consideration. "How spotty?" Could *that* be the reason for the mask? But what then of the twins? Spots and paint would hide the resemblance of twins.

"Plagued, poor girl," his brother said.

"The pox?"

"Just pimples. The explosive, pustulant kind."

"Could they have been twins?"

"And also the Misses Gillsett?" Bey's brows rose. "A farce complex enough for Drury Lane. Alas, all four were in the inn at the same time, and perhaps I did not mention that the Misses Gillsett are elderly."

"Not disguised to look old?"

"Not from the reports. Also, they are regular customers here."

Relief surged through Brand. Not the Misses Gillsett, then, so not twins. In that, at least, she had been true. Yet the Misses Gillsett had sent a note and his mysterious lady had used their name. Was she careless enough to leave such a trail?

Was it a trail to a trap?

He put that aside. He'd not be fooled again. For the moment, it seemed very likely that his partner in sin and delight was either the painted lady or her spotty maid.

He looked at his brother. "You can't have lost this Lady Richardson. I know you."

"I don't lie to you, Brand," Rothgar repeated. "If you suggest it again, I'll meet you at dawn. Lady Richardson announced her destination as York, and her coach took that route. It has not, however, been seen on the York road. Presumably it turned off, but we have no information as to direction. I have reports from various locations of coaches carrying two women, but none matches our lady and maid. Checks of the posting inns tell me that she definitely did not stay in any she could have reached last night. I have people checking all private houses of substance within a few hours' drive. The lady was disguised, but her afflicted maid is memorable."

"And have you any leads?"

"Absolutely none."

Brand couldn't help laughing. "Cunning, mysterious lady. I think she's beaten you, Bey, and that's an achievement."

"I've hardly started yet," his brother said coldly, "being for some reason concerned about my wretched, worthless brother. I have men out making deeper enquiries—"

"Call them back." Brand still didn't know what had happened, or what he wanted to do about it, but he didn't want his brother involved. Bey was too inclined to be harsh when anyone harmed the family.

Brand folded the notes and put them by the bed. "As I said, it's personal, and it's over. The last thing I want is to meet the woman again. Once I've rested a bit, I'll have plenty of business to discuss with you. Agricultural business."

"I look forward to it with tremulous delight."

Which, since Rothgar's interest in innovative land management was slight at best, made Brand laugh despite everything.

Once his brother left, however, he lay back. She'd desperately wanted him to leave and never return. It looked as if she'd done her damnedest to make sure of it. And yet, if so, why come here? Why put herself in such danger of exposure? It didn't fit. It seemed to be a Malloren trait, this need to have the pieces to fit together smoothly, for the world to make sense.

He closed his eyes and tried desperately to force clear memories of his last hours with his mysterious lady, but he couldn't even be sure that sudden vision of her offering him a poisoned cup was real. Veils shielded everything.

Déjà vu indeed. But at least this time he knew who he was. And in time it would all come clear.

Chapter 17

Rosamunde finally arrived at her home late the next day. She ached with forbidden loss, but also with joy to be back at Wenscote, back in safety, back where her role and duty were clear. The sight of the clustered village, and the solid stone fortified house brought tears to her eyes.

The high wall dated back to the days of the Scottish raiders, and had been one of the things she'd loved about Wenscote when she married. It had shielded her. Behind it, she had worked in the gardens out of sight of the world. The wall was her friend. Even without her special feelings for it, it was not forbidding, for it was softened by waves of ivy, soapwort, and phlox, and the iron gates always stood open in welcome.

As the coach turned through them and stopped, she sat still for a moment, savoring the music of Wenscote—the Ure flowing swiftly by, chuckling over rocks; the soft cooing from the dovecote; the hum of bees; and birdsong and crow-croak. All this was sweetly misted by perfume of lavender, honeysuckle, and rose. All spoke to her of security and home.

Digby came to the door, beaming his delight, and she dashed out of the coach and ran over, laughing, into his arms.

Sir Digby Overton was a big, hearty man and his arms enveloped her. "Ah, Rosie, I've missed you sorely and that's the truth. Welcome home."

She smiled up at him, but had to force the smile to stay when she saw his high color. And he was wheezing just from the effort of coming out to greet her.

All Edward's doing, she had no doubt.

"Come in," she said, linking arms with him. "I'm dying for a cup of tea, and I want to tell you all my adventures!"

He chuckled, and pinched her cheek. "Gallivanting in Harrogate, eh, pet?"

There was a question in his eyes—a shamefaced, not-to-be-spoken question that she answered with a smile. She wasn't sure she could tell him directly what she had done. She hoped he'd guess it had happened. And approve.

She poured his tea just as he liked it, and passed it to him, then sipped her own. "Ah, that is so good. I've traveled hard today to get home. I hope you didn't mind my staying at Arradale for a few days?"

"Not a bit of it, pet. So, tell me about the masquerade. It's past time you had such fun. Exciting, was it?"

"Immensely." Rosamunde grasped her courage and nodded firmly for him. Only then did she realize that he'd assume it had happened at the masquerade. Better so.

He closed his eyes, and to her horror, tears leaked. She leaped to her feet. "Digby . . . !"

He opened his eyes and waved her back. "I'm fine, love, fine. Very fine." He pulled out his handkerchief and dabbed at his flushed cheeks. "Oh, Rosie. Such a brave girl you are. Such a good, true wife."

Rosamunde had to swallow tears then. He meant it, and it soothed her conscience and her soul. If only she could tell him the whole truth—how it had really happened, how she'd felt, how she'd loved. It wouldn't be fair to put that burden on him. It was hers to bear alone.

"There were hundreds at the masquerade," she said with determined good cheer, "and the costumes were truly marvelous. Knights, pirates, nymphs, monsters. And the masks! You should have seen them, Digby. Animal faces. Birds. Hawks and eagles, even. Some made me shudder, and it was completely impossible to guess who anyone was!" She chattered on, falling eagerly into truth, and also giving him what he wanted to hear.

He smiled and nodded. "You must go to such things

again, Rosie, now you've come around to it. It's no good you being stuck here all the time."

"I like being stuck here. But perhaps we can both go about more. I know you've often stayed home because I didn't like to meet strangers."

"I'm content at Wenscote, too, pet. Especially these days. Did you see your family at Arradale?"

"Mother and Sukey. And Aunt Arradale, of course. She sends her regards. . . ." News of her dinner there, including the promising romance between Mr. Turcott and Mrs. Lampwick, passed a bit more time. Rosamunde began to feel the effort however. Surely it hadn't been so hard to find things to say, before. . . .

Then she knew what she was contrasting this with.

She firmly closed that door, and concentrated on her husband. Oh, please God, let there be a child. It will be the child of his heart, and will be so loved and wanted.

And of Brand's body.

A little bit of Brand.

She closed the door again. Locked it. Barred it.

"Widows ought to marry," Digby was saying of Mrs. Lampwick. "Not right to be alone. Especially young widows."

Rosamunde just smiled. "Widows with children have enough to fill a life." It was a promise of sorts, and one she meant, though not one she wanted to have to fulfill. She desperately wanted to have Digby with her for decades.

It was a reminder, however, that even if Digby died, Brand Malloren had no place in her life. Her life was quiet, isolated Wenscote. His was in grand estates, court, and nobility.

Stop it, Rosa!

Forget him.

To change the subject, she said, "I understand Edward came here with another Cotterite while I was away. I wish you wouldn't let him bother you."

Digby sighed and shook his head. "He's my heir, Rosie. Now, at least. And we're far enough from other resting places. I can hardly turn him and a companion from the door as the light's going, can I?"

"Doubtless why he turns up as the light's going."

"Aye, you have the right of that. I grant, it does fair fret me to see him in that stupid getup, mincing and praying at every little thing, making a to-do about eating plain food. Pulling a face at the sight of drink or a maid's full bosom." He winked. "I told Polly to ease down her shift another inch and to be particularly particular in her attentions to him."

"Digby!" Rosamunde burst out laughing. "You wicked man!" Polly was a house maid with the most generous of endowments, made more so by a tiny waist. She was not a wicked girl, but she had no reluctance to flaunt her pride and glory.

Digby chuckled, too, dabbing his eyes again. "I swear to you, pet, he turned purple at one point! Mind you, to give him credit, George Cotter didn't turn a hair."

Rosamunde stopped laughing. "Who?"

"Aye, pet. Edward's companion was none other than George Cotter himself, start of all the trouble. And Edward making a damn fool of himself, as if he had the King by his side."

"George Cotter!" With sick certainty, Rosamunde asked, "An ordinary-looking man in rather threadworn clothes?"

"That hardly singles him out, love, though I know what you mean. I was surprised by him. Do you mean you've met?"

Rosamunde suddenly felt icy. "He passed by the dower house while I was taking the air. He didn't give his name, but he did say that he was staying here with Edward for the night. I would have rushed home if they hadn't been leaving the next morning."

George Cotter. She tried desperately to remember what she had said in that idle chat, whether she might have raised suspicions.

"Aye, well, I'll not deny Edward upset me as usual, but Cotter was no trouble. Truth is, he seemed a reasonable man, and his honest talk about God and justice strikes home in any rational mind." After a moment, he added, "Dangerous, that."

"Very."

"Clever, too," Digby added. "Very clever."

Rosamunde heard the question in his words, a question echoing her own concerns. "We just shared commonplace courtesies."

He nodded. "And where've you been since then, pet? Your note said you were off to Richmond with Diana."

More lies. "You don't mind, do you? Diana had some errands there. One of them was to visit a friend of hers who used to be in the theater. We discussed face paint."

"Aye?"

"This lady showed me ways to cover my scars so they aren't so noticeable. Diana thinks I should do that when I want to go abroad."

"She might be right, love. Not that I think you need to cover up anything, of course," he gallantly lied. She noted that he was sitting to her good side as usual. "But I know it frets you, and you can't spend the rest of your life hiding up here."

"I feel so strange all painted up. Not like me at all."

"Well, you'll have to put on the paint and let me be the judge, eh?"

Rosamunde ran her finger down the long scar. "I will, then. In truth, Digby, I do feel a little less afraid of showing myself after this adventure. Everyone has been right all along, that my scars aren't so bad. George Cotter acted as if there was nothing wrong with me at all."

"Good of him," said Digby, gruffly. "As I said, in his own way, he's a good man. Come, give me a kiss, love, and then I'll take a nap. Knowing you, you'll want to be off checking everything. Hera dropped her foal while you were away."

"What?" Rosamunde leaped up, then obeyed the first instruction and kissed his too-red cheek. "The thoughtless jade. She wasn't due yet."

"Women," he teased. "No relying on them at all."

She cheekily stuck her tongue out at him and hurried off to the stables to check on the offspring of her best mare and Lord Fencott's Friesian stallion.

On the path to the stables, however, she paused in the herb garden to collect herself. That had gone well. Digby really was happy at what she'd done, and eased by hope. Despite common morality, perhaps she had done the right thing.

If only she hadn't let the worm of forbidden love into this blossom. It was for her to prise it out and crush it. Her situation would only be truly honorable if she put Brand Malloren out of her mind forever.

Weeks later, with her mind largely under control, and harvest keeping her too busy for folly, Rosamunde received an unexpected visit from Diana. Rosamunde was helping Mrs. Monkton and a maid lay apples on racks in the cool room, but a glance at Diana's face was enough to have her abandon the job.

Trouble.

She'd thought all safe by now.

She hurried out into the privacy of the garden. "What?"

"The Marquess of Rothgar has virtually invited himself to Arradale."

Rosamunde put her hand to her mouth. "He suspects? How?"

"I don't see how," Diana said, with a helpless gesture so very out of character. "Perhaps it's coincidence. He's moving around the North making enquiries about the New Commonwealth, and Arradale is an obvious base for Wensleydale. He requests my knowledge and opinion, though it's likely only a polite excuse."

Coincidence. It had to be. Rosamunde commanded her heart to slow its panicked beat. "If he's able to do something about the sect, I'll be pleased."

Diana looked at her. "Does it still matter?"

Rosamunde knew she had turned red. She'd not spoken of this to anyone. "I don't know. . . . But . . . I am late."

"Rosa! This will be such a wonderful thing. Does Digby know?"

She shook her head. "I haven't said anything yet. I can't be sure. I'm as regular as the church clock usually, but I can't be sure."

"Will it be all right?" Diana asked, taking Rosamunde's hands. "With Digby?"

She smiled, tears forming as they often did these days. Joyous tears. "So right, Diana. I wasn't entirely sure, but he's showing me in so many little ways." She pulled out a handkerchief and blew her nose. "I can't wait to tell him."

Diana pulled her into a deep silent hug. Then she put her away again and took a breath. "Now, Rosa, listen. I've had time to think this all through. Since I must play hostess for Lord Rothgar, I'm holding a house party and throwing a ball. It will be expected, and it will serve to distract him from me a little."

"He'd never recognize you!"

"I pray not. You, of course, must stay out of his sight. That should be easy since you are not in the habit of attending large social gatherings."

"But what of Digby? You know he enjoys a chance to get together with the neighbors."

"But he attends without you. This time must be the same."

"Of course."

Diana nodded. "I thought I'd better make sure, because everyone's noticed that you're going about more these days." Diana gently touched the side of Rosa's face, touched the tinted paint. "It's excellently done."

"Dulcie helped me. But it doesn't change this. Of course, I won't come."

"On what excuse, now you have attended other events? I didn't mention this, but . . . Rosa, it is just possible that Lord Brand might accompany his brother."

Rosamunde felt as if someone had poured ice and fire through her veins. "No!" she said, shaking her head. "No. I can't. . . ."

"Quite." Diana seized her hands again. "Don't panic. If you stay up here, you won't meet. It will be all right, love."

Ice of fear, fire of need. Rosamunde put need behind her. She wouldn't ruin everything now by giving in to the temptation to see Brand Malloren one last time.

"Perhaps Digby won't want to go," she said. "He's

not well. He seems to find it impossible to follow a plain diet. He tries for a day or so, but then he's tucking into puddings and drinking bowls of punch again."

"I'm sorry for it, but it serves our need."

"Once I'm sure of the child, he'll try harder, I'm sure. Perhaps I should tell him now." Her hand slid down to her belly. "I am, Diana. I can feel it in the most extraordinary way. I've been hesitating for fear that I'm deluding myself, but I know. Everything is suddenly different." She shook her head. "I can't let anything spoil it now!"

"Nothing will. I promise."

"What of you and Lord Rothgar, though? What if he suspects who the spotty maid was? He would make a very dangerous enemy."

"No more dangerous than I," Diana retorted, "and he'll be on my territory. Anyway, how could he possibly guess? I assure you I intend to be dignified and grand enough to please even Mama. No trace of a scrubby servant girl."

Rosamunde relaxed. In truth, it would require mystic powers to pierce Diana's secret. "And I will not attend, no matter what. We're safe."

With relieved smiles, they turned to stroll back toward the house. At the trellis arch, burdened by late fragrant roses, Rosamunde stopped, however, hand again to where her womb would soon swell.

"I need to say this once, Diana. Once, and never again. This is Brand Malloren's child, and I wish for his sake and my own that I could tell him, and share it with him. It is Digby's child and will save us all, but my heart weeps for the other."

Diana hugged her, saying nothing. She doubtless understood all that was unsaid.

Rosamunde's future was now fixed at Wenscote. The child, the whole reason for this, must be raised here, raised as a simple Yorkshire landowner who would love this land and stay on it. She had always known this, known the consequences of her decision, and accepted them. She had never anticipated, however, how painful, how agonizing, that acceptance might be.

*Please, Lord, let Brand not come with his brother.
Please don't make me have to be near him again.*

Brand rode up Wensleydale toward Arradale House,
Bey by his side, but the carriages of servants and baggage far behind. He'd only decided to come at the last
moment, and had been in the mood for mindless speed.
They'd visited a few studs around Leyburn to pursue
Bey's interest in racehorses, but Brand's excuse for coming was the heavy horse breeding he'd heard about farther up the dale.

Of course he wasn't riding the dales in the hope of
meeting a certain lady. A lady with an interest in animal
breeding. A lady who didn't like spindly legs and nerves,
but preferred the heavy horse. . . .

His lips twisted at his own folly. Every day, every
breath, he searched for her, even though he didn't know
what he wanted to do if he did stumble across "Lady
Richardson."

Assure himself of her safety?

Hold her?

Seduce her?

Throttle her?

"Good country," Bey remarked as they walked the
horses for a spell along a leafy lane between harvested
hay fields. "But rises to rough rather soon."

True, the fells weren't far away, already divided in
places by the new gray stone walls. "Sheep country,"
said Brand. "There's nothing wrong with sheep."

"In the form of tender lamb, true."

"And wool. Sheep have always been the staple of England." Brand looked all around. Though they were in
the fertile valley, he could see for miles. "I like it here.
Up on the moors, a man can truly feel alone."

"Perhaps I should have set you to the navy."

"A chance to feel alone?" Brand countered with a
grin. "The land suits me perfectly."

"I would never have guessed," said Rothgar dryly.
"But a person can be too alone in these parts. If dumped
here unconscious."

Brand sighed. "Leave it be."

It was too much to hope that Bey would forget an assault on the family, but Brand was weary of fencing over this. He'd long since remembered everything that had happened, everything, and decided for sanity to put it behind him. She clearly hadn't felt as he did, or she'd never have tricked him into drinking that potion.

"Are you not yet ready to act?"

Brand simply urged his horse back to a canter.

He'd been tempted to give his brother everything he knew and permission to do his worst. She deserved it, the cheating jade. But then one day he'd received that bleak note, sent on with other papers from London. It melted anger, but fueled despair.

All the same, he hadn't been able to ignore the fact that it had been written on the Three Tuns's paper, in the same handwriting as the note delivered by the Misses Gillsett. She had been either Lady Richardson or her spotty maid, but both had vanished like creatures from a myth. They'd outwitted even Bey, which was almost a unique achievement.

What did it matter?

The note told him there was no hope.

If only it was as easy as that. Dreams, rage, and questions swirled in him constantly, misting the words in a book or the figures in a ledger, stealing his mind in the middle of speech.

He hadn't been able to resist the long journey up into Arkengarthdale, to the isolated home of the eccentric Misses Gillsett. He'd hoped to learn something there. Even though they were elderly, there had to be a connection.

The tough-skinned old ladies had refused to tell him who had given them the note. They had, however, expressed cryptic duet opinions on men who dallied with married women, trying to lure them from their lawful husband and children.

Children.

He'd never imagined his lady with children, and he'd ridden away in a state of shock.

He'd tried to seduce her from her elderly, neglectful husband, but could he steal her from her children, and them from her? He was sure she was a loving, beloved mother. Perhaps that was the unscalable barrier that had stood between them. It was a barrier he had to respect.

Even with this, he was a Malloren and thorough. He needed to know. Riding back down Arkengarthdale, he'd slipped into conversations with local people and learned that the old ladies had no close relatives, none with a title. No one there had ever heard of Lady Richardson.

It was a dead end and more proof that his lady was clever. He'd returned to Thirsk with yet more respect for her determination and quick wits, with yet more bitterness at losing her.

He'd never been a romantic, never believed in the concept of the one-and-only, but now it was as if part of him lay dead. Heroine or jade, she had captured him, and despite the brutal severing, she had not set him free.

So here he was, working most of his waking hours, seizing every chance to travel, just to pass the days. And of course, despite all his resolutions to put it out of mind, everywhere he went, he couldn't help searching. For a spotty maid. For a lady with a hint of the familiar. For the house where he'd spent two days and lost his life.

One tree, however, looked much like another, and that was all he'd been able to see from his prison's window. Trees, a small garden, and a trace of a passing, quiet road.

He found himself doing it now. Checking a nearby building for anything familiar. Damnation, his prison hadn't been a four-room cottage! It was over and better so. He had a life to live.

The road split, the right arm pointing up the dale toward Aysgarth and Hawes, the left toward Arradale House. They went left, and for a while the countryside did not change. Then a hedge started, lining the winding road, and in the distance a great house could be glimpsed between trees.

Brand pulled up. "Arradale, I assume."

Bey halted, too. "Impressive, especially for this part of England." He pointed with his crop to the hills beyond. "I believe that is the ruin of the family's home in generations past. Arradale Castle."

"A striking fortress in a powerful location."

"The family gained the land just after the Conquest due to the bloody labors of a man known as Ironhand. The earldom came for fidelity to the Stuarts."

"And the right to pass it to the female line, I gather."

"The gentleman in question was a great favorite of Charles the Second, and had only daughters. The castle had been destroyed in the war, so the new earl built a more modern home."

"To the greater comfort of all, I assume." Brand urged his horse forward at a walk. "Do you ever meet anyone without gathering information?"

Bey raised his brows. "Do you visit an estate without knowing something of the area?"

"True. I was engaged in that sort of research when I was abducted."

"My investigations are much safer, and done by others. I recommend it. The late earl married below him to a local woman, one Sarah Ludley. It was only permitted because he was the second son. However, the older brother died in a carriage accident before marrying. It seems to have been a happy union, despite the imbalance, though blessed by only one child, a daughter. The countess is still young. She came into her inheritance three years ago at the age of twenty-two."

"Three years older than you when you inherited," Brand pointed out.

"I was never young."

Brand feared that was true. Bey had been present when his mother murdered her new daughter, but being young himself, had been unable to stop it. It had shaped everything. Brand knew it was why his brother found it so hard not to pursue anyone who attacked his family. He was always defending because of the one he had failed to defend.

"She takes her duties seriously," Bey was continuing, apparently unmoved. "She's held in respect by the people of this part of Yorkshire, though there's some indulgence in it. It would seem she was not an orderly young person."

"A hoyden?"

"Anyone can be allowed a little recklessness in their youth."

"I don't remember you allowing us a great deal," Brand teased.

"I knew the dangers all too well."

Brand returned to safe subjects. "So, what sort of person is the madcap countess now?"

"Strong willed and determined, I gather. She shows no inclination to marry, though of course she is besieged by suitors. The woman does own and control a large part of the North."

"Since you don't plan to marry either, you can hardly carp."

"I never carp. Lady Arradale is still young, however, and I'm sure she is pestered."

"Whereas at your advanced age, you are left alone."

"If only," said Bey, "that were true. Politically, the countess is of the peace party. She's at one with the King there. She's High Church and fun loving, and staunchly opposed to the Cotterite movement."

"A woman after your own heart."

"Don't be foolish. She has one strange quirk. She has ambitions to take her place as equal among men of similar rank, even to bring about a change in custom so that peeresses such as she can take a seat in parliament."

"The deuce you say! She wants to join the men's clubs and smoke a pipe?"

"I have no idea if it goes that far. However, you can be sure that during our visit I will treat her as far as possible as a man of equal rank. I recommend that you do the same."

"Poor thing. You're a manipulative devil at times."

"All the time, I hope. That's how I've built our power."

Brand suddenly felt sorry for the young countess. "Don't hurt her, Bey. You know you can be damned seductive if you've a mind to be."

Bey stared. "My dear, I never seduce men of equal rank."

Brand laughed, and by then they could see the gate house, a magnificent stone arch with cottage attached, and wrought-iron gates standing open. It seemed somewhat pointless without a wall around the property, but it was an impressive statement of power and wealth.

"Reconstructed, stone by stone, from the castle, at the lady's orders," Rothgar murmured, as they rode forward. The gatekeeper was running out to bow and wave them through. "Delusions of grandeur?"

"As I said. A match made in heaven."

"Our coronets and convictions would clash."

In moments a horn sounded, telling all that noble guests were arriving.

The formal drive of Arradale ran straight toward the house between disciplined lines of glowing lime trees. To the sides, however, some modern landscape work had been done, creating admirable vistas. Here a small lake was crossed at one end by a miniature stone-arched bridge. There a Grecian temple could be glimpsed through a careful arrangement of trees. Deer cropped the grass, also keeping the lower trunks of the limes tidily clear of growth.

The house was a solid block with two flights of steps curving up toward grand central doors. Servants spilled out from the sides to take the horses, and the doors were opened by liveried footmen.

Brand smiled. Perhaps this was the usual grandeur, or perhaps the countess was intent on impressing the Marquess of Rothgar.

They climbed the steps and entered a paneled hall hung with enough weapons to arm a significant force, and found the countess waiting for them. At least, it must be her. Straight spine, determined chin, and gracious smile. Despite a charmingly feminine yellow dress and a fashionably frivolous muslin-and-lace apron, despite glossy chestnut curls crowned by a lace-and-ribbon confection that hardly deserved the name of cap, she gave a clear impression of authority.

Brand wondered whether she habitually disguised it

this way, or whether it was a performance put on especially for Bey. 'Struth, it was to be hoped the lady hadn't abandoned her determination to remain unmarried and decided to set her pretty cap at a marquess!

"We are honored and delighted to have you visit us here at Arradale, Lord Rothgar," she said, extending a hand for a greeting salutation. That was when Brand noticed her rings, flashing brashly in a sunbeam. Far too many rings, all large. A conundrum, the Countess of Arradale. She might amuse Bey and distract him from Brand's affairs.

Brand kissed her hand in turn, then she gave one hand to each and led them toward a grand staircase leading up to a balcony edged with columns of rose marble, glowing warmly in shafts of afternoon sun.

"I have invited some of my neighbors to stay for a few days, my lords," she said. "People who will be pleased to make your acquaintance, and whom you will like to meet. Tomorrow, there will be a ball." Arriving at the balcony, where yet more servants waited, she added, "I will have you shown to your rooms to refresh yourselves, but then perhaps you would honor us with your company in the drawing room."

"If you can excuse our riding clothes, Lady Arradale," said Bey. "We have outpaced our baggage."

"Of course, my lord."

She was the epitome of the gracious hostess, and Bey was at his smoothest. Brand felt as if warning bells were sounding, but couldn't imagine why.

Perhaps she was in marital pursuit and Bey was aware of it. For his part, Brand had no interest in such silliness.

Once in his room and alone, he sighed, thinking that coming here had been a mistake. A house party and a ball. Though he enjoyed good company, he had little patience with the more superficial society gatherings. As he washed and tidied himself, he took comfort in the fact that he would soon be able to escape for daily rides around the area. Bey could play social games with the countess without anyone holding his hand.

Drying his face, he smiled at the thought of his teasing on the road. The countess was hardly Bey's usual type, but she might be a worthy challenge. Unfortunate, perhaps, that she and Bey were unlikely to lock horns. It could be amusing.

He reknotted his cravat, wondering why she wore so many rings. He was no expert on such things, but he didn't even think them of significant value. Just large and faceted for greatest sparkle. . . . He paused. That sparked a memory.

Rings?

After a moment, he shook his head, accepting that whatever memory had flickered had died.

He joined his brother and they returned to the lower floor, where a footman guided them to a handsome drawing room, decorated in the latest Chinese style. The countess again came forward to greet them and introduce them to her guests. Brand began to relax. Though mostly of the upper class, the guests were country people rather than courtiers, and likely to be interested in matters that interested him.

He saw his brother watching the countess now and then, as if searching for something about her. He put it aside. Whatever Bey was up to had nothing to do with him.

He settled with a group of ruddy-faced men and began to learn about animal breeding in Wensleydale.

Chapter 18

In the end, simply because she knew he wanted to go, Rosamunde had urged Digby to attend Diana's party. She knew she should keep him at home, but he did so love these events. Since their marriage, he had stayed with her at Wenscote so often, a sacrifice she hadn't always appreciated as much as she should.

Let him have the pleasure of time with his old friends. What harm could it do? He knew nothing of a connection between her and the Marquess of Rothgar.

She couldn't help weakly wondering whether Brand had accompanied his brother. She felt she should know if he were so close, but that was nonsense. Better not to know. She wasn't sure she could resist the temptation to try at least to see him.

She was particularly pleased Digby was away when her nephew, Edward, turned up again. As usual, he'd arrived as evening fell, so it was impossible to send him on his way. At least this time George Cotter wasn't with him.

"Digby isn't here," she said with satisfaction as she led him to his usual room.

"No? It's rare he leaves home."

"He's at Arradale. The countess is holding a house party with a ball tomorrow night in honor of the Marquess of Rothgar." She couldn't resist adding, "I understand the marquess is in the North looking into the activities of the New Commonwealth."

Edward, virtuously trim in dress and build, put his bag on the bed. "If he investigates, he will only find wisdom for his damned soul."

"Damned? Just for asking questions?"

"Damned, Aunt, for his wicked life. George Cotter knows all about the marquess and his questions, and does not fear them."

His quiet certainty of absolute virtue always made her want to say something outrageous. She turned to leave, but he spoke again.

"Do I gather my uncle is in good health, then, if he feels able to indulge in parties and balls?"

Ah, so that had caught him on a raw spot. "I doubt Digby will dance," she said, casually, "but he is fine fettle. I think he's heeding your advice about a simple, healthy life."

"God has answered my prayers, then." If she didn't know better, she would have believed him. "And you?" he asked. "I hear you have put aside vanity and go about more."

True, he'd been urging her to face the world. Edward had a gift for giving good advice in a way that made it intolerable.

But then he looked closely at her for the first time. "What is this, Aunt?" he asked, stepping closer. "A miracle . . . ?" But then he stiffened. *"Face paint?"*

Hiding a spurt of wicked glee, Rosamunde touched her cheek. "This? Why yes. Wonderful, don't you think?"

He raised a thin hand as if fending off the devil. "You should accept the way God made you!"

"God did not make me scarred."

"God's will speaks in all things." He actually seized his Bible and held it in front of himself as if needing protection. "So why, being so wickedly transformed, are you not at Arradale with your husband, prancing and flirting, and showing off your body in lewd silken garments?"

"Raw cowardice. I am still not comfortable with strangers, so I made an excuse of not feeling well. I would love to be braver," she told him. "To be prancing and dancing in silken garments."

He sighed. "Aunt, I know you do not favor my cause, but can you not see how wicked the world has become, how much change is needed? In Lancashire, people wept

to hear George Cotter speak, to hear the simple guid-
ance from the Bible that would lead them to sober, honest lives. You are not lacking sense. Look at England!
We are ruled by kings and nobles who flaunt their mis-
tresses, drink themselves unconscious every night, and
gamble away their heritage without a thought of those
on the land they play with. Do you really think the wild
extravagance of Arradale, the likes of the Marquess of
Rothgar, the excesses of masquerades, the deep dissolu-
tion of drink, the wickedness of fornication and adultery—"

"Stop!" The word escaped Rosamunde before she
could help it. Her heart scurried as if he knew, as if he
were speaking of her. "My goodness," she said shakily,
"you are learning your trade well. I warrant you stir
them from the pulpit."

He preened. "I hope I am receiving the Lord's gift of
words, yes. Though not from the pulpit. Following our
leader, we speak simply on level ground with those who
will listen. In a barn, a hall, or even in a field." He
stepped forward and took her hand. "Can I hope that
my words touched you, Aunt? That you might one day
see the light?"

She supposed he was sincere in his own way. "I do
agree that excess drink and gambling is wrong, yes. And
fornication. Someone who can bring people to live honest, sober lives is doing good in the world. But you know
I cannot agree with everything about the New Commonwealth. Joy is not evil. Dancing is not a sin. You need
to be more tolerant."

"God's servants must be rocks. There is no place for
half measures. We of the New Commonwealth will turn
England into Jerusalem, one acre at a time. When I am
master here—"

She snatched her hand free. "When?"

"Aunt, Aunt! One day, all men must come to dust,
earthly possessions forgotten. Thus, one day this will be
mine, and likely soon. Your devotion is admirable, especially to an old man who must disgust you—"

"How dare you!"

"Come, come. Speak the truth. You do your duty admirably and that is to your credit, but had you not ruined your looks by your folly, you would never have married here."

She flinched from the bitter truth. "I *love* Digby, and he doesn't disgust me in the slightest. You, however, do! For all your talk of God and sin, for all your study of the Bible, you have forgotten Christ's preaching about charity and humility!"

With that she swept out, but as she hurried down to the kitchen to check on the meal—and to tell Polly to twitch her bodice down a few inches—she knew she should have kept her temper. The only way to deal with Edward was to put up with him and get him on his way as soon as possible.

She couldn't help shivering slightly at the thought of his reaction when she revealed that she was with child. Thank heavens Digby would be by her side.

Tasting the soup, Rosamunde couldn't help thinking about the gathering at Arradale. Diana's feasts were always splendid. She did hope Digby would keep to his moderate eating and drinking, though she knew it would be hard for him.

She wondered what he would make of Lord Rothgar. She'd enjoy his impressions. What would he make of Brand—

No! She would *not* think of him.

Brand relaxed at the long, gleaming table, sipping fine brandy. He was slightly stuffed, for the food had been truly excellent, but not unpleasantly so. The ladies had recently left to take tea in the drawing room, and snuff and pipes had come out. Though clay pipes were not uncommon, he wasn't sure he'd ever seen so many in use in such grand surroundings after a sumptuous meal. He was charmed.

The company was pleasant, too. Brand accepted an invitation from Sir Malcolm Bursett to inspect his sheep, and one from Lord Fencott to visit his stud. But then the enthusiastic young viscount towed him around the table to a high-colored, older man. "Since you're interested in the plow horse, my lord, you must meet Sir Digby Overton. He has a neat little breeding program. . . ."

Sir Digby, puffing on a pipe, was a typical country-man—grizzled hair, bushy eyebrows, and ruddy skin. His build was British bulldog, wide of chest, strong of jaw, but heavily overlaid by fat. He was drinking deeply and cherry red with that and good humor. Brand suspected that he was just the sort to keel over one day with a fatal seizure, but from his merry smile, he would have lived life to the full in the meantime.

"Lord Brand," the man said, "I hear you're a true land man, despite your rank."

"Thank you, Sir Digby. As for rank," he said, taking a place vacated for him, "I'm a younger son, and forced to be useful."

"Wish they were all so forced," the man said bluntly. "There's a good many wastrels and rogues come from that stable."

"Doubtless why my brother put us all to work. I understand you have an interesting stud."

"Ah, that." He topped up his glass and offered the decanter to Brand. Brand took some to be sociable.

"It's my wife's little hobby," the baronet said, "but folk around here will persist in seeing it as my work. Don't think it's quite the thing for a woman to be involved in breeding, you see. Well, except for babies of course." He coughed and drank half his glass straight down, clearly embarrassed. Brand hid a smile. Men like Sir Digby would talk about mares and ewes without a blink, but choke to speak of their wives in a familiar way.

"We live quietly, you see, my lord," the man hurried on, "so it keeps my wife amused. A grand lass, my Rosie. She likes to keep busy."

Brand envisioned a woman rather like the bluff Misses Gillsett and was charmed. "I understand she was unfortunately too unwell to attend this gathering."

"Just a bit under the weather, my lord." He dropped his voice. "Womanly thing, you know."

Brand was slightly surprised. He'd assumed Lady Overton to be past the age of "womanly things." Perhaps there were others besides the obvious. "I was hoping to have a chance to visit your stud, but I would not wish to put Lady Overton to any inconvenience."

"Inconvenience? Never that, my lord. She's not been in the way of welcoming strangers—"

"Well, then—"

"But that's changed these days. I know she'd dearly love to talk about her horses to an interested party. I have to admit," he said in an embarrassed voice, "that I can't see the beauty in those huge beasts. Useful, of course, but not a pretty sight. But don't let that on to her."

"If you're sure she wouldn't mind . . . ?"

"Not Rosie. She'd talk about her beloved horses on her deathbed!"

He must have reacted to that, for Sir Digby laughed and topped up Brand's glass again. "A figure of speech, I assure you, my lord. She's fit as a fiddle, the Lord be thanked!" Then he sighed and pushed away his own refilled glass. "I can only pray He'll be as kind to me. Rosie would scold me fiercely to see me drinking so much."

"Takes care of you well, does she?"

"Aye, bless her heart." He seemed to stare into the distance, then pulled out a snowy handkerchief, and dabbed at his eyes. "Such a good wife. I pray God send you one as fine, sir."

"I pray so, too," said Brand, touched by this devoted couple.

Sir Digby fiercely blew his nose. "Stop by anytime, my lord. Anytime. We live quietly, but you'll always find a welcome at Wenscote, and my Rosie will be happy as a robin to meet a fellow enthusiast."

Brand rather wished he could take up the invitation first thing tomorrow. At least it would get him away from all these people. Like a damn melancholy poet, he felt a strong inclination to isolation, perhaps even to attempting a maudlin verse or two.

The gathering was serving Bey's purpose, however. In his usual way, he was sifting through gossip and chatter for grains of the New Commonwealth, for any hint that the gentry could be secretly involved. He had a remarkable memory, and hardly ever forgot a detail, which had led to his reputation as devilishly omniscient. It was almost true, as his family had frequently found out.

As the men finally rose to walk—or stagger—to the drawing room to join the fairer sex, Bey found chance for a quiet word with his brother. "Discovering anything useful about our saintly friends?"

"Merely stories that reinforce what we know. As preachers, they're rivaling Wesley in popularity. He's in the area, too, you know."

"Is he connected?"

"Not at all, though I suspect he'll rock English society in his own way. It could do with a good rocking. Wesley's movement is a different matter entirely from the New Commonwealth. There's no such fanatical control of the membership, nor a greed for land. The Cotterites stand to inherit an estate in this area."

"Inherit? In a will?"

"Not with the owner's consent. The heir is a member of the Cotterites, so when the present owner dies, they have it."

"The will can't be changed?"

"There's a long-standing settlement on the estate. A place called Wenscote."

"Wenscote?" Brand glanced to where Sir Digby was making his ponderous way up the stairs, clearly affected by drink and perhaps wheezing a bit. "Then the Commonwealth may not have long to wait. That's the present owner. A genial gentleman, but asking for a seizure. I wouldn't have thought him the type to raise a Cotterite son."

"Nephew." Rothgar studied the older man. "No wonder they all seemed worried."

"Shame his wife's past childbearing."

"Is she? One man suggested there might still be hope."

" 'Hope springs eternal . . .'? I gathered that she was close to his age, but perhaps the womanly complaint that keeps her home is of the more obvious variety."

"Then she is, alas, not with child. And even if it is

still barely possible, after many childless years, it is not to be looked for. Feeling around here runs solidly against the New Commonwealth." As they began to climb the stairs, he added, "Except, perhaps, for our hostess."

"The countess! A less likely candidate . . ."

"In a brief exchange, she rather pointedly supported an improvement in morals, sobriety, and industry."

"Don't we all?"

"Not, I think, if applied to ourselves. And it was clearly a rapier point directed at me."

Brand laughed, but he wondered if he should warn the countess about crossing swords with his brother. Blades or wits, he was rarely matched. He shrugged. Bey wouldn't do the woman serious damage, and if she was up to mischief, she doubtless deserved a lesson.

The next day, Brand found that the countess had arranged a wide choice of pleasurable activities. That was to be expected, but he was disconcerted to be steered firmly by her toward the River Arra where guests were trying for trout.

"You believe angling is my favorite occupation, Lady Arradale?"

She looked up from under a charming flat hat crowned with artificial marigolds. "Is it not? All gentlemen . . ."

"I could say that all ladies enjoy stitchery."

Her look was sharp, and indeed, he wasn't sure why he was debating with her. "I can sew," she said. "I have been trained in all the feminine arts."

"And I can fish. However, at the moment, I do not care to. If it would not discompose you too much, I would prefer to stroll about your delightful park."

Now, why did she frown? However, she could hardly object. The fleeting frown was replaced by a charming smile. "I think you will enjoy it. There are some pleasing walks over near the river," she said, pointing to the left.

Thanking her, he took her direction, but he was intrigued. What, pray, was the countess up to? Some plan to do with his brother? Once out of sight, he altered course and worked his way back in the opposite direction from the one pointed out to him. He didn't for one moment think Bey would need help, but if the pretty countess was going to play seductive games with his brother, he wouldn't at all mind coming across them.

However, a short time later, as he stood at the top of a small rise admiring the vista of the house below, he saw the countess ride out accompanied by two grooms. Not intent on seduction, then.

A wonderful piece of horseflesh, he noted, and a magnificent rider. And, by gad, she rode astride. Watching the flash of chestnut horse and crimson habit gallop out of sight, Brand thought for a fleeting moment that it was a shame that neither his brother nor the countess were at all interested in each other.

Rosamunde was in the stud stables when Diana came up behind her, saying, "Rosa!"

Despite an urgency in her cousin's tone, Rosamunde held up her hand. "Hush." She didn't take her eyes off the scene in front of her. She was observing the enclosed covering yard from a small unglazed window, watching as her newest prized possession, a Flemish stallion, called Dirk, approached a mare.

"Odd's life!" breathed Diana close behind her. "No wonder she wants to get away. He'll kill her."

Rosamunde realized Diana had probably never seen this event before. The fact that the stallion was large, and he and the mare were each controlled by two men probably would give it a strange effect.

"Don't be silly. Sinda's been flirting with him for hours like the worst whore in York."

"I've never seen a whore in operation, and neither have you. But I see what you mean. She's virtually shoving her rump at that stallion. Oh!"

That, Rosamunde knew, was because Sinda had just let loose a stream of urine. Not appealing to humans, but apparently as good as a "Come on, sailor!" to a stallion. Dirk snorted, and moved forward to accept the invitation.

Voice hushed, Diana said, "The way she's holding her

tail out of the way is positively wanton. I wonder," she added thoughtfully, "what the equivalent is with humans."

"Diana!" Rosamunde didn't take her eyes off the horses, but she was blushing, and not over horses. "I thought you had all those books."

"They're dull reading without . . . Well, without." Diana was leaning against Rosamunde's back to see through the small window, her chin resting on Rosamunde's shoulder. "That stallion is quite well mannered, isn't he?"

"Doubtless as well. An unwilling mare can geld a stallion with an angry kick."

"If only men were as well trained, or women as well equipped. By gemini!"

Dirk mounted, nipping at Sinda's neck. The mare squealed, but settled to the business as enthusiastically as he did. Rosamunde heard a sort of choked gurgle from her cousin and grinned. She'd felt exactly the same disbelieving embarrassment the first time she'd seen a stallion's tail pumping merrily in tempo with other parts of him.

The tail stopped, and Dirk's handlers drew him back, off the mare. Sinda was led away while the stallion stood like a statue, as if expecting everyone to applaud his mighty achievement.

"Males," muttered Diana, still sounding slightly strangled. Rosamunde turned, and found that her cousin was bright pink. She feared she was, too, for other reasons. That was the first covering since her night with Brand, and it had stirred heated memories, perhaps enhanced by Diana's body pressed to her back.

She could almost hear him whispering, "More? Please." Hot and throbbing, she wanted to speak the words. To him.

Diana took her arm. "Are you all right?"

"Yes, of course! That went well, didn't it?" she asked breezily. "That's a new stallion, so I wanted to be sure he was well behaved. They are so big that I worry, though Hextall points out that any horse is big and dangerous, so it doesn't matter that much when they're extra big."

She was chattering nonsense, and waited for searching questions.

Diana, however, said, "I have something important to talk to you about, Rosa."

That chilled her heated thoughts. "Trouble?"

"Lord Brand is at Arradale."

It hit like a blow. "I prayed. . . ."

"Prayers don't always work." Diana tugged Rosa out into the open near the paddock. "The real problem is that Sir Digby has invited him here to see the stud."

Rosa slumped back against the wooden rails. "That's sunk me, then."

"Will he recognize you?"

"Of course he will! I might fool him in passing, or even for a brief meeting, but not over any length of time. Oh, why couldn't he go back south, where he belongs?"

"Because he's a man, and men never do the sensible thing." Diana paced, slashing at tufts of tall grass with her riding crop. "You'll have to take to your bed. It's the only thing. Nothing too serious, but enough of an ailment to keep you in bed. Lord Brand will only come over for a few hours, and Digby can show him the stud."

Despair lifted a little. "I suppose that might work. I'll have to get rid of Millie for a while. He'd recognize her in a heartbeat." Underneath coherence, an incoherent part was gabbling, *Here. So close. I could see him. Can I stand it?* "What about Digby, though?" she asked, forcing weak thoughts away. "It will worry him to death if I seem to be ill, especially now. And he mustn't suspect who it might be. Ever."

"I thought you said he didn't mind."

"He doesn't. But he believes it happened at the masquerade. Anonymously. I don't know how he'd feel if he knew the man involved."

Diana put an arm around her shoulders. "He won't find out. We'll manage."

After a moment, Rosamunde couldn't stop the question. "How is he? Brand, I mean."

"Suffering no ill effects."

"Thank God." Then a new fear stirred. "Butterflies! What of the dower house, Diana?"

Diana rolled her eyes. "It's sitting there like a barrel of gunpowder just waiting for a match. There's no reason for him to go there, but if he does, he's bound to recognize it. I tried to get him settled down at the river today, angling, but no, he wanted to walk. At least I directed him in completely the wrong direction."

Brand stood at the edge of an artfully contrived wilderness, staring at the square, stone house. He'd been seeking the familiar for so long that now he doubted his eyes. Of course, he had no idea what his mysterious lady's house looked like from the outside, but the layout of the grounds seemed to match the view from that window.

There was one way to find out.

He followed the path that ran close to the passing road, pausing at a tangle of blackberries. Picking a lingering fruit, he tasted it, then shook his head at his own folly. Ridiculous to think he could recognize a blackberry from the remembered taste of juice on a lady's fingers, or a spicy alcoholic cordial. Ridiculous to think blackberries important at all. They lined every country lane.

Determined to settle this, he cut briskly across the lawn toward the house, seeking the back door. Before rounding the corner, however, he turned back to survey the setting. It did look devilishly the same.

But how? Why? The only young lady in the area was the countess, and he knew she wasn't his mysterious lady. He'd have to feel something in her presence, he was sure.

He knocked sharply at the door. It was opened by a thin young maid who curtsied, but showed no hint of recognition. "Yes, sir?"

"Whose house is this, girl?"

"Why, 'tis the dower house of Arradale, sir. But no one lives here at the moment."

The aroma of cooking and baking seeped out around her. Disregarding courtesy, he pushed past into the large kitchen. "You cook for the faeries?"

She was gaping at him. "I mean none of the gentry

live here, sir! Mr. and Mrs. Yockenthwait are caretakers here."

At that moment, a tall, raw-boned woman stepped into the kitchen, eyes taking in the situation. Did they show momentary alarm? He wasn't sure he was capable of judging such things. Every sense hunted for sounds, smells, objects, anything to confirm that this was the house where he'd stayed for those brief, shattering days.

"Sir?" the woman asked, stepping between him and the maid. "Is there some way we can help you?"

"You must be Mrs. Yockenthwait."

"I am, sir."

And the sort of woman one tangled with at one's peril.

He could think of no approach but the truth. "A few weeks ago, did you take care of a sick man here?"

The woman's face could have been made of stone. "Here, sir?"

"Yes, here." He thought then to look at the maid, but she was wide-eyed and useless.

"No, sir," said Mrs. Yockenthwait.

"My lord," he snapped, willing to use his meaningless title to intimidate. "Lord Brand Malloren."

The woman did twitch at that. Flinch, even. But her only clear response was to curtsy. "My lord."

"So, you have had no guest here in the past weeks."

"No, my lord. If you could tell me what bothers you, perhaps I could help."

He looked around as if the whitewashed walls, the stone sink, or the hanging hams could speak. Despite the woman's convincing denial, instinct told him this was the place. Who was she protecting? The obvious answer was Lady Arradale, but it didn't make sense. She wasn't his lady.

There was one way to be sure. Find the room. He put the woman aside and headed for the door into the rest of the house.

She grabbed his sleeve in an astonishingly strong hold and towed him back. The next he knew, she was between him and the door, a cast-iron frying pan in her hands. "What do you think you're doing, my lord? If you are a lord, which I'm beginning to doubt!" Before he could answer, she added, "Jessie! Run and get Mr. Yockenthwait, and any other men you can find."

The door slammed after the fleeing maid, and Brand winced. Hands raised, he spoke as soothingly as he could, "I apologize for alarming you, Mrs. Yockenthwait. I merely wish to inspect the bedrooms."

"And as caretaker, I should let any stranger who pushes his way into the house free to wander the place as he wills?"

"You may accompany me if you wish."

"And you may go up to the big house and ask my lady's permission!"

"Since I'm a guest there, that won't be too difficult a task!"

And that hit her, he saw. A moment later, however, he realized it could merely be because she feared her mistress's displeasure at upsetting a guest.

It was all moot, for two men stormed through the door. "What's this, then?" one asked, a wiry man a bit shorter than Brand, but probably able to do real damage. The other was a strapping young farmhand with forearms like prize hams.

Brand raised his hands placatingly, having no desire to get into a fistfight over this. "My apologies, mistress, gentlemen. I see that it's unreasonable to expect you to let me to wander freely here to satisfy my curiosity." He bowed to the Amazon. "I will ask for Lady Arradale's permission, mistress. In fact, I will obtain it in writing. Will that suffice?"

To her credit, she did not thaw. "You bring my lady's instruction to me, my lord, and you will have everything she wishes you to have."

It sounded as if she hoped it was poison.

Which was close to what he'd been fed in this house already, if his suspicions were correct.

He looked around one last time, thinking he might recognize a cup or coffeepot. Such things were not kept on open shelves, however, so, keeping an eye on the wary, pugnacious men, he made his escape. When he stepped outside the door, he found the young maid hov-

ering, hand to her mouth. At the sight of him, she
squeaked and moved back a step.

"Jessie, isn't it?" he said with his most charming smile.
"I'm sorry for alarming you."

She just stared at him.

"Are you sure you don't know me from before?"

Wide-eyed, she shook her head with violent conviction.

"And no man stayed here?"

"No, sir!" she squeaked, finding a voice of sorts. "Not
since I came to work here last winter, sir!"

"Jessie!" Mrs. Yockenthwait appeared in the doorway, weapon still in hand. "Get in here and get on with
your work." With a final glare, she slammed the door in
Brand's face.

He looked at it, then walked back to the side of the
house he thought his room had been on. Plague and
tarnation, it had to be. There was the path he'd seen his
lady on with her companion. . . .

Now *there* was a lady who could be the countess. The
one in the pale gown and big hat. Though in truth, he
was beginning to wonder if Lady Arradale could have
been his mysterious lady. How far could he trust his
memory and instincts on this? She was the right height,
build, age. . . .

But he felt nothing for her, not affection, lust, or recognition. He couldn't believe she was his lady. But then,
he couldn't believe his lady had coaxed him into drinking that potion, even sipping from the same cup to
pledge her love!

Then again, there was that letter, the one he carried
everywhere in his pocket. The one written at the Three
Tuns when Lady Richardson had been there.

He froze as a fugitive memory stirred itself. Hadn't
Bey asked about rings, talking of Lady Richardson, who
wore a lot of rings? And the woman had apparently
been ill. Add that to this dower house, and surely the
Countess of Arradale was in it up to her pretty neck.
Either she used the place for the purposes of fornication,
or she lent it to others. Perhaps it was a regular occur-
rence. That would explain the servants' convincing deni-
als. Secrecy was doubtless part of their job.

So, what did that say about his lady? If she wasn't the countess, and instinct told him that, then what? Had all her confusion, her shyness, been acting? Did she play this game a dozen times a year, laughing at the poor dupes who fell in love with her?

He jerked into motion, striding back down the path.

Plague take them all. Doubtless the ladies involved in this little game shared their stories, and the countess was laughing at him behind her pretty fans. She'd be in fits over the story of him bursting into her den of sin and being driven off by her servants.

He pulled out the letter, tearing it into pieces and scattering them as he went. If not for the ball tonight, he'd leave immediately.

First thing in the morning, however, he'd be away, shaking the dust of Arradale from his shoes.

Chapter 19

Diana listened to Jessie's whispered message and felt ready to give up. Brand Malloren had found the dower house! The servants had done their best, but surely he must have recognized it. And after she'd tried so hard to keep him away.

Perhaps she should have stayed to keep an eye on him, but she'd needed to speak to Rosa in person. She was trusting nothing in writing, particularly with Edward Overton in the vicinity.

Edward was claiming to have twisted his knee, limping and bemoaning the fact that he couldn't ride, and couldn't leave Wenscote. A likely tale. Sir Digby had the coach here at Arradale, but Diana had suggested that it be called back to take Edward on his way.

Rosamunde had decided not. "He cuts up my peace, but as long as Digby's not here to be fretted, I don't mind. Trying so hard to get rid of him might look suspicious. And anyway," she'd added with a grim smile, "it's rather pleasant to watch him smirking over 'his' estate, and imagine how put out he's going to be when he discovers he's no longer the heir."

Diana had left Wenscote, thinking that they had matters under control, but she'd returned to find Jessie waiting with this disastrous message.

She sent the girl back to the dower house with praise for the way everyone had handled the problem, then sought the only true peace in the crowded house, her bedroom. She tossed her tricorn on the floor, and flopped back on the bed to think.

She could see no further maneuvers. They were sunk.

So, could she still manage matters to keep danger away from Rosa?

What would Lord Brand do now?

Presumably ask for permission to inspect the dower house. How the devil was she going to get around that?

Once he knew the truth, what would he think? What would he do?

Could she convince him that the house had been used without Arradale's knowledge? She could accuse the servants of setting it up, and reward them handsomely for the slur. That would leave Lord Brand little further forward except that his lover was presumably from this part of Yorkshire.

What if he involved his formidable brother in the mystery? Diana shuddered. The Marquess of Rothgar set on finding out the truth, and presented with such a clear clue, was not something she wished to think about.

She pushed upright, reminding herself that, like Good Queen Bess, though she had "but the body of a weak and feeble woman, she had the heart and stomach of a king." Of the ruler of an earldom at least. The blood of the mighty Ironhand ran in her veins and she would not give up. If the Mallorens knew about the dower house, perhaps she could coax them out of revenge.

Coax the diabolical marquess?

Suppressing a shiver, she slid off the bed and rang for her maid. Coaxing the Mallorens, she decided as she worked her way out of her habit, was probably best done as the weak and feeble woman. They would surely hesitate to hurt a lady. So, she would act with complete innocence, be the young Lady of Arradale that everyone expected.

With her maid's help, she changed into her frilliest, most girlish dress, one embroidered with pink roses and trimmed with cotton lace. As Lucie redressed her hair in a soft style, Diana fretted over whether to tell Rosa about this new development. She decided against it. There was nothing Rosa could do, and in her condition, she shouldn't be worried more than necessary. There was still no means by which the Mallorens could find out who the lady at the dower house had been.

Chilly with vague images of torture—she wouldn't put it past the marquess—Diana added pearls and a touch of pale powder, then ventured out. Perplexingly, however, Lord Brand was keeping to his room, and the marquess was attending to paperwork. After hours of polite conversation with her guests, Diana began to pray for them to emerge, for battle to begin.

By the time she had to change for dinner and the subsequent ball, she felt as if she sat under the sword of Damocles, listening to the string fray in a sequence of audible snaps.

Brand was about to go down to dinner when his brother entered his room, glorious in black satin, wondrously embroidered. The stitchery was in gold thread, the buttons rubies.

"Impressing the locals?" he asked with raised brows.

"A hint of the weapons available."

"Weapons? I wasn't aware we were at war."

"Conflict lurks in astonishing places." Bey surveyed Brand's perfectly adequate blue velvet suit. "Is that the best you can do to uphold the family's glory?"

"I generally try to fit in, not blind."

"And you look at me and think of the new plows you could buy with the cost of my gold thread alone."

Despite his mood, Brand had to laugh. "Sometimes."

"Investments, my dear. Investments." He strolled over and took Brand's chin. "Not a hint of powder on the skin? Not a patch? Faith, child, you look like a country bumpkin."

Though Bey wore no patches, he was prepared as if for court—hair and skin powdered. Heaven forbid that a nobleman look as if he ever went out-of-doors.

"I've endured hair powdering," Brand said. "That will have to suffice." He rose. "Is it time to go down?"

"Time for a discussion." With a gesture, Rothgar dismissed Kenyon.

Brand warily settled back on the bench before the dressing table. With knowledge of the dower house churning inside him, the last thing he wanted was an inquisition.

"Could Lady Arradale be your mistress?" Bey asked.

Brand's heart pounded a warning. "In the future? I suppose she *could*."

Bey looked at him. "Could she have been the lady who brought you to grief?"

Having stolen a moment to think, Brand decided to give a cautious answer. "It's possible. She's the right height and build. But highly unlikely, wouldn't you say?"

"Voice?"

"Similar. But so are many ladies' voices." He was going to have to lie. "We didn't talk much."

Bey was watching him far too closely. "So I am to take it that you feel no sense of familiarity, no recognition, when you are with the countess."

"None." He could say that with confidence, and only realized a moment later that it had been unwise to change tone. Plague take it. He was in no condition for a duel of wits with his brother. "Why would you even think it?" he asked. "Would such a haughty lady risk her reputation in a clandestine affair?"

"You find her haughty?"

"In your eyes, she's doubtless a quivering mass of insecurity."

Bey's lips twitched. "Hardly that. She has, however, chosen a difficult path. Since she wishes to rule her earldom, she has a natural disinclination to marry. Unlike an earl, however, obvious sexual conveniences are denied her. To take lovers and conceal her identity might appeal."

"Drugging them to be sure of it?" One of Brand's greatest torments was that his lady might not have rescued him, but arranged his drugging in the first place. Before the dower house he'd not believed it, but now . . . ?

"She has the will for it," Bey said. "And she wears many rings."

Ah. So Bey had noticed that, too. Of course. Suddenly protective, Brand said, "So do many ladies."

"But few can afford such excess of brilliance."

"I've noticed that most of Lady Arradale's are not of great value."

"Chosen for their glitter. A strange quirk. However,

in Thirsk, Lady Richardson wore one magnificent ruby. Did your lady drink any of the potion?"

Brand considered for a heartbeat and then told the truth. "Yes."

"Lady Richardson was unwell. It could have been the same cause."

"We are agreed that Lady Richardson could have been my persecutor, but I never set eyes on her. You did. Could she have been Lady Arradale?"

"She was certainly much younger than she appeared. So yes, she could have been. I doubt it, however."

"Why?"

"I don't think she could steal your heart."

"My heart is unaffected," Brand snapped.

"As you will."

"So, Lady Richardson is not Lady Arradale. We are no further forward." Aware of a ridiculous relief, Brand stood, pulling his waistcoat into line. Besotted fool though he was, angry though he was, he didn't want his lady at Bey's untender mercies. "Why are you tormenting this?" he demanded. "I asked you to put it aside. It was unpleasant, and I wish the harpy in hell, but I want nothing more to do with her. I've decided to leave here tomorrow. This sort of gathering stifles me, and there's plenty of work to do."

Bey rose, too, unperturbed. "I thought you planned a visit to Sir Digby's estate."

"I might still do that." Brand adjusted his cravat, aware that he was fiddling, feeling like a fish trying to wriggle off a hook. "Judging from the man, it might be an unpretentious kind of place."

"Are you calling Arradale pretentious? What must you think of Rothgar Abbey?"

Brand gave his brother a rude gesture. After a moment, they shared a smile. Bout over.

"Leave if you will," Bey said. "But it will suit me to have you visit Wenscote, it being in danger of Cotterization. Report anything unusual you find there." He led the way to the door.

To uphold the family dignity, Brand slipped on one

sapphire ring in addition to his signet. "And you'll drop your speculations about my affairs?"

"Not if they amuse me. And I must confess, the countess amuses me."

"As a trout amuses the angler."

Bey smiled as he opened the door. "Perhaps. But since you wish it, I will keep anything I discover to myself."

Two other guests were passing in the corridor, so Brand stifled his protest. Bey was right. He didn't want to know.

If Lady Arradale was his lady, however, did he want Bey on her trail? But when she came forward to greet them, almost rivaling Bey in magnificence, nothing stirred. Not memory, desire, or hate.

It could not be she. His lady was still safe.

"My lord!" she declared giving Bey's magnificence a rather amused survey. "You light up this benighted part of Yorkshire."

Bey gave her a full court bow. "My Lady Arradale, no place could be benighted when illuminated by your brilliance."

Certainly her ruby-red figured silk, ruched, and ribboned was grand enough for court. They made a startling study in red, black, and gold.

She flipped open her gilded fan. "Then perhaps together we are in danger of dazzling the company into blindness, my lord."

"Excellent. As Oedipus observed, 'Blind, they will enjoy the music even more.' Will we dance the first minuet, my lady? Such a wonderful opportunity for dalliance."

She eyed him over her fan. "What point to a ball, my lord, if one does not flirt a little?"

With one finger, Bey pushed the shielding fan down. "Perhaps I should warn you, Lady Arradale, that I never do things 'a little.' "

The lady's eyes widened. Perhaps she realized at last that though she was the one dressed in red, she was playing with fire. Brand might feel sorry for her if he didn't think her a jade, if he didn't know she had a part

in his undoing. On her right hand, amidst a constellation
of glitter, shone the deep luster of a large, fine ruby.

Brand left for safer quarters, a little sorry for the
countess, despite everything. His brother was suspicious,
and was going to test those suspicions in a crucible of
seductive play. She doubtless deserved every minute of
it.

Rosamunde slipped into Arradale House, guiltily
aware of her folly. She'd tried to tell herself she was
coming here to check on Digby, but it would be an outright lie. She was here, against all sense, for a last
glimpse of Brand.

Easily avoiding the servants, who were all busy with
the ball, she found her way to the small neglected gallery
that faced the larger one holding the orchestra. It had
been hers and Diana's favorite childhood spot for spying
on the adult gatherings.

Being larger now, and encumbered by the wide skirts
of her habit, it took some effort to squeeze herself into
the dusty space concealed by a curtain. Once settled, she
put her eye to one of two carefully cut holes and the
glittering assembly burst into view—brightly colored
silks, gold, and jewels, shimmering under an extravagance of candle chandeliers.

For a moment, she wished she were down there in the
magic. But then, perhaps not. She was not part of that
world, and up here, she felt like one of the fleshy gods
and goddesses watching from the ballroom's painted
ceiling. Watching human folly. She saw Lord Fencott
pinch Mrs. Masham, and Mrs. Masham not object. Saw
the way Lady Coverdale was glaring at her old enemy
Mrs. Pyke-Herries.

Where was Brand? Would she witness him flirting
with some beauty? Distressingly, in the mass of pale-
powdered heads, she couldn't pick him out. Surely she
should know him on the instant!

Then her eye caught a tall man entering, startling in
dark, magnificent silk, with gold and embroidery like fire
sparks in the night. The marquess. And there, at his
side, Brand.

She smiled with joy and relief. She would have known him, and she loved the ordinariness of him still. His clothing was suitably fine, but not extravagant, and he wore it casually, without ostentation. He was already smiling at an acquaintance, and moving to talk with some of the men.

Rosamunde glanced back at the marquess. He was talking to Diana, and from her godlike view, they made a startling pair, he in black scattered with gold and rubies, she in ruby red, frothed with gold and black. Rosamunde knew that tilt of her cousin's chin, as well, and the way she was wielding her black-and-gold fan. Crossed swords, though in the most charming, social manner.

Oh, Dinah. Don't. Don't challenge the marquess. Then she had a suspicion. Was Diana drawing enemy fire? After all, the dower house was a connection to Arradale, not clearly to Rosamunde. Could she allow this? She had to, for Digby and Wenscote. After all, the Mallorens couldn't prove anything, and would never seek to destroy the Countess of Arradale.

She let her attention shift back to Brand, following him with her eyes as he moved around the room, clearly already liked and welcomed. Of course, he was. He was thoroughly likable, and showed courteous interest in all. He even seemed to be able to coax a few words from pretty, shy Miss Mifflyn.

The orchestra struck the note for the opening minuet and the company shifted, moving toward the walls and leaving the center area free for the dance. As the lady of highest rank, Diana would begin the ball with the partner of her choice. It was inevitable, Rosamunde supposed, that she choose the marquess, if only from rank.

Of course, completely trained for their roles, they both danced perfectly, but from her elevated view, it seemed as dangerous as a sword fight. The locked gazes, the stately steps and constant contact of the hands, seemed like a challenge in the making. It was a relief when Lady Fencott stepped in, and then the other ladies in order of rank, each with her partner.

It was a shock, however, to see Brand partnering Miss

Mifflyn. Rosamunde immediately controlled her mind. Was he to attend a ball and not dance?

She knew it was worse than that, however. She didn't want him to dance with young women. She hated the way he was making Celia Mifflyn smile and even talk. She was known to be afflicted by almost paralyzing shyness with strangers. Though Rosamunde was back with her husband and building a life that did not include Brand, she did not want him to so much as smile at another woman.

Enough of that. She fixed her eyes on him and wished that he enjoy other women. More than that. She prayed that he soon would find the perfect life companion and settle to happy marriage. Perhaps even with Celia Mifflyn. She was a good-hearted young woman, honorable, kind, and not stupid. Just shy, and if anyone could coax a shy bud into flower, it was Brand Malloren.

Inescapably, her thoughts leaped back to their day and their night. She had been shy, and she'd blossomed with him. Celia would have all that and more. She would laugh with him in the day, and flower in the secret times of the night.

Rosamunde jerked back so the magical world became just a glitter of light in a musty curtain. So be it. The most loving thing she could do for Brand Malloren now was to set him free.

After an hour, Brand would gladly have escaped from the ball, but he knew his duty. The attendance of a marquess raised this event to one in a lifetime, and as the said marquess's brother, he carried a little of the glory. Dances with him would be treasured memories, and so he dutifully danced every one, each with a different lady. Whenever possible, he danced with the shy and the wallflowers.

He saw Bey, through necessity, working his way down the ladies by rank, charming each one, but with the edged charm of the slightly perilous. How many Yorkshire hearts would flutter in memory of the way he kissed their hand, giving solid, faithful wives material for wicked longings.

He suppressed a grin. It was a performance, but one played so often over years that it must be second nature by now. He was sure his brother was well aware of his effect and in control of it. In his own dangerous way, Bey was quite kind.

It was probably as well that duties meant that he couldn't apply his perilous charms to the countess, herself moving courteously through the company. Whatever had happened in the Arradale dower house, it was past, dead. There should be no more suffering over it.

That was reason speaking. He looked again at the smiling countess. She knew. *She knew.* The temptation to force the knowledge out of her burned in his gut like acid. She knew. Her very silence about his visit to the dower house was incriminating.

And, against sense, he needed to know. As he'd done his duty this night, he'd searched the room for his mysterious lady. She wasn't here. Not, therefore, part of the local gentry. Who?

Bey came up beside him. "You frown?"

"It's nothing."

"I thought you weren't interested in pursuing it?"

There was no point in denying it. "Very well, it irritates like a flea bite. I would like to know, just to ease the itch."

"You are sure it is not Lady Arradale?"

"Certain."

"You'd know her even blind?"

Brand stared at his brother. "What's that supposed to mean?" But Brand remembered saying he'd know her in the dark, and by her kiss. . . .

"Samson, blinded by love," said Bey, "ignoring his beloved's obvious deceits. I recommend that you reread your Bible."

"I'll just avoid razors."

"And sleeping drafts." With that neat hit, Bey moved away to speak to the dowager countess, who smiled warmly upon him.

Puzzled by his brother's comments, Brand went to Arradale library to consult a Bible. "Vexed unto death," certainly described his state. Samson, however, had been blinded by the Philistines, not by love of Delilah.

Closing the book, he saw what Bey meant. Delilah was rather crude in her deceits, and any man not blind should have seen through them. So, it was love that had made Samson willfully blind long before his eyes had been put out.

At the end, he'd noted, it didn't say that Delilah was among the Philistines killed when Samson tore down the pillars in Gaza.

Love. If he'd known she was there, Brand suspected Samson could never have done it.

Chapter 20

Rosamunde settled her horse into the Wenscote stables, and slipped into the silent house, weary, but strangely at peace. It was over—

A figure emerged from the gloom, making her gasp. Stark moonlight showed her Edward Overton's stern face. "You frightened me!"

"Where have you been, Aunt? Out with a lover?"

"For a man of strict religious beliefs, Edward, you have a low mind. I've been down to the stud stables. One of the mares was in some distress." It was true, though the matter had been a simple one, taking up very little time, and the stud was too close to ride to. With luck, Edward would not see that.

"It is not seemly for a woman to be engaged in such matters, Aunt, or for her to be out of the house alone at night."

"It is not seemly, in your eyes, for a woman to show her hair, or her arms, or her chest. It would seem you New Commonwealthers are very easily tempted."

His lips tightened. "All men are easily tempted."

"Then perhaps *men* shouldn't be allowed out of the house at night," she pointed out, trying to sidestep him.

He blocked her way. "Before heaven, Aunt, you have an unseemly tongue and need to be taught better!"

"With a whip?" She looked him straight in the eye. "Edward, I despise you, your beliefs and sanctimonious—"

He slapped her.

For a frozen moment, silence reigned, Rosamunde with her hand to her stinging cheek. Then: *"Out!"* she cried, pointing at the door. "Out!"

"You have no right—"

"Shall I rouse the servants and have them throw you out?"

"You cannot—"

"Out," she repeated, snatching up the poker and advancing on him, burning with a rage she'd never have thought was in her. "Out, out, out!"

He backed. "You can't throw me out. I'm the heir—"

"You're *nothing* until Digby dies, and with God's will, you'll be dead by then yourself, choked on your own sanctimonious bile!"

"He'll be dead within the year. And then we'll see!"

"When he's dead, you can return here, Edward, but not a moment before."

He was up against the door and fumbling for the knob. "Uncle Digby will never permit that."

"He will when I tell him you hit me." She jabbed the poker at him. "Out. Out. Out."

He staggered back through the open door. "It's dark. Where do you expect me to go?"

"To hell for all I care!" Rosamunde slammed the door in his gaping face, turned the key, and added the scarce-used bar for good measure. Then she turned and sagged against the oak. My, but that had felt good. She should lose her temper more often!

Had it been dangerous, though?

No, she decided, straightening and rubbing her stinging cheek. Having an excuse to bar him from Wenscote would save Digby a lot of strife. And now that she was with child—she was sure she was with child—it would soon become irrelevant.

She hugged herself and did a little dance around the silent hall. She'd banished their grim grayness in every way, and now everything was perfect.

The Arradale footman answered the banging on the doors with some surprise. The night was well advanced and no more guests were expected. At the sight of the plainly dressed man in the steeple hat, he started to close the door again.

The man pushed through. "I am Edward Overton. I must speak to my uncle, Sir Digby, on a most urgent matter!"

Well, that put a different face on it, even if it was a plaguey Cotterite. James reluctantly led Mr. Overton to a small reception room. "I will see if Sir Digby can be found, sir."

"Lose many guests here, do you?"

My, my. James stalked off, suppressing a smirk. Those saintly New Commonwealthers weren't supposed to lose their tempers. Good for whoever upset this one! But as James trotted up the stairs to find Sir Digby, he felt a little concern. Perhaps it was worry, not anger. Perhaps there was trouble at Wenscote. The only family there was Lady Overton, and no one would want to wish further trouble on the poor lady.

He found Sir Digby in the card room, half in his cups, and laughing with a bunch of the old cronies, and whispered his message.

"On my life. What's to do?" the man asked of no one in particular as he heaved himself up. He made his way ponderously toward the door, clearly as concerned as James, and clearly drunk. James hovered all the way down the stairs, praying he could catch the portly gentleman if he slipped.

Everyone knew that Sir Digby stood between Wensleydale and the New Commonwealth. Long life to the man.

Once he'd seen Sir Digby safe into the reception room, he blew out a relieved breath and shut the door.

"Is something amiss?"

James turned to see the countess coming down the stairs, and stood a little straighter. Truth was, he had some spicy daydreams about the pretty countess in her lovely silks, but he rarely had a chance to talk to her in person. "I don't know, milady. Mr. Overton has ridden over from Wenscote with some urgent message for Sir Digby."

His lady's brows came together in a frown, and then she marched over, high heels clicking on the tile floor.

He hastily swung open the door for her, and she passed through into the room. Then, alas, he had to close it.

"Lady Arradale!" Edward Overton protested. "This is a private matter."

Diana observed him, trying to conceal her dislike. "My apologies if I intrude, Mr. Overton, but if anything has happened to my dear cousin . . . Sir Digby? Has there been an accident?"

Sir Digby was sitting in a chair, hands on his spread knees, looking flummoxed. "An accident? Stap me vitals, but I don't know! Here's my nevvy telling me that Rosie has thrown him from the house in a fit of mad spite."

Diana turned to the younger man. "Upon my soul, what a strange affair. And you did nothing to offend, Mr. Overton?"

The man drew himself up. "I have no doubt she took offense. I discovered her sneaking into the house after dark and advised her on wiser behavior."

"Somewhat impertinent, wouldn't you say?"

"I am a man, she is a woman. What is more, I am now a speaker in the New Commonwealth. I preached in Lancashire to a most gratifying response. It is my duty to advise sinners."

"Only those in your flock, I think."

"For the New Commonwealth, all mankind is our flock."

Diana raised her brows. "Are you saying you would attempt to advise *me,* Mr. Overton?"

He looked down his nose at her. "It would be my duty, though I would harbor little hope of success."

"Lud, sir, but you will soon have preached your way out of another bed for the night."

"I have no intention of staying here," he said, as if invited to lie in a pigsty. "I expect my uncle to return with me to Wenscote and discipline his wife."

"And I refuse to permit such a thing. Sir Digby should not exert himself in that way."

"Uncle?" Edward Overton turned from her to demand compliance from Sir Digby.

The older man shook his head. "Stap me, but it's a pickle. To tell the truth, though, nevvy, I don't fancy a trip back up to Wenscote just now. I was just about to seek my bed."

"You would feel more up to such things, Uncle, if you forswore drink."

Diana hoped Sir Digby would put down such impudence, but he pulled a shamed face. "Aye, and you're right about that, Edward. Rosie would be cross, too, to see how much I've ate and drank. It's time I mended my ways. Especially—"

"Especially when drink is making you feel unwell, Sir Digby," Diana hastily interrupted. This was no time to tell Edward Overton about the pregnancy.

"Not so much the drink as the puddings, me dear," he said, easing undone the buttons of his stretched waistcoat. "I'm resolved to make a change."

"I am glad of it, Uncle," Edward put in.

"But since Rosie is all right"—Sir Digby heaved himself out of the chair—"I'm not about to jostle and bounce my burning stomach through the dark to Wenscote. I'll go in the morning to sort this all out. Anyway, Lord Brand Malloren's coming up with me to look over Rosie's stud. I can't go without him."

"And you must stay the night, too, Mr. Overton," Diana said, cutting off further protest. "We can find you a very simple room that will not offend your principles. It is gone midnight and doubtless my cousin is in her bed by now."

"Very well," he said stiffly. "Since my uncle is unwell. . . ."

"How considerate you are." She led the way to the door. "And how fortunate that your knee has healed."

He colored slightly. "In truth, it still pains me, but I had no choice."

"How very brave. Tomorrow you can return to Wenscote in the coach, which will be a relief to you."

Diana arranged for his room—by requiring some upper servants to share another one—and for the hovering footman to be sure Sir Digby made it safely to his bed.

Then she worried. What on earth had so upset Rosa? Could it have any connection to the Mallorens? How?

And why had she been sneaking back into the house at night? With sudden certainty, she knew Rosa had been here, and a quick message to the stables confirmed it.

Oh, Rosa. The sooner Brand Malloren was away from here the better, and Diana wished desperately she could see a way to prevent the visit to Wenscote tomorrow. It fretted her that he hadn't asked about the dower house, but she let herself believe that he wasn't sure. If so, and if Rosa could stay out of sight, they still might escape with their skins.

Brand finally escaped the ball when the local guests piled into lamplit carriages to travel home under the full moon. Once in his room, however, he found he was in no mood to sleep. Fighting a tendency to look at the moon and pine, he settled to a dull, informational book, cursing himself whenever his mind slipped to another book, and a certain mysterious lady.

He would like to read the rest of *Planned Breeding Programs,* but he hadn't dared buy himself a copy yet. It carried too many dangerous associations.

Even in bed, he lay wakeful. Perhaps he should dress, creep across the park, and break into the dower house. Why, though? He knew the room was there, and what more could it tell him? Could it tell him who his lady was? Or that she had been true and loving? He laughed at his own folly. Despite everything, he was a blind prisoner in Gaza, still hoping to learn that his Delilah hadn't betrayed him, even as he remembered the poisoned loving cup she had set to his lips.

With dawn, he gave up any attempt at sleep and wandered the misty grounds, listening to the first fervent birdsong, but keeping well away from the beckoning dower house. He hoped he looked normal at breakfast and when he took his leave of his hostess and his brother. Doubtless not in the latter case. Bey was devilish about reading people.

All he said, however, was, "Don't forget to keep your eyes open at Wenscote."

"Why? It's a straightforward case. The heir is a Cotterite and he'll take over the property when Sir Digby dies."

Bey drew him down the front steps toward the waiting coach, carefully out of earshot. "He became the heir upon the death of another nephew, William Overton."

"Not unusual, surely?"

"What if William Overton was murdered?"

Brand stared. "It's not like you to chase wild theories, Bey. If the death was suspicious, we'd surely have heard of it."

"William Overton was a man very like Sir Digby, and not a great deal younger. He ate and drank 'merrily' as people put it, and suffered the consequences. No one was greatly surprised when he keeled over one day after a large meal."

"But you suspect foul play?"

"Exactly the same thing happened last winter to a Mr. Josiah Crayke, heir to an estate over near Northallerton."

"Northallerton?" Brand echoed, his mind starting to stir.

"There *are* estates near there," Bey said sharply, clearly irritated by Brand's abstraction.

"Yes, of course. Who owns it now?"

"One Samuel Barlow, a recent convert to the heavenly rewards promised by the New Commonwealth. Mr. Crayke left two daughters, so Squire Barlow has settled money on them and the widow, but the estate has been given to the Cotterites. He's taken to the life himself, even sharing his house with a number of unmarried farm laborers."

"And Crayke died of an apoplexy?"

"Or something of the sort."

Brand's attention was caught, by that and other matters. "It could be coincidence."

"I am always suspicious of coincidence. It's remarkably clever. So many men are feeble through food and drink. If Sir Digby Overton keeled over one day after a hearty dinner—a respectable time after his nephew's demise of course—would anyone be surprised? Really,"

Bey added with asperity, "both he or his senior nephew should have attended to the matter of the succession."

"That's rich, coming from you." Then Brand wished he could bite the words back.

"I have brothers," Bey said, unmoved. "Some of whom seem naturally enthusiastic about marriage and procreation. You see now, I hope, why I want you to pay attention to more than cart horses at Wenscote."

"Yes, of course. It would be a shame for Sir Digby to come to an untimely end."

"It would be a shame not to catch them in the act. You will apparently be traveling with the heir, who has spent the night here."

After little sleep, Brand wasn't fit for mental gymnastics, and he stared at his brother. "I'd hardly think he was one for balls."

"Apparently Lady Overton threw him out of Wenscote, so he came running to his uncle."

"Lord, Bey, how do you always know everything?"

"If I knew everything, my life would be a great deal easier. Find out what caused Lady Overton to react that way."

"Yes, sir!"

"Brand," said his brother with obvious forbearance, "you say you want to know nothing more about your lady, yet she is sitting in your mind like a canker. This is dangerous."

Brand closed his eyes for a moment, knowing he should tell his brother about the dower house. He couldn't. He didn't know what Bey might do. "Did you find out anything from the countess during the ball?"

"If she enjoys dalliance, she does not indulge at public functions."

"You tested her?"

"I did my best, within polite boundaries, to invite myself to her bed."

" 'Struth. Would you have gone?"

"Noblesse oblige. She's quite skilled at that game, but seemed remarkably untempted. I guessed as much. Unless my instincts are seriously dulled, she is a virgin, though not a naive one."

"So, not my lady. I didn't think so. Perhaps she knows, but short of torture, there is no way to make her give up the knowledge."

"I doubtless have the thumbscrews in my baggage somewhere. . . ."

Brand laughed, but his mind was swirling over other things. "The inn I remember last," he said, "the place where I was probably drugged, was near Northallerton. And I've just realized why the name Barlow sounds familiar. Is the estate called Rawston Glebe?"

"Yes."

"It lies next to one I was looking over for us. I was asking questions about Rawston Glebe, since neighbors are often as important as the estate itself. Probably asking questions about the New Commonwealth. So if they murdered Mr. Crayke . . ."

"Especially if they knew who you were. Did they?"

Brand shrugged. "I travel incognito, but I don't make a performance of hiding my name."

"And I have no doubt word had already traveled north that the King is fretted about the New Commonwealth and had appointed me his investigator. Your sufferings could well be laid at my door."

"At the Cotterites' door, you mean. By gad, but I'll be glad if you bring them down. And I thought George Cotter not a bad sort of man." He glanced over. "Here comes Sir Digby and his nephew. I must go."

Rothgar put his hand briefly on Brand's arm. "Take care."

"You think they might attack again? I'm not after them."

"But they don't know that. Be careful what you eat and drink."

"I've learned that lesson."

Brand walked over to the waiting coach, mocking himself for the joyous warmth that stirred inside. If he'd been drugged by the New Commonwealth, then at least his lady hadn't abducted him for her pleasure. She really had rescued him.

Some of it had been honest, after all.

Most of it, in fact. She'd claimed all along to simply be taking payment for her help.

Edward Overton was already in the coach, all gray disapproval, but Sir Digby was just climbing in. He settled with a blown-out breath. "Odd's death, I think I truly will reform my ways. My head's pounding and all I could put in my stomach this morning was a bit of toast. I enjoy a good breakfast."

Brand had intended to ride, but that would leave poor Sir Digby alone with the chilly-looking Cotterite. He ordered his horse tied to the coach, and climbed in, taking the backward seat without protest. He wondered briefly whether Sir Digby could have been fed something noxious last night, but accepted that it was simply overindulgence.

"Moderation does have its blessings," he said to support Sir Digby's good intentions.

"Are we to understand," asked Edward Overton, "that a Malloren lives moderately?"

"Yes, Mr. Overton. No one has ever accused me of excess."

"A virgin, are you?"

"Hey, nevvy!" Sir Digby intervened. "That's no way to talk!"

"No," said Brand, almost amused, "I'm not a virgin. Do you truly think *any* sex excessive?"

"Outside procreation within marriage, yes."

"Then I assume you are a virgin."

A little color flared in the pale face. "I was a sinner once. . . ."

"Oh, shut up, Edward," said Sir Digby with a groan. "My head's pounding and you're being damned impolite to Lord Brand. Come to that, you should be sitting with your back to the horses, humble servant that you are."

Edward Overton pursed his lips and turned to watch the passing scenery. Brand shared a slight smile with Sir Digby. He did like the older man.

Though the rough road twisted up the dale, it took less than an hour to reach the small village by the river, and the gray stone house that dominated it. The coach turned between the open gates that broke a high stone wall.

"Very defensible," Brand remarked.

"Aye. Well, the place is three hundred years old," Sir Digby said, "and there's been times when good walls were welcome."

The coach drew up between the house and a charming garden. Beyond, screened somewhat by trees, Brand saw stables, but not of a size for a stud.

"Rosie's stables are outside the walls," Sir Digby said as the steps were let down and a manservant hovered to assist him to alight. "I wonder where she is? I sent word I was bringing a guest."

Brand wondered if the lady regretted her ejection of Mr. Overton—though he was sure it was justified. He hoped he wasn't going to be witness to embarrassing family arguments.

Climbing down after Sir Digby, he breathed in the perfumes of a precious garden. He couldn't resist wandering closer to the waving banks of blossom. Someone had lavished care on this over many years. It might just be an excellent gardener, but he suspected Lady Overton had played a part. The garden spoke of a very personal kind of love, and conveyed a powerful sense of sanctuary.

When Sir Digby called, he went into the cool house. "I was admiring the garden. It's as lovely as I've ever seen."

Sir Digby beamed. "My wife's work, of course. She's a dab hand with plants. It was just a garden before she came here. Now it's something more."

Brand caught a pinched look on Edward Overton's face. "You don't approve of gardens?"

"We do not believe in wasting good land and labor on useless plants. Not that we ban flowers altogether," the man conceded. "There are many that have practical purposes."

Talking to Edward Overton would never lead anywhere pleasant. Brand was surprised Lady Overton hadn't ejected him years ago. Sir Digby, swarmed by happy dogs, had marched to the bottom of the dark oak stairs and was yelling, "Rosie! We've guests, love!"

A middle-aged woman in apron and cap came bustling out of the back of the house. For a moment Brand thought she was Lady Overton, for she looked the type, but she curtsied and said, "I'm sorry, Sir Digby, but Lady Overton's not well. Ate something that didn't agree with her."

Brand twitched to alertness. Surely the New Commonwealth wouldn't have need to poison the wife.

"She was well enough last night to venture out of doors," said Edward Overton frostily.

"Happen what did it, sir," the housekeeper said. " 'Course, she wasn't feeling quite the thing before or she'd have gone to Arradale, wouldn't she? Can I serve you something, Sir Digby?"

Sir Digby blew out his breath and turned to Brand. "I'm sorry about this, my lord. I'll be up and see her in a moment. Perhaps she'll feel better later. But of course, there's nothing to stop you checking out the stables. Her stable man can tell you anything you want to know."

"Then I'd be glad to do that. And I won't stay, since your lady is unwell."

"No, no! None of that. It's a long way from here to anywhere you'd want to be unless you go back to Arradale, and you didn't seem in the mood for more of that sort of nonsense. You'll stay here the night, my lord, just as we arranged. Now, do you want any refreshment, or should I send for Hextall?"

Brand declined refreshment and was soon strolling toward the stables with a quite young man who clearly knew his business and thought very well of his mistress. All in all, Brand was content to be on his way to interesting matters and out of the house while the family sorted out its problems.

Wenscote kept country hours, so he was summoned back for a meal in the late afternoon. He'd spent an enjoyable time, but was hungry. Once he'd found his room and washed, he returned to the main floor without any sight of Sir Digby's wife. It was a shame, because he'd enjoy her opinions. The stud was run on the latest principles by well-chosen servants who thought the world of her.

"She's sulking," Sir Digby muttered with a frustrated scowl, drawing him into a paneled parlor. "Says she won't come down while Edward's here. Says he hit her. He says she's making it up. What's a man to do?"

"Trust his wife?"

"All the time?" Sir Digby asked dubiously. "They're strange creatures, women."

"Delightfully so. But if a man marries, he must trust. What sort of life will he live otherwise?"

Sir Digby looked flummoxed. "You're something of a philosopher, my lord. But unmarried, I would point out."

Brand gave him that telling point. And anyway, he would have married his mysterious lady, and that clearly would have been folly.

"If only William hadn't died," the older man said. "I tell you, my lord, there's been no peace since!"

"Can the estate not be left elsewhere?"

"Nay, it goes to the children, males first, then females. Then to the collaterals in the same manner. It's been that way for generations and no trouble before."

"I see. But even so, you don't need to see or speak to your nephew. It's clear he cuts up your peace."

"Aye, aye." Sir Digby stumped over to a brimming punch bowl and scooped large amounts into two glasses, passing one to Brand. What had happened to abstemious living?

"I'm a family man at heart, my lord," Sir Digby said after a deep drink. "Me and William, we were like father and son. I keep hoping . . ."

"I doubt Mr. Edward Overton will change."

"Aye." He sighed. "I look back now and think how it might have been if I'd married sooner and had children. But there was William such a likely lad, and a woman about the place is a lot of bother. . . ."

"I think we all look back and think of might-have-beens."

Sir Digby glanced over furtively. Brand hoped he wasn't about to be confided in.

"Stone," Sir Digby said.

He was.

"Stone?"

"The stone. Bladder. Gave me terrible grief all my life. Never thought to marry with that till Rosie. Got cut a few years back for her sake, and it's been a mighty relief to me. But sometimes the operation . . . Well, you know. . . . I . . . er, wanted you to know, my lord, that I wasn't lazy about my duties."

"I never entertained the thought."

"And William married a poor filly," Sir Digby continued, filling his glass again. "Five miscarriages and two stillborn. Terrible hard on a man, that sort of thing. When she died, I didn't press him to wed again. I still had hopes that Edward would get over this silliness." He drained his glass and looked around. "For that matter, where the devil is he? Come on. Sit down, my lord. We'll start without him. Dinner!" he bellowed, that clearly being notice to serve in this house, for the housekeeper hurried in with a tureen of soup.

Brand took his place, hoping food would end the confidences.

"It's Wenscote I fret for," Sir Digby said, tucking his serviette into his stock. "When any of this matters, I'll be past caring, and Rosie's provided for. But it's bitter to think of Wenscote passing into the hands of those carping gray folk."

Brand took soup from a lushly endowed maid who looked likely to fall out of her bodice at any moment. "They're good farmers."

"Aye, so I gather. But a cold sort of Christian. Christ fed the five thousand," Sir Digby said, breaking his bread and dropping pieces in the soup, "but those lot look at good food as if it's the devil's work. He went to a wedding feast, didn't He, and changed water into wine? But they don't celebrate their weddings and don't drink wine. How's that following the Bible, I ask you?"

Brand attended to the soup, for there was nothing to say.

"And they'll plow up Rosie's garden. . . . Ah, there you are, Edward. You're late!"

Edward Overton slipped into his chair. "My apologies, Uncle. I was reading my Bible."

"With blinkers on. Eat your soup, if it isn't too wicked for you."

Brand was startled to see Overton actually scrutinize the soup as if judging it, but at least he did take some. As it turned out, that was all he ate, though he took two bowls and a piece of bread, consuming them slowly as the other courses came and went. He drank small beer diluted with water.

Sir Digby's color deepened, and Brand suspected it was more at the sight of his nephew's meal than at the effects of his own, though he was eating far too much. Brand was heartily wishing that he hadn't accepted this invitation.

"So, Uncle," Overton said, as he dabbed his lips and carefully folded his serviette, "I trust Aunt Rosamunde is repentant."

"Let be, Edward."

" 'Suffer not a woman to usurp authority over a man!' " Overton quoted. "You risk your place in heaven, Uncle, if you let a woman rule your house. I will continue to visit here."

Sir Digby scraped the last trace of pie off his plate. "Aye, well, as for that, perhaps it would be best if you didn't come around so often for the next little while. It's not as if you take interest in the management of the estate."

"It will be managed according the principles of the New Commonwealth."

Sir Digby glared at him. "There's no *purpose* to your coming here other than to upset my Rosie."

"Of course it is not my purpose—"

"But it's what you do! Give over. I don't know why you come. We don't please you. The food don't please you. The maids offend you. Go do your preaching!"

Edward Overton stood abruptly. "That young woman will be the death of you, Uncle!" Brand was startled by the word "young." "And she's clearly no better than she should be."

Sir Digby pushed to his feet, a deep red by now. "Don't you dare imply—"

"I *caught* her, I tell you! Sneaking into the house, stinking of sin. And where was she when I visited a few weeks back? Gallivanting in Harrogate, was it not?"

"There's no harm in that! As it was, she didn't like it—"

"So she says."

"She came back early, I tell you!"

"Then where was she when George Cotter was here?"

"Spending a few days with her cousin, that's all, and me well aware of it! I'll not have you casting stones at Rosie, Edward. She's the best, truest wife a man could have."

"Sometimes, Uncle, I think you are willfully blind."

Brand sank back in his seat and imagined a comfortable hole opening up, one he could slip into and pull a lid down on top of while the fire blasted overhead.

"With her cousin, indeed!" Edward Overton ranted on. "As if the sinful countess was any sort of companion for a decent woman."

Brand took more interest.

"Sinful?" Sir Digby echoed. "You can't go saying things like that!"

"I speak the truth! Her very nature sins. She does not accept the true place of woman. She apes the man. She wears breeches under her skirts and rides astride."

"Been looking under her skirts, nevvy?"

Edward Overton braced his hands on the table and leaned toward his uncle. "God knows what she does, she and your wife, at that dower house. And I mean that literally, Uncle." He pushed straight and raised his right hand. "God knows, and He will consign them to hell's flames for it!"

As the outraged Cotterite stormed out of the room, Sir Digby filled his wineglass again and knocked it back in one gulp.

Brand sat stunned.

Lady Arradale and Lady Overton. The dower house. They'd been there a few weeks back when George Cotter was in the area. A well-run stud. It was all he could do to sit in his seat, not to race up to find the room where Rosie Overton skulked.

He swallowed and hoped he could speak calmly. "I gather your wife is young, Sir Digby."

The man looked a bit awkward about it. "Aye, she's quite a bit younger than I am."

"Still of childbearing age?"

"Oh, aye. She's not yet twenty-five, my Rosie."

"Then perhaps God will be kind and send you an alternative to Edward Overton."

And tears glimmered in the corners of Sir Digby's blood-shot, half-drunk eyes. "We have hopes, Lord Brand," he whispered, clearly forgetting that he'd already confided his impotency. He touched the side of his nose. "Not saying anything yet. But hopes."

As he'd suspected. Collusion between husband and wife. And doubtless the whole of Wensleydale was in on it. Brand stood. "If you'll excuse me, sir."

Sir Digby nodded, doubtless assuming Brand was finding the necessary. Without subterfuge, Brand climbed the stairs and found the most likely door. He opened it, went through, shut it, then seized the woman he found sitting reading an all-too-familiar book. He hauled her up and drove her back against the wall. "A planned breeding program, perhaps, Lady Overton?"

She went a strange color—stark white with creamy blotches.

Then fainted.

Chapter 21

"Christ." Brand swept her into his arms and laid her on the big old bed, his heart pounding with panic and guilt.

Tapping her cheek, he said, "Rosie?" finding her name awkward on his tongue. It was his lady, though. This was the body he knew so well, the face he'd sensed beneath the mask.

His Delilah. The woman who'd tricked, drugged, and used him. Bitterness and anger, however, were melting away.

He saw something on his fingers. Rubbed them together. Grease?

Then he realized that the right side of her face was painted. Looking closer, he thought he saw marks underneath.

He went to the washstand, dampened a cloth, and came back to rub at the paint. Her eyelids fluttered, and she put up a weak hand. "Don't."

Ignoring her, he removed most of the thick paint, uncovering scars. A network of jagged purple scars ran beside her eye, one streaking down her cheek. He touched that, only able to think how painful and frightening it must have been at the time.

Her eyes opened, saw him, then squeezed shut as if she could make him go away.

"Wake up, Lady Overton. We have things to discuss." He was clinging desperately to the defense of fury, but deep inside other feelings stirred. He remembered their laughter, their lovemaking, their sharing of minds.

She was certainly as lovely as he'd thought. Scarred, but lovely, with long lashes, and smooth skin dusted with freckles across the bridge of her nose and the tips of her rounded cheeks. His eyes lingered on the full lips he still hungered for.

Catching a breath, he stood and put distance between them.

She opened her eyes, fearful, watchful.

"So? Are you with child?" he asked.

She struggled into a sitting position. "Why do you ask that?"

"What sort of a fool do you take me for? I can see a plan when it's so clear."

She winced as if he'd hit her. "I'm sorry."

"So, are you with child?"

"I think so."

"My child."

But she stiffened at that. "Digby's child."

"I could prove that not to be true."

"You'd find it hard."

Damn her. "With all the servants in on the scheme, I suppose I would. I could take you away from here by force."

She shrank back. "Why?"

"Because you're stealing a child from me."

"It's as much mine as yours. More!" They were both keeping their voices low, but it was as if she screamed it.

He turned away. Hell's fire, he didn't want to take her child. He wanted *her*—Samson indeed—but he couldn't have her. She was another man's wife. He could even appreciate the need here. In their position, I too would do almost anything to save this lovely place from the New Commonwealth.

But had there been nothing true between them? He realized that that was why he was here, why he was attacking her. He needed to believe that beneath the betrayal, beneath the cold-blooded plan, there had been something real.

He turned and walked to the bed. She began to scramble back awkwardly, hindered by her tangled skirts. "Stop it!" she hissed. "This is my husband's room, too, you know. He could come in."

"He's doubtless snoring off his dinner." But a glance

confirmed what he'd ignored before. No question of separate rooms here. She shared this room, this bed, with Sir Digby every night. Rage flaring again, he grasped the front of her bodice and towed her close. "Don't I deserve something for stud duty?"

"I saved your life!"

And it was true, as was so much more. He knew it and he wasn't blind. He changed his grip and held her close. After a moment, she stopped fighting.

"Tell me about the scars," he said. "What happened?"

Her neck relaxed a little and her head rested against him. "A carriage accident. We were going too fast in the fading light."

"We?"

"Diana and I. Lady Arradale. We're cousins. Almost of an age. Always up to trouble."

"How old were you?"

"Sixteen."

She'd married at sixteen. Because of the scars? "What were you up to?"

She looked up then, rueful mischief in her eyes. "We'd talked the coachman into taking us to the Richmond Races—something our parents wouldn't permit. It was just mischance that the coach left the road as we hurried home."

He traced the long scar. "And your cousin escaped without harm."

"She was unconscious for two days. And she's always felt guilty. It was her idea."

"I'm sure they all were." Brand felt a strong temptation to take a whip to the wild, feckless Countess of Arradale.

"You underestimate me, sir. I was well able to come up with a good adventure now and then." Then her humor faded. "Before."

"Before you married Sir Digby. You were forced?"

"No!" She sighed. "It looked far worse then. Everyone hovered over me, pitying me. I couldn't stand their pain. I couldn't stand being 'poor Rosie,' living at home forever with no hope of marrying. When the idea came up, I seized it. They could all stop worrying. I'd be safe at Wenscote behind the walls. . . . He didn't really want to marry, you know. I didn't see that then."

"Someone should have advised you to wait."

"Everyone was as devastated as I was." She looked into his eyes, calm and mature. "It was a long time ago."

"But has led us here."

"A blessing, then. We'd never have met, you and I, except for that accident."

"Strange logic, but true." Then he had to add, "I wish you had trusted me. Was I not trustworthy?"

Tears glistened. "It wasn't my secret to risk. Please don't spoil this, Brand. It's not just me. It's—"

"Hush. I know." He wiped one tear from her cheek. "It's Sir Digby. It's Wenscote. It's Wensleydale."

"Edward must never suspect."

"Edward already suspects." At her alarmed look, he added, "Not your pregnancy, but your virtue."

"He'd suspect the virtue of a hermit in a cave. He'll never be able to prove anything unless you help him."

She wasn't trying to tempt him, he knew, but she was, just by being herself. His Delilah. His beloved. The one, the only. But forbidden. For a moment, he considered seduction, but even if he could fracture her strong will, she lay on her husband's bed, and even a kiss would be sordid.

He took his arms away and moved from temptation. "I won't betray you. You have my word. Trust me this time. But don't underestimate Overton and the Cotterites. Make sure Sir Digby sticks to his resolve to make him stay away."

She put a hand to her belly. "He might try to do something?"

"He'd probably see himself as the avenging hand of God. You are perpetrating an illegality, you know. If he could prove it in a court of law, I'm sure there are penalties for this sort of thing."

"He couldn't prove anything, without you."

"So, he might try rougher justice. I'm still tempted to carry you away from here, simply to protect you."

Her chin firmed in that precious way she had. "I'd

fight. This is my home, Brand. This is my place. I am fixed here, like the rose trees in the garden."

It was a message, one his mind accepted and his foolish heart spat out. "Without Sir Digby or a child . . ."

"That will not be."

Her resolute words stole his breath. Before he knew it, he had hard hands on her shoulders. "I have one price for my silence."

Shrinking beneath his grasp, she whispered, "What?"

"If you are not pregnant, if something goes wrong. If you think to try again, send for me. Promise me that. I'll give you to Sir Digby and Wenscote, my lady, but I'll be damned if I give you to another philandering, chance-met man."

She bit her lip and tears spilled, but she nodded. "I could not do it now," she whispered, "with any other man."

He wanted to ask her then whether Digby still demanded anything of her in this big old bed. The man had hinted he was incapable, but he might still try. He might . . . It was not something he had the right to ask, and he didn't want the wrong answer. Beating like a trapped bird in his mind were the words "Mine. Mine."

In reality, she was not, and could not be.

Reason defeated passion. He let her go, and walked to the door. There, he paused to look back. "It would be madness not to see this as the end."

Tears tumbling now, she nodded. "Good-bye, then, Brand Malloren."

"What should I call you? Rosie?"

"That's my childhood name. My name is Rosamunde, but I'd like you to call me Rosa as Diana does."

"Then God, and my love, be with you always, Rosa Overton."

He opened the door, checked that all was clear, then left. Downstairs he found Sir Digby sprawled in a big chair, hounds over his feet, snoring. Brand wanted to shake the man awake and tell him to take care of himself, that his wife needed him. A bitter other part wanted Sir Digby to die, now, before he could ever share a bed with his wife again.

Instead, he did one last service for his lady. He ordered Sir Digby's coach and his own horse, then went in search of Edward Overton. He found the man sitting on a bench in the lovely garden—Rosa's garden—reading his Bible.

"Even useless flowers are pleasant company, Mr. Overton?"

Overton closed his book on a finger. "God's open air is healthful, Lord Brand."

"I am leaving, and you are coming with me."

The man stiffened. "Why do you say that?"

"Sir Digby asked that you leave. I am offering escort."

"I have no intention of leaving a place I consider my home."

Brand plucked the Bible from his hand and put it on the bench, then hauled him up. "You consider it your *future* home. For now, you are leaving with me, conscious or unconscious."

Overton's eyes bugged and his cheeks reddened. "How dare you! What business of yours is all this? Help! Ho! *To me!*"

"Do you really think anyone here will come to your aid?" He shook the man. "I warn you. I'd enjoy beating you."

"You can't . . ." Overton spluttered, but he put up no resistance as Brand towed him to the coach, only insisting on picking up his Bible. The servants there acted as if there was nothing unusual in a man being thrust into a coach by force.

Brand slammed the door, for he'd no intention of enduring Overton's company for hours.

"My possessions!" Overton demanded, sticking his head out of the window.

"Are packed and in the boot. Though, of course, as a true follower of Christ you have little thought to such matters." Brand swung onto his horse. The groom gave him an approving wink, and despite everything a grin broke free.

Though he suspected his lady—Rosa—might be watching from a window, he resisted the urge to look up. The only other service he could give her now was to never raise any suspicions.

For that reason, he did not look back as he rode away from Wenscote and his no-longer-mysterious lady.

They passed Arradale without stopping. Brand would have liked to speak to Bey, to make sure he would put aside all enquiries and thoughts of vengeance. Doing that straight from Wenscote, however, would be as good as raising a flag blazoned with the discovery, and he couldn't be entirely sure his brother would obey his wishes. Bey tended to think he always knew what was best.

The ride to Leyburn passed in a bittersweet haze. Rosa Overton. Rosamunde. Like a love-sick poet, he found himself murmuring it to himself. Rose of the world. Fair Rosamond who'd been trapped in a maze for a king's pleasure. Trapped . . .

He remembered the sweet weight of her as he'd carried her to the bed. Devil take him for a wretch for frightening her! Every curve, every line, every breath had been instantly familiar, and desired.

He'd not thought himself a thorough Malloren. His ambitions were modest. He didn't take offense easily. He didn't expect to win whatever he reached for. Now, however, he wondered if he'd simply not wanted anything before. Not wanted as he wanted his lady.

The one woman he could not have.

What would Bey do in his situation? Impossible to imagine, of course, but Brand suspected that his brother would have ridden off with her, confident that he could make everything right.

Brand, however, could not violate her right to choose, especially as he understood her plan and her need. She and her husband had come up with a means to circumvent the law and do justice, and she had bravely carried it through.

He remembered her awkwardness, her naiveté, her desperate resistance to her feelings. Proof, every one, of courage under fire. Now, he no longer doubted the magic, their instant bond, or that she felt the pain of parting as fiercely as he.

She was a heroine. The least he could do was be her worthy hero.

That and remove the thorn in her side.

At Leyburn, he asked Overton where he wanted to go.

"It makes no difference. I intend to return to my uncle's house."

They were sitting in an inn, eating a meal—a somewhat inaccurate term for the stewed vegetables Overton was consuming with his watered beer. Brand resisted the temptation to attack him with one of the sinful pork chops on his own plate.

"You will not return. I have instructed the servants there to tell me if you turn up uninvited again." He didn't add a threat, which was surely unnecessary.

"Why?" Overton demanded, color nearly as high as his uncle's. "Why take this unseemly interest?"

"I like Sir Digby. He told you to leave and to stay away. I'm making sure you act as a good nephew should. I'm sure any Cotterite would approve."

"We prefer to be called saints."

"Then live up to the name."

Overton subsided into simmering silence. Brand had to admit that though he wasn't given to autocratic meddling, he was rather enjoying himself. He wondered if Bey found the same wicked amusement in watching the victim flail helplessly in the net like a landed trout.

"Take me to Rawston Glebe," Overton said as he finished his meager meal.

"What?"

"It is an estate near Northallerton."

"I know where it is."

And something flickered in Overton's eyes, something shifty.

"I was near there a while back," Brand said carefully. "It marches with an estate I'm thinking of purchasing. Run by the New Commonwealth, isn't it?"

Lips tight, Overton nodded.

"I met George Cotter in an inn there. An interesting man."

"A true saint."

Brand nodded. "You may be right. I have to wonder about some of his followers, though. Base motives creep in past prayers sometimes, don't they?"

Reading Overton's tangled expressions, Brand decided to write a report for his brother after all. If Overton dabbled in potions, he might have had a hand in Brand's problems and in his cousin William's death. Did this pose a threat to Rosa? Not as long as Overton and his fellow "saints" were kept well away from Wenscote.

He rose and tossed some coins on the table for the meal. "I'll have the coach take you to Rawston Glebe. I'm for Thirsk. Show your nose at Wenscote again, Overton," he added, "and you will likely transform from a saint to martyr."

Brand tipped the Wenscote servants generously, though he didn't think they needed incentive to make sure Overton reached his destination. Then he rode on to Thirsk, to his rooms at the Three Tuns and the mountain of work waiting for him. He welcomed it more than ever. It was his only defense against a lovely home, a precious woman, and a slowly forming child.

A feeble defense. At every opportunity, his thoughts leaped back. Seven months or so from now. Despite all good intentions, he couldn't cut all contact. He had to know whether it was a son or daughter, that she came through childbirth safely. How could he find out without raising suspicions? If he took a particular interest in the stud and visited now and then, would anyone see a problem in that?

Probably not, but it was far too dangerous. His willpower would hold only so far. He winced every time he remembered the battle he'd waged that last night, a battle to make her betray everything she loved, to betray her honor. The problem was, he couldn't be sure he'd never do it again.

What if something went wrong? What if she lost the child . . . ?

Despite selfish greed, he could never wish that grief on her. All he could pray for was a safe birth and a healthy child, and long life to her husband.

All he could do for her was to stay away.

Forever.

When Rosamunde heard how Brand had removed Edward, she had to fight tears. He was her knight errant after all, driving away the monsters from his lady's bower. He stayed on guard as well. She soon discovered he'd told Potts, Digby's man, to inform him if Edward returned.

It was dangerous, that lingering, tenuous connection, but precious, too. She wouldn't let it come between her and Digby, and so she could hold Brand's chivalry to herself, something precious to soothe her in the secret sadness of the night.

At all other times, she banished him.

Exploiting Digby's shame at having snored away the afternoon instead of throwing Edward out himself, she bullied him into better health. She forbade Mrs. Monkton to make the rich foods he loved, and rationed his brandy. If he showed signs of resisting, she raised the subject of the child, and he immediately made new resolutions to live well.

To strengthen his resolve, she told him all the little signs of change in her body. How her breasts were larger and more sensitive. How her waist was already thickening. How the smell of the stables was beginning to make her nauseated, though she'd escaped actual sickness thus far.

"You shouldn't be going down there then," he said as they passed the stud on the way to the nearby fells. Dr. Wallace said exercise would help, especially walking up gentle hills.

"But I enjoy it, Digby." Rosamunde breathed in the fragrant evening air and suddenly twirled, reveling in life, and nature, and beauty.

"Hey, Rosie, be careful. I'm not sure I'm up to catching you if you turn dizzy!"

She stopped and teased, "You'll soon be able to carry me. Except that by then I'll be as big as an elephant!"

They laughed, and her laughter was pure joy. She wasn't deluding herself. He was looking better, and she thought he was feeling better for all that he kept complaining about the boring food and drink.

"Perhaps we'll have you fell racing soon," she added.

He roared with laughter at that. "Now that'd set the dales talking! Not that I didn't run some races in my youth, you know."

As they walked, he entertained her with stories of his younger exploits. She wished she'd known him then, in his vigorous prime, and yet life was perfect now.

Close to perfect, at least.

She would not think of other things.

She even had Brand in her life in an innocuous way.

The first contact had been a polite letter of thanks to Digby for Wenscote's hospitality. Inevitable, that, but it had included a request for permission to write to Lady Overton from time to time on the matter of horses.

Rosamunde had struggled with it, but Digby had been pleased and she'd let herself believe there was no danger. She trusted Brand now, and knew he wouldn't try to use the correspondence for secrets. He simply wanted contact, and so—weakly—did she.

There had only been two letters so far, and two replies. Letters she'd read to Digby, and replies she'd shown him "in case he wanted to add anything." She'd made sure to tell Brand that the letters were shared with her husband, but she knew it wasn't necessary.

Sometimes she wondered if she was foolish to trust him as absolutely as she did, but she knew she was not. It sprang not from their time in the dower house, but from the moment in her room when he had not kissed her.

The need had been raging, in her as much as in him, the more so when they were meeting face-to-face for the first time. But he had not even tried, and she knew why. And thus she knew she could trust him, completely, forever.

So she had become glad of the letters, though each reopened wounds. Apart from the precious contact they gave her, Brand had the right to know how things were with his child. He would hear of her health, of the birth, of the sex and name. If the letters continued, he could follow his child through the years.

His child.

The child he had so generously given her, not in those lustful days in the dower house, but when he'd ridden away from Wenscote without argument or a backward look.

Chapter 22

A fortnight after his visit to Wenscote, Brand was drinking ale in the inn taproom with a local farmer and arranging purchase of a couple of prime rams, when they were interrupted by his brother. The first sign was when Bill Stalling stiffened. Bey had that effect on many. Not dislike or fear, just a lack of ease.

As Bey came toward them, Stalling brought the conversation to an end and took his leave. Bey took his place, pushing the half-full tankard to one side. "I intend to return south next week."

"You've finished with the New Commonwealth?"

Rothgar picked up a nut from the bowl on the table and cracked it between his fingers.

"Good," Brand said, meaning it. "You have proof of murder?"

"Proof? Perhaps not, but an incriminating pattern. Geographically, the deaths have occurred throughout the north, and thus were not easily detected."

"Except by someone like yourself with a far-flung net for information."

"Precisely. Enquiries about medicinal substances purchased by the sect have been illuminating as well."

"Opium?"

"That's the least of their weapons. It's rather alarming what concoctions are possible with the right knowledge."

"Collecting recipes?"

Bey's lips twitched. "How well you know me. But, when the whole picture is presented to a court, it will convince. Especially as a Cotterite was present at every victim's last meal."

"Is Edward Overton involved?"

"Up to his weak, sanctimonious chin. He is assistant in their apothecary at Rawston Glebe, and was present at three deaths, including that of his cousin William."

Brand did his best not to show his relief, or even his interest. He'd no doubt Bey had found time among all this to search for the people who had drugged him, but he couldn't have discovered anything. Now Rosa was safe from Edward Overton, and from Bey.

"I didn't have a seizure, though," he pointed out. "Why not?"

"Their victims were carefully chosen. All men in danger of such attacks. A young healthy man with powerful connections was another matter entirely. For you, they had to create an accident."

"So what did they use?"

"I suspect a potion they use on members who try to express doubts about the community. Opium and some other ingredients. Deep long-lasting unconsciousness, followed by suffering. The unconsciousness gets the malcontent out of the way for a while, and the pain doubtless deters future rebellion."

"It would deter me, that's for sure."

"Another useful recipe."

Brand laughed. "You deter rebellion without need of such crude tactics."

"How strange then that people so often fail to follow my plans." He leaned back in his chair. "This enquiry had been a fascinating insight into the dangers of power. George Cotter, as best I can tell, began his crusade as honestly as Wesley."

"I'd have said he was still that type. There's no guile in him." Brand wondered, however, if Bey was also speaking of himself. The responsibilities and temptations of power were enormous, and could corrupt.

"It is possible that Cotter is being kept in ignorance," Bey agreed, "but more likely that his Godly purpose overwhelmed his judgment of the means."

"Then it's a damn shame. He's right about so many things."

"You do have a generous soul, don't you?"

Brand shrugged. "Clearly a sin in your eyes."

"Wrongs must be avenged."

"Very Old Testament. What happened to turning the other cheek?"

"One of Christ's more difficult recommendations. But then, being rich, I have to fit through the eye of a needle, so the minor details hardly matter. Perhaps in the Cotterite recipe books I will find an elixir of smallness."

Brand shook his head. His brother was in a strange mood.

He thought back to the assault on him. "So, they drugged me; then to be sure, dumped me on the open fells. If I'd lain in that bog for the night, I'd doubtless have been a corpse."

"So, the Mallorens owe thanks to your rescuer. To your mysterious lady."

Brand sipped from his glass. "She set her price, and I paid it."

"Indeed? An unusual transaction. You know no more of her?

"Bey, let's not get back to that."

After a moment, Bey said, "Very well. Now, if you have time, I would like to involve you in this New Commonwealth matter."

"I thought you said it was done with."

"My investigations, yes. I'm intrigued, however, by George Cotter's part. Either he's very clever, in which case he might escape my noose, or he's an innocent, in which case he could help me. I'd like you to find out."

"What?"

"Whether he's saint or devil. I'm bringing in troops under pretext of a sweep against smugglers on the coast. Within days, we'll take over the New Commonwealth estates for investigation. In the end, the ringleaders will be put on trial, and the sect disbanded."

Brand stiffened. "You can't break up a farming community with harvesttime coming."

"That's one area in which I need your help. You're going to oversee that."

Brand groaned. He might have known he'd be dragged into a cartload of work.

"For the moment, however," his damnable brother

continued, "and before I bring them down, I want you to find Cotter and see what you make of him. If you think he's innocent, get him to help punish the sinners in his midst."

"Even though it will destroy his whole movement?"

"If he's righteous, he'll realize he's created a tree of evil not of good." Rothgar rose. "I must deal personally with one matter, but I will return in two days. Take care."

"Take care, too. These people sound mad."

"It's distressing how frequently religion has that effect. What is one to make of it?" With that philosophical whimsy, he left.

Brand paid the tab, and followed, wondering idly what was so sensitive that Bey had to handle it himself. Above all, his brother was a master of delegation—as in deputizing him to sort out the mess of the New Commonwealth estates. He'd planned to escape south this week. Wenscote and Rosa sat in his mind like a beacon on the horizon, calling him to folly and dishonor. Excuses for the half-day journey popped into his head a dozen times a day, and the hunger never eased.

Duty called, however. Someone had to make sure the New Commonwealth land was cared for, and bring the harvest in, and it seemed it was him.

Edward Overton opened the message and thumped down onto the plain chair of his small room at Rawston Glebe. No!

He read the note again. Despite the coldness toward him at Wenscote, he'd found one servant willing to keep him informed, for a price. He'd *known* his aunt was a whore, and here was the proof. His spy had overheard his uncle and aunt talking about which room would be the nursery. He doubted even his uncle could believe the child his, but Sir Digby would wink at the wicked deception in order to keep him out of his legal rights.

He screwed up the paper, trying not to panic.

Wenscote was *his*. His to turn into Jerusalem. What they were doing was a bitter sin—outright theft—and could not be allowed. Moreover, he had the means to correct it.

He rose to circle the room, horrified by what he was planning to do.

When he'd chosen to work in the apothecary, he'd thought only to heal and succor. Then he had been asked to help in other matters.

It had been for the good of all and the glory of God. He believed that. See how many saints lived pure lives on estates once poorly managed for the idle luxury of the few. On a Commonwealth estate, each saint had his own equal piece of land and could grow his own food, raise his own meat. No earth was wasted for ornamental gardens, deer pasture, or follies.

He could bring Wenscote to this glorious state, and he would. To let them get away with their deceit would be stealing from God! Uncle Digby was living on borrowed time, anyway. It wouldn't be like Cousin William—

He put his fist to his mouth, remembering his cousin's last moments. That had been entirely his own plan, but not selfish. He'd acted only to clear the way for God's purpose.

He was righteous.

He was a saint.

They had sinned, not he.

Firm in his purpose at last, he went to the dispensary and carefully filled a small bottle from the lotion for bruises labeled "Poison. External use only." It was rarely used, being ineffective. He then consulted a book, and found what he wanted—the recipe called, ambiguously, "A means to preserve the menses." He mixed that and filled another bottle.

With both concoctions in his pocket, he humbly asked permission to visit his uncle, who was unwell. Soon he was riding toward Wensleydale on one of the placid cobs held as communal property of the saints.

He fretted a little about Brand Malloren, who had warned him to stay away, who'd said the servants would tell him. He'd no taste for another encounter with that fire-eater. By the time word reached Lord Brand, however, Sir Digby would be dead, and the whore's child would be swept away in blood.

And he, Edward Overton, would finally be able to put Wenscote to God's purpose.

The next day, Rosamunde prepared to mount her horse in her parents' stable yard. Since the servants must surely soon guess, she'd plucked up courage to come and tell her parents about the baby before they heard rumors. She'd worried about what they'd think, but their joy and congratulations had been genuine. If they had any suspicions, they were keeping them to themselves.

She knew her mother must have recognized Brand at Arradale, but she'd never said anything. Had she told Rosamunde's father? It all made her feel young and shivery, but it was done. The plan was going to work.

Her mother kissed her, and her father handed her up onto the mounting block from which she carefully eased herself onto the sidesaddle. She was taking no risks. She was leaving early because she'd walk the horse all the way back to Wenscote.

Her groom mounted to accompany her, his saddle hung with baskets and bags. Her mother clearly thought her poorly fed at home! She knew it was just caring, though, and turned to wave as they rode out onto the track leading across the fell to Wenscote.

Though broken by clouds, it was a lovely day, a dales day that sang to her of how fortunate she was in so many ways. She would not allow her losses to take anything from her blessings. As she looked forward along the path home, she looked forward to a good life.

She was in the last dip before home, Wenscote almost in sight, when four men rode out of some scrubby trees and trapped her startled groom between horses and pistols. What on earth . . . ?

She broke free of bemusement and whipped her horse forward toward Wenscote and help, cursing the fact that she was riding sidesaddle. Before her startled mount could gather speed, a gray horse charged forward to block her, and a hand seized her reins.

"Lady Overton, I assume."

The Marquess of Rothgar! Rosamunde came close to
fainting again.

"Sir, what are you doing?" she asked, not needing to
pretend fear. He knew! He knew and he'd come to exact
revenge. One thought screamed in her brain. She
mustn't let him hurt her baby.

"Don't be afraid," he said, his expression unreadable.
"I'm simply taking you to safety."

"My home is not far from here. I will be safe there."

"Perhaps not—"

Rosamunde slashed for his hand with her whip. It was
caught and wrenched from her, but for a second she was
free and she urged her horse to speed.

Toward Wenscote.

Digby.

Safety.

She was gathering breath to scream when his big gray
thundered alongside and cut off her horse again, making
it rear. She needed all her skill to keep herself in the
saddle.

When she faced him at last, hot and shaken, he
seemed unmoved. A quick glance showed her poor
groom on the ground, bound hand and foot and looking ashamed.

"This isn't your fault, Ned," she called to him. "You
couldn't be expected to fight four bullies."

Lord Rothgar's henchmen were as unmoved by her
scorn as their master. They were already remounting,
and soon moved to circle her, making any further break
for freedom impossible.

"What do you want with me?" Her voice shook. This
couldn't be happening. Not now.

"You will be taken south, Lady Overton, out of danger. We have a coach on the road." He indicated the
way and set his horse and hers to a leisurely walk, as if
abduction were a casual matter. Hemmed in, she had no
choice but to go with him.

"I am in no danger, sir, except from you. Who are
you?"

"You know well who I am, and you must know you

are in no danger from me. Brand would never forgive me."

Oh God. Brand was part of this? She'd trusted him, and he'd failed her. "No danger!" she snapped in anger. "I was nearly thrown, thanks to you."

"I won't underestimate you again."

He was like a rock, but there must be words to chip at him. "Why are you so kindly abducting me, Lord Rothgar?"

"The New Commonwealth is being brought to an end, Lady Overton. Some members are already under arrest on charges of murder and assault. They have been using poisons to acquire estates, including, I fear, Wenscote, through the death of William Overton. I prefer to see you clear of all danger."

Could he be sane after all? "But what of my husband?"

"My concern is with you and your child."

"Child?" It was a foolish echo, but she couldn't think what else to say.

"Surely you know the facts of reproduction, Lady Overton, being an animal breeder."

"Of course, I do. I simply cannot conceive of any interest you could have in my child."

"*Cannot conceive* is an interesting term, wouldn't you say?"

"Brand told you," she said bitterly.

"No. He has kept your secret most faithfully, as have your people here and at Arradale. It wasn't hard, however, to find that Lady Arradale has a cousin to whom she is very close, and that the cousin is Lady Overton, devoted but young wife to Sir Digby. Everyone knows that if Sir Digby does not produce an heir of his body, the New Commonwealth will spread its tentacles into Wensleydale. And I'm afraid that Brand did carelessly put the final brick in the wall. He visited Sir Digby's estate, and suddenly his itch to know who you are died."

Rosamunde was daunted and impressed by his logical powers, but puzzled by one thing. "My lord, how could you possibly suspect a connection to Lady Arradale?"

"Rings, Lady Overton. As Lady Richardson you wore many, as Lady Arradale does."

"That is not unique."

"But the magnificent ruby you wore in Thirsk is. And the countess wore it at her ball."

"I wish," she said bitterly, "that I had thrown up all over you."

"It would merely be another sin in your balance."

Rosamunde fell silent. He knew all, and despite his cool manner, anger simmered. She could sense it, like a storm rumble on the air. She had to escape. She had to! Even if the marquess did not harm her, he was going to ruin everything.

She tried honesty. "Lord Rothgar, you are opposed to the New Commonwealth. Surely you see that my child is important."

"The New Commonwealth is broken, Lady Overton, and Mr. Edward Overton with it. He will likely hang. There is no longer any concern about Wenscote."

"But my child will still be heir to Wenscote!"

"By what right of blood or necessity?"

They were at the coach, and she let him help her off her horse, dazed by the unexpected blow.

"There is another heir, I believe," he was saying. "A Dr. Nantwich, distant cousin of your husband's. Do you intend to defraud him?"

Under pressure of this change of view, she could hardly think. Her child had no right . . . ? She had no right? Wenscote was lost to her?

He touched her arm, perhaps gently. "Do not distress yourself, Lady Overton. We will take care of you and the child."

"We?"

"Rosa!"

They both turned to see a horse and rider hurtling down a steep incline toward the road and coach, tufts of grass flying from under scrabbling hooves.

"Diana!" Rosamunde gasped. She'd surely fall.

Lord Rothgar muttered something and his hand tensed on her arm. But the horse slithered onto the road, quivering and white-eyed, and Diana leaped off and raced over, her hat flying away. "Rosa! What's happening? What's going on?"

The marquess stepped back as if by instinct, leaving a path for Diana to Rosamunde. Diana stopped short of an embrace, however, and swung behind him. "I have a pistol pressed into your back, Lord Rothgar. Do exactly as I tell you."

Everything froze. Rosamunde sagged against the coach. Could anything possibly become more bizarre?

"Most people are not truly willing to pull a trigger," the marquess said. "Are you, Lady Arradale?"

Rosamunde could see that Diana's hands—she was using both to hold the horse pistol—were shaking slightly. He could probably feel it.

"The man who taught me to shoot made the same point, my lord. He told me to prepare my mind to kill as effectively as I prepared the pistol. I have done that. If you think I'm directing the ball away from the most vital points out of stupidity, you are misjudging a woman again. If I shoot you, it will be in a place that gives you a chance of living. Not a good one, but a chance."

"I see. So, my lady, what now?"

"First, your men disarm themselves and release Rosa's groom. I have a force with me, out of sight."

"An interesting notion. Do we believe you?" Even so, he ordered his men to obey her.

Diana called, "Come forward!" and a small army did rise from over the hill. "I have chosen this route to avoid bloodshed, my lord, but if you want to make a battle out of it, we will engage."

Shock and reaction made Rosamunde want to giggle. Diana's army consisted of armed grooms and local people. Some of them had guns, but most just sticks or even farm implements. They came down the slope cautiously and hovered there, nervous, but clearly ready to fight to the death.

"Oh, well done, Diana!" Rosamunde said.

"Well done indeed," the marquess agreed as if he were not defeated.

"So," said Diana, a little more steadily, "do we fight, my lord?"

"Not at all, Countess." He turned slowly. "The King would be displeased at open warfare between his nobles."

"What were you doing with Rosa anyway?" Diana demanded, taking a few cautious steps back.

"Taking her to safety."

"What danger is she in?"

"A complex variety. She will doubtless explain."

"Even so, it is no business of yours."

"I have an interest in her welfare."

"You have no interest in anything here, Lord Rothgar. I recommend that you return south to your proper sphere."

"No thanks for breaking the New Commonwealth?"

Diana inclined her head. "All thanks to His Majesty, whose servant you are."

He returned her bow, cynically. "As are we all."

A gesture had his horse brought over by one of his men, and he swung into the saddle. "You have claimed your right to protect Lady Overton, Countess. Do it well. The end of the New Commonwealth has only just started, and Overton may not yet know his fate. If he knows of the child, he might try to destroy it. And consider carefully the legalities of your cousin's situation. None of us is ever served by selfish violation of good order."

He turned to Rosamunde and bowed quite deeply. "Your servant, my lady." To Diana, he simply said, "Until we meet again, Countess."

Surrounded still by storm rumbles, Rosamunde watched him ride away, his men and coach following. The army of Wensleydale let out a mighty cheer, shaking their motley weapons after the defeated southerner and loosing the ancient war cry of Arradale. "Ironhand!"

Diana laughed and, raising her cocked pistol, she fired it into the air. "Ironhand!" she cried.

A moment later, however, she sat with a thump on the ground, lowering her head as if she feared to faint. Rosamunde knelt beside her. "That was amazing. My heart was in my mouth when you rode down that slope!"

Diana raised her head and shook it a little. "So was

mine! Poor Cyrus. I'll have to give him extra special care after demanding that of him." She gripped Rosamunde's hand. "Thank heavens I was in time. Where was he taking you?"

"South, he said. I don't understand it. But"—she sat down in the dirt beside her cousin—"he was right."

"Right? To take you south?"

"That if the Cotterites are done for, and Edward with them, this child has no right to Wenscote."

"Nonsense. Who else?"

"There is another heir back up the family tree a bit. I'd forgotten him, but Digby keeps in touch with him. He's a doctor in Scarborough."

"Who'll never know," Diana protested, scrambling to her feet, then giving Rosamunde a hand.

"I'll know. Digby will, too. If Edward's out of the way, he won't want to foist a cuckoo into the Overton nest." She put a hand over her belly. "What's to become of the poor thing?"

"That's what he meant about violation of good order, plague take him. I—" But she fell silent, clearly as tangled and distressed as Rosamunde. "Oh, come on, love," she said at last, wrapping an arm around Rosamunde's waist. "Let's get you home. We have months to sort through this mess."

"Not really. If the child can't inherit, it can't exist."

"Rosa!"

But now Rosamunde shook her head, not willing to talk about it until she'd thought some more.

Accompanied by Diana's six grooms in case the marquess tried to snatch Rosamunde back, they rode to Wenscote. At the sight of the high stone walls, Rosamunde thought perhaps she'd order the gates locked tonight for the first time in years.

But then she saw Dr. Wallace's gig outside the front door, and her heart missed a beat. She slid from the horse with a thud and ran into the house.

"What?" she asked Millie, who was standing there, weeping.

"Oh, milady! It's Sir Digby! He was taken ever so ill after his dinner!"

No! Rosamunde picked up her skirts and raced up the stairs to their room. She stopped outside for a calming breath—she mustn't upset him—then opened the door quietly. Perhaps this time he'd take the warning seriously.

He lay in the bed, eyes half open, skin gray. A chill swept through her. "Digby?"

A hand stopped her rush to the bed. She turned to see Dr. Wallace's sober face. "I'm sorry, Lady Overton. You are too late by minutes. He has just left us."

She stumbled over, fell to her knees, and took his still-warm hand. "No. Come back, Digby."

Then Diana was there, holding her. "Hush, love. It's over."

"My dear aunt." Another hand rested on her shoulder. "Lady Arradale is correct. My poor uncle has gone to his heavenly reward and as Christians, we must be glad of it."

Rosamunde stared up at Edward Overton. "What are you doing here? You were told to stay away!"

"Not forever. My uncle did not mean that. I feared our distance might be distressing him."

"Your presence distressed him!" But as she pushed to her feet, sick fears churned. He turned up. Digby died. The marquess had implied strange murders. Poison . . .

She turned to the doctor. "What caused his death?"

The man shrugged pityingly. "Need you ask, Lady Overton? I have been warning him for years, but he seemed completely unable to be moderate."

"It was his heart? You're sure?"

"As sure as a medical man can be."

She faltered. She'd known this was coming, too, despite every attempt on her part to help him to be healthy. Probably Edward had agitated him into this, but that couldn't be called murder.

She gently closed Digby's eyes, accepting the two pennies from the doctor to place on the lids. Then she gathered his flaccid hands and crossed them over his breast. When she bent to kiss his forehead, her tears fell onto his lifeless skin. How fast the spirit fled. She dabbed them off with a corner of the sheet, then pulled it up over his face.

What now? What was she supposed to do now?

Her grief tangled with her horrible moral dilemma. Should she claim her child as Digby's heir, or conceal it? Though some of the servants must have suspicions, thus far she'd only told her parents. They could be asked to keep silent. She could bear the child secretly, far away. . . .

What would Digby have wanted? If only she could have asked him. She couldn't think of all this now!

With Digby dead, however, she had to. Within days, the legal wheels would start to turn. If the marquess was right, Edward wouldn't inherit, but Dr. Nantwich hovered in the wings. By right, Wenscote was now his.

All she had to do, however, was announce that she was with child, and Wenscote would be her child's, and thus, for many years, hers. Wicked, but oh so tempting.

She looked rather helplessly around the room. Mrs. Monkton was there, weeping into her apron.

"What do we do now?" Rosamunde asked.

"You must not worry about anything, Aunt," said Edward. "I will take care of all the details. I will look after you."

No, you won't, she thought, but kept it to herself. She thanked him for his concern, and led the weeping housekeeper away. "Let me take you back to the kitchens, Mrs. Monkton. I must have a word with the staff, too."

As they went downstairs, the housekeeper said, "It was fast, milady. That's one blessing. One moment he was enjoying his dinner. The next, he came over funny and was unconscious."

Suspicion revived. Food. Unconsciousness. Death . . . "Did Edward do anything to upset him?"

The woman shook her head. "I wouldn't say so, milady, any more than by just being himself. Seemed to be trying to be careful, in fact. Even told the master not to eat the fried collops." She began to cry again. "I'm right sorry about that, milady, but he asked special like! Do you think they killed him?"

"No, no," Rosamunde soothed, though she was exasperated. Had Digby been sneaking forbidden foods every time she was away from the house? Perhaps the collops had caused his death, but other suspicions would not go away. She must try to confirm or deny them.

In the kitchen, she was met by somber, anxious faces. "Sir Digby has just died," she said. The maids began to weep. "We should all take time to think about him and recover from the shock. Don't worry about your work for a while. Why not go out and walk in the garden for a half hour?"

They looked bewildered, but she shooed them all out, even the housekeeper. Alone for a moment, she hurried to the dining room where the remnants of the meal still lay untouched by the distressed servants.

Diana came in. "What are you doing?"

"Not the soup," Rosamunde muttered. "Edward ate that."

"What?"

Rosamunde picked up Digby's plate, still half full of rabbit stew and fried collops. "It's his second helping, too. I can tell from the amount left in the dish."

"Rosa, I know you're distressed, but leave this. Even if he ate the wrong foods, it doesn't matter anymore."

"Oh yes, it does. Go and find Potts. I want witnesses. I'm not mad, Diana. Please."

With a pulled face, Diana went. Rosamunde considered the wine, but the inch or so left in Digby's glass seemed clear, and she doubted a potion could be disguised in straight wine. It had to be the spiced stew.

Perhaps she was mad with grief, but she didn't feel it. She burned with righteous anger. The marquess had implied that Edward's goose was cooked, but if he'd murdered Digby, she would be sure of it.

Diana came in with Digby's red-eyed manservant.

"Potts, I want you to watch something, but I also want you to hold your tongue about what happens here. Do you understand?"

"Yes, milady. But—"

"Just observe."

Digby's hounds were upstairs, mourning outside his room. Rosamunde went to the one hound left behind, poor old Snapper, too crippled now to climb the stairs. She put the plate in front of her. The bitch lifted her sad head to sniff at the plate, then lurched up painfully to enjoy the treat.

Rosamunde watched as the bitch licked the plate clean then collapsed down again. For a moment, she thought she'd been wrong, but then the animal gave a kind of cough, stiffening. Then another. Then after a few horrible twitches, she died.

Rosamunde knelt and stroked the hound's bony old head. "I hope you're chasing rabbits in heaven, Snapper. Or romping with Digby."

"I'll arrest the wretch!" Diana declared.

"No." Rosamunde looked up. "The marquess has plans, and we don't want to interfere with them."

"Oh, don't we?"

Rosamunde shook her head. "Also, I want Digby's death days to be untarnished. Once he's in the ground, we'll see what to do next. You both are witnesses if needed. Yes, Potts?"

"Yes, milady."

"You're going to pretend this didn't happen?" Diana protested.

"Just for a little while. If it looks as if he might go free, however, I have the means to destroy him. Potts, you may go now. Remember, say nothing."

"Yes, milady, though it will be bitter not to spit at him."

The man left and Rosamunde put the plate back on the table, ladling the rest of the stew onto it to disguise her act. Then, thinking of something, she tipped the plate to smash on the floor.

"What was that for?" Diana asked.

"In case one of the servants decided to polish it off."

" 'Struth. I think I'll employ a food taster after this!" Then she came over and wrapped an arm around Rosamunde. "You're so pale, love. And see, you're shivering. Come up and lie down. I'll get Mrs. Monkton to make a possett for you."

Suddenly drained, Rosamunde let Diana shepherd her up to a spare room, where she slipped off her shoes and lay back on the bed. Diana pulled a thick eiderdown out of the chest and fluffed it over her. She gathered it round gratefully, even though it was a warm day. She lay there, trying to accept the fact that Digby really was dead, that nothing she could do would bring him back.

"Rosa," Diana said, "I don't want to bother you, but if you don't say anything about the stew, what's to stop Edward Overton from playing havoc here in the next few days?"

"Send for Mr. Whitmore. There are legal ways, I'm sure." But then it all seemed to break through the shell around her. The death. The baby. The murder.

And Brand. Always, always, the forbidden fact of Brand Malloren. "Brand. It's his child, too," she whispered, to the one person who understood. "What am I going to do?"

Diana spread her hands helplessly, and Rosamunde broke into soft, deep tears.

Chapter 23

Mrs. Monkton bustled around making her favorite oatmeal possett for her ladyship, glad to have something to do. If only she'd not made those fried collops!

It was only to be hoped that their suspicions were right and the lady was with child, no matter how that'd come about. Otherwise it'd be Mr. Edward and those Cotterites. There'd be no joy cooking for the likes of them.

She added the ale, wine, and sugar, and set it to stand and cool a little. When she turned from the fire, Mr. Edward was watching. "What are you making?" he asked, quite pleasantly. "I have taken the study of medicines and such as part of my labor for God, so I have an interest in these things."

"It's just an oatmeal possett, sir. It'll steady the lady and give her strength."

He asked about ingredients and did seem to have some knowledge. When she put the dish on a tray, he said, "Let me take it up. I'm sure you have much work to do."

For a moment she was tempted, but then she remembered how much the poor lady disliked him. She didn't need more upset at a time like this, so Mrs. Monkton thanked him and took the tray up herself.

Mr. Whitmore arrived before Rosamunde's message had found him, for the news was already spilling down the dale like the river. As an old friend of Digby's, he was much distressed. Rosamunde felt better for the cry and possett, so had energy to comfort him. She offered him a glass of brandy.

He sipped it gratefully. "Such a terrible shock."

"Yes. Edward is here."

"He heard so soon?"

"No, he arrived this morning." It was tempting to share her knowledge with this trusted family friend, but it was better kept quiet for now. "I'm sure he's pleased he had the opportunity to speak one last time with his uncle."

The solicitor nodded, but without conviction.

"What is the procedure now, Mr. Whitmore? As far as the running of the estate. Financial matters and such."

He put down his glass and became businesslike. "You must not worry about a thing, dear lady. I and your father are executors, and can authorize any payments in the immediate. And of course you are provided for through the settlements."

"When will I have to leave?"

He sighed. "That will depend on Sir Edward, of course."

Rosamunde started. She'd forgotten that Edward had inherited the baronetcy as well. She couldn't help a spurt of malicious pleasure. "I don't think he'll enjoy the title."

Mr. Whitmore's eyes twinkled for a moment, but then he turned sober. "I doubt you would want to stay here, Lady Overton, once the New Commonwealth takes over."

"No, of course not. When must that be?"

He tapped the table, thinking. "Well, as to that, nothing can be settled in such a case as this until it is proved that the lady is not . . . er . . . with child."

Rosamunde met his eyes. Did he know?

"Of course, it is unlikely," he said quickly, "but it must always be assumed to be so before an alternate heir is given access to the property."

Time. Time to think. "How long?"

At that moment, the alternate heir came into the room, pinch-faced. "Aunt, why was I not told Mr. Whitmore was here?"

"I wished to consult with him first, Edward. About my position here, my jointure and such."

He turned to the solicitor. "I will see to Lady Overton's welfare."

"There is no need, Sir Edward—"

"Please!" Edward shielded himself with his hand. "We do not use such titles."

"Very well, *Mr. Overton,* as you doubtless know, Lady Overton is well provided for through the marriage settlements. And unless she wishes otherwise, she is entitled to live here until your inheritance is proved."

"That can hardly take long."

"Two months, perhaps."

"Two months!"

"When there is no direct heir of the body, sir, the widow is assumed to be with child until it is clearly otherwise. We must wait for at least two months before you can be given unrestricted access to the property. However—"

"Since there can be no question of a child. . . ." Edward turned to Rosamunde. "Can there?"

"I do not care to speak of intimate matters, Edward, but it is not *impossible.*"

Mr. Whitmore cleared his throat. "Quite so. Quite so. Two months is not so long, Mr. Overton, and you will be permitted an allowance from the estate in the meantime. For the moment, however, everything must remain unchanged. No property may be bought or sold or substantially altered. No commitments entered into, debts incurred." He rose to take his leave.

Two months. Rosamunde rose and spoke. "Mr. Whitmore, Edward . . ." She turned to him, keeping her eyes lowered in case he read the expression there. "Though of course you must stay the night, Edward, I . . . I cannot feel at ease to have a young, unmarried man in this house for longer than that."

"Then perhaps you should leave, Aunt. Your family would be pleased to have you."

"Sir!" protested the solicitor. "Lady Overton has every right to stay in her home until the matter is settled, and you must respect her delicate feelings."

It was clear what Edward thought of her delicate feelings, but he was balked. "It shall, of course, be exactly
as you wish, Aunt."

As he stalked out of the room, Rosamunde shivered.
What now? Would he try to poison *her*? She would be
extremely careful about what she ate tonight.

Edward was no longer the real threat, however. Her
poor innocent child was. What was she to do? Once the
solicitor had left, she went to sit by Digby's body, and
it took very little thought to accept that she could never
claim the child as his. Once Edward was finished, Dr.
Nantwich would be the new owner of Wenscote.

She sighed. If she bore the child openly, telling everyone that it wasn't Digby's child, she'd never live down
the shame. She might take up that burden, but it would
be a terrible stain on Digby's memory, that his wife had
deceived him in his last months.

For Digby's sake, therefore, she must hide the pregnancy and bear the child far away. What then? She immediately thought of Brand, but there was no hope
there. Even if he wanted to marry her, they still couldn't
have the child together. This child couldn't exist without
shaming Digby. The only honorable solution was to give
the child to others to raise.

The child would not suffer. Only she would. Ah, but
it would hurt.

Then there was Brand. He knew about the child. He
had a right to some say, but would he fight her over this
as he'd fought her that last night in the dower house?
What did he care about the honorable memory of a
Wensleydale squire?

She covered her face with her hands, drowning in despair. She'd only tried to do her best for Digby, and now
her life lay in ashes. . . .

The door opened and Edward walked in. "We are
arranging the vigil through the night, Aunt. Do you wish
to take part?"

Rosamunde resented Edward taking charge, but at
this point she could hardly care. "Of course. I believe
Mrs. Monkton will want to take part, and Potts. They

are the two here who have been with him the longest.
What part of the night do you prefer?"

He gave a little bow. "I will accommodate myself entirely to you, Aunt."

He really was being too pleasant, but she couldn't
chase after that either.

She summoned the two servants, and after some polite
debate, it was agreed that she would take the first watch,
Edward the second, Potts the third, and Mrs. Monkton
the dawn period.

For the sake of the household, she tried to be calm
and composed, to attend to all the little details. Still, her
mind kept scurrying in destructive spirals of fear and
hope, crashing again and again into the fact that Digby
was not here, would never be here, would not come in
smiling to support her. That a part of her life, her whole
adult life in fact, was over, leaving her as alone and
frightened as she had felt at sixteen.

*Ah, Brand, weak though it is to think it, I wish you
were here.*

When she heard her mother's bells, she ran out to
greet her, to fall into her warm, sensible embrace. Despite reality, she felt that nothing terrible could happen
when her mother was in charge.

By the time she went to sit vigil, Rosamunde felt truly
at peace with her situation and her soul. Her mother
and Diana were both staying the night, and both had
offered to keep her company, but this was a time for
her and Digby to be alone one last time.

At first she tried lowering the sheet, but the shrunken
gray features didn't look like Digby anymore, so she
covered him up again and sat nearby, remembering him
when alive.

Her mind swirled from thought to memory, but then
settled into speech. "I suppose I was dreadful sometimes. Sixteen, angry, scared. You gave me Wenscote,
didn't you? To play with. Did you really like the garden?
I hope so. And the stud. And the sheep. You probably
didn't want your comfortable life turned upside down by
a restless, bitter child. How much of the time did you

stay here with me, saying you liked the peace of your home, when you'd rather have been at Richmond races or the sheep fairs at Hawes and Masham? Like a heedless child, I took you at your word."

She put her hand on the covers that lay over his hand. "Thank you. I hope I made you happy in the end." She sighed, and spoke what needed to be spoken. "You know everything now, I suppose. I hope you aren't hurt. I never saw the danger until it was too late, or I would have prevented it. I didn't know about love like that, you see. Oh, that sounds wrong, too. I did love you. I do." She brushed away some tears. "You can read it in my heart."

She tested her own heart, and was at peace. She had loved Digby. Everything she had done, except perhaps for that one wicked night, had sprung from her love for him. Her love for Brand took nothing away.

"I wish you were here to help with the tangles, though," she said. "Would you want me to keep Wenscote for the child? I don't think so. You were as troubled as I was by bringing a stranger's blood into it." One hand still on his, she put her other hand over her womb. "It is the child of your heart, though, Digby. Be a special angel for it. It will need you."

A feeling of such sweet peace came over her that it was like a blessing, one that made her weep. He'd always made her feel this way. Safe, warm, protected. She knew now he'd do the same for another needy child.

Smiling sadly, she rested her head on the mattress and let her thoughts wander over eight years of a special kind of love. . . .

When the clock struck one, Edward tiptoed in. Rosamunde rose, stiff and tired, glad to be going to her bed, but sad to be taking a final farewell of her husband. This wasn't him, however. He'd moved on. It didn't seem wrong to leave Edward with this empty shell.

She nodded to him as she passed.

Then was caught, hand over her mouth, an arm shackling her.

She'd never have imagined he was so strong! She

writhed and kicked, but could not break free. His grip switched so he had his arm tight around her neck. She tried to claw it down or scream, but he tightened his lock, almost throttling her.

"Try to call out again, and I'll really throttle you," he whispered. Then something cold pressed against her neck.

"Yes, a pistol, Aunt. One of Uncle's. How kind of him to insist that I learn to use it."

He slowly released her neck, and she gasped for breath, putting a hand to her aching throat. "You won't shoot me. Everyone would know."

"Perhaps I can make it appear suicide. But I don't want to kill you. Just to get rid of that devil's spawn in your womb." He presented a small glass bottle before her eyes. "Drink."

Teeth and lips clamped shut, she desperately shook her head.

"It won't be too unpleasant, and it will cleanse you of your sins." He sounded as if he believed he could persuade her! "Otherwise, I will kill you, and your babe will die, too. Come, come. Your life will be easier without a child. You'll be able to find a young, handsome husband then. Perhaps the one who planted the unrighteous seed."

All Rosamunde could do was shake her head, and keep her mouth clamped shut. She was afraid even to scream for he might manage to tip the stuff down her throat.

He suddenly jammed the pistol into the base of her skull, jerking a cry from her, but she sealed her mouth again before he could act. "Open up!" he snarled, mashing the cold bottle against her lips. "Swallow your medicine, you foul trollop. Purge yourself of your abomination!"

He kicked the back of her leg and she went down on her knees. He hit her with the pistol barrel so she couldn't help but gasp. Some liquid splashed into her mouth.

She spat it out and tried to twist away.

He grabbed her hair in his pistol hand and pulled

back, trying to jam the neck of the bottle between her lips. . . .

Diana came suddenly awake. The house lay silent, but something was wrong. She and Rosa were sharing a bed, but Rosa wasn't here yet, so it couldn't even be one. She felt around on the table for her watch then held it into a beam of moonlight. Surely it said ten past one.

Then she heard something. A bang? Not on a door, but as if someone had stumbled against a piece of furniture in the dark. Downstairs?

Heart pounding, she eased out of bed, took her pistol out of her valise, and crept toward the door, more afraid of making a fool of herself than of real danger. She opened the door and peered out. They didn't have housebreakers up in the dales. It had to be a servant moving about below. Yes, there were footsteps in the hall below. She relaxed, but then she tensed again. Was that a noise from Sir Digby's room?

Where *was* Rosa?

Then, shocking after silence, steps pounded up the stairs, preceded by a candle's wild flare. A man appeared, rushing for the master bedroom.

Brand Malloren!

Diana raised the pistol in both hands. "Halt!"

He charged through the doorway as if deaf, and true to her training, she pulled the trigger. The flame from the barrel blinded her. The detonation deafened her and rocked her backward.

Then she heard screams.

She stood, frozen in ice. No, she hadn't prepared herself. She'd not prepared herself to hear that sobbing agony that went on and on. . . .

As people called and doors opened, she dropped the pistol and staggered into the room. Rosa sprawled on the floor. She hadn't hit Rosa had she? A man crouched over her. Another jerked and cried on the floor, blood spreading.

Not Brand Malloren.

Edward Overton!

She looked back at Rosa, and saw Brand was the man with her, supporting her unconscious form.

She fell to her knees by them. "Is she dead?"

"Fainted." He held her closer. "Rosa, love. It's all right. Wake up . . ."

Potts ran in. "Saints preserve us!" He went to Overton, who weakly begged for something. Help, death, mercy . . .

Mrs. Monkton appeared at the door and began to scream. Short, repetitive, high-pitched screams.

Rosamunde's mother arrived, slapped the housekeeper, and went to Rosa, who had come around. In moments, she was taking her daughter away.

Diana just knelt there, still hearing the explosion of the pistol mixed with whimpered pleas. A gaggle of servants in all stages of dress stood wide-eyed in the doorway now, while the housekeeper sat collapsed in a chair. Blood was pooling on the floor. Voices were blending to a dizzying buzz.

This would never do.

Diana forced her weak legs to support her. "Now," she said, proud of her level tone, "would someone tell me what is going on here?"

Unfortunately, at that point the buzzing drowned her thoughts and dark rushed in.

Chapter 24

Brand looked around, feeling as if he was emerging from an insane fire. Two bodies lay on the floor. The Countess of Arradale and Edward Overton. Someone had called "Halt," then fired a pistol. They must have shot Overton instead of him. Overton had been screaming, but he was quiet now.

Someone had taken Rosa away. That was as well.

He could hardly feel the passage of time between riding toward the house and seeing into this window—seeing Rosa struggling—and being here now with the aftermath.

Rosa was safe, though. That was all that mattered.

He knelt by the man lying in a pool of blood. The servant shook his head. "Not quite gone, sir, but soon. Took him right in the side and it's in there somewhere. Did you . . . ?"

"Best not speak about it." Potts had sent word that Edward Overton had returned to Wenscote. Brand had raced up here, driven by the certainty of danger. He picked up the pistol that must have fallen from Overton's hand. Not fired. A bottle had spilled its contents on the floor.

"Poison?" Potts gasped. "Again?"

"Again?"

Potts gestured to the bed, and for the first time Brand saw the shrouded shape. "Sir Digby?"

"Aye, milord. But I was told not to mention . . ." he whispered. "I'm pleased, milord, that you shot Mr. Edward, and glad he suffered. That's the truth, unchristian though it might be!"

Brand didn't correct him, though he had no idea

who'd fired the shot. It couldn't have been Rosa. Who else was there?

He rose to stand by the corpse, looking down at the remains of a man he'd liked, a man who had stood between him and his heart's desire. His conscience twitched that he'd not sent a warning. He'd never thought Overton would go this far, but had he been selfish?

With honesty, he could say no. To serve his lady, however, he would arrange matters here as best he could. The first thing was to get rid of the wide-eyed servants. The housekeeper, though glassy-eyed, seemed to have some of her wits back. "Why don't you make some tea, Mrs. Monkton?" he suggested. "For everyone."

With a nod, the woman staggered off, shooing away the servants as she did so.

Now what? He wanted to go to Rosa, but the damned countess was lying there. Stupid woman to be fainting when she could be of use. He gathered her into his arms, arranging her frippery silk-and-lace nightgown for decency. Then he smelled powder on her hands, and saw dark dust on the white silk.

'Struth! *She'd* fired the shot? The woman needed a keeper. He carried her into the corridor, listened, then went toward voices. As he hoped, he found Rosa sitting on a bed, her mother comforting her.

"Diana!" Rosa gasped, quickly making room on the bed.

He placed the countess there. Rosa's mother produced smelling salts and waved them briskly under the countess's nose until she spluttered and came around.

She pushed the pungent stuff away. "I hate that!" she complained, then sagged back, a hand over her eyes.

"Stop that, Diana," the older woman said briskly. "Just because you're embarrassed to have fainted."

"I never faint," Lady Arradale muttered. "Never."

"You've doubtless never killed anyone before," Brand pointed out. "If your aim had been better, you could have killed me!"

The countess sat up, glaring. "If you rush into people's houses, you must expect to be shot."

"I rushed in because I saw what was happening!"

'Struth, he must be in shock himself to be squabbling with the woman. He turned to his pallid beloved. "Are you all right?" Of course, she wasn't. Why could he never comfort her when he wanted to?

"As well as can be expected," she said, with a gallant attempt at a smile. He could see that she had no more idea how to behave in this situation than he did.

He fell back on convention. "I'm deeply sorry about Sir Digby."

"Thank you." She tried the same approach. "Have you met my mother, Mrs. Ellington? Mother, you know Lord Brand Malloren?"

"We met at Arradale," said the plump, sensible-looking woman in nightgown, shawl, and nightcap.

Brand bowed as if he was in a drawing room, feeling increasingly unreal. "Your servant, ma'am."

"You must have traveled a long way, Lord Brand."

"From Thirsk."

Devil take it, they'd be talking about the weather next. Everyone here must know the true situation. He perched on the bed near his lady's feet, and took her chilly hand. "You're safe now, love."

"I know. It's all right." But then she swallowed, looking only at him. "He wanted to . . . to . . . Brand." She began to shake, and then she tumbled herself toward him and he was free to gather her preciously into his arms at last.

For a moment, that was all, a connection too long denied, and deeply hungered for. Then she whispered, "He wanted to get rid of the baby, Brand. He was trying to make me swallow something."

"Hush."

"I kept my mouth shut. I couldn't even scream—"

He held her closer. "Hush, love. It's over. I'm here. I'll take care of you."

If only he could. He longed to lie with her, comfort her, and protect her, but this was her husband's house, and Sir Digby lay dead not many yards away.

He was going to have to leave again.

He couldn't bear it.

Suddenly, the countess slid off the bed. "I need tea. With brandy in it."

Rosamunde's mother rose from her chair and nodded. "Excellent idea."

She bustled past and briefly—amazingly—pressed her hand to his shoulder.

Well, who was he to go against a mother's wishes? As the door closed, he sank onto the bed, his lady safe at last in his arms. She spoke wildly for a while, going over and over what had happened, what Edward had said, how she'd fought, the shock, the explosion, the screams. . . .

He just held her and eventually she quieted, and finally slept. Arms around her, he kept watch over his lady through the night, as a true hero should.

Rosamunde woke. In someone's arms? Digby?

No, not Digby.

She opened her eyes, hardly daring to hope that her final memories hadn't been a dream. It was Brand. Heavy-eyed, but watchful and with her.

"You saved me. Or rather, the child."

"Wouldn't any father save his child?"

She closed her eyes. "Brand . . ."

"Hush." His fingers weighed gently on her lips. "I've had the night to imagine all the troubles. But we can triumph over them. I don't think you know my family's unofficial motto."

"Let me guess. 'We are gods and do just as we wish.' "

His smile crinkled his eyes in the most delightful way. "Close. 'With a Malloren, all things are possible.' "

She looked directly at him. "What do you want to be possible?"

"I'll be hurt if you don't know."

"I need you to say it."

"I want to marry you, Rosa, and love you, and cherish you, and guard you, and delight you forever and ever, Amen."

She laughed, fighting tears. "You almost make me believe." Then she touched his face, roughened with stubble again. After his long journey and adventure, he was close to the Brand she'd rescued. "Does it happen often, this sudden force? It doesn't make sense."

"I don't think sense has anything to do with it."

She expected—half-feared—a kiss. She didn't know what to do, what to wish for in this extraordinary situation. "Brand, I'm so confused. The baby . . . I'll have to . . ."

"Hush. We'll find a way. Just tell me, do you want to marry me? I won't force you."

Could he doubt? "If I'm silly enough to object, please use force!"

He laughed softly, laying his head against hers. That was all, however. That was one of the things she loved so dearly about him, his honor and his true sense of what was right.

"Rosa," he said, "we can't do anything just yet, but I will find a way. Trust me."

She stroked his hair. "I trust you. And we can be together, as long as we give up the baby."

He looked into her eyes. "You won't want to give up your child."

"We can't always have what we want. I'm resigned to it."

"I'm not. 'With a Malloren, all things are possible.' If you don't believe me omnipotent, perhaps you have faith in my brother."

Faith wasn't the word for her feelings there. "He won't try to stop me concealing this child, will he? I won't shame Digby."

He smiled. "You look so fierce. And formidable. You realize, Lady Richardson and her spotty maid outwitted the Marquess of Rothgar. It's unique."

She thought of the kidnapping, wondering if he knew of that defeat. She was sure the marquess must be plotting revenge. "He frightens me, Brand. Don't let him interfere."

" 'Struth, love, there's no avoiding that. But the plan will be as you wish. Only let me try to find one that gives us everything we desire. Everything."

She looked at him almost with exasperation. Didn't he know, Malloren or not, that some things simply couldn't be? They couldn't marry and have their child with them without shaming her and Digby. She'd give him what trust she could, however. Taking his hand, she said, "I will pray for a miracle, then, my love."

The air stilled. The pull of the forbidden kiss swayed them closer. But then, he said, "This is Sir Digby's mourning time. We'll both regret it if we forget." He rolled off the bed to stretch and yawn as if it were just another morning. He was tousled, stubbly, beautiful, and impeccably honorable. All this at least she would one day have. She would not let loss of the other shadow it.

It would be enough.

He turned to her. "I must leave. Will you be all right?"

She wanted to keep him here. "We've parted too often in our brief time. . . ." But she found strength to add, "I have Mother and Diana, and my family will be here soon to walk Digby down. You don't want to stay for that?"

"I have no place here. Yet." He was deftly restoring himself with the aid of the small mirror. It pleased her that he didn't need a manservant for every little thing.

"Where will the service be?" he asked.

"In Wensley."

"I'll be at the church there, then. Just an acquaintance paying my respects."

"And afterward?" She couldn't leave matters so profoundly unsettled. "I can't marry you soon, Brand."

"I know."

Did he? Did he really understand? "Not until after the baby's born. After—"

He put his fingers over her lips again. "Trust me."

He waited for her nod, then straightened and winked. "You're lucky I'm a very patient man, Rosa Overton, or I'd be off seeking another woman to make me into her willing love-slave."

Having reduced her to fiery blushes, he left, pausing only at the door to say, "Remember. Remember in the coming months that I love you, Rosa, till death us do part and into eternity. You will have everything you desire."

"How?" she whispered, but thank heavens, he was already gone.

Tears threatened, but she controlled them and put all future problems to one side. Instead, she blew her nose, and rose to face this day, Digby's mourning day.

When she emerged from her room, she found that Brand had already accepted responsibility for Edward's death, and had taken his body with him to Lord Fencott, the magistrate. He'd also dropped hints that the New Commonwealth was being investigated on many charges, including using poison to remove inconvenient people.

As a result, the gathering to escort Sir Digby on his final journey fairly buzzed with shock and speculation, but also with enormous relief. There was even laughter at times. She didn't think Digby would mind. He was missed, and he'd know it, but he'd always enjoyed good cheer.

No one seemed to find Brand's intervention suspicious. They all knew he'd met Digby at Arradale, and taken Edward away by force when he left. That story had been too good not to fly around the dale.

Did they suspect other things? She really didn't think so. The servants at the dower house had kept their mouths firmly shut. Those at Wenscote who had suspicions were doing the same. Perhaps her plan, at least, would work—to bear the child secretly and find it a good home.

Then she'd marry Brand and have other children.

It would be enough.

The men of her family arrived—uncles, brothers, and brothers-in-law, as well as her father. She felt bulwarked and secure, but couldn't help wondering how they would treat Brand in the future. Because he was an executor, she'd had to tell her father that her child was not Digby's. He'd not condemned her—she was sure he understood—but he'd sighed and shaken his head, clearly seeing the problems as she did.

Accepting her part in it didn't mean that he'd accept Brand's, but it didn't matter if there was coldness. Once married, she'd live in the south. Looking out over the dales, she flinched under a raw new loss.

But she'd have Brand. It would be enough.

Digby was nailed into his coffin. Rosamunde put the flower garland she had made on top, and eight men took up the burden for the first stage down the dale. Rosamunde and Diana rode with the men behind. Her mother drove Mrs. Monkton in her chair, the bells removed for this journey.

All along the way, people came from cottage, field, and inn to bend their heads at the passing of a good man of Wensleydale, and as they approached Wensley in the afternoon, the church bell began to toll. When they entered the cool church, it was packed. Tears fell, but not really of sorrow. This was almost a celebration of Digby's warm-hearted, honest self.

She wept during the service, and as she watched him lowered into the ground, but he was already elsewhere, in a better place. She felt sure that the peace around her was his gift.

Brand was doubtless among the mourners, but she hadn't looked. As people passed by to give their personal condolences, however, she knew he would eventually be one of them and worried a little. It passed without incident. He simply bowed and said, "I am honored to have been of some small service to you and Sir Digby, Lady Overton."

She did not let her eyes follow him. Their time would come. It was not now.

Having paid his respects to the widow, Brand hovered, chatting to the various people he'd met at Arradale, but really standing guard in case anything should happen to disturb Rosa's peace. He hoped he wasn't giving anything away.

It was hard to stand here as a mere acquaintance, to leave her care and comfort to others. They'd had so little time together, and none of it peaceful.

He wanted more.

He couldn't have what he wanted, however, and he was, as he'd told her, a patient man. He was used to starting land development and breeding programs that would take years to show results. He had ordered the planting of trees that would buy the pleasures of future generations.

A year was not so long.

At the moment, however, it seemed a damned long time, especially when they must hide their feelings for most of it. At least he could watch her, as long as he was careful not to let his heart show in his eyes.

It was the first time he'd seen her with people, almost the first time he'd seen her out of doors. What a strange relationship theirs had been. She was a little shy, he saw, even with neighbors. A little reserved. She tended to tuck her head down sometimes, perhaps from a habit of hiding her scars, though the paint made them hardly visible now.

At some point in the past they must have been a terrible burden to her. He wished he'd been there for her then.

Despite shyness, she was kind and gracious to all, and clearly well loved.

He observed her family around her, pleased at the obvious closeness. Three tall, strong men were probably her brothers, and he'd liked Mr. and Mrs. Ellington when he'd met them at Arradale. Solid, sensible people who'd care for her well.

In fact, he liked the people of Wensleydale. They could be taciturn and sparing with their smiles, but there was a rootedness in them, a strength formed by one of England's harsher climates.

With a start, he realized how much this was Rosa's place on earth. She'd said her roots ran deep as rose trees, and it was true. He didn't know what that was like. He was used to a wandering life, living in almost constant circuit of Bey's properties.

The idea of roots was strangely pleasant. 'Struth, but Bey was likely to be put out if the plans forming in his mind came to anything!

Realizing his eyes had rested on her too long, he headed toward the inn's stables. His control was faltering, so he'd better leave. He was paying the groom and preparing to mount when a voice said, "Young man."

Brand turned and found Rosa's father there, hands clasped behind him, weathered face bland.

"Mr. Ellington?" Brand wondered uneasily if Rosa's brothers were nearby.

"I'd appreciate a word with you, if you don't mind, my lord."

Brand tethered his horse and moved into a more private spot. "Yes?"

Mr. Ellington eyed him like a farmer eyeing a bull at a sale. Or one at the slaughtering block. "Not to wrap it in silk, my lord, I gather my daughter is carrying your child."

A hint of Malloren pride made Brand want to give a cool response, but instead he said, "So I gather."

"Yet you seem to be leaving."

Brand suspected those stalwart dalesmen brothers of hers were hovering nearby, possibly with cudgels in hand. "Rosa prefers it this way."

"Women sometimes don't know what's best for them."

"Really? I don't find that. Are you saying you want me to marry Rosa now? I'm willing, but I don't think it would be wise."

The older man relaxed a bit. "Ah."

"Mr. Ellington, Rosa and I will marry. However, the situation is delicate, as I'm sure you can appreciate. I ask you to trust me to arrange matters."

The man relaxed even more. Slumped even. "It's hard to see how it can be arranged, and that's the truth, my lord. Perhaps if you marry her quietly and take her away."

"I hope to do better than that. Tell me one thing. Some people may suspect that she carries a child. A few know I spent time with her. If given another story to match the facts, will they keep knowledge and suspicion to themselves?"

The man nodded. "For one of their own, yes, my lord."

Brand put out his hand. "Then I hope to be welcome in your family one day soon, Mr. Ellington. Myself, Rosa, and our child."

After a moment, the other man shook it. "Well, if you can pull that off, it'll be as good as a miracle, my lord, but it's good of you to try."

Brand found the Three Tuns in the organized chaos of his brother's removal. Bey's own rooms were orderly, of course, despite constant traffic and a flow of crisp orders. While his people prepared for his journey, he was organizing the last moves against the New Commonwealth.

"I've put Cotter in hiding," Brand said in a moment of privacy. "He had no idea what his overenthusiastic followers were up to. He thought all the convenient deaths were God's will."

Bey read a note and put it with others. "He doubtless doesn't know either that some of the cursed fools were planning treason. They intended to do away with the Crown."

"The deuce! So the King was right."

"I'll make sure to compliment him. They'd never have pulled it off, but it makes Cotter's situation impossible. He'll face charges of treason."

"Be hanged, drawn, and quartered? He's a good man, Bey."

"He's a naive fool."

"Look, he wants to take his message to America. Can we do that? Get him and his family away?"

His brother thought for a moment. "We don't need any more heads on Temple Bar. Will he compromise enough to wear ordinary clothes?"

"I think so."

"Very well. On your head be it if he ferments treason in the colonies, too. They're restless enough as it is."

Bey dealt with another report and issued instructions while agreeing in passing to some question from Fettler about his baggage.

"Get Cotter and his family to Liverpool," he said when they were alone again. "Bryght should be able to find a safe ship. We have a number that sail that route. Then return here and pick up the agricultural pieces."

At Brand's silence, he looked up. "You object?"

"You didn't notice my recent absence? I do have concerns of my own. Sir Digby Overton is dead, and Lady Arradale says he was poisoned by his nephew."

Bey went still. "I'm sorry for it. I never thought he'd go that far. What does the countess have to do with it?" It seemed a strangely sharp question.

"She observed Lady Overton feed the remains of Sir Digby's last meal to an old hound. It died."

"So we have evidence if we need it."

"You won't. Edward Overton is dead, too. The countess shot him."

Bey stared, clearly, for once, almost shocked. "What an interesting time you've been having."

"Don't be too impressed. She was aiming for me."

"Is she admitting that?"

"We didn't discuss it. Bey, Lady Overton is my mysterious lady."

His brother was singularly unastonished. "I had put the pieces together. So, what are you going to do? She can't keep Wenscote."

It shouldn't surprise him that his brother had the whole matter clear. "She doesn't want to."

"What does she plan for the child?"

"To bear it in secret and find it a good home."

Bey looked at him. "And you agree to that?"

"No, but to preserve her husband's memory, she insists that it never be known as hers. I have to agree with that."

"I will raise it for you if you wish. A bastard, but a Malloren."

Brand nodded. "Thank you, but I hope to do better. In fact, that gives me an idea." He turned it in his mind for a while. "She plans to remove immediately to Harrogate to pass her early mourning there. Before the baby shows, however, she'll need to go farther. I can't play an obvious part. Will you see to her travel from there to some safe and quiet spot?"

Bey became suddenly interested in his ruby signet ring. "It would seem your lady is very discreet."

"What's that supposed to mean?"

Bey looked up. "Is it likely that one day you will tell me the whole story of this mysterious affair? Having met Lady Overton—briefly, alas—I find it hard to imagine the details."

"You've met her?"

"That is why I called her discreet. She hasn't told you."

Though Brand would trust his brother with his life, a chill crept down his spine. "Told me what?"

"I tried to take her into custody. Purely for her own safety, though I confess that the idea of restraining the woman who had brought you such suffering had its appeal."

"You . . . And *failed*?"

"Lady Arradale summoned her forces and defeated me. I mention it, only because Lady Overton may not care to travel in my care."

Brand could read his brother somewhat. "What did you do to her?"

"I seized her neatly and efficiently. However, despite the lessons Elf has taught me, I seem to be in the habit of underestimating apparently conventional young women. She made an excellent attempt at escape. I stopped her, and in the process I could have caused her an injury. I should have let her go." He shrugged. "I was angry with her on your behalf."

No wonder Rosa had seemed frightened of Bey, but it wasn't Brand's way to rant over matters past and done. "If she had come to harm, it would have driven a wedge between us. As it is, I'm sure she will forget it if you do."

"A tolerant woman. You will suit."

It was, in its way, a blessing. Brand wasn't sure his brother would approve of all his plans, but he'd fight those battles later. They quickly arranged the details, agreeing that their sister Elf was the best one to handle Rosa's affairs. No one could be afraid of Elf. No woman, at least.

After that, Brand settled to healing a small wound. Bey had, in his own way, confessed to mishandling a situation and apologized. He must be bleeding. Brand poured wine from the decanter and passed a glass to his brother. "As penance for abduction, relate to me exactly how Lady Arradale overwhelmed you."

Chapter 25

After the funeral, Rosamunde found herself more shaken and exhausted than she'd expected, perhaps because of her pregnancy. She left Wenscote immediately, smothering the sense of bitter loss. After a few days with her family, she moved with Millie to Harrogate and truly did relish the rest and calm.

She longed for Brand, however, for even a word, a letter, but knew they must not reveal their connection. He hadn't said yet what plans he'd formed. She assumed he was coming to realize that everything wasn't possible.

A year, and then they could be together. It stretched before her like an endless empty road, with the painful valley of her child's loss still to be traveled. But it was not endless. And in the end there would be Brand, at least. It would be enough.

Then, one day, a maidservant passed her a letter. She opened it to find it was from Brand. This was too risky! But the middle-aged maid touched her nose. "With a Malloren," she said quietly, "all things are possible. If you want to reply, milady, just give it to me. Name's Dora."

Hurrying to the quiet of her room to savor the letter, Rosamunde knew the Malloren in charge of this was the marquess. He'd kept out of her way, but she knew Brand was right. Nothing would stop him from interfering. This interference was a heavenly blessing!

Not a love letter in the usual sense, but she read the account of harvest and the sowing of rye and winter wheat in that way. She commiserated with him over the tangle of Cotterite affairs, and rejoiced at his successes. He even included some stories that made her laugh.

As soon as she'd finished, she hurried to her desk to write a long letter back, one similar in tone to his, but about the characters of Harrogate and her lazy days.

Weeks drifted by, made precious by almost daily letters, but increasingly painful because he was so tantalizingly close. How easy to make the short journey to Thirsk. Why couldn't she bump into her husband's friend, Lord Brand Malloren, and at least see him, talk to him . . . ?

Kiss him.

Love him.

Then, one day, in a Harrogate street, he was there. He bowed and said, "Lady Overton. I'm pleased to see you looking so well."

Rosamunde hastily told Millie to sit on a nearby bench and moved some distance away. "What are you doing here? This is too risky!"

"One visit won't start a scandal. You are looking well."

"I am."

"And the baby?"

"Well. Brand . . ."

"Don't look at me like that, or we will start a scandal." He tucked her hand in his arm, and strolled down the street. "I came because I have something important to discuss."

"Trouble?"

He glanced at her, shaking his head. "No. A plan. I want you to leave here and travel to Wales. Apparently you have an aunt living in quite a remote spot there, and you are going to stay with her."

"I'm to have the baby there?"

"No. We'll make the connection more tenuous. You'll only appear to travel there. In reality you'll live in a village in Herefordshire as a captain's wife."

"Expecting a child? No one will believe that old tale."

"They'll pretend to, if given to understand that you are, in fact, mistress to a lord, bearing his child."

She looked at him. "I'm to live there as a wicked woman?"

"Is it too much?"

After a moment, she laughed. "No. I'll just think like Lady Gillsett."

"I thought perhaps you could use the blander name— Mrs. Richardson."

They laughed together over that, but then she asked, "And this might mean we can keep the baby?"

"But yes. Who do you think is the lord in question? That's the beauty," he said with obvious satisfaction. "I'm going to accept the responsibility of my own child. I'm hoping," he said, with a special smile, "that my future wife will be forgiving, and take it into our household."

Fragile hope swelled. "Can it work? Can it?"

"I don't see why not. You'll have to give up the child for a little while after the birth, but once Lady Overton arrives at Rothgar Abbey and becomes my betrothed, you will be together again." He sobered. "It means you will not openly be your child's mother, but—"

"But I'm resigned to that. Brand, this is perfect! Truly, I believe in Mallorens. We have everything."

"Perhaps we can have more."

"What? What could possibly be more?"

But he refused to answer that question. He took her to have tea and cakes, and they caught up on news in person, struggling all the time not to tumble headlong into betraying delight. This at last, however, was real. This was ordinary days. This was their future.

Truly, it would be enough.

Brand had to tear himself away from Harrogate, and their brief glorious hours there only made torment worse. He could only be relieved when Rosa's move was accomplished, and she was days away instead of hours.

The letters had to cease, too. No way to disguise daily messengers in a sleepy village, and no one would believe a lord would take that much interest in an ex-mistress, even one who carried his child. Bey found a carter who traveled through Waltham Green, however, and who would deliver and take messages. For all Brand knew, he was already one of his brother's people, gathering information as he traveled.

Thus he heard about a comfortable cottage, and the first time she felt the baby move, and she heard that his duties were coming to an end.

Fired by mischief, and since the village knew of her noble ruin, he arranged delivery of a lavish basket of fruit from the hothouses at Rothgar Abbey, along with extravagant quantities of flowers.

In her next letter, she chided him for extravagance, and he was shortly embarrassed by three enormous potted palms delivered from York. They were so large, they could not fit up the stairs in the Three Tuns and had to decorate the entrance hall. He laughed himself silly over them, and set everyone to clear up his work.

He could surely make one visit without ruining everything. He needed to see Rosa, who clearly liked to tease, and who was swelling with their child.

He rode into the village of Waltham Green on a damp winter's day, and asked for Pate's Cottage. It turned out to be a simple place, built of gray stone. Doubtless in summer the garden had been a bit more lively, but he'd rather his beloved was in grander quarters. A mansion. A palace, even.

He smiled. Rosa wouldn't want a palace. He knew what Rosa wanted, and was working to get it for her. Everything she desired.

Everything.

Stripping off his gloves, he walked down the path to knock at the door, but then heard her laughing voice from the back.

She had company?

Jealousy stirred. He went around, then paused to drink in the sight. Rosa, his Rosa, beautifully rounded and laughing, was dragging a ribbon for a playful young cat. She was so engaged, he managed to creep up on her and swoop her into his arms.

She shrieked, then gasped, "Brand!"

"Don't faint on me again!" he said hastily, frightened by his own folly.

"Then don't leap on me like that!" But she glowed with health and welcome, and her arms were around his neck. "What are you doing here? I thought we weren't supposed to—"

He kissed her quickly, then lingered. Then realizing they were in the open, he stopped, stepping back toward the concealment of the building. "There's self-control, and then there's bloody martyrdom. How are you?"

He could see, though. Perfect fruit, and now she was truly ripe.

"Well. Very well." Tears shone. "It's been so long. Sometimes . . . I didn't realize what it would be like, being so long."

"I know." He slid her slowly to her feet, but kept his arms around her, drinking in her beauty. "I've longed for a portrait. I'd even have treasured that damned mask."

She slid her hand into a pocket and pulled something out. She showed it, and he recognized a miniature done of him about five years ago.

"Lord Rothgar gave it to me. He has been very kind, but he still frightens me sometimes. Oh, he hasn't done anything. It's just the way he is!"

"I know, love. He's the man you'd want by your side in trouble, though."

"No, he isn't. You are."

He grinned. "True enough." He held her back slightly, taking in every detail—a deep green gown and brown shawl which both suited her healthy skin and glossy hair. "I feel like a starving man faced with a feast. Inclined to gobble, but wanting to make it last and last."

"It will last. If we want it to."

He supposed it was reasonable that she have doubts after all this time. He was glad he'd come. Letters weren't enough. "I want it to," he said, rubbing chilly noses with her. "The baby feels strange. Like a ball between us."

"I've had more time to get used to it." She pulled away a little, holding hands. "Come in out of the cold. Or do you have a horse to attend to?"

"I left it at the inn." They strolled hand in hand into the cottage, where he found Millie huddled in shawls, but willing to make them tea. They waited in the small and simple parlor scattered with books and needlework. Her room, shaped by her. He picked up a white cotton garment and said, "Will it really be this small?"

"So they say." With a rueful smile, she put her hand on her abdomen. "It already feels bigger than that."

It was strange to sit and talk when he wanted nothing more than to carry her to a bed and love her for days. But this was right. They'd never spoken of it, but he didn't think he misread her. They'd wait.

For the moment he was content to watch her, and catch up in person with months of life. With whole lives. They'd shared so little. When the black-and-white cat leaped onto his lap to be stroked, however, he was glad of the contact.

It wasn't enough. As soon as they'd finished their tea, he pushed the cat off his lap and held out his hand, praying she'd not balk. With a smile, she came and sat on his lap, wound her arms around his neck, and kissed him.

Hearts don't break, especially with joy. Their first real kiss, and he could have wept with the perfection of it. This was certainly enough for now, especially as it went on and on. Then she broke free and put his hand against her belly. He felt a little bounce.

"By heaven," he said, grinning at her. "It's a miracle."

She laughed and shook her head. "And you a farming man."

"Very well, then, wench. I'll think of you as just a mare with a foal."

Laughing, they fell into another lingering kiss, then rested entwined, savoring mere togetherness after an eternity of separation.

He stayed only the one night, however, and at the inn, for he shouldn't be here at all. Over the next months they made do with planned casual encounters in nearby towns. And letters. What a collection of letters they both had by now.

Their year was passing and it should be enough, but it wasn't. At times, slogging away at work that had lost its savor, he felt like tearing the world apart to be with her. He fought the impulse. This was simply the price to be paid for a perfect future.

For everything.

And he was beginning to hope that he could truly give her everything, have everything. If only sluggish time would pass.

He plunged back into work, finding some escape there, and also preparing for the changes to come. Then he received the message he'd been waiting for.

The end at last, and the beginning.

Rosamunde collapsed back in the birthing stool. Brand's arms came around her from behind. Despite the midwife's protests, he'd refused to stay out of this womanly affair.

She was glad of it, and found the strength to grin at his disheveled, frantic state. "Relax," she gasped. "Mare with a foal. Remember?"

"I worry about my favorite mares, too, you know." He wiped a damp cloth over her face just before the next push started.

Recovering from that, feeling the baby huge between her legs, she muttered, "Only 'favorite,' am I?"

"Only," he said, and kissed her cheek. Her scarred cheek. He had a way of doing that which during the past few months had turned the marks into a blessing. But then the next push caught her and her body dragged her into ferocious effort.

"Ah-ha!" declared the midwife, smiling up at her. "Here we are!"

Rosamunde looked down and saw the miracle of her baby's head, dark and sticky, before the next push swallowed her. Half-conscious and dazed from the effort, she felt the baby slide free and reached down. "My baby!"

By then, the child was loosely wrapped. "A daughter," the midwife said cheerfully and placed the bundle in Rosamunde's arms. Brand's arms came around them both, his head resting next to hers.

"As beautiful as her mother," he whispered, touching the trace of dark hair, kissing Rosamunde's cheek at the same time. "Was that as terrible as it looked?"

"It was wonderful," she murmured, adoring her perfect, miraculous daughter.

"You're deluded, love."

"No. Pity poor males who cannot do that."

She heard him laugh and knew he didn't believe her, but it was true. A dangerous ecstasy, but ecstasy all the same. And such a naturally powerful thing. If enemies burst in now, she felt as if she had power and to spare to fight or flee, to defend her young.

The midwife reminded her to put the rooting baby to the breast, and in moment she was gasping under a new sensation. Not entirely pleasant, but satisfying all the same. The baby obviously agreed, for she went limp with contentment.

Time passed and all was well. Rosamunde ignored everyone, even Brand, as they cleaned her and moved her. Eventually, in the big comfortable bed, she looked at him. "The idea was that you take the baby away now."

He was sitting on the mattress, still in disordered shirtsleeves, hair tumbling loose. With a wry smile, he said, "I've guessed. You're not letting the baby out of your sight for a moment."

"I'm sorry, Brand. I can't. Anyway," she said, looking down and stroking the baby's fuzz of hair, "I want to feed her. All the time. I'm sorry." Tears ached in her eyes. Hadn't she always known it was too much?

Instead of showing anger, he laughed. "After going through that with you, I'd not leave her with strangers either. I'll come up with another plan. Trust me?"

She still didn't see how it could work, but she meant it when she said, "Always. And with everything." She was beginning, almost, to believe in the Malloren motto.

A week later, he returned with a wet nurse. When she protested, he sent the young woman to wait in the kitchen. "I think I can work this, love, but you won't be able to be with Jenny all the time, and you'll want her to be fed. We were always going to need a trustworthy wet nurse anyway, if only for appearances. Jenny can't be known to be yours, so someone has to be feeding her."

Her baby was sleeping in a cradle by the window, and she had an urge to rush over protectively. She didn't want any other woman feeding her child.

"Trust me, Rosa."

She fought a battle and won. "What's going to happen?"

Only when he smiled did she realize that he'd seen her struggle. She held out her hand, and he came to her. "We're going to go forward much as before. We only need to separate at the last moment, so Jenny appears to arrive separately. Coincidence can happen."

"Can that woman be trusted?"

"I think so. She's a genuinely good girl abandoned by a lover. She'll do anything to keep her baby and earn a living. I judge her to be honest and intelligent."

Trust, she reminded herself. She had him bring the wet nurse, Edie Onslow, back in. Only eighteen, poor thing, and frightened, but daring to hope, just as she had. She was clean, and seemed healthy. As Brand said, she was intelligent and seemed honest. An instinct to cling to her baby, to protect her from strangers, still burned within Rosamunde, but she couldn't not try this.

For Brand. For herself.

For everything.

The next day, they set off for Rothgar Towers, an anonymous family with wet nurse and baby. A few miles from their destination, the party split, with Edie and a groom going ahead with two babies, while Brand and Rosamunde took a circuitous route.

Despite logic, Rosamunde watched with fear as her baby disappeared. He gathered her into his arms. "I know, love, but trust me. We'll be back together within hours."

It went perfectly, and in the huge, awe-inspiring abbey, feeding Jenny was easily arranged. Spending time with her was even easier, for Rosamunde was now betrothed to Lord Brand Malloren. It was her duty to get to know his child.

Time together was now permitted, too, though by silent accord, they restrained themselves to kisses. Heated kisses. Heated touches. But nothing more for now.

Safely strolling on the moonlit terrace, she said, "It is going to work, isn't it? Thank you, Brand."

His fingers twined with hers. "I'm arranging my own paradise, too."

"Everything," she murmured.

"More?"

Startled by memory into heat, she laughed at him. "Don't!"

"There's nothing more you want?"

Home, she thought, but suppressed it. That she could not have, neither Wenscote nor the dales. Her life would be here with him and their child, and that was more than she'd ever thought possible.

Weakly, something escaped. "Is it possible that we be married from my parents' home?"

It seemed a terrible thing to ask, but he said, "Where else?"

"But Brand, it's so far. Three or four days' journey! Just for a wedding?"

"Just? If you wish," he said extravagantly, "we'll marry on the moon!"

She looked at the huge full moon. "Even with the Mallorens, that is not possible, you foolish man."

"Hmmm. Is that a challenge?"

She pulled his face to hers. "I do love you, even without the moon. All I want is to marry you in Wensley Church with my family around me."

And truly, it would be enough. To visit. To see her family again. To introduce them to Jenny. And then she would settle to this strange life in the south.

Strange.

Terrifying.

A small threatening cloud on her horizon.

Her first ordeal had been their betrothal ball. Brand said they need not have such grandeur if she didn't want, but she was determined to be part of his life. In cosmetics, powder, and fabulous silk, she had braved it and survived it, with him at her side.

With him at her side, she could brave all of this.

Now, through days of smaller celebrations with neighbors and tenants, her nerves were steadying, and she was grateful to have faced the challenge. She could do this. She could live this life, and country people were not so different all in all.

Tomorrow, however, they were moving to London. It was apparently essential that she be presented to the King and Queen at the Queen's drawing room. In this, she was given no choice. Apparently, now they had begun to make grand gestures, this one was essential.

"As if the King cares!" she snapped a week later, quaking in her absurd gown. "And why do I have to dress in eight-foot-wide panniers?"

Brand, tricked out in unusually glittering finery, just fanned her, endlessly tolerant. "Never question court protocol. It just is. Chin up, Rosa. It's just the King and Queen."

She stared at him in disbelief, but then suddenly, it was something she could do. She didn't have to like it, but she could do it. Chin up, she accompanied him into the magnificent room and managed her court curtsy perfectly.

There. Done. But then the King, instead of moving to the next person, paused to talk to Brand about farming matters. What was worse, he then bombarded her with questions about Yorkshire, her stud, and even her cousin. She'd heard he loved new information, but she felt like a prisoner of the Inquisition.

She flashed a glare at the marquess, well aware who must have alerted the King to her interests. The marquess merely bowed. Answering a royal question about climate, she remembered the maid Gertie, and was threatened by an attack of the giggles. *He knows the King as well as I know Mr. Baines the butcher!* It was clearly true. The young king treated Lord Rothgar as one of his closest confidants, and Brand as family.

Giggles wavered into panic. She couldn't do this after all. She couldn't live like this, talking to the King, spending hours in stuffy over-perfumed rooms in absurd dresses, crushed by protocol and artificial expectations.

The King's concerned face began to waver in front of her eyes.

She came to in an anteroom with her stupid panniers sticking up in all directions, and Brand hovering by the chaise on which she lay. "Are you all right? Don't worry, it's not that unusual to faint at these damn things."

But did many women faint, she wondered, from the horrifying fear that some things are impossible, even for the man they love beyond reason?

"What is it, Rosa?" He hunkered down beside her, strange in brocade and jewels.

I want to go home. I don't like it here.

A moment later, to her horror, she realized she'd said it.

"Home?" he said, with amazing calm. "To the dales? To Wenscote?"

"Wenscote isn't my home anymore."

He took her hand. "It can be, Rosa. I can lease it for us if you want."

She struggled up. "Lease it? What? Why?"

"Why? Because it's lovely. Doctor Nantwich has taken a devil of a time to make up his mind. I think he quite fancied being the country squire. His wife, however, absolutely refuses to leave her family and the civilized life in Scarborough. Finally, she's worn him down. I received his letter today."

"But what use is Wenscote to you? You have two fine estates here in the south. We'll live at one of those."

"Not unless you want to. They've always been investments to me. I've lived a gypsy life, traveling from place to place. I'd be happy to settle at Wenscote and begin to put down roots."

She shook her head. "No! I'll have no more sacrifice. We will live where you want. This,"—she gestured around—"this is your world."

He burst out laughing. "Oh love, I'm sorry, but even Bey would dissolve into laughter at that. I've always hated this sort of thing." He took both her hands. "I like Wensleydale. I loved Wenscote at first sight. Perhaps in time we can break the settlement and buy it. If not, we can live there for many years. I want it. Trust me?"

Tears were streaming down her face. She must look a mess. "I'm not sure I can about this. You are too gener-

ous. You can't really want to live in the isolation of the
dales. What of your work?"

"I've hired new people. I'll still keep an eye on things
and travel a bit, but I'm tired of that life. I'm telling you
the truth. I want to put down roots. At Wenscote. You
spoke once of the force of sudden love. It was like that
for me, before I even knew that Wenscote was your
home. We arrived, I looked around, and fell in love."

"I see," she said, struggling to make sense of it. "You
only wanted me for my garden."

"And your stud, and your land, and your sheep, and,
always, for you."

Searching his face, she whispered, "It's so perfect, it
feels wrong."

"Everything? At last?"

Her heart ached, but with joy. "Yes. Everything." She
put her trembling hand to his cheek. "Thank you."

He kissed her palm. "Not quite everything. But that
will come, my love, on our wedding night."

Epilogue

Lord and Lady Brand Malloren escaped their wedding feast and rode up the dale to Wenscote. They talked and laughed about the strange mix of weathered dalesfolk and perfumed southerners, and how well everyone had behaved.

Rosamunde was astonished at how perfectly everything was going.

They'd traveled north as part of an astonishing cavalcade of Mallorens—ten coaches with outriders—for the whole clan, except for Lord Cynric and his wife, currently in Canada, had decided to attend her wedding. Since this included six children—including her own Jenny—a number of dogs, and even two pet rabbits, she wondered if some of the inns were glad to see the back of them.

Probably not. The marquess paid magnificently for good service. Servants rode ahead so every halt, every night's accommodation, awaited them in perfect preparation, complete to their own bedding and pillows.

She'd broken into giggles at one point thinking of her captive lover, whom she'd thought an ordinary sort of man. The giggles were also partly nerves. What would the Wensleydale people think of all this? It made the marquess's previous appearance seem positively casual.

Wensleydale, of course, took it all in stride and there'd been nothing but smiles at Wensley Church this morning, nor during their triumphant ride back up the dale, scattering pennies to the children along the way, nor at the merry gathering they'd just left.

And now, they were on the last step of a long journey. The short ride to Wenscote. Tears fell when she found how little it had changed. The garden had grown a little wild, and the honeysuckle was in danger of overgrowing the front door, but it was Wenscote. It was home.

She glanced once at Brand, wondering still if this was what he really wanted. His smile convinced her.

Everything they desired, here in their hands.

Or almost.

Tonight.

They went immediately to the nursery where Jenny lay, fascinated by her toes and a beam of sunlight shooting through the window. At the sound of their voices, she smiled and stretched out. Brand picked her up, making her crow a little, then passed her to Rosamunde to feed, while Edie slipped away.

Brand watched, as he often did, giving the baby his finger to clutch as she sucked. Familiar contentment, but today, amid the music of Wenscote, it was heaven.

They were home, at last.

"This is a lovely nursery," Rosamunde said, sparing a glance for the first time at whitewashed walls and bright curtains with yellow flowers.

"For you and Jenny."

"Your work?"

"My orders, at least. Who else?"

She'd already glimpsed subtle changes in the house. He was the most amazing man.

When the baby was fed, they took her with them to introduce her to her new home. Soon, they wandered out to inspect their domain, finding two new foals in the stables, and crops growing tall. Familiar by now with their shared enthusiasm for things that many others found boring, they analyzed and inspected, making plans for future improvements and preservations.

Often, by fence or hedge, they stopped to kiss, but lightly because of the baby. Perhaps they'd brought her deliberately, to restrain their appetite. It was almost as if they wanted to tease out this perfect anticipation to the finest possible thread.

Unless it was nerves.

With her, a little of it was nerves. They'd had so little true time together, and it had been so long ago. And her body was still a bit thickened and flabby from the pregnancy. Her breasts sometimes leaked. . . .

Eventually, as the sun began to set and Jenny fell asleep, they wandered back, Brand carrying the baby soft against his shoulder. This was in a way, she thought, perfect happiness—Wenscote in the evening and Brand, their tiny baby safe in his care.

They gave Jenny into Edie's care, and found the bedroom at last. She'd worried about this—that it would remind her too much of the past. The bed was new, however, and a rich Chinese rug lay upon the floor, its jewel colors catching the evening sun.

It was enough.

"Well, my lord," she said, grasping her courage, but almost wishing for a mask, "you have me in your power at last. What do you command?"

He took her hand, and kissed it by the wedding ring he had placed there not many hours ago. "Everything, of course." He traced her scars, then kissed them. "Thank you."

He'd asked her to marry him without paint. "Without a mask," as he'd put it. In the end, it hadn't been difficult. The paint had served to bridge a gap in her courage, to enable her to face the world, but she was beyond that now.

He kissed her lips. They sank onto a chaise and kissed as they'd kissed in recent times, as if kissing was all and must be given its full due.

All fears and doubts fell away.

He was skilled at extracting a lady from her clothes, and proved it. She had little practice with men's clothing, but she was enthusiastic, hindered only by her joy in his emerging, beautiful body. Soon they were laughingly naked, facing one another hand in hand in the hot shades of the setting sun.

She was breathless with desire, which shimmered in the room like a heat haze.

"Did I ever mention," he said unsteadily, "how very grateful I am to you for saving my life?" Before she could reply, he added, "I'm sure I have not even begun to pay my debt. No, no"—he swung her into his arms and kissed both breasts—"don't demur, dear lady. I insist. I insist."

He laid her on cool, blossom-scented sheets and placed a hand possessively between her thighs. "I insist on paying my debts to the full. It might take a lifetime, but I insist."

"Am I arguing?" At an increase of pressure, she sucked in a breath and reached for him. "This is everything. Come to me."

His lips swooped down her cheek from eye to lips, and sealed them as he spread her legs and moved over her. Slowly, he slid into her. Resting there, he raised his head and smiled into her eyes.

"Everything," he said. But then, with a wicked twinkle, he added, "And more?"

Author's Note

First, I invented the Cotterites. They do fit, however, with the 1760s.

Warning, brief history lesson follows!

Back in the 1640s, King Charles I had blundered and stumbled into civil war. His opponents were a motley group, some mainly interested in curbing the king's power through a strong parliament; others in weakening the Church of England so that alternative forms of Protestantism such as Presbyterianism could flourish. But the king's opponents were united in one thing—a terror that Charles might try to bring back Roman Catholicism, which was still remembered in terms of Mary Tudor, who had burned Protestants at the stake.

When Charles fell, so did the Church of England, and sects flourished. The Levellers were radical republicans. The Diggers opposed private property and took over open land. Fifth Monarchists believed Christ's Kingdom was imminent. Muggletonians believed their leader was divine. Ranters indulged in sexual license and blasphemy.

However, the government was now in the hands of the Puritans.

The terms Puritan and Quaker are often used interchangeably, but in English political terms, "Puritan" describes the extremist religious faction during the Civil War and during the subsequent republic led by Protector Oliver Cromwell. Quakers, on the other hand, were and are the pacifist Society of Friends who were even persecuted at times by the "Commonwealth of Saints."

Rule by stern, self-appointed saints was predictably unpopular, made more so by Cromwell's virtual martial law. After Cromwell's death it all fell apart and Charles I's son was invited—begged!—to return. Charles II's reign was the Restoration, when everyone celebrated by swinging to the other extreme. It also brought a period of prosperity, and a flourishing of arts, science, industry, and trade which continued into the eighteenth century.

By 1762, the cost of excess was becoming obvious. We are not long past the time when gin—introduced in 1690—was cheap and plentiful and ruining many lives. (See Hogarth's painting "Gin Lane.") After many attempts at control, heavy taxes in 1756 made it impossible for most people to over indulge, and matters began to improve. In 1754, chaotic marriage laws had been changed, reducing thoughtless marriage and bigamy.

However, life was still unruly in many ways so there was a movement toward sober living, one in which the Wesley brothers were active from 1740 onward. The Yorkshire dales, particularly the mining areas, became staunchly Methodist.

So, my New Commonwealth fits into the historical background and the current movements, but it never existed. If it had, however, I'm sure George III—remembering his ancestor Charles I's fate—would have dispatched his *eminence noire,* the Marquess of Rothgar, to sort things out.

Of course this period was also the time of the agricultural Revolution, when land usage in England changed, shaping the country we see today. Having grown up in the North and visited the dales frequently, I was startled to discover that the familiar dry stone walls are not ancient, but were built in the mid-eighteenth century as part of the enclosure and reorganization of the land.

I love learning new things. I learned a great deal about heavy horses, land drainage, crop variety, and animal breeding as I worked on this book. As you'll notice—probably with appreciation!—not much of it is included. That's as it should be. I needed to know in order to fit comfortably into my characters' heads.

I even took a trip to England to touch up my research, because, having set some scenes in the Three Tuns in

Thirsk, I discovered that it is still there and in operation. I just had to go, and it certainly didn't harm to wander Wensleydale with an adult, observant eye.

Arradale is based very loosely on a place called Bolton House in Wensleydale, which does have the ancient Bolton Castle looming up on the hills behind it. The only connection, however, is in the castle and the location. The style of house, family history, etc. is all fiction.

I loved Thirsk, and recommend a stop there if you're ever traveling in England. It's a small market town, just a little crowded because it's also where the vet who wrote as James Herriot had his real practice. The square is a lovely feature, and the Three Tuns sits on it, the coach yard still behind, the original stable blocks now used as storage and garage areas.

If you wish, you can stay in the Tuns. It's not particularly expensive. Or you could have a drink or meal in the dark-oak pub. Or take tea in what I designated the Guests' Parlor. Or you could just stand at the base of the staircase and think of Rosamunde trying to gather strength for the climb.

For even more Georgian ambience, however, I recommend that you drive or walk to the attached village of Sowerby, which has a truly wonderful, hardly changed, Georgian Street. When we were there, the daffodils were blooming beneath the trees set in the wide grass verges. These verges divide the roadway from the footpath that runs in front of the long rank of varied Georgian houses. No danger of splashing from passing coaches.

I found it easy to imagine Rosamunde and Brand on a visit to Thirsk, strolling there one lovely evening, perhaps with a few happy children running along the grass beside them.

For those of you new to the Mallorens, the previous books about them are: *My Lady Notorious* (Cyn and Chastity); *Tempting Fortune* (Bryght and Portia); and *Something Wicked* (Elf and Fort). The first two are presently out of print, but the third can be ordered by your bookstore or through the direct order form in this book. And yes, there will be a book about the Marquess of

Rothgar—at last. It is scheduled for publication in May 2000.

Happy reading and happy endings, always!

I love to hear from readers. You can write to me care of my agent, Alice Harron Orr, 305 Madison Ave., Suite 1166, New York, NY 10165. Please include a SASE to help with the cost of a reply. Or e-mail me at jobeverley@poboxes. com. I keep an e-mail list, and use it to notify people of upcoming books or other special news.

I also have a web page at http://www.sff.net/people/ jobeverley. You'll find interesting background to my books there, and also a complete, annotated booklist.